Yellowcake

BOOKS BY ANN CUMMINS

Red Ant House: Stories

Yellowcake

Yellowcake

Ann Cummins

Houghton Mifflin Company

BOSTON · NEW YORK

2007

For information about permission to reproduce
selections from this book, write to Permissions,
Houghton Mifflin Company, 215 Park Avenue South,
New York, New York 10003.

Visit our Web site: www.houghtonmifflinbooks.com.

Library of Congress Cataloging-in-Publication Data
Cummins, Ann.
Yellowcake / Ann Cummins.
p.   cm.
ISBN-13: 978-0-618-26926-6
ISBN-10: 0-618-26926-6
1. Uranium miners — Health and hygiene — New
Mexico — Fiction. 2. Family life — Fiction. 3. Navajo
Indians — Fiction. 4. Conflict of generations —
Fiction. 5. New Mexico — Fiction. I. Title.
PS3603.U657Y45 2007
813'.6 — dc22   2006023453

Book design by Melissa Lotfy

Printed in the United States of America

MP 10 9 8 7 6 5 4 3 2 1

ACKNOWLEDGMENTS

I would like to thank the supportive and inspiring readers who saw this book through many drafts: first and last, my husband, Steve Willis. Susan Canavan, editor extraordinaire. Tilly Warnock. Nancy Johnson, Ann Packer, Sarah Stone, Ron Nyren, Lisa Michaels, Vendela Vida, Cornelia Nixon, Julie Orringer, and Angela Pneuman. For their help with the Navajo language and medical details, Ellavina Tsosie Perkins and Warren Perkins. For putting up with me, my sisters and brothers, Mary, Tom, Steve, Trish, and, in spirit, Kathy. Georgia Briggs, whose stories have been a guide for many years. The Lannan Foundation for its generous support and haven in Marfa. The wonderful Jenny Bent.

Tell me what's the matter with the mill.

MEMPHIS MINNIE

Yellowcake

1

THEY COME AT ten o'clock in the morning. Ryland's wife, Rosy, is at the fabric store with their daughter, Maggie, who's getting married next month. Ryland goes ahead and opens the door against his better judgment. He always opens the door when somebody rings, though he usually regrets it. He is not afraid of muggers. Muggers, he figures, will leave sooner rather than later. He's afraid of the neighbor lady, Mrs. Barron, who always leaves later, and the Mormon missionaries, who like to fight with his wife, they always leave later. And Pretty Boy across the street, old Hal Rivers, who waters his lawn in bikini swim trunks, parades young girls in and out, day in, day out, lady's man, though he has a gut and a little bald pate — still, the girls like him, which only goes to show that it's not the looks but the pocketbook. Old Hal stopping by every now and again to chew the fat terrifies him, though Ryland makes sure the man never knows but that he's welcome.

This man and woman, though, Ryland doesn't recognize. He lets them in because of the young Navajo woman with them. She has to tell him who she is. Becky Atcitty.

"You know my dad," she says.

"You're not Becky Atcitty."

"Yes I am."

He stands for a minute and admires the young woman little Becky has become. He tells her that when he first met her she wasn't any bigger than a thumbnail. Now they sit across from him, three of them on the couch, and Becky begins telling him how Woody is sick.

Ryland shakes his head. He likes Woody. "Your dad was a good worker. Every time somebody didn't show up for a shift at the mill, I'd call him and say, 'Woody, got a cup of joe with your name on it,' and your dad'd always say, 'Okay, then.'" Ryland looks over Becky's head out the front window to the ash tree in the yard. The leaves are green-white, dry. Rosy has hung plywood children in plywood swings, a boy and a girl, from the tree limbs. The children aren't swinging, though, because there's no hint of a breeze.

"He has lung cancer," the woman with Becky says. Classy. Dressed like a TV news anchor in one of those boxy suits. Hair any color but natural — one of those poofed-up, clipped, and curled deals that hugs her head.

"Your dad's a strong man," Ryland says to Becky. "Don't you worry." Becky is sitting between the man and the woman. The man is looking all around, beaming at the pictures on the wall. His hair is pulled back in a little ponytail. Skinny guy in jeans.

Becky says, "We just think that maybe the mill workers should get some of the same benefits the miners got."

"We're just at the beginning of this process, Mr. Mahoney," the woman says. "The mill workers like yourself and Mr. Atcitty are entitled . . . Tell him about the air ventilation in the mills, Bill. Bill's a public interest lawyer —"

"I don't have cancer."

The woman stops. She blinks at him. He watches her eyes slide to the portable oxygen tank at his feet.

"Of course not," she says. "We were wondering if you kept medical histories on your workers, and if by chance you still have . . ."

"You people like something? I could put on some coffee. Rosy'll be home any minute. She's going to be mad if she sees Becky Atcitty here and I didn't give her anything."

Becky says, "They think if you've got any records on Dad it might give us some place to start."

"Mr. Mahoney," the woman says, "as I'm sure you know, we

made great strides when the compensation act passed, but it does us no good if there's no way for victims to collect. The mill workers like yourself and Mr. Atcitty are entitled . . . Bill, tell him about the—"

"He doesn't have to tell me anything," Ryland says.

The woman blinks again. She smiles.

The lawyer gets up and walks over to the pictures on the wall. "Is this your family, Mr. Mahoney? Handsome family."

Ryland stares at the man staring at his family.

The woman says, "This is simply about workers who were continually exposed to toxic—"

"Your daddy doesn't know you're here, does he." He peers at Becky, who leans back into the couch. They had a party when she was born. He brought cigars and cider to the mill. Sam Behan, his old chum, teased him. "During working hours, Ry?" Sam said, and Ryland said, "Who's the boss?" They all raised a glass and toasted this girl's birth.

Ryland leans forward. The girl stares at something over his shoulder. He can't read her. Navajos. Never could read them. But her dad, Woody was a good man. Didn't truck with unions. When they wanted to bring the union in, Woody said he had a family to support. This Ryland knows for a fact.

"Don't you worry about your dad," he says. "He's a strong man." He looks at the news anchor lady. Her eyes are as bright as a child's, and her grinning teeth are blue-white. Her hands, laced in a fist on her lap, are white, too, and the skin pulls so tight it looks like her knuckles are about to bust through.

"One of the best men I know," Ryland says to her. "Woodrow Atcitty. This girl's dad."

But Rosy catches them as they're leaving. Now the four of them sit around the kitchen table drinking coffee. Ryland sits in his chair in the living room. ". . . little chance the Navajo miners with legitimate claims can file. The red tape is prohibitive," the lawyer's saying.

On the TV a fancy man is breaking eggs into a dish. The man

uses one hand to break the eggs—egg in the palm of the hand, little tap, then presto! On the egg-breaking hand, the cook wears a Liberace ring. One of those rings that stretches from knuckle to fist.

The lawyer says they've only just begun to organize. He wants to have community meetings. He wants to educate and motivate.

Moneygrubbing lawyer. Ryland would lay bets that guy's on the clock. The man isn't sitting at his kitchen table out of charity.

Liberace says, "Whisk it up good." He's making a confection. Ryland watches him stir sugar into eggs.

Rosy wants them to know about Ryland's handkerchiefs. "All those years that he worked in the uranium mill, his handkerchiefs were always stained yellow from mucus he blew out of his nose. I have many questions and no answers."

"We all have questions," the lawyer says. "Maybe you'd like to join us next week. We're identifying key people in the region who might form a planning committee."

"Sure," Rosy says. "Any day but Tuesday." She says something about a doctor's appointment Tuesday. Ryland strains to hear. He hits the mute button on the channel changer. She's saying he's got some sort of test scheduled.

"What test?" he calls out.

The kitchen goes silent. Ryland can feel them looking at each other. Then Rosy yells, "I told you about it. We scheduled this a month ago, Ryland." He stares at the thick confection as Liberace pours it into a bowl. Now he hears a chair skidding on the kitchen linoleum, and he watches his wife's reflection in the TV screen as she comes into the living room. "You agreed to it," she says quietly. She says that Dr. Callahan recommended this test, that they're going to take a little tissue from his lung. That's all. "It's just a precaution," she says, and he turns, giving her a look. "It wasn't my idea," she hisses, her dark eyes fiery. He wonders about that. "Don't you remember?"

He looks back at the TV. He can see her hands, tiny fists in the screen's reflection. He says, "You're my memory."

2

H E CAN'T QUARREL with them. They have their evidence. He's heard all about it for years, what uranium does to people. How could you quarrel? He's seen the pictures: pictures of tumors, pictures of soft-gummed miners whose teeth have fallen out. Maybe it was the uranium exposure. Maybe it was something else, like cigarettes. But nobody was complaining back then, not on payday. It isn't that he wants to pick a fight; it's that the quarrel is beside the point. He doesn't really know what the point is, just that the steady drone of moneygrubbers taking up this cause and that cause makes him sick.

The thing is, it hasn't been a bad life. They've done okay.

Sometimes he dreams he is there. In the heat of the crusher room, midafternoon when the shift was new. On a swing-shift afternoon in the uranium mill, sunlight bored hard through the smeared windows in the room where the crushers split yellow ore for the yellowcake they made. At a certain angle, in the heat of the day, golden dust filled the air above the conveyor belts, and entering the room was like entering an oven. You didn't want to go in. You didn't want to begin. Once there, though, the heat took you. You got the rhythm of the place. The clickety-click of the bearings in the conveyor belts, the steady pounding of the crushers grinding rock to bits, dust the texture of chalk. Mouth and nose coated. Entering the mill when the heat-seared walls and ceiling began to sweat was exhilarating, like moving hard into a fast hot wind.

· · ·

Of the eighteen men who moved down from Colorado to New Mexico with him in 1964 to operate the mill on the Navajo reservation, he supposes some have died. He doesn't know, doesn't keep track. Rosy keeps track. She reads him Christmas letters written by wives, wives who don't seem to die. It's always old Mr. So-and-So died, never Mrs., which seems a little like a conspiracy to Ryland, how the women just live on and on to write their Christmas obituary letters.

Sam hasn't died, though. Against all odds, Sam Behan is still alive. Sam is his oldest friend; they are both sixty-five years old and have been friends for fifty-eight of those years. Sam called Ryland from Florida last week to tell him about a new kind of tin roof. It takes Ryland exactly twenty-two rings to get out of bed, put on his slippers and robe, start the portable oxygen tank rolling. He takes his time getting to the kitchen to answer because he knows Sam won't hang up. Drunk or not, when Sam wants to talk, he's a patient man. Sam had been watching TV in some Florida bar and saw a commercial about the roof. "Twice as durable, half the cost," Sam had said. Old Sam. Sitting in a bar, thinking about hard New Mexico winters and Ryland's roof. Though they talk once, sometimes twice a month, Ryland hasn't seen him in seventeen years, ever since the mill closed. Lily, Rosy's sister, divorced Sam that same year when she found out about Alice. Sam had been having an affair with a Navajo woman, Alice Atcitty, the entire time they were on the reservation. For Sam there always were women in the wings. It surprised Ryland, though, that he let one of them monkey up his marriage. Ryland and Sam had married Lily and Rosy Walsh in a joint ceremony three years after the war. They'd been best man for each other.

It was Sam who went down to the reservation with him that first summer, before any of the workers or their families came, to get the place ready. They bached it, slept in sleeping bags on a bare floor in one of the company houses. Everything seemed pretty bleak then. None of the mill families wanted to move from Colorado to that godforsaken place. He and Sam drove down that first week into a sandstorm that didn't let up for three days. He remembers pulling hard against the wind, trying to get furniture moved into the mill office, remembers yelling himself hoarse, trying to mobilize the newly hired Navajo workers. Taking care of business despite the red eyes and grit and howling wind in the ears, then sitting with Sam late into the night, worrying.

"You want this to work," Sam was fond of saying, "you're going to have to please the wives."

The wives didn't want to move down from Durango. Who could blame them? They had been displeased from the moment whispers about the transfer south started circulating. Rosy had worried about it for a whole year while the company bigwigs worked out details with the tribe. She prayed the Indians wouldn't grant the lease, even though the move meant a huge promotion for Ryland. In Durango he was a shift foreman; in Shiprock he would be the mill foreman. The boss. Still, Rosy resisted right to the end. Before she ever saw the housing compound, the square block where they all lived, and then for the ten years she lived there, she called the place Camp, as if it were temporary, something you could break down and leave in the dead of night.

They set out, he and Sam, to please the wives. He remembers sitting on the stoop of one of those empty houses, drinking whiskey, smoking cigarettes, thinking about it. Sam came up with the idea of planting grass. The housing compound — the whole village — was bald, the exact opposite of their Rocky Mountain homes, where they all had lawns and gardens and mountains outside their kitchen windows. Ryland had called Henry Ritter over in Cortez because Henry knew grass and he had grass. Henry advised Bermuda. Took good in alkaline soil. It took three days to lay five acres of Bermuda sod around the empty houses.

That night, sitting on the stoop, two A.M., bone-tired and tipsy, Ryland felt good. He remembers it to this day, how fine it was to sit there with his friend, to smell wet grass and feel dampness in the desert air. The whole adventure felt possible that night. They had government contracts for uranium to fuel new power plants and for vanadium. Enough to keep them in work for a long while. They had the mill, the houses, and they had grass.

"What do you think?" he asked Sam that night. "Will the wives be pleased?"

For a long time Sam didn't say, just sat looking out. The stoop they sat on faced the highway, and beyond it the trading post, which was dark, and beyond that fields, and the river, and the mesa where the mill was. A barbed-wire fence between them and the highway. That night, and every night they'd been there, they'd seen a line of horses, a dozen or so, crippling along on the other side of the fence, their back legs hobbled, rumps twitching. Sway-backed and thick-bellied, not the scrawny desert horses. These were horses somebody owned, out taking their evening constitutional. At the compound cattle guard, they would stop, one at a time, and look in. Pretty things.

Watching the horses pass, Sam said, "Just as soon as you fix one problem, here comes another. How long do you think those horses are going to stay on that side of the fence? You know what they see over here? Good grazing." Ryland laughed. "You think I'm kidding? You're going to have to secure the garbage cans. The wives," Sam said, "aren't going to want garbage all over their yards, and once those horses get in here to the grass, they're going to be spilling the garbage."

"Sam, you're a comedian," Ryland said.

Sam hunched into himself, his shoulders rolled, head sunk low, scowling at the world. "You know what?" he said, but then didn't say what. He shot up, pitched his cigarette, and ran across the field yelling, "Hai! Hai!" and the horses turned as a unit, bolting across the highway, away from Sam Behan's waving arms.

3

L ILY BEHAN SITS at a picnic table in Durango's Santa Rita
Park, twisting the gold posts in her ears and listening to the
soft shush of the muddy Animas River behind her. Around and
around the earrings go. She is waiting for Fred Steppe to bring
groceries from the car. Half an hour ago, he'd knocked on her
door and told her he had salami and champagne in his trunk. So
today her new beau has arranged a surprise picnic, and yesterday
... Yesterday, while walking by Thorton's Jewelry, they stopped to
admire the earrings in the window, and Fred went right in and
bought these pearl studs.

Lily is sixty-two. For the first time in her life, she has punctured
earlobes. How long, she wonders, will it take Rosy to notice that
the pearls in her ears are attached to posts, not clamps?

Lily knows what her sister will say about her ears, the same
thing their mother used to say: "If God had intended for us to
have holes in our ears, he would've put them there." She knows
what Rosy will say about Fred, too. "He's a walking heart attack."
Lily supposes he is. He is a fatty. But a good dancer. At any rate,
Lily's heart is not attached to him. That's what she'll tell Rosy if
ever she meets Fred: "Here today, gone tomorrow." Rosy will say,
"You cannot take a gift from a man you intend to leave." But why
not? Anyway, she doesn't intend to leave him today. She wants
pampering, and Fred seems willing.

"What we ought to have, we ought to have fish," Fred calls as he walks over the grass toward her, a bag of groceries in each arm. "River's so low I can see them in there."

"I'm not fond of fish," Lily says.

"Are you crazy?" He sets the bags on the table, wipes his forehead with the back of his arm. He's not bad to look at, Lily has decided. His face is more thick than fat, a broad-chinned Saxon face with kind brown eyes, though they sink a little too deep, appear smaller than they are, pillowed by puffy flesh. Still, it's a kind face, not at all bad to look at, and he seems comfortable in his skin. Today he's wearing loose jeans belted with a plain sand-cast Navajo buckle, a white button-down shirt open at the throat, sleeves rolled up. These are his work clothes. He sells life insurance.

"I like tuna salad," she says.

"You are crazy. You're in the middle of trout country."

"I know that."

Fred begins pulling plastic deli containers and packets of white butcher paper from one bag.

"I like it in lots of mayonnaise with chopped dill pickle. I guess you could say I like fish if I can't taste it."

Fred shakes his head. He pulls out two sturdy china plates, white linen napkins, and forks, real forks from his home, not plastic, he hates plastic, already she knows this about him.

"My husband fishes. My ex-husband."

From the other bag, he pulls out a bottle of champagne, holding it so she can read the label — French. His eyes shine. She wishes she knew something about champagne, because this bottle's clearly a prize.

"That would be Sam," he says. He takes two champagne glasses, carefully wrapped in paper, from the sack.

"Uh-huh."

Fred begins twisting the wire on the bottle. Lily unwraps the glasses, then begins opening deli containers. One has plump raviolis in pesto, pine nuts sprinkled over the top, another assorted olives, another roasted red peppers.

"Now that's one sport I could never get into," Fred says. He covers the bottle with a napkin and begins pushing the cork up with his thumbs. "Never could see the appeal of sitting on water and getting eaten by mosquitoes." He pops the cork, which makes a satisfying crack. He fills the glasses, clinking his against hers, and says, "Here's to you, pretty lady."

Lily smiles, sips, enjoying the champagne mist that sprays her nose and cheeks. She wonders how her life would have been had she met a good, caring man like Fred at the beginning instead of now. She knows, she is absolutely certain, it would have been better, and it makes her mad, really, the years she lost to Sam. Fred is here now, though, and she supposes she doesn't care, certainly she shouldn't care, that he's a little on the heavy side, except it's hard to imagine sleeping with him. She hates herself for feeling this way. She does and doesn't want to talk with Rosy about him. Rosy might lecture; Lily usually regrets confiding in her sister. But Rosy can recognize a phony. She's almost always right about people, and Lily is almost always wrong. The fact is, Lily cannot trust herself in character assessment, thank you very much, Sam Behan. He ruined her.

She rolls the base of her glass between the table-top slats. The table is splattered at one end with bird droppings, and initials and names — HH, ST, LORI — have been carved into the wood. People and birds have left their marks. Lily pushes her tipless tongue against her teeth. Sam's mark on her. A little love bite. Once he had put her through the front window of his car, and she bit the tip of her tongue off. Stupid. He had been trying to race a train. He heard the train, saw the tracks, and before she knew it, he was flooring it, the car flying over the tracks, but it landed hard, and the next thing she knew she was on her knees in the dirt, blood gushing out of her mouth, and he was beside her, cupping the blood, holding her head, apologizing, whispering, "I'm sorry, God, I'm sorry, I'm so sorry," and then they were just very still together, as if they were kneeling on fragile ground, praying. He was good in a crisis, always rose to the occasion. Too bad she couldn't make a crisis every minute for Sam. The marriage might have worked.

Fred pours more champagne into her glass and begins opening the packets of butcher paper. "We've got provolone and Swiss,

hot salami, corned beef and roast beef. Anything you don't like?"
He begins spearing slices of cheese and meat, piling them on her
plate.

"Just a little, not so much," Lily says. She sips the champagne.

Fred takes some of the slices off her plate and piles them on
his own. Lily, watching, presses her lips together and looks away,
twisting around to take in the river and Smelter Mountain behind
it. She pulls her legs out from under the table, turning to lean her
back against it.

Fred turns so that he's facing the river, too, bringing his plate
with him. He sits close enough that his arm brushes hers. She can
smell the spiced meat, which he rolls into logs and eats with his
fingers. "What do you say I take the rest of the afternoon off and
we move the party to my house? I've got a very nice Merlot."

Lily smiles. She gazes upstream at kids walking down the center of the river, carrying yellow rubber rafts over their heads. She
can feel Fred's eyes on the side of her face.

"Lil?"

She says, "Somebody ought to tell them they need water to
float." She glances at him. He's studying her, his eyes half closed.
She takes a slice of salami from his plate and pops it into her
mouth. "Why is it that food off of somebody else's plate always
tastes better?"

He looks downriver at the disappearing rafters. He doesn't say
anything. Lily leans into him, pressing her thigh against his. He
sits still, moving neither away from nor toward her, and for a moment she feels dizzy, like she used to with Sam, as if she were leaning against a hollow body.

"Well," he says, turning and putting his plate on the table, picking up the container of raviolis and turning back. He forks a rav-
ioli, holds it out to Lily, who takes it between her lips, and he
watches while she chews and swallows, then takes his napkin and
wipes the oil from her lips. He is himself again. The hollow man
has disappeared. He is not like Sam. He's smiling at her. "On the
other hand," he says, "I should probably get back to work."

But she doesn't want that, either. "Work?" She doesn't want to be alone. She just wants to sit here, that's all. "Get me liquored up and then leave me?"

He laughs. He puts his arm around her, pulling her to him, nuzzling her hair. She can smell the spiced meat on his breath, and she feels like she's being pulled rapidly underwater.

"Okay, then," he says. "That Merlot has your name on it."

Sun glints off patches of the Animas where water still flows. Once she watched Sam dive from a rock just upstream from here and torpedo headlong through the rapids. He was drunk, of course, and she was certain that he'd crack his skull, but he didn't. Like an animal navigating on instinct, he wove in and out of the shallows, a white fish, then pulled himself out right about here. Just like a child.

When Lily stands, her temples throb and her legs feel water-logged. She turns to help Fred pack up. He's leaning over the table, gathering food. His shirt has come untucked, and she can see the rolling country of his lower back, a broad pink swatch of skin, which makes her want to cry. The thing she never tired of was Sam's body, solid, compact.

She drains her glass. She says, "What a lovely day, Fred. What a lovely picnic. Thank you. This is the kind of thing my ex would never do."

Fred looks at her, a funny look in his eyes, and snaps the lid on the raviolis.

4

A T THE MARATHON MARINA, it's always cocktail hour after dark, and tonight, when Sam Behan steps out onto the deck of his houseboat, he can hear martinis in the lilting voices. All around him there's a mumble of languages, Spanish and English, and he can smell fish grilling. He takes a pack of Winstons from his shirt pocket, shakes one out, and lights it. He leans against the railing, smoking and looking over the line of boats from here to the shore. They bob in the water, some glowing like Christmas, with lights running up masts and soft yellow lights in kitchens, where he can see people, women mostly, standing at counters while men tend the outside grills. Across the way, there's another row of bobbing houses.

When he's done with the cigarette, he pitches the butt into the water and goes inside. If Alice were here, she'd tell him to eat. She likes to say that he's the only man she knows who needs to be reminded. Liked to say? Alice didn't winter with him here last year. She said it was because she had to stay on the reservation and help her mother with the farm. He wonders, though. For the past seventeen years, Alice Atcitty has spent the winter months with him here on the boat. Spring and summer she follows the rodeo. But Alice's winters in Florida have gotten shorter over the years. He wonders if there might be another man in the picture.

It's a little after nine o'clock. He makes coffee, then takes the carton of eggs from the refrigerator and breaks three into a bowl, whisks them with a fork. From the dish drainer he takes the frying pan, puts it on the burner, and starts the heat. It's one of those no-stick fancy pans Alice left here. While it's heating, he switches on the little battery-operated radio. Radio Martí. Cuban jazz. He's been lucky on these clear nights. The station comes in good. He opens the cupboard over the stove and takes down his gray tackle box, puts it on the table, opens the lid. He also takes down packets of feathers and synthetic foams.

When the eggs are ready, he stands over them, eating from the pan and looking over the tackle box on the table. It's a tiered box with hooks, eyes, and colorful threads — shimmering greens, corals, and silvers — in the top tier. His tools are in the tier below, vises, pliers, bobbins, threaders, and bone — actually plastic sticks that look like bone. Fish bone.

Finished with the eggs, he pours himself a cup of coffee and sits down, taking ten sticks from the box and arranging them lengthwise in front of him. Twelve inches long, they will make spines for tempting lures to attract big fish that are easily tricked by flash and color. A flash of silver, a streak of coral — it isn't necessary, Sam knows, to make a pretty fly. The right presentation of color, a fly well tied, light and sturdy. A fat marlin will blush when teased with the right fly.

He takes out vise, wire, and epoxy. It's big-fish season. For little fish he'll use single hooks and tie on feathers from guinea hens, mallards, ostrich, hair from elk, deer, rabbit. But he needs bulk for big flies, so he uses synthetic foams with names like secret streamer hair, crystal flash, and ice chenille. Mostly Sam ties flies by touch. His eyes can't focus on the fine close-up work anymore, but he has always been able to trust his hands. At the uranium mill he kept the machinery in repair, working blind when an ore roaster blew, feeling into the parts of the machinery for fissures and flaws. It was what he was good at, and now he's good at this, fly-tying. Jorge Molina will give him a dollar a fly for little flies and two-fifty for the big ones. People want Sam's flies, according to Molina. Jorge says Sam has built himself a little reputation.

From another compartment, he takes ten more sticks, these

four inches long. He dabs epoxy near the top of the long sticks, lays the smaller sticks across them, pressing down, then gets up, finishes his coffee, and pours more from the pot. He opens the freezer. The top shelf is still full of yellowfin, finless now, gutted and cleaned, chopped into steaks, each in its own baggie, the baggies crusty with freezer burn. He and Alice brought in the big fish together two seasons ago. He's saving the steaks for her.

From the bottom shelf, he takes out a bottle of Stoli. He prefers gin, but he ran out today . . . Yesterday. One of the days. This bottle was a gift from Tom Leroi, who has a little yacht three docks over. Last weekend Leroi caught a one-hundred-and-fifty-pound marlin with one of Sam's fancy hand-tied flies and showed his gratitude with the Stoli. Sam pours a couple inches of vodka into his coffee, leaves the bottle on the counter.

He's been thinking it might be time to take a trip out west. He hasn't been back since the divorce from Lily. He has an excuse to go. Yesterday he got an invitation to Maggie Mahoney's wedding in the mail. On the bottom of it, Ryland had penned a message that made Sam smile: GET ON THE DAMN PLANE AND COME TO THE DAMN WEDDING.

Rosy sent a photo at Christmas. Ryland's eyes were sunken and tired, his lips blue-rimmed. Sam should go see Ryland.

Money is an obstacle. Sam doesn't have much on hand. He hasn't been keeping up, hasn't been to Molina's to sell flies in six, seven weeks. He keeps his cash under the mattress, but the stash has been dwindling. He sends money to Alice. Last month he sent an envelope full of twenties. He sends the money for the kid, their kid, Delmar, though the kid's hardly a kid anymore. Last Sam heard, his son was in jail.

To get money, he needs to sell a shitload of flies. He's been making them steadily. He has grocery bags stuffed full of flies just getting moldy in the boat. He could go to Molina, sell his inventory, and get cash, but Moley might give him trouble. He doesn't like to keep stock in the storeroom. Molina's motto: "Keep people wanting 'em, they'll keep paying."

"Moley," Sam says, shaking his head. He picks up one of the

skeletons, testing the epoxy's hold, which is strong. Outside, the cocktail hour is getting louder. Somewhere a motorboat buzzes, and the floor under him begins to buck gently with the churning waves. On the dock very close to his window, a girl says, "Shut up," then says it again, "Shu-ut up." She is laughing, and a male voice is talking low, teasing.

Alice is in her midforties. Forty-four? Forty-five? He can't remember. Women at that age frequently start needing a little excitement. Last time he saw her, she'd added a layer to her hipless hips, and her hair had long strands of gray here and there.

He winds the thread tightly where the bones cross, pinching down, leaving a thread loose on one side, catching its mate, looping in a spiral across the T-bone to the end, affixing a hook, front hook down, tying off, catching the loose thread and spiraling, a tight wind, across the other side of the T, affixing the other hook, tying off, sipping the coffee, cool now from the frigid vodka. He works in a line, ten Ts, ten flies, he is a human factory, and the tide is coming in, his house shivering. In Cuba tonight the jazz is live, piano and horn. Static. Then music.

Fifty-six minutes into it, he has ten synthetic mackerel that will hold their own against any live bait. He stretches his arms, ripping through the stale cabin air that always seems to cocoon around him when he concentrates. He just made twenty-five dollars, double his hourly wage at the uranium mill.

He made it if Molina will pay it.

5

SUMMER WEEKENDS when there's a little wind, Becky At-citty and her friend Arnold Gardner go to Morgan Lake to watch the windsurfers. The Saturday after her visit with the Ma-honeys, Arnold picks Becky up in his new Saab, and they cross the San Juan River, heading up Power Plant Road, windows open. Becky breathes deeply, hungry for air that isn't contaminated by the stench of illness. Six months ago, when her father relapsed, she gave up her apartment in Farmington and moved back to her parents' house in the valley just outside of town to help her mother. Becky's mother doesn't drive, and now her father is too weak, so Becky spends much of her free time chauffeuring her fa-ther to doctor appointments and running errands.

Morgan Lake is an artificial lake at the base of Four Corners Power Plant. The water supplies coolant for the plant, which cre-ates a wonderland of artificial weather on the mesa. Cottony white smoke blooms from the stacks, painting the sky with clouds on a cloudless day, and even when there isn't a hint of breeze any-where else, something magical and warm stirs the water, which in turn massages the air over the lake, making windsurfers happy. It wasn't always so. Becky is twenty-five. When she was a little girl in the early seventies, the clouds coming from the power plant were black, filled with toxic particles that made her cough, and nobody went to the lake. Now the stacks are filtered, the fish thrive, and the scenery is easy on the eyes.

Arnold pulls off the road and onto the lake's bank, which is baked clay in the dry season but turns the texture of wet cement when it rains. A mud-plastered pickup is embedded in the bank near the water, buried to its hubcaps. It's been there since last August. Today a group of surfers are milling around the truck, which holds their gear and coolers of beer.

There's no shade on this side of the lake, just gray reeds and scrubby trees at the water's edge. Arnold parks near some boulders, and they get out, leaving the Saab doors open. Bob Marley and the Wailers blare from the tape player. As a tribute to the tenth anniversary of Marley's death in May 1981, Arnold has been listening to nothing but the Wailers all summer. Becky has now memorized everything Bob Marley ever wrote.

They sit on the ground, propped against the boulders. Surfers are tossing around bottles of sunscreen, rubbing lotion on themselves and on each other's backs. "That one," Arnold says, watching a longhaired guy in baggy white trunks head into the water with his board, his back a perfect, muscled V, the trunks roped low on his thin hips. As he gets far enough into the water for the wind to catch the sail and for him to climb on the board, the trunks turn sort of transparent, so that even from a distance Becky and Arnold can see sculpted butt and chiseled thighs.

"That one?" Becky says. "That guy's why you should join the gym. He works there. He's really funny. Even when he's training people he watches himself in the mirror. I mean constantly. Actually, he's just your type."

"Do I have a type?"

"You definitely have a type. You just don't get any action." Arnold sighs audibly. "Which is completely your fault," she adds.

"Grr."

Any local action, she could say, but doesn't. Arnold's the king of one-night stands "abroad" — abroad being at least two hundred miles in any direction from Farmington and the reservation. He'll come back from Albuquerque or Denver, moody and sullen about barroom trysts. On home ground he might as well be a monk.

"Why is it my fault?"

"Because you don't try."

"Yeah, like you try."

"I've tried."

"Sure you have."

"Anyway, who has time to try?"

Arnold leans forward, squinting at badly sunburned Ricky Longacre, the quarterback on their high school team seven years ago, whose arms are longer than his legs and whose mouth is foul. "That one," he says.

"For you."

"For you."

She raises her chin, as if considering, then says, "Too red."

Arnold's dimple—he has only one, and he complains that it makes him look lopsided—creases his broad cheek. "See," he says, "you're prejudiced." He breaks off some squares of Hershey's chocolate from a king-sized bar and hands them to her. "To me color doesn't matter. Me, I'm democratic."

Becky laughs. "Sure you are."

"So what'd you find out about Mr. Zahnee?" Arnold says.

"I could not find any evidence that he's married." A promising specimen, Harrison Zahnee, opened a checking account at the bank a few weeks ago. Becky is a loan officer at the First National, and Arnold's a security guard. She found out that Mr. Zahnee has just taken a job at the college as a Navajo language specialist. "He's got a single-party checking account. He didn't mark anything for marital status, but his beneficiary is somebody named Carlee Zahnee."

"There you go," Arnold says.

"Yeah, but he didn't put anything under relationship. She might not be his wife."

"Oh, please." He peers at her out of the corner of his eye, his lip curled in an Elvis snarl.

"Don't be mean," she says. He smiles and looks at the lake.

Despite Becky's claim that she's tired of being terminally single, Arnold says she unconsciously chooses married guys—the last two were married—because she's afraid of real involvement.

Becky met Arnold her sophomore year in high school, ten years ago. He had just transferred from an all-Indian boarding school in Albuquerque. The first day of class, their homeroom teacher asked the students to introduce themselves and say a little about their hobbies. Half the room listed fellowship in various local churches as an interest. Fruitland is a churchy community. Becky's mother was raised there, the youngest daughter of Baptist missionaries. Becky's father follows the Navajo Way. Della agreed to marry Woody only on condition that their children be raised Baptist.

When it was Arnold's turn to introduce himself, he announced that he belonged to the church of Cecil B. De Mille. Becky had no idea who or what that was. When she found out, she began paying attention to the weird new guy who sat in the back of the room and who always said something off the subject. She craved anything Hollywood. The only movies she ever saw were the ones Aunt Alice occasionally took her to — *Star Wars, Blade Runner.* At school they sometimes showed uplifting old movies like *Seven Brides for Seven Brothers* and *Paint Your Wagon.* When she could, Becky bought movie magazines, hiding them in her locker.

She'd never met anybody like Arnold. He seemed to know so much. He was not her type. He was buttery and soft. She liked athletes and had a crush on a hurdler who was as graceful as a cougar. The cougar she watched, but Arnold she hung out with. Whenever she thought she could get away with it, she'd skip her Wednesday night youth fellowship meetings to go to Arnold's and watch movies. He had a VCR and a good collection. He especially loved Kurosawa and anything Eastwood. He could recite the entire soundtrack from *Dirty Harry* and *A Fistful of Dollars.*

Four windsurfers are dipping in and out of Morgan Lake. Power plant machinery percolates a rhythmic metallic breath. The air smells a little like chlorine — some sort of cleansing chemical coming from the plant.

Arnold breaks off more chocolate and offers it, but she waves it away. A battered maroon station wagon is speeding along the road toward them. It veers suddenly onto the dirt shoulder, dust rolling behind it. The car slows, pulling off onto the bank about a hundred yards away. The car doors open. "Mmm, mmm," Arnold says. "Aim for the heart, Ramon."

"Don't even think about it," Becky says. Her cousin Delmar has just gotten out of the passenger's side. He looks in their direction, shading his eyes with both hands. He's with a white girl who looks familiar. The girl pulls a baby from a car seat in the back. Delmar opens the back door on the passenger's side, sticks his head inside, and a minute later a little boy climbs out, immediately running for the water. Delmar runs after and picks him up, swinging him as if to toss him in, and the boy screams.

"I want hair that color," Arnold says. Delmar's hair, the color of a shiny penny, gleams in the sun. "Those kids his?"

"Not that I know of. Let's go."

"Go? It just got interesting." Becky glares at him. Delmar has been nothing but trouble the last six months. A couple of years ago he was busted for stealing cars, dismantling them, and selling the parts. He was given a three-year sentence, but he got an early parole. He's been out since February. The board put conditions on him, though. He can't have a car or get a license until he's kept his nose clean for a year. So Becky is Delmar's ride. All spring and summer he has badgered her to drive him places. He calls her at the bank: pick me up, take me here, take me there, come get me — ordering her around as if she were his slave. They are practically brother and sister. When they were growing up, Delmar was at her house as much as at his own. His mother, Becky's aunt Alice, would drop him off for months at a time.

"Oh look, they're coming over," Arnold says.

Delmar carries the little boy under his arm like a sack of flour, the boy smiling serenely. The boy has his mother's dirty blond hair and green eyes. Becky recognizes her now. Crystal Rebeneck. She and Delmar were always getting in trouble when they were teenagers. Becky doesn't really know her, just knows of her and has seen her around, though not for a while. She looks a lot older, her long face gaunt and her hair, in two waist-length braids, dull. She carries the big, sleeping baby in a tummy harness, his fat pink legs and feet bouncing off Crystal's bony hips.

"This guy's a flying fish," Delmar says, tossing the little boy up as he screams, then catching him, twirling him around, the boy trying to speak: "I'm — a — flying — fish."

"Stop it," Crystal says. "He'll wet his pants."

"Don't wet your pants, and don't go in the lake. There are sharks," Delmar says. He puts the boy down. The boy wobbles, trying to walk, then falls, bursting into tears.

"You made him dizzy," Crystal says.

"Tofu. Are you dizzy?"

"His name's Torry," Crystal says.

"He likes Tofu," Delmar says. The boy cries. "Hey, look what that guy has." Through teary eyes, the boy looks at the chocolate bar in Arnold's hand.

"You want some?" Arnold asks the little boy. "Can he have some?" he asks Crystal. "Hi, Del." He glances at Becky, his dimple dimpling.

"*Yá'át'éhéii.* Sure, he can have some," Delmar says, taking the bar from Arnold, unwrapping it, and letting the little boy scoop melting chocolate with his finger. "This is Stuck," Delmar says, jerking his head toward Crystal, "and sleepy Kylie."

"Crystal," the girl says, lowering herself onto a boulder. The baby kicks, fussing but not waking.

"Stuck," Delmar says. He hands the bar, unwrapped but on its wrapper, to the little boy, who sits on the ground, legs stretched out, the candy before him.

Crystal rolls her eyes, smiling. "That's his name for me."

"Stuck at Stuckey's," Delmar says. He grins, sliding his hands into his back pockets — he wears black jeans that look hot and a faded red T-shirt, not really tight but threadbare, and when he moves, his pecs and abs show clearly. Delmar has been living and working at their grandmother's farm on the reservation near Shiprock since he got out of jail, and he's in good shape. Becky watches Arnold's little smile as he eyes Delmar, and when Delmar's not looking, she kicks him. Arnold ignores her.

Delmar walks back toward the Saab, the Wailers singing, "Chant down Babylon one more time."

"Stuck's the employee of the month at Stuckey's Pecan Shoppe," he says. "Nice car."

"Which Stuckey's?" Becky says.

"In Grants," Crystal says. Grants is a hundred and eighty miles south. "We just came up to see Del for the weekend."

Becky looks over her shoulder, watching Delmar stoop to look at the Saab's dash. She nudges Arnold, who twists around, then looks at Becky in alarm as Delmar slides in behind the wheel. Arnold doesn't let anybody behind the wheel of his car. "Hey, Arnie. Nice stereo," Delmar calls, and Arnold's eyes widen.

Becky smiles. She whispers, "That one?" She ignores Arnold's fingers scratching her arm. "How old's your baby?" she asks Crystal.

"Kylie's one and a half. Torry's four." Little Torry's face has a chocolate smile from cheek to cheek.

"These speakers come with this?" Delmar says. "You ought to upgrade."

Arnold digs in. Becky puts her hand over his and removes it from her arm. But she gets up. "We should go," she says. Arnold scurries up, grabs the pack, and hurries toward the car. He stands by the driver's door, waiting for Delmar to get out, which Delmar slowly does, though he doesn't move out of the way so Arnold can get in.

"They've got good upgrades at Radio Shack. You can get surround-sound. *Ree*ally nice car," he says again.

Arnold smiles thinly.

"How's *Shidá'í?*" Delmar says, leaning against the door frame, looking over the car top at Becky.

"I don't know. Worse." Her father has started having burping fits, awful to listen to, a metronomic gasping or croaking that can go on for hours.

"*Shimá sání* wants to come see him."

"Shall I come pick her up?" Becky says.

"Nah. *Shimá* will bring us." Delmar is saying that their grandmother is still mad at Becky for taking her father to the *bilagáana* doctors, who she believes have made her son sick. If her grandmother had had her way, Becky's father would have stayed far away from the hospital. The last time Becky saw her grandmother, the old woman gave her the silent treatment.

Delmar looks over the door toward the lake. He says, "Hey, Stuck. Your kid's going to drown." Torry is standing at the water's edge, and now he's walking in, leaving his tennis shoes on the bank. Delmar steps out of the doorway, brushes by Arnold, who slips quickly into the driver's seat, slamming the door and starting the engine. Delmar runs toward the water's edge, chasing and grabbing the little boy.

6

E VERY MORNING RYLAND'S breakfast comes with a pink
pillbox. The pillbox has seven compartments. Each compartment has six pills. He empties a compartment a day, and on
Sunday he empties the last. Monday morning the boxes are magi-
cally full again. He never sees Rosy refill them. Rosy keeps track
of the pills and their aftereffects. She has a little notebook. Sometimes he peeks in the notebook to see how he's doing.

The book is full of important words: Cipro, Prilosec, Vicodin,
Percocet, Reglan, Furosemide. Pills that keep him running. He
forgets on purpose exactly what each one does, but he knows that
something in him will stop working if he skips a pill.

He has lots of good days. It says so in his wife's scrawl, right
there in black and white. Some days aren't so good. Some days,
without warning, he'll react to one of the pills, or at least that's
what Rosy says: *Got nauseous today, maybe the Cipro? Very hy-
per today, must be the Reglan. Check for allergies?* She's almost always right. He'll think back to one moment in the day when he
got himself into a little temper, one moment when he thought
he'd explode if he had to stay in the house any longer, and know
it wasn't like him at all, and that it had to be the Reglan or some
such.

He has his favorites among the pills. Prilosec, that's a good one,
though not as good as Xanax. Happy pills. The Xanax doesn't get
a little pink compartment. The Prilosec does. Prilosec is for ev-

eryday, the Xanax for special occasions. Rosy keeps the bottle of Xanax on the top shelf above the stove, where the grandkids can't get it. He can help himself if he thinks he really needs one, though she advises half a pill, not the whole, and he ought to forgo it if he can, because Xanax can be a little meanie. Sometimes it calls to him like a siren, usually thirty minutes after he's eaten half of one. The other half, the amputated half, begins to whine, and if he were a stone, he could ignore it, but he is flesh and blood, contrary to what anybody thinks.

On Sundays he takes half a Xanax before church. This is routine because Mass is more an ordeal than a pleasure. Too many people. He wouldn't mind if the church were empty. Sometimes he takes the other half when he gets home, because most Sundays the family comes to dinner. He likes the family dinners better after he takes that little pill.

Standard Sunday fare: Rosy roasts beef and potatoes, with that good brown gravy and homemade bread. On Sundays, Ryland gets to choose between regurgitated bird food—a little can of something called Ensure that won't upset his stomach—or Rosy's roast beef. He has been known to choose the bird food, though not very often.

This Sunday, the third Sunday in August, the NFL season begins, so Ryland has the game on, the volume muted. He doesn't want to contribute to the noise. His son Eddy's kids are running around screaming, and everybody else is in the kitchen—Maggie and her fiancé, George, Eddy and his wife, Sue. Teri, Ed's youngest, has just come into the living room and is staring at Ryland's feet. His feet are on Teri's chair, his footstool.

Though Teri can't talk yet, she has a book under her arm that he knows she wants to read to him. Two years old, but she still talks a line of gibberish. He pulls his feet from the stool and says, "Have a sit-down." He doesn't like to play favorites, but she is his favorite by far and has been from the day she was born. She looked him in the eye from the incubator, stuck out her lower lip, and he fell in love. In her own little way, she seems to prefer his company, too. Now she sits, opens the book, holds it in two hands, and begins reciting like a schoolmarm. The sounds make good enough sense.

Teri isn't afraid of him. The two older girls, Pooh and Sandi, are afraid of the tube in his nose and the cup, his spitting cup. *Look in it. I dare you. I'm not going to look in it. You look in it. Ask him. You ask him.* But Teri seems to take the tubes and dials and pills in stride.

Eddy comes in from the kitchen with George behind him, both holding Coors cans. Ryland likes Maggie's fiancé. George has big, goofy feet that come flopping into a room, and he always seems to be blushing. Tall and awkward. He's twenty-eight years old, same as Maggie, but George looks like he is still growing into his body, his arms almost as long as his legs. He doesn't say much, not with his mouth. Ryland can tell why Maggie fell for him, though. Can see in his eyes that the kid's no fool.

"How you doing, Mr. Mahoney?" he says.

"Okay."

Eddy sits down on the couch opposite Ryland, and George sits in the overstuffed chair. "She bothering you, Dad? Come here, Ter."

"She's not bothering me. Are you? She's my pal. Aren't you?"

Teri frowns and scolds a line of gibberish. She's teaching. He should shut up and listen.

"Who's winning?" Eddy says.

"Dallas," Ryland says.

Eddy shakes his head. On this they agree: they have no use for Dallas.

"I always thought I'd have roses at my wedding," Maggie is saying in the kitchen.

"Have what you want," Sue says.

"Do you know how much roses cost?" Rosy says.

"Look at that!" Eddy jumps, and beer sloshes onto his knee. Ryland watches Troy Aikman sprint from the thirty-yard line, holding the football out in front of himself. "Showboat," Eddy says. Aikman sashays over the line, hoisting the ball over his head.

"Teri, take your thumb out of your mouth," Eddy says. Teri is twirling her hair with one hand, sucking her thumb with the other, completely absorbed in the book. "Dad, take her thumb out of her mouth, will you?" Ryland leans over, wiggling his big finger like a worm in front of her. Teri scowls at the finger, then grabs it with the hair-twirling hand, grins, and continues to suck, so Ryland wiggles the fingers on his other hand. She laughs, dropping the book on his lap, grabbing a finger with her wet hand. Their hands dance together until a wave catches in Ryland's throat and he has to shake loose to cough. And cough. His first good cough of the day, the ball of it rising from his stomach, hurtling through the rusted pipes, whipping metal bits against his throat; he doubles over, groping his stomach. *Dear God,* he prays, a torrent of hard nothing whiplashing through, and behind it the something that never comes — oh, he wants it out, the thing that never comes. He watches Teri through his watering eyes, sees her freeze like they all do. Freeze and listen. But he's coughing now, his stomach in his throat.

They told him the breathing problem was in his head. Six years ago, when he first woke gagging and gasping, out of air, and Rosy rushed him to the emergency room, they told him it was psychosomatic, said he was suffering panic attacks. So he started exercising more, wore himself out walking miles each day, but still he woke gasping in the middle of the night, and when they finally took him to the specialist, the man said his lungs were working at about half capacity. No cancer. Just shrunken sacks, all worn out.

When he comes out of the fit, Teri is the only one still watching and listening, her eyes saucers, though not fearful, watching the way she always does when some part of his galumphing body spills into the world. He is her favorite thing in the zoo. He shakes his head at her. She shakes hers back.

Something in the kitchen begins to sizzle. Maggie's saying she'll settle for lots and lots of gaudy autumn arrangements for the wedding. "There are sunflowers growing all along the irrigation ditch in Shiprock."

"What irrigation ditch?" Rosy says.

"In Camp."

"What were you doing in there, for goodness sake?"

"Just looking around."

"Maggie, I don't like you going there. Those houses are dangerous."

"Mom, it's part of my job." Maggie has been working as a gofer for some environmental research group that investigates the deaths and disappearances of desert plants around old tailings sites. She got the job two years ago, and now she thinks she's some kind of an authority. She'll huddle up with Rosy, giving her all kinds of things to read about radiation poisoning and whatnot. Ryland tells her she ought to thank the nuclear industry. His generation got paid to make a mess, hers gets paid to clean it up. Everybody wins.

"Why did they let those houses go?" Sue says.

"Who knows? It's such a waste," Rosy says.

Ryland thinks about the other half Xanax in the bottle over the stove. His throat and chest are aching now. It's only noon. They'll be cooking for another hour, then eating, and then there will be coffee and dessert and digesting, and they won't go away until late afternoon. It's always the same.

"I blame the Navajo tribe," Rosy says. "They could've kept those houses up. They were perfectly good, solid houses."

"They say the houses are witched," Maggie says.

"Who says that?" Rosy says.

"The Indians."

Ryland leans his head back. They're talking about the company houses. He's seen pictures. The roofs, caving in now, look like they were made of straw rather than asphalt shingles and tile. The grounds have all gone to weed, and the paved road leading into the development has crumbled.

Sue says that for her money the tribe should just let private developers come in and do something about those properties. "People love the landscape, and Shiprock's a prime location because of its proximity to the San Juan." She says she doesn't understand the concept of reservations anyway. "The Indians would be better off if they opened the borders and let some money come in."

Sue's voice is an irritating chirp. Ryland can hear happiness in it. She used to be sour, and he liked her better then. In the last few years, her real estate business has taken off. He believes her new money makes her happy. She now makes more than Eddy, who works in the oil fields. Ryland wonders how his son feels about that. If it bothers Eddy, he doesn't show it.

"Who do you like for the season, Mr. Mahoney?" George says. It's halftime. The majorettes are twirling their batons. Maggie comes in holding a glass of green liquid and sits on the arm of George's chair.

"For the season?" Ryland says. "Dallas'll take the season."

"I don't know," Eddy says. "You might be surprised."

George says he'll pick a dark horse and go with Tampa.

"Tampa!" Eddy and Ryland say together.

Maggie kisses him on the head. "You big lug," she says.

Sue is telling Rosy about a sale she has pending up on Whitaker Mesa, a new gated community that everybody says is a desert paradise. "Why don't you come up with me tomorrow?" Sue says. "We can go to Edna Friedan's house."

"Can't tomorrow," Rosy says. She tells Sue about the uranium coalition and their organizing meeting tomorrow. "Don't like to leave Ryland too long." He smiles. Rosy gives herself an outing a day, never longer than two hours. She thinks he needs looking after.

"So that's tomorrow, then Tuesday we'll be in the doctor's office for most of the morning." Ryland hears the word "bronchoscopy."

He leans forward, gripping his chair. First appointment of the morning, she says, just a precaution, no reason for worry, and she begins telling them about the procedure, the tube that will go down his throat, the lung scraping. Ryland's stomach gurgles. The smell of roast beef has started doing bad things to it.

Ryland watches Maggie lean into George and whisper something. Maggie's whispering makes him tired. Teri looks tired, too. Her left eyelid sags a little. She was born with the look of a droopy-eyed skeptic. She scoots forward and puts her cheek on Ryland's knee. He rests his hand on her head and leans his own head back. He's beginning to think the regurgitated bird food will win out over the beef today. A shame.

Teri gets up and wanders away, leaving the book with him. It's a cardboard book, gnawed on the corners. He runs his finger over the ragged edges. The Cowboy cheerleaders are climbing on top of one another, making a pyramid, and Sue is telling Rosy about a Mercedes she's got her eye on, which she's planning to pay cash for when her deal closes. Maggie, whispering to George, is not in the kitchen helping her mother, which irritates Ryland no end. He stares at her, willing her to look at him, but she doesn't, so he says, "Somebody ought to be helping her mother in the kitchen," then he eyeballs her, registering the surprise on her face.

7

S AM IS NOT SICK. Ryland keeps coming back to that. If the stuff is so deadly, who should be sick if not Sam? Rosy ought to ask the uranium coalition that. Sam was in direct contact with the stuff the whole time he worked in uranium. While Ryland worked his way up, out of shift work and into the office, Sam never got out of the mill. Never wanted to.

The first time they ever saw it, the raw ore, Sam got gold fever. They were teenagers, fishing on the Dolores, and they saw yellow streaks in the cliff face. Sam and he climbed up there with their pocketknives and dug out chunks, which they took to the assayer in Durango. He told them it wasn't gold, just uranium, and they weren't rich.

Who knew? Later, after the war, when the mines started springing up everywhere and the government started talking nuclear power, Sam bought himself a Geiger counter. He wanted to stake claims, get a drill of his own. While Ryland went to school, Sam was out running around the country digging for ore. Ryland had told him he ought to use his GI bill, let the government buy him an education, but you couldn't tell Sam anything. He was always broke in those years. He'd scrape together enough to stake a claim, which would turn out to be barren, or the ore would be too deep, and he'd break drills trying to get to it, and he'd get drunk and stay drunk.

It was 1957 before Sam surfaced from his get-rich-quick

schemes. Ryland had been at the mill for three years by then and was already on his way out of shift work. He put in a word for Sam with his boss, and Sam took the job, though he resented Ryland's meddling. He never wanted anybody doing anything for him, and he passed up every opportunity to advance. Ryland tried, did his best for him. Sam seemed happiest tinkering with the ore roasters and climbing on the tailings pile, which grew steadily. When the wind blew, fine silt covered everything. You could see it on Sam. His hair, eyelashes, and eyebrows, normally white-blond, turned pink on a windy day. Ryland's hair was black then. On him the stuff disappeared, he seemed to absorb it, but underneath his hair, his scalp would be like sandpaper. He can remember his jaws aching because he clamped his teeth together, trying to keep the silt out of his mouth. Rosy complained and complained because his work clothes would turn her wash a muddy brown, and she had to wash his stuff separately.

For years the tailings pile wasn't news, and then all of a sudden it was. It wasn't uranium anymore. It was chemistry. Polonium, bismuth, lead; it was all about the chemical breakdown, what happened when the ore was blasted, and there were all kinds of speculations about toxicity in the tailings after they processed the stuff. They said the radiation in Durango's air was ten percent above safety levels. There were editorials, weeks and then months of them in the *Durango Herald*, the *Rocky Mountain News*, the *Denver Post*: "You can't see it, you can't smell it, you can't taste it — this deadly gas."

Just before they moved the operation south to the reservation, some honcho in New Jersey got the bright idea of planting grass on the pile to keep it from blowing. Didn't work. Radiation levels stayed the same. But they planted. Sam spent a few weeks climbing the pile, seeding the tailings, rigging sprinklers. Someplace there's a photo of Sam on the catwalk they erected at the top of the pile, standing up there smoking a cigarette, on the clock, his face a study in indifference, Superman, to look at him.

Who, if not Sam, should be sick?

8

MONDAY MORNING. Several people crowd around the table in Bill Lowry's law office. Becky sits closest to the door. Lowry asks them all to introduce themselves. Lowry's assistant sits next to him, and next to her are two women from Shiprock Chapter House, then a man from Shiprock's Public Health Service. Angela Bistai is here from the Nenahnezad Chapter House. Becky knows her slightly. Becky's father goes to Nenahnezad chapter meetings — or did when he was well enough — just across the river from their house in Fruitland, off the reservation. Her mother didn't want Becky in reservation schools. She worried that they were too lax and, in the eighties, too dangerous. LA gangs had started moving into the reservation by then. Della fretted every time Becky or Woody went to Shiprock to visit Becky's grandmother.

The pastor from Farmington's Unitarian church is here and the one from the Navajo Methodist mission. Rose Mahoney is here. Her husband is not. A very tall white man is sitting across the table from Becky — at least the half she can see is tall. He introduces himself as Terry Conrad, representing a Dallas company, American Geological Exploration and Resources — AGER. There are also people from Navajo Mines and from the Bureau of Indian Affairs.

"Let me begin," Bill Lowry says, "by going over key events that have brought us here, though I know this is familiar territory for most of you."

The door opens behind Becky, a voice says, "Sorry I'm late," and Lowry says, "We're just getting started." She turns to see Harrison Zahnee. She sits a little straighter. He opens one of the folding chairs leaning against the wall, and she scoots over to make room for him. He smiles at her.

"As you know, the bill that passed last year, the Radiation Exposure Compensation Act, RECA, is an insult to those injured by the uranium industry in our area," Lowry says.

Harrison is wearing a blue shirt and jeans. His hair, in a tight braid, falls to the middle of his back. When Becky looks at him out of the corner of her eye, she can see a hint of crow's-feet behind his shades. From his bank file, she knows he's twenty-nine, four years older than she.

"Only miners who actually worked in the mines before the EPA safety initiatives were adopted are eligible for compensation," Lowry is saying. "Only those who have a specific kind of lung cancer are eligible, and only if they can document precise exposure to radiation, supplying medical records of specific treatments —"

"Which, of course, the majority of Navajo miners can't do, since most of them didn't have access to medical care and most don't — didn't, in many cases, since many have died — speak English," his assistant says. Her lips gleam, cotton-candy pink.

Lowry begins reviewing events that led up to RECA, the dam break in the southern part of the reservation, which flooded the Rio Puerco with waste from the underground mines and produced what he says was the biggest single release of radioactive poisons on American soil since the bomb tests at White Sands. "That single devastating event finally got some attention in Washington. We're seeing the effects of the industry everywhere. One study has found that organ cancer rates among Navajo teenagers living near mine tailings are seventeen times the national average. But, of course, organ cancers like kidney and liver are not even covered under the act." He tells them that the mill workers are not covered. People in the path of wind-borne tailings, people who have drunk from contaminated water sources, children who have drunk milk from cows that grazed on contaminated plants — none are eligible.

"There's some evidence," the assistant says, "that houses and hogans in mining and milling areas have high levels of radiation, and it's thought that people used radioactive materials scavenged in the area to build their houses."

"So," Lowry says, "let's start talking strategy."

Harrison interweaves his fingers on the table in front of him, long, straight fingers, the nails beautifully curved and glowing like mother-of-pearl. He wears a wedding ring, but on the little finger of his right hand. A simple Navajo band with inlaid turquoise, dark lines separating each stone. Looks old.

"We should begin, I would think," Lowry says, "by using the tribal infrastructure and enlisting the chapter presidents throughout the reservation. Another thing I'd like to do is to contact the downwinders in Nevada who are fighting the same battle and see if we can join forces. And we need money."

"The tribe may have funds for this, don't you think?" Anita Bistai says.

"Why should the tribe pay for a situation created by the mining companies?" a Shiprock chapter representative says. "The Diné entered into business in good faith. The mines ought to pay."

"Well, that's not going to happen," the assistant says.

"If I may," the man from Texas says, "my company has an interest in grass-roots organization around this issue. We have a non-profit component dedicated to education, and if the community shows support, AGER is willing to match it."

"What does that mean, Terry?" the assistant says.

"It means we will provide matching funds for any monies generated in the community. The funds are targeted for education only, not lobbying."

"Really?" Rose Mahoney says.

"Yes."

The assistant asks if AGER administers and distributes.

"No. We're not set up for that." He gazes around the room. He looks like he's about Becky's age, maybe a little older. Five o'clock shadow. Hazel eyes. Long, handsome face, in good proportion to his body. "I'd recommend choosing a not-for-profit host organization. The library, for example. Or the college. Mr. Zahnee might be in a prime position to administer," he says, smiling and nodding at Harrison, who sits back, crossing his arms and ankles, saying nothing. "What we've done in other areas is help get efforts off the ground by organizing town meetings and inviting key community leaders. People with resources. We could start there. Take Farmington's temperature. See if there's interest. Then move into smaller towns and into the reservation. Build momentum."

"Good idea," Lowry says. He suggests they form a subcommittee and asks anybody who's interested in organizing a town hall to join him and Mr. Conrad for coffee at the café across the street directly after the meeting. Then he begins mapping out a plan of action for the next six months.

When the meeting ends, Harrison turns toward Becky. In his mirrored sunglasses, she sees two miniatures of her face. He says, "Coffee?"

He sits next to her in a large round booth packed with other committee members. He says something to her in Navajo, but her family did not speak Navajo at home when she was growing up. She has only a few words. She smiles.

His eyebrows rise, thin brown frowns above the mirrored glasses. He says something else.

His glasses are irritating. There's no good reason for them — the windows are shaded. They seem an affectation, an old-fashioned warding off of the evil eye.

"You don't know your language?" he says.

"My language?" she says.

"Oh. I thought you were Diné."

"I am."

The lenses study her.

"Does your wife like those sunglasses? Because I guess she always has mirrors whenever she's with you. She can do her hair."

The frowns rise a little higher, his forehead wrinkling. He smiles and says, "I'm not married." He takes the glasses off and puts them in his shirt pocket.

"Thank you," she says.

"'*Aoo'*." He gazes at her—eyelashes long and straight. She swallows, looking away.

They begin talking about where they might hold the meeting and how to publicize it. Terry Conrad tells them how he's seen it done in other areas, turning to her at one point and saying he's glad to have a representative from the bank here. He asks if she has the combination to the vaults, and she says, "Actually, I do," and they all laugh.

"I don't see that we need a huge amount to get us started," the assistant says. "Our firm is willing to offer legal advice on a contingency basis—isn't that right, Bill."

"With the expectation," Lowry says, "that some form of class-action initiative might be put in place. For the town meeting, we could get a meeting room and equipment donated. It would be good to tap locals as motivational speakers."

"People who've been there," Conrad says.

"Becky," Lowry says, "if we asked your dad to speak, would he?"

"No. He's not well enough. Plus, he doesn't go for that kind of thing."

"Maybe you'll speak on his behalf?" the assistant says, brown eyes bright, joyful, a little creepy.

Becky feels Harrison turn and look directly at her. "Go for it," he whispers.

"Maybe," she says.

"How about you, Rose?" Lowry says.

Harrison is still looking at her, she can feel it. She glances at him. His eyes are teasing, full of laughter, and now he seems to be trying for eye contact, making a point of it. When the waitress comes to refill their coffee, Becky asks him to pass her the sugar. He hands her a packet but doesn't let go. She tugs. He smiles. Lets go. He says, "'*Ahéhee'*," which she knows means thank you.

She says, "You're welcome," and rips open the packet.

He smiles widely, as if she's just made his day, and her stomach flips.

Later, walking out, he says, "You should take my class."

"Why?"

"Because."

"Because why?"

He shrugs, putting the sunglasses on. "Maybe you'd like it." They walk into the sunny parking lot, a cloudless furnace, which feels good after the frigid air-conditioned room.

"Are you a good teacher?"

"Some say so. I've seen you over there, you know—at the bank."

"You have?"

"'*Aoo'*."

"How come you never said hello?"

"You always look so busy. Looks like they work you hard. You like it?"

"It's okay. I like the numbers. Not so crazy about the customers."

"You're not a people person?" He laughs, his laugh whispery, airy.

"Are you?"

"There's nothing like people."

They watch Terry Conrad fold himself into a green Dodge Dakota with tinted windows. "How tall do you think he is?" she says.

"Six-seven."

"You think?"

"He told me. *He* signed up for my class," he says, his tone challenging.

"I thought he lived in Texas."

"'*Aoo'*. He's just sitting in for a couple of months. He wants enough Navajo to get by on."

"What does that mean?"

"Good question. Yeah, he comes to my office a couple of days ago. He wants to learn hello, goodbye, how's the weather. Like that."

A truck engine starts, and the Dakota pulls out, rolling toward them. Terry Conrad salutes with two fingers as he passes.

Harrison nods. He doesn't seem to care much for Conrad. Becky wonders if that goes for all white people or just him. "So are you going to sign up for my class?"

"Maybe."

"Maybe? I'm telling you, you'd like it." He grins. "Five o'clock. Monday through Thursday this fall. There are only two spaces left. You better sign up now if you want to get in."

"I guess you're popular."

"'*Aoo*'." He steps aside so she can open her truck door, saying, "*Hágoónee'*, Becky Atcitty," as she slides in. "See you in class."

At work she tells Arnold about Harrison. "You guys with the language. You're so full of yourselves. You act like you're more Indian than the rest of us."

"Aren't we? Just kidding, just kidding. But really. You should. Go to school. You'd see him all the time. You could visit him during office hours." Arnold laughs, low and dirty.

"Like I'm going to put myself in the position of being graded by him."

"Girl, you are so chicken shit."

"He wears a wedding ring, but he said he's not married."

"And you believed him? You are a child."

She sort of feels like one. She feels almost chipper. "Chipper" is one of her dad's words, something he picked up years ago from the mill workers. "You're chipper today," he would say when she was little, and Becky would howl, "Chipper, chipper, chipper like a bird." For a while everything was chipper. Hamburgers were chipper. The moon was chipper. She's thinking of this as she drives the ten miles from the bank to her folks' house late that afternoon. She notes chipper things along the highway, the wrecking yard that goes on for miles and miles, growing a little more every year, a metal monstrosity, today a chipper one, and she doesn't even notice the absence of worry, which usually starts the minute she leaves work and grows into full-blown dread by the time she gets home, until she makes the turn into her parents' lot and sees her father dozing on the porch swing, wrapped up in his Pendleton blanket, even though it must be ninety degrees out. A lump instantly clots her throat.

"Hey, Dad," she calls, getting out of the truck and walking over to him. He opens his eyes. Face the color of ash, lips tinged purple, oxygen tank at his feet. "What are you doing out here?" she says.

"Waiting for the army." His lips peel back to expose colorless gums. It's Monday, and Becky's aunts Katie and Pip will be on their way. Soldiers in the Army of the Lord. Her mother's unmarried sisters have been coming three or four evenings a week since her father relapsed, helping with housekeeping and dinner, sometimes staying after the dishes are cleared to do their crafts. Becky's mother is a beader. Katie knits, and Pip does needlepoint. Her father will wait to say hello, then will disappear out back when the prayer circle forms. Since the relapse, he's been first and last on the prayer list. Becky thinks it creeps him out. Though she'll join the circle — her aunts insist — it creeps her out, too, and has since she began cutting Bible study when she was nine. Over the years her aunts have gotten more and more zealous about their faith. They tell Becky she's walking on Perdition Road because of the movies she watches (so violent) and the company she keeps (Arnold). Her mother has toured Perdition Road, too, from the aunts' point of view. Della is the youngest of six, three brothers, two sisters. She is not related to them by blood. Their parents, Swedish missionaries, adopted Della at birth. She is the only Navajo.

It was dancing that got Della started down Perdition Road. Becky's mother loves to dance — she taught Becky how to country-swing to old Merle Haggard records when Becky was very young. "It's not the dancing that's sinful," her aunts chided. "It's what it leads to." In her mother's case, it led to marriage to a pagan.

"Something smells good," Becky says.

"Can't smell," her father says.

"Smells like cinnamon."

"Yeah, she's baking something." He nods toward the house. "You running today?"

"Soon as it gets cooler." She and her father, both long-distance runners, have run two marathons together. Before he got sick, her father could run a marathon in under four hours, usually finishing at the top of his age group. He's forty-six.

An old black and white Datsun pulls into the dirt yard, Aunt Pip honking as she comes. She swings the car in a wide arc to park under the willow tree, the only tree in the yard. The car's bumper is plastered with stickers. Today there's a new one: AS SURE AS GOD PUTS HIS CHILDREN IN THE FURNACE, HE WILL BE IN THE FURNACE WITH THEM.

"Hello, hello, hello," the aunts call. They open the back doors, and pull out baskets of craftwork.

Pip and Katie look so much alike they could be twins; they're treelike women, solid and shapeless, strong-limbed, long-fingered, long-necked. Their chins are broad and square and always tilted slightly skyward, as if in prayer. Their cheekbones are high, and their eyes are silver dashes. Their hair, once sunflower yellow, has darkened over the years and now is the color of autumn wheat. They usually wear it braided and wrapped around their heads. When she was little and stayed with them in the house they share in Farmington, Becky would sit quietly and watch the long unwinding and brushing of the hair at night, and she thought they were as beautiful as angels. She loves them to death. They would do anything for her, she knows. In her moments of doubt, when she worries that the fiery hell they so fervently believe in might really exist, she holds on to the hope that they'll sweet-talk whoever's in charge and get her into heaven.

Delmar's old dog, C3PO, has come out from under the porch and begun to bark. "Oh, hush," Katie says, stepping up on the porch. "How's everything? We brought peaches."

"Where'd you get them?" Becky says.

"At the fruit stand. Hush, smelly dog."

"Don't let him in," Pip says.

C3PO scoots between Katie's legs and into the house. Pip follows, crossing her eyes at them.

Becky's father begins struggling up from the swing, and Becky helps him. "Tell *Shízhánee'* I'm out back," he says.

She replies, "I'll come, too."

But Aunt Pip calls, "Becky, do you want to join the circle?"

She meets her father's eyes. "Too late," he says, smiling. She watches him totter down the steps and around the house.

They don't care if she doesn't contribute to the petitions, as long as she's holding their hands, a part of them. They pray in the large living room, with its cedar walls, which her father built. These days it smells as much of sickness as of cedar, and the smell irritates the lump in her throat, though today the sick smell is almost hidden by whatever's baking, and by C3PO, smelling way too doggy in the hot weather. Eyes half closed, Becky watches her mother, whose face has started to take on the gray hue of her father's. In the last six months, spidery lines have appeared at the edges of her mother's mouth, which always seems downturned, so unlike her. Her mother rarely gives in to moods — she thinks that's sinful — but depression has been pulling at her. Her father's luck — *shízhánee'* — doesn't look so lucky these days.

They have always seemed to be in love, her parents, unlike her friends' parents, many of whom are divorced or who seem to live to quarrel. Her father says it was love at first sight. He first saw Della at a community basketball game. He was playing for Shiprock, she was rooting for Fruitland. With seconds left in the fourth quarter, he had the ball when he saw her, a delicate, doll-like Indian sitting calmly in the middle of a pink crowd. He threw wildly, and swoosh — the rez team won by three points. He had given Della her name: *Shízhánee'*, Lucky.

When they're through praying, Becky says, "I'm going to go run," but Aunt Katie clutches her hand, tugging her toward the table, while Aunt Pip steers her mother toward the kitchen. "Your grandparents sent something for your dad," Aunt Katie says. Becky's maternal grandparents have been running a mission in Argentina for the past ten years. Katie takes an envelope from her craft basket and hands it to Becky. There's a check inside for three thousand dollars. "It's for a casket."

"Wow," Becky says. "How'd they come up with so much?"

"They prayed for it," Aunt Katie says, her eyes full of the unsaid lesson — that Becky could get on that money train, too, if she only would.

"Caskets cost that much?"

"More. But this will buy a cherry-wood one. Isn't cherry his favorite?"

Her aunts have been having these hushed conversations with Becky about the funeral costs for a while, trying to save her mother the pain of making arrangements. They mean well, she knows. In the prayer circle they always pray for the miracle of health, but they are practical women, ready to do what needs to be done.

Her father has been worrying about money, too. Since the mill closed, he's been making a meager living farming, and her mother makes a little with her beadwork. They have huge medical bills, and there won't be any farm income this year. Though the house is paid off, property taxes keep rising, and he's been worrying about how Della will pay them on her own.

"He'd probably prefer a less expensive one. He likes cherry wood, but . . ." Becky says.

"He deserves it," her mother says hoarsely. Becky turns and sees her standing in the kitchen doorway. Her chin quivers.

"Go for your run, sweetheart," Aunt Katie says, hugging her hard.

9

C AN YOU JUST put your head down?" Dr. Callahan is saying to Ryland.

It had been down. Now it's up again. Ryland has turned into a
turtle this afternoon; his head, poking up out of his carcass, wants
to see what's going on. He forces it back on the little paper pillow. He's lying on an examination table, and he's wearing a paper
gown that ties in the back. Socks and underwear. That's it. The
nurse, Rae Freitag, a woman he knows from church, has covered
him with a thin cotton blanket, so not everything in this room is
paper.

The day has been horrible. They sat in Dr. Callahan's waiting room throughout most of the morning because he had been
called to the hospital for an emergency. Finally, the receptionist
told them they'd better reschedule, so they went home, but then
the office called in the middle of the afternoon, saying the doctor
was back and wanted to do the procedure now. Ryland was against
it; the man had wasted enough of their time, but the receptionist
said they'd better come now because the doctor was going on vacation in a week, and he wanted to do it sooner rather than later.
So they went back. Now Rosy is in the waiting room, where Ryland banished her. At the very last minute, as they were walking
down the hall toward the examination room, he said, "You don't
need to come with me."

"Are you sure?" she said. She wanted to come.

"Yes." He was sure.

The doctor is speaking in a tone that makes Ryland feel as if he's a very young child. "This is the villain," he says, holding up the rubber contraption he'll use to take the tissue sample. He waves it in front of Ryland's face so that he doesn't have to lift his head from the pillow. The first test of the afternoon: Can Ryland control his damn neck muscles and keep his head on the pillow? He feels as if he is drowning, and they haven't even started yet.

"Now, are you comfortable?" Dr. Callahan says.

Rae Freitag has put his oxygen tank on a shelf that pulls out from the examination table, and now she hands him the tube. Overhead, the plastic case covering the fluorescent lights is completely clean. Admirable. Very admirable.

Rae gave him a shot to relax him, and now she is inserting an IV into his arm. Before they started, she asked him if he needed the toilet, and he did, and now he needs it again, but she is holding his arm and telling him to be still. His arm is shaking. He's afraid his bladder is going to burst. He doesn't want to wet himself. Not in front of Rae. She's a nice woman.

"What we're going to do," she is telling him, "is pass this tube through your nose. This other tube here is oxygen. So you're going to be getting plenty of air. You don't need to worry about that. Okay?

"Now Ryland, when the tube passes through your vocal cords, you may feel like you can't catch your breath. Don't worry about that. Everybody feels that, and after a minute it'll pass."

Dr. Callahan stands to his right, wearing a green mask. "If you get at all worried that you can't breathe, Ryland," he says, "you just raise your hand and I'll stop whatever I'm doing and let you catch your breath."

"What if I need to cough?" Ryland says.

"That's not going to happen. That's what this IV is all about. It administers medicine that relieves the need to cough. You're getting a good dose of steroid here, buddy." Above the green mask, behind the speckled glasses, the doctor's eyes smile. "Ryland, you're in a doctor's office. If you get into trouble, where better?

Now you can help by taking slow, shallow breaths through your mouth. Can you do that?"

Ryland breathes.

"You ready?"

He feels the tube when it enters. The other tube, with oxygen, is cold, this one hot. He feels it scraping into the soft upper part of his palate.

"Try not to talk while the tube is in your lungs. Talking can make you hoarse or give you a sore throat after the procedure."

Ryland blinks. He thinks about pissing into his helmet when he was in the service. Crammed in a foxhole with a dozen other men. Nobody wanted to sit in piss. They pissed into their helmets, but he doesn't have a helmet. He can't trust his eyes not to tear.

"You may feel pressure or tugging when the specimens are taken. How you doing? Remember, raise your hand if you want me to stop."

He remembers what he forgot to ask the doctor. He wanted to ask exactly how long the tube was going to be in his lungs, and how he would know when it got there, and how long it took to get there, and how long he needed to hold his breath, because he could hold it quite a while. It was a trick he used to stay awake in the foxhole, and on the graveyard shift, and when he was a boy and needed to stay awake until everybody else in the house was asleep. He could hold it for four or five minutes in his prime, but he isn't in his prime now, so he needs to know what's expected of him. He tries to raise his hand. He is raising it. He's pretty sure he is raising it. The green mask is in the way. He can't see a thing because the doctor's damn green mask is bearing down.

Afterward, when Ryland is dressed again, the doctor comes back in and tells him they'll send the samples down to Albuquerque. Might take a week, maybe longer, to get the results. "If there's anything, anything at all, I'll call you. But if you don't hear from us, don't worry. In this case, no news is good news. I'll have the results sent to you. Okay?"

"Okay."

"So when's the big day?"

Ryland stares at him.

"The wedding."

"Oh. Soon. Six weeks."

"Little Maggie. I remember when she was born."

Ryland smiles, nods, and swallows, his throat burning where the instrument had scraped.

10

S AM STANDS JUST inside the door of Molina's Fish and
Tackle holding two large grocery bags and blinking while
his eyes adjust to the dim room. He puts the bags down next to
five others he's brought in. Molina's wife, Mary, is behind the cash
register, and Molina, a trim man with a thin mustache and thick,
wavy brown hair, is talking to a customer. He nods at Sam, Sam
at him. It's a tiny room, stinky with fish, the floor gummy. Bait
bags of ready-to-go live bait cover most of the counter where Molina stands. The customer, a willowy man in a Hawaiian shirt and
shorts, rubber thongs on his feet, a Yankees hat on his head, tow-
ers over him.

Sam walks along the edge of the room to the fly bins and sees
that the cubby where Molina keeps his fancy flies is empty. Two
teenage girls crowd in, looking in the cubbies. He moves on to the
frozen cases, reading labels on boxes he can barely see through the
frosty glass: Mullet, Squid, Pilchards, Ballyhoo, Spanish Sardines,
Cigar Minnows, Chum.

"My friend Sam might disagree with you, *verdad*, Sam?" Molina calls. "What'd you bring me?" Sam walks back to the door,
picks up two bags, walks over to the counter, and puts them on
top of it. "People around here have been having luck with Sam's
ties. *Buenas dias, señor. Donde estabas?*" Molina says, stretching
his hand out.

"Moley," Sam says, shaking it.

He returns to the door, picks up two more bags. Behind him, Molina clicks his tongue.

"*Hola*, Sam," Mary says.

"Mary." Mary could be her husband's twin, they look so much alike. They're nearly the same height, though Mary is fleshier. Her hair is a longer version of her husband's, thick and wavy, and both have mild brown eyes.

"What'd you bring me, *viejo?*" Molina says again. "*Pesces largos?*" He grins. Sam scoots a bag toward him, and he opens it, pulling out one of the fake mackerels. "We can't keep these in stock," Molina says to his customer. "Not this month, not next. Try one of these, my man. Test your luck."

"Wouldn't use artificial bait," the man says.

"Artificial's starting to take off," Molina says. "Works, and it's not so smelly."

"Live bait and a Carolina rig," the man says. "Can't miss. Did you ever try that?" the man asks Sam. He pulls a snapshot out of his shirt pocket and hands it to Sam. Molina smiles, ducks his head, and occupies himself with Sam's flies. Molina spends his weekends listening to the weekend fishermen tell their stories and show pictures of their catches. "People don't understand the Carolina rig," the man says. "They don't trust it. Pure ignorance."

Sam stares at a picture of this man standing in a boat, holding what looks like a good-sized bass attached to a hook and line that must be this Carolina rig. The man in the photo stares solemnly at the camera's eye. Sam nods and hands the photo back. He watches Molina count his flies by twos.

"Carolina rig with live ballyhoo."

"I count twenty-five, *verdad*, Sam?" Molina says.

"Twenty-five," Sam says.

"Fifty bucks," Molina says.

"Working's one thing," the man says. "Working better is another."

"What else you got?" Molina says, nodding at Sam's other bag.

Sam pushes it across the counter and reaches for two more bags on the floor. Molina opens the first and looks in.

"Yes, indeed, I was up on the Potomac with a friend of mine when this picture was taken. Have you ever fished up there?"

"What I'm going to do with these?" Molina says. He pulls out a handful of the white flies Sam tied last fall, getting ready for Alice before she didn't come. Sam has named these Florida Ghosts. When the mackerel start running, a little white fly on the top of the water will bring them in. He's seen Alice land twenty in an hour. Schools of mackerel start running in November and December. "How many you got here, Sam?" He drops the handful on the counter.

"Hundred."

"Hundred? What I'm going to do with them?" He shakes his head, gathers the flies up again, and drops them back in the bag. "Can't use them, Sam. In a month or two, yes." He pushes the bag toward Sam.

Sam pushes it back, and pushes another alongside it. "Wets," he says. "Blue Dun, Black Gnat, Coral Moth, Mirth. Red-winged Moth, Silver Speeder ... What you want, Moley? You don't see it here, I'll do it special."

Molina peers into the four bags on the counter. "Been busy, eh, *tío*? Well, I wish I could. The *pesces largos* are the ones that are moving right now, Sam. I could use maybe another twenty-five. As for these others ..." He pushes the bags back across the counter. "Mary, give me seventy-five dollars. We'll advance you on the next batch."

Mary rings up a sale. Sam watches her take money from the register, shuffling bills, counting them, crossing the room. "Oh, these are pretty. Aren't these pretty," she says to the customer. She picks up one of Sam's big flies and offers him the money, but Sam doesn't take the bills. She puts them on the counter.

"Tell you what, Moley," Sam says. "I'm going to make you a deal on these flies. I've got five hundred dollars' worth here. I'll give you all of them for three hundred, plus I'll make another twenty-five for the wide-mouths." He pushes the bags back across the counter.

Molina clicks his tongue and shakes his head. He pushes the

bags back. "You know the story. No storage and not much ready cash. Just write me out a receipt for seventy-five dollars."

Sam folds his arms. He doesn't touch the bags. He's nodding and feels cold in the sticky room. He eyes Molina, and Molina's eyes shift down. Moley's got cash in a safe in his hurricane shelter, lots of it. Sam has seen it. Moley knows that. They got drunk together in that shelter once, and Moley showed him the safe.

"Okay, I guess I'll have the ballyhoo," the customer says, picking up a bag of bait. He puts it in front of Molina on the counter, pushing one of Sam's bags out of the way. The man steps in front of Sam, looking into the glass display case, tapping his finger on the glass. "So that's a Marlin II reel? Can I see it?"

"You know the score, Sam," Molina says. "Your flies sell good. I want to sell them for you. I got no storage space." His eyes shift away.

"Three fifty," Sam says. "You just missed out on my good deal. Still, it's a savings, Mole. Three hundred and fifty right now today. If you want to see me again."

"What do you mean by that?"

Sam nods. "Known you a good while, Jorge."

Molina closes his eyes and shakes his head. "You haven't been coming around regular, Samuelito. You bring me some in a couple of weeks, I'll be ready."

"Now that's a dual-mode, isn't it? Can I just take a look at that?" the customer says, and Sam turns around, walks out of the room, leaving the flies and the money behind.

He crosses the parking lot quickly, pulling his flask from his back pocket, taking a drink, then another. He opens the truck door and gets behind the wheel, slams the door, turns the key, puts the truck in gear, starts to back up, then stops. He stares at the open door. He says, "No sirree, no sirree," just under his breath. He turns the key off and folds his arms. After a few minutes, Mary steps out on the porch and looks at him. She's holding the cash and a bag. She starts to step down but stops when Sam shakes his head, a precise back and forth. He says, "No sirree." He takes a drink. Mary shrugs, hesitates, then turns and steps back in.

Cars and trucks come and go in the parking lot. The day is sweltering, and the air in the pickup is rank, a little like rotting meat. A mosquito plays in and out of the window, buzzing around Sam's right ear, but he pays it no attention. He opens his glove compartment, where he keeps a receipt book and pen. He takes the book and writes Jorge's name and the date at the top of a receipt, and below that $350, and below that Cash. He tears the receipt out, lays it on the dash, opens the glove compartment, puts the book and pen back in. He takes a drink.

The man in the Hawaiian shirt comes out carrying his bait bag. He glances at Sam and quickly away. Sam can see Mary through the open door, standing in the shadow where she probably thinks he can't see her. Other customers come and go.

Forty-five minutes later, Jorge comes out. He stands on the porch, glowering at Sam, shaking his head. He steps off the porch and starts toward Sam's truck. Halfway across the parking lot, he stops. He shakes his head slowly. Sam nods. Molina's cheeks fill with air, then deflate. Finally he turns and walks around the store toward the backyard, where the hurricane shelter is. Sam nods, keeping his right foot pressed hard on the brake. When Molina comes back around the corner, his hands are stuffed in his pockets. He walks to the driver's side door. Through the open window, he hands Sam a wad of bills. He says, "*Diablo.*"

Sam hands him the receipt, stuffs the bills into his pocket, and turns the truck key.

"Don't you want to count it?" Jorge says.

"I trust you," Sam says.

Molina shakes his head. "Don't do this again, Sam. Come in regular. Okay?"

Sam eyeballs him.

"*Ladrón,*" Molina says, and spits on the ground.

Sam says, "I don't know what that means, Moley, but I'm going to take it as a compliment."

11

TUESDAY NIGHT, Rosy called Lily and asked her to drive out to their storage unit to look for old files from the mill. They had rented the unit together in Durango before moving to Shiprock because the company houses were a fraction the size of their mountain homes and they couldn't stand to part with everything. Just before the Shiprock mill closed, Ryland had taken a file cabinet full of his personal files up to the storage unit. He turned everything else over to the company.

The unit is in a city of asphalt — rows and rows of padlocked cubes. Lily walks along the cement floor, Tom Jones singing, "It's not unusual to be loved by anyone," through the invisible speakers overhead. She inserts her key into the heavy-duty padlock on I-12, unlocks it, slides the bolt, opens the door, steps inside, and switches on the light. She pulls the door shut behind her.

Lily got rid of all the furniture she had shared with Sam. There are still a few pieces from her and Rosy's childhood — an old birch coffee table that they'd secretly inscribed as kids, crawling underneath to crayon their names and, as teenagers, boys' names; the chrome dinette table that had been the family's kitchen table; a clawfoot bathtub that had been in their grandparents' home. There's a mountain of boxes full of junk. Lily has always been a collector. As a girl and after she married, she kept scrapbooks with relics from every important event — pictures of her and Rosy dancing with Sam and Ryland at Grange Hall dances, pressed leaves, the first colors of fall each time fall came around, a pressed mum — the first corsage Sam gave her. She has no pictures of Sam in her house. No pictures, no scrapbooks, just the bills for the storage unit.

Ryland's file cabinet is just inside the door, along with several cardboard boxes full of mill stuff. Lily's own file cabinet, a smaller one, is full of important documents: old tax returns, old bank statements, her birth certificate, her divorce papers. Which Lily never filed and which she will not worry about today. She has wasted enough of her life worrying and feeling guilty. Yesterday Fred talked to her about her useless feelings of guilt. She'd been telling him how she was blindsided by Sam's infidelities. How could she be married to a man for nearly twenty years and never know he had affairs? Was she an idiot? Fred said that some people are just expert liars and it wasn't her fault. She disagreed. She believes in her heart that she knew but just ignored her instincts and that she's guilty of betraying herself. Fred asked her how long she was going to blame herself for her marriage, because, he said, if it was going to go on for much longer, he would probably be spending less time with her, which he didn't want to do. "I like you, Lily." That's what he said. And he is right. She has spent far too much time beating herself up over her divorce.

Except technically she's not divorced. Lily shudders, glancing at her little file cabinet half buried under a pile of boxes.

She opens the top drawer of the large cabinet from the mill. She stares at a row of faded yellow file folders with color-coded tabs. The folders are dated and labeled: Budgets, Contracts, Transportation, Equipment. But they are all empty. She closes the top drawer and opens the second. Personnel files. Her name, Behan, leaps out at her. Sam's file. She flicks the file open with her fingernail, peering in. Empty. Someone has cleared these out. Lily laughs silently. Like her marriage. Empty.

She supposes she figured at the time that given all the lies, she'd never had a real marriage, so why should she have a real divorce?

Overhead the neon light flickers soundlessly. On the Muzak channel Engelbert Humperdinck blends seamlessly into John Denver, who sings about sunshine on his shoulders.

It's not that she deliberately didn't file the papers. It's that Sam wanted out so fast. They agreed on the terms, signed the documents, and he gave her a cashier's check for half of his pension from the mill — ten thousand dollars. Then he left, taking the truck. Left the papers with her to file. Left her to do the packing. Left her stranded on the reservation without a vehicle. She had to rely on Ryland and Rosy for transportation. It was horrible, having to make arrangements to get places, go through paperwork and memorabilia from twenty years of marriage. And then pack it all up, haul the boxes to Durango, find a place to live, get the utilities hooked up and the phone started — and she had to do everything by herself, which her sister has never done. Rosy has never found her way in the world alone. She complains that she's tired, but she doesn't know tired. She chose Ryland, a good man, a man who would never do what Sam did. Though Rosy doesn't say that, it's implied. Actually, it seems to Lily that Rosy chose Sam for her. He was Ryland's good buddy . . .

No. She is not going to fret about Rosy today and she is not going to feel guilty.

She closes that drawer and opens the third, which has no folders but is packed full of loose papers. Mostly numbers and charts. She flips through them to bound stacks underneath, some of which seem to be data collected for the Atomic Energy Commission, letters from scientists, physicists, people she doesn't know, never heard of, studies, all with different dates, some as early as 1946.

Should she take all of this stuff? There's so much to carry. It really would be better if Rosy came and looked for herself, though Lily knows that Rosy's plate is full now, what with getting ready for Maggie's wedding, plus she can't leave Ryland alone for long. He has fallen twice in the last six months. Poor Rosy. Lily thinks that pretty soon Rosy will have to face the fact that she cannot take care of Ryland by herself. Ryland is failing, it's clear. She will have to start looking into long-term-care options. Which they cannot afford. She's not good with money. Rosy and Ryland have never been good with money.

Lily is good with money. She and Fred are alike in that way.

They are financial equals. Lily invested her half of Sam's pension in real estate here in Durango, a very good investment, as it turned out. She now owns a string of apartment buildings up near Fort Lewis College, highly desirable, a steady ninety percent occupancy, and she employs property managers who do their jobs and don't bother her. Fred likes that about her. "Do you know how many women your age are looking for husbands to take care of them? They find themselves divorced or widowed and have no idea how to support themselves. Not you, Lily." He said he wanted a woman who can hold her own in all things, a true equal, financially, emotionally . . .

Lily has tried to talk with Rosy about what she's going to do if Ryland needs expensive long-term care. Rosy says she'll piece something together. Lily suspects she's figuring on her sister's nest egg as a large part of the piece.

Oh, she hates herself for thinking this way. Rosy would do anything for her, Lily knows this.

She pulls several of the reports out, drops them on the floor, closes the drawer, and opens the fourth. She just hopes Ryland holds on for another few years. She wants to travel, and Fred wants a travel partner. He's just about where he wants to be financially and is planning to retire in November, while he's still young enough to enjoy it. He wants to see the Yucatán. He's something of a history buff, he told her. He wants to explore Mayan ruins, see Chichén Itzá. He showed her pictures in his *National Geographic*. It looks so exotic, and now Lily can't stop thinking about it. He's thinking November. He asked her if she's free then.

The fourth drawer has notebooks in it, several of them tied together in twine, daily logbooks. These, she supposes, might be useful. She drops them on top of the reports. There's also a photograph of the old tailings pile in Durango. Sam poses on a wooden walk at the top of the pile. He had seeded the pile with grass, and for a few years the pile looked like a grassy knoll. He looks so young, a sleepy-eyed, hollow-cheeked miner, serious and sad. His gaze so cool. A mask for his lust. Her stomach flutters. In those days he was always at her. She couldn't wash his smell off, he was in her so much—before his shift began, then again the minute he got home, and in the middle of sleep she'd wake to him in her. There were no other women then. There could not have been.

Now the grass is gone, the pile is gone—everything that used to be is gone. Where the mill once was there are office buildings and shops. The old rope bridge across the Animas that she and Rosy used to play on, that's gone. They'd grown up in a house across the river from the smelter. As children they'd go to the middle of the rope bridge, jump, and set it bucking. It was great fun, and often they'd cross to the other side of the river to pick blackberries. But one day—she was a teenager then—Lily crossed the bridge and was stopped by an armed soldier. Overnight the army had come in, and that side of the river was suddenly off-limits. They turned the smelter into a mill for uranium. And so Durango did its part for the war effort, and when the soldiers came home from the war, the army sold the mill to private industry, and the soldiers all had work in uranium, which was, they thought at the time, so much more profitable and cleaner than fossil fuels.

When they married, Rosy and Ryland moved uptown, five miles from the mill, but Sam and Lily converted the upstairs of her parents' house into an apartment, where they lived for ten years, and every time the wind blew, they were directly in the path of the windborne tailings. Had she only known.

There should have been two babies. There almost were two. In 1957 she carried one for six months, a little girl, buried at the foot of her grandmother's grave. She lost the other at three months. Sam was so sweet about that. "There will be more, Lil, don't worry."

But there were no more babies. They tried and tried. That's when she should have paid attention to her instincts, because everything changed. After a while there was no more lust, no appetites, just a quiet, almost pitying politeness, as if something was wrong with her. He had done his part. He had gotten her pregnant. She couldn't do her part.

She tosses the photo of Sam back in the drawer, then picks it up again. She'll burn it. She blinks, loosening tears, swallowing. No. She won't cry for Sam Behan. Never again.

Suddenly she wants to be quit of him. For good. She closes the drawer, scoops up the logbooks, and struggles to her feet, her legs achy and stiff from kneeling. She's cold, chilled to the bone in this artificially cooled building.

She will make an appointment with her lawyer. But how can she ask him openly? She can't bear for anybody to find out about the divorce papers. God, she *is* an idiot. Why didn't she file them?

Well, she'll just pose a hypothetical situation to the lawyer. A vague question. She has to see him this week about some investments. Just inquire about the legalities. That's what she'll do.

What would Fred say if he knew she wasn't actually divorced?

He'll never know. She'll make sure. Blinking, she slides the door open and walks into the gray light of the windowless hall.

12

B ECKY SPENDS FRIDAY morning at the bank processing loan applications. She's just getting ready to stop for lunch when she looks up and sees Delmar in the customer's chair on the other side of her desk.

"I want to apply for a loan," he says.

She doesn't smile. It's one o'clock, an hour past her usual lunch break, and she's hungry. But she doesn't want to tell him it's time for her lunch, because Delmar will want her to buy him lunch. She says nothing.

"Let me borrow your truck," he says.

"No."

"C'mon. You don't need it. You're working."

"You don't have a driver's license."

"I'm not going to wreck it. C'mon."

"Why?"

He grins at her. "So I can go cruising."

She just looks at him.

"I've got a job interview." He's wearing ratty blue jeans and a white T-shirt.

"You have a job," she says. His job is helping their grandmother with the farm. That was a condition of his parole.

"I don't," he says.

Becky stares at him. He smiles. She had gone with her aunt Alice and her grandmother to the parole hearing last January. That was just before her father's relapse, and her grandmother was still speaking to her. She watched her aunt go into action, making a case for Delmar's release, pleading on behalf of her half-blind seventy-year-old mother, who she said needed looking after. Alice had been living with her mother, but it was rodeo season, and she wanted to be on the road. Delmar was the only one in the family not doing anything, just sitting there in prison. Alice described the farm as a desolate, prisonlike place, which it isn't — it's on good land near the river. For her part, Becky's grandmother sat as regal as a queen, her walking stick between her knees, legs covered by her green velveteen squaw skirt, and wearing her weight in turquoise, all decked out for her trip to the city. It was probably having her there, acting blinder than she really is, that made the case.

"*Shimá sani* and *Shimá* don't mind," Delmar says. "They think I need my own money."

"You're not going to get a job dressed like that."

"It's a gardening job," he says. "They don't care how you dress. C'mon. I'll have it back here by five, when you get off. Really. I'll put gas in it."

"Why can't Aunt Alice drive you?"

"She took *Shimá sani* to the eye doctor in Durango."

"How'd you get here?"

"Hitched." He's wearing transparent brown shades that seem to magnify his eyes — the yellow-brown of a coyote's eyes. He's cunning, Delmar. She knows she'll give him the truck. She doesn't have a choice. She's a little afraid of him, though he hasn't given her any real reason to be since they were little. When he was very young, he had a terrible temper, would kick and scream and throw punches when things didn't go his way. Once, just after his mother had dropped him off at Becky's house and taken off for Florida, Delmar went into a rage and bit her, breaking the flesh on her arm, the bite so deep it could have been made by fangs; she still has four little white scars on her forearm, plus she has the memory of pain from the bite and from the tetanus shot she had to get. He seemed to outgrow his temper as he got older, to develop a sweetness that she has never quite trusted. In junior high he was solitary. He loved to sing. She sometimes followed him on his walks in the desert, listening to the songs he sang just under his breath, songs he heard on the radio. He didn't tell her not to follow him, he just ignored her. He once told her that being with her was like being with nobody, which was why he liked her.

"What gardening job?" she says.

"Landscaper. I promise I'll take good care of it and not go cruising. Pretty please?" He blinks at her.

Becky shakes her head, but she reaches for her purse. She imagines her beautiful truck, which will be paid off in a year, a tangle of chrome and metal. She hands him the keys. "Two hours," she says. "No more. Be back by three. I get off at three." This isn't true; she gets off at four.

Delmar grins. She stares at the dark spot in his front tooth where the enamel chipped when a baseball hit him in the mouth. He was ten. She remembers the blood and how he didn't cry, but he came to her for nursing, and she had put Vaseline on it.

"Wish me luck," he says, tossing the keys in the air. Catching them.

She's worrying before three o'clock comes around and is not at all surprised when Delmar doesn't show, even by four.

At four-thirty she goes out to sit on the bench in front of the bank. If he shows at five — she believes he will, since that's the time he had in his head — she'll still be able to get a run in. It'll be light until eight. She needs a run tonight.

The afternoon was a waste. She added columns of numbers over and over again, getting different totals each time. He better not wreck her truck.

Across the river, thin clouds rest above the Navajo Indian Irrigation Project — NIIP — fields, where the tribe has piped in water and turned the barren mesa top into a green field of corn and wheat. The irrigation system has changed the climate a little. More humidity, more clouds, still no rain. Yesterday evening her father said he wanted to go up to NIIP to see the crops, so she was going to drive him there, but he wasn't halfway to the door before he changed his mind and teetered back to the couch, his thin legs just feeble walking sticks under folds of flannel pajamas.

Delmar doesn't come at five or five-thirty. Arnold had left at four, when the front doors closed, telling her to call him at home if Delmar didn't show. The air smells and tastes like exhaust. Sluggish cars and trucks roll by on the street in front of her, some of the drivers staring straight ahead, some giving her a bleary-eyed look. All look resigned to the slow roll of rush-hour traffic. She's been doing mental calculations. Her truck payments are $225 a month. She wonders if her insurance covers her cousin. What if she has to buy a new truck, pay off the one he wrecks, plus pay somebody's medical expenses? She's already budgeted so tightly there's nothing left over at the end of the month. Since her dad relapsed, she's been paying on the loan her parents had to take out to pay the hospital bill. She cosigned.

If Delmar gets hurt, she won't pay—not a dime.

The bell in the steeple of the Catholic church begins to chime. Six o'clock. She's just looking for change to call Arnold when a Dodge Dakota with tinted windows pulls up to the curb in front of her. She hears the electric buzz of the passenger window rolling down. Terry Conrad is behind the wheel.

"Hi," he says.

"Hi." She gets up and walks over to him. It's a nice truck. She smells leather.

"What are you up to?"

"Not much."

"I drove by an hour ago and you were out here."

"Yeah. My cousin has my truck."

"You need a ride?"

"It's out of your way. Fruitland," she says.

"That's right on my way." He smiles, leans across the seat, and opens the door for her.

He takes her on what he calls the scenic route. It's the long way, across the San Juan River, up the mesa and through the Upper Fruitland district on the reservation side of the river. Ivory bluffs line the road on the left, with farmhouses, double-wide trailers, and butane tanks scattered on the sandy land to the right. The autumn sunflowers are in bloom, clusters of them sprouting along the road.

"Where were you going?" she says.

His smile, though thin-lipped, has something sweet and boyish about it. "Just driving, really."

"Oh."

"To be honest, I spend a lot of time just driving around. I don't know many people here."

"I hear you're taking Harrison Zahnee's Navajo class this fall. You'll meet people there."

"Yeah, I'm looking forward to that. It's a hard language. I ordered tapes, but I couldn't get anything from them. I'm better in groups." He shifts, gearing down as the truck climbs the mesa. When they top it, Shiprock blazes crimson and blue directly ahead. Though the rock is twenty miles away, the day is clear, and she can see the two peaks, one a little shorter than the other, two sails that don't look at all like sails, but the rock stands alone in that swath of desert like a ship on the sea. To the right, Hogback, a ragged beige mesa that looks like a giant hunkered-down pig, bisects the land, and to the far right white smoke plumes from the stacks at Navajo Mines. From up here it's possible to see both power plants, the larger Four Corners on the left.

"You sure live in pretty country," he says.

"You mean the power plants?"

He laughs. "Dallas is flat and getting smoggier all the time. Ever been there?"

"I've never been anywhere."

"A homebody?"

"Not really. I may travel some day."

They're driving through the NIIP irrigation project now. There are no houses, just square plots of full-grown corn.

"How's your dad doing?"

She shrugs. "Not good."

"What'd he do at the mill?"

"Everything. He started as a welder, but he was a shift foreman by the time they closed."

"What does he think about all this?"

"It's complicated. He blames himself. Apparently they had protective face masks and gloves, but he never wore his because it was too hard to do the work with them on."

"Ah. He shouldn't blame himself. He was in the industry during its dark ages."

"He doesn't like to talk about it, but I've been reading through EPA papers on the Shiprock mill-site cleanup. I read where the workers raked yellowcake in open pans. Steam-heated pans."

"That's only a small part of it."

"Yeah, and when they tore the ceiling out of the processing building, they found an inch of yellow dust. It had been accumulating for years."

They drive in silence for a while, the road veering right toward the river and down into the valley, past the Nenahnezad Chapter House. The land is greener here, the sand giving way to richer dirt. Overgrown salt cedar, cottonwoods, scrub oak, and sage crowd the narrow road, occasionally brushing the side of the truck. They cross the bridge over the sluggish San Juan and drive off the reservation.

He wears a cologne that reminds her of the scent white boys used to wear at junior high dances, boys she would slow-dance with and whose cologne would come home with her, keeping her awake in her bed. Only a handful of Indians went to the public school in Fruitland. This white man seems familiar.

"Neanderthal days in the uranium business. It's not nearly so dangerous now, and I foresee a future where nuclear could be the safest fuel choice we have."

"Really?"

"Yeah. The huge risk is in ore extraction. Now nearly everybody's looking at in situ leaching—leaching the uranium from the rock without removing it. Ore extraction's the reason so many uranium miners are dead now. You pull the ore out, release toxic gases, breathe it in, and die, plus the gas stays around, embeds in the soil, the kiss of death for generations. See this is part of what we do at AGER — research progressive and safe mining techniques. Nobody'll be extracting ore in the next phase."

"Turn here. The next phase?"

"That's how I see it. I think nuclear has to be an option in the next millennium because the sad thing is, there won't be any more fossil fuel. According to our stats, this ol' earth will be out of oil in forty or so years. Solar's an option, wind's an option. But those alone won't begin to meet world energy needs."

"Man."

"Sorry to be depressing."

"Yeah."

Her parents' land appears, a green acre in the midst of yellow fields. Years ago her father planted a juniper hedge as border to the property and let it grow up high; now it nearly hides the house. "That's it," she says as they approach the turnoff. He pulls in and parks under the willow. Her truck isn't here. She'd been hoping Delmar would be waiting. The only car in the yard is her father's little Honda, which he took apart a few months ago to find out why it knocked. He hasn't felt good enough to put it back together.

C3PO struggles out from under the porch, barking. "Who's that?"

"That's C3PO."

"Old dog."

"Ancient. Somebody left a litter of puppies at the mill once, and my dad brought home two, one for my cousin, one for me. We were into *Star Wars,* so he called his C3PO. Mine was Princess Leia. She got pregnant and ran off. My cousin likes to say that his dog's a good dog because he always does exactly what a dog should do — eat, sleep, and get his sister pregnant."

Terry laughs. "Well, I'd like to meet him, this cousin of yours."

"I'd like to kill him." She steps out of the truck, shutting the door behind her, propping her arms against the door frame, and looking at him through the open window.

"Oh?"

"Long story."

"Maybe I could come by the bank some noon, take you to lunch, you could tell me." She hadn't expected this. She hesitates, and he quickly says, "No strings attached. I'm a lonely guy. Just looking for a little conversation."

She shrugs. "Okay. Maybe. Thanks for the ride. I really appreciate it."

13

T HE FOX TURNS TAIL and runs along the garden path between the acid leach and the cool clear water. Ryland cannot move. It's so hard putting one foot in front of the other. The leach is green like mucus. He can barely see the path. Two seconds is all it takes for the acid to eat through leather. One one-hundredth of a second to eat through cotton. One one-thousandth to eat through skin.

Now he is in a kitchen. A woman kneels at his feet and picks shreds of green cotton from his leg. He watches the skin corrode. Under the shredded work pants there is no bone. There's only skin turning in on itself, red, raw. The woman's hands are brown, but as she picks the skin from his leg, they begin to mottle, to lose pigmentation, and he is back on the path and it's breaking up under his feet. Acid has splashed his leg.

Now he is not so much dreaming as drifting. He is aware of the pillows at his back and an ache in his side. The grandfather clock in the living room putt-putts a warning, machine-guns a warning — *Well, you wouldn't be able to hear the clock if you didn't insist on sleeping with the door open.*

And now he is awake.

The neon numbers on his bedside clock say it's 12:35; 36. He had been dreaming about a little red fox they used to see out near the leaching pond at the mill in Durango. They called it the garden path, the narrow walk between the leaching and rinsing ponds, and the night shift always looked for that little fox; it was a lucky night when somebody saw it.

He reaches for the aspirin on his bedside table. His throat aches and has for four days, ever since the doctor scraped his lungs. A scorching poker drilling up and down. There'd been nothing wrong with Ryland's throat on Tuesday. He wonders if he might have picked up an infection at the doctor's office.

The pills in the bottle rattle, and that's how he knows his hand is shaking. He can't see his hand. The little night light down the hall doesn't reach this far. The light Rosy insisted on so he can see when he gets up to use the bathroom—*Gets up to use the bathroom five, six times a night. I hear him, bless his heart. This is why I'm always tired.*

Rosy doesn't sleep with him anymore. Three months ago she moved down the hall to the spare bedroom. It was his suggestion. He got tired of hearing her tell everybody how tired she was. Now, though, he thinks it's her absence that wakes him. He's used to her sounds, her breathing and jostling the sheets. The only thing he can hear in the middle of the night is the brown oxygen tank percolating in the corner of their—his—room, and the puny air raking his throat. The clock. The traffic on the street.

He opens the pill bottle and takes three aspirin. Maybe they'll help him sleep. He has tried turning the light on and reading when he wakes at night, but the words are all black dots. He can't breathe if he tries to focus. Breathe or focus, one or the other. His eyes are roving little animals, working day and night. Even when he is asleep the eyes turn inward, look and look for something, which is why he has to have the door open at night. The eyes want to see what's coming when it comes.

Outside, cars are racing up and down Cactus Drive. Kids. And cops. Every now and again there'll be the whoop-whoop of the siren.

Wide-awake now, he sits up, throws the covers off, swings his feet to the floor, and turns on the light. He toes under the bed for his slippers, which are not there. Which means Rosy has put them away. She scoots them far under the bed skirt because she doesn't like to have anything visible on the floor, and she doesn't care that he has to get on his hands and knees to fish them out. He drops to his knees, lifts the curtain, reaches for his slippers, but his eyes fix on his shoes. He is wide-awake. He is wide-awake because he sleeps all day. He doesn't do a damn thing but sit in his chair and sleep. He can't sleep at night because he never gets any damn exercise. He thinks maybe he should take a walk, and adrenaline shoots through him. He reaches for the shoes quickly before he changes his mind. Go for a walk now, change your mind later, he tells himself.

The oxygen cart chitchats behind him. His leather soles slap the sidewalk. This is a good sound. He is marching. Pick your feet up, soldier, he orders himself, and he picks them right up, just as if he weren't old. Behind him the house is quiet. He has gotten out and to the best of his knowledge he did not wake his wife. AWOL. He looks both ways across Cactus Drive, steps off the curb, and crosses to the other side of Sunshine Street.

What truly amazes him is how good he feels. No part of him hurts, no part nowhere. How had that happened in fifteen minutes? His throat doesn't even hurt. Could be the aspirin kicking in. Could be that Rosy's right. "Your throat hurts because you're thinking about it." If he had an infection, aspirin wouldn't be strong enough. He feels good, and he feels warm. What's the temperature? This time of night it'll be 70 degrees. Today it reached 102, and he sat out on the front porch in that heat so he could get warm. His regulator's all off. But he feels warm enough now. He's got a little pinching in his calves, which are tight from lack of use.

He's walking alongside an adobe wall that's taller than he. Branches heavy with crabapples stretch over the wall above his head. Everybody has crabapple trees, but nobody plants them. They are volunteers. In another month the sidewalk will be gooey with rotting fruit. The scent of apples reminds him of his mother. She loved applesauce. She used to say, "Bury me in applesauce." She also said, "Bury me in butter." She was a big woman, his mother. She liked to eat.

It has been a while since he came this way, because Cactus is

71

so busy. He can't sprint through the daytime traffic on that busy street. At night the kids have the street, but the kids move in swarms, like bees, all over town. At the corner of Sunshine and Ute, he stops and shakes his legs, first one, then the other, holding on to his oxygen cart for support. His right calf muscle has balled up, on the verge of spasm, the way it used to when he played football in high school, and his knees feel a little rubbery.

There's a dog that lives at the house on this corner, a little yapper, the cemetery dog. She howls during funerals at Desert View Cemetery, just down the street. She's a little finger of a thing — he calls her Lady Finger. During the day she makes enough racket for a whole pack. Tonight she must be sleeping inside. A funny little thing. Though she lives blocks from him, she can hear him the minute he hits pavement, and she barks with good gusto until the moment she sees him, then shuts up. She'll race up and down her side of the fence, furious but mute, until he has passed, and then she'll start up again. He's given Lady Finger a license to drive. Once, in a little bit of a temper, he can't remember why, he sailed his license across the fence at her. It's still there, wedged between the fence and the lawn, out of lawnmower range.

The night air creeps down his coat. He shivers. He's got to keep moving, to keep the blood flowing. He steps off the curb and crosses Ute.

He's just out of shape. That's because he's grounded. He used to get around a good bit. Used to fly planes. Army Air Corps, 1941 to 1945. Put him behind a C-54, he'd know exactly what to do. C-54, B-17, P-40, C-87. P-38 Lightning.

The man who considers himself unfit for combat flying or who is considered unfit by the flight surgeon or the unit commander is obviously inefficient.

He remembers those words from his flight manual. He didn't get them then, and he doesn't now. If a man considered himself unfit, wasn't that efficient? If an unfit man considered himself fit, now that was inefficient.

Well, he tries to be efficient. He never takes two steps where one will do. He steps off the curb and crosses Supai, stops at the

72

chainlink fence, and stares into Desert View Cemetery. His breath is shallow now, the waves in his chest just offshore. He thinks about the breath worming through his shriveled lungs. A respiratory therapist at the hospital advised him to visualize his breath: "Can't catch your breath? Try to see it. Visualize it. It's white, healing air running through you."

He has a headache brewing. He ought to sit down and visualize his breath. He walks a little way along the fence and lets himself in by the side gate, which is never locked.

Rosy says it's morbid that he likes coming here, but he has liked cemeteries ever since he was a little boy. Rosy says that's the Irish in him. He is the self-appointed captain of a troop of deaf-mutes. The skeleton crew. They'll do exactly what he says. He says, Sleep. That's an order, boys.

There's a boulder near the gate where he likes to sit He lowers himself carefully, holding on to his tank for balance, and leans back against the fence. His legs are shaking. He curls them up toward his chest, planting his feet solidly on the ground, then checks that the plastic oxygen tube is in his nose.

He can't help wondering about Rosy's timing. Why have this test done a month before the wedding? What if it's positive? Had she thought about that, about what kind of wet blanket that would throw on the festivities? No. She doesn't think. She's got her lists of things to do but never really thinks of the repercussions.

He's sorry he let Rosy talk him into these tests, these doctors. His mother hadn't believed in doctors. She said doctors make you sick. She was a great believer in mind over body. If he or one of his sisters came down with a cold, she'd say, "Go to your room and get rid of it," though if the illness was serious, she took on the battle herself. There was a scarlet fever epidemic in Durango when he was a kid. The hospital set up a quarantine unit, and many children died there. His sister Frieda got the fever, but his mother refused to send her away, believing that the hospital would be her morgue. She'd sent the rest of them — he, his sister Natalie, and their father — to his aunt's house. She stayed with Frieda. He can remember going by the house every day to wave to them in the upstairs bedroom where Frieda was confined. The two of them looked so happy, Frieda holding up her books and dolls, nothing to do but play. He remembers being jealous of his sister getting their mother all to herself. When Frieda got better, his mother scoured the house before she let them come back, and she burned all of Frieda's books and cloth dolls. Frieda was inconsolable, but his mother had no patience for her tears. "You're alive. Go to confession and get rid of your sin of ingratitude," she said.

She didn't truck weakness, his mother, and she didn't truck meanness. In the middle of the Depression, there was no work in Durango. His father had gotten work up north at the Idarado silver mine, which was open off and on in those years. During the summer, when school was out, the family moved up to be with him. Ryland loved it there. No chores. They lived in a tent and he fished the Uncompahgre. But being seasonal, he was an outsider. A group of year-round boys ruled the camp.

Early on, though, Ryland found a way to get their attention. There was always a woman at the river beating the filth out of the miners' clothes. Ryland had discovered blasting caps in the pockets of his father's dirty clothes, and he figured there might be caps in the pile of clothes by the river. So one day he threw some lit matches on what turned out to be a highly flammable pile, and the clothes exploded, pow, pow, pow, making him an instant celebrity among the camp boys. But Ryland's mother had been so ashamed of him. The woman's husband had died in the mine that spring, and the pennies she made washing clothes supported her and her son. Ryland felt rotten, then, both that he had increased the woman's pain and that he'd been reckless with his father's pay, because his mother gave that week's wages to the woman to cover the loss.

His mother insisted that he apologize to the woman and her boy, which he readily did. They lived in a boxcar on the edge of the camp. The boy was a thin-shouldered towhead with pretty, girlish features. That was the first time Ryland saw Sam Behan.

When Ryland began stammering about how sorry he was, Sam

shot him a contemptuous smile, as if to say, If you're going to do something that swell, don't apologize. He jumped down from the boxcar and walked away without a backward glance. Ryland instantly hated him.

They might never have become friends had Ryland not accidentally found a way to even the score. The boys loved to sneak into the full ore carts and ride them down the mountain. One day Ryland found himself in the same cart with Sam, Sam on one end, he on the other. After a few minutes Ryland saw that they weren't alone. It was so well disguised, the body there in the corner of the cart, right next to Sam. A copper-colored corpse, same color as the ore. When somebody died on the job, it was the miners' custom to send the body down on the carts. Ryland figured Sam's father had probably gone down that way. But it turned out that this man wasn't dead, just asleep.

Sam rode along, as cool as water, his hair a fractured halo flying from his face, watching the scenery as if he were alone in the cart. Ryland waited until they were almost down before he said, "Hey, kid, you got company." And he watched that blond boy jump, then blush.

After that Sam didn't turn his back on Ryland anymore. They started palling around. Sam knew every cave on Red Mountain, and he knew where the fish ran, and he had schemes for getting liquor and cigarettes.

When Sam was fourteen, his mother died—a complication from pregnancy. The baby was stillborn, and nobody came forward as the father. Ryland's mother got word that Sam would become a ward of the state. She insisted that he come and live with them, and he did, for three and a half years. When Ryland and Sam turned eighteen, they enlisted, and by the time Ryland's tour was over, his mother was dead from pneumonia. He hates that —that he went away to war and never saw her again.

Ryland is listening to the whop of bugs smashing the streetlight at the alley's edge—solid-backed green torpedo bugs, moths the size of golf balls. He puts his left hand on his oxygen tank, his right on the boulder, and pushes once, then again. He stands, shaking and heaving, his night vision blocked by the dots that swarm before his eyes, and he remembers what he wanted to tell the troops, the skeleton crew, that the real dangers of the jungle are not the timid beasts but the tiny flies that get in your eyes, the parasites that carry germs.

He grasps the handle on his oxygen tank. His hands and feet are ice. He walks along the fence to the sidewalk. He steps onto it and wishes it would move. It doesn't, so he does. His heart is pounding in his ears. This is a good thing, he tells himself. He can't hear his old feet shuffling.

To keep his mind off his feet, he takes inventory of everything the army told him he needed to survive in combat. Gun and ammunition. Compass. *How are you going to know where you are without your compass, soldier?*

He has a tickle in his throat. He doesn't want to cough.

Big five-celled waterproof flashlight.

Pocketknife.

Pinchot-Lerner lightweight emergency fishing kit.

Presents for the natives: glass, mirror, tobacco, salt. *The natives are friendly. Remember how the natives helped the troops in the Solomons, New Guinea, the Philippines. The natives will help you if you gain their confidence with a smile.*

Something squishes under his foot, something wet. He jerks upright and lets go of his tank, which rolls, pulling the tube from his nose down to his neck. He lifts the foot, twists to catch the tank, and feels a little ping in his back, a spitball of pain. He grabs wildly at a tangle of bushes to his left, clenching dry, stickery twigs, and the cough catches him, hurling him into the bush, hacking and hacking.

When he straightens up, the spitball in his back balloons, spreading from left to right kidney, then bolting upward, a lightning pain that makes him inhale but won't let him exhale. He leans his whole body into the bush, dry-heaving, trying to catch his breath, and smells shit, which is what he stepped in — dog shit. He strains to breathe and closes his eyes against headlights bearing down from the street. The car passes. He breathes, though not deeply. Hurts too much.

An engine revs behind him. He turns his head and sees that the car has stopped and the backup lights have come on. He presses further into the bushes, and his heart begins to thud. He fumbles with the oxygen tube at his throat, finds the breather, pushes it back into his nose.

"Hey, mister" — windows down, front and back, kids, a car full of them, thick Spanish accent — "you all right?"

"I'm okay," he whispers. He can smell liquor from the car and poop under foot. *Dear God.* A door opens, the back door, and a boy gets out — big boy. Young man. Big-bellied, baggy pants.

"You want a ride, *viejo*?" he says. Breath like gasoline. "Where you live?" He touches Ryland on the arm, then lets go. "You smell like — *eeooo!* He stepped in caca." He starts to back away, but a girl in the car says, "Let's give him a ride."

"If he takes his shoes off," the driver says. "Berto, tell him to take his shoes off. Don't want no caca in my car."

"I'm okay," Ryland whispers.

Berto sticks his face close to Ryland's. Ryland can see his eyes now, clouded with drink but laughing, and it's difficult to hear. His ears are roaring. "Where you live, old man?" Berto takes his arm and pulls him from the bushes.

"Make him take his shoes off," the driver yells, and for an instant the car opens up to Ryland like the ground over Palau had. For an instant, what he wants is the dark cushiony depth of the kids' car, just like he'd wanted — he can remember this — the impact of metal and earth while flying low over Palau one time. Just let this boy take him home, or wherever. But he says, "I'm okay. I live right up here."

"Get his money," somebody in the back seat says, and there's laughter from the others in the car. Ryland's shoulders flare.

He straightens, reaches into his back pocket, yanks his wallet out, and says, "Here. You want my money? Take it." He shoves it toward this fat boy, into his chest.

"Whoa," Berto says. He steps back, raises his hands. Ryland lunges forward, waving the wallet in his face.

"You all want my money?" he hears himself yell.

Berto lowers his hands. They stare at each other.

Then Berto's upper lip curls, his lower protruding. He spits on the ground by Ryland's foot. He says, "We don't want your money, old man."

"Get his money," somebody sings from the back seat, but Berto turns around. "Fuck him," he says. He gets back into the car, closes the door, stares straight ahead. After a few seconds, they peel out. Ryland watches the car fishtail down the street until it disappears and he can't hear the engine anymore.

Heart racing, he looks up the way toward the house. He is only two blocks away. He can see headlights glide by on Cactus Drive. His eyes have clouded, black dots congealing in the corners, tunneling his vision the way they do when he's almost out of oxygen, though there's plenty of air in his tank. He tries to pull breath from his belly. He feels as though he has split in two, the upper half empty, the lower half ripped open—a searing back pain.

He begins to walk. The globbing insects in his eyes spill over and run down his cheeks. With the back of his sleeve, he wipes the little buggers away. *We don't want your money old man.* He wants to smash him, that fat Berto.

He crosses Cactus, walks tear-blinded up the path to his porch. The smell from his feet makes him want to vomit. He tries to scrape his shoes on the stoop, but the stink doesn't want to come off, so he takes hold of the railing, toes the shoes off, still tied, and leaves them tucked under the porch.

14

ROSY IS SHAKING HIM, saying Maggie's here and they're going for a walk by the river. He blinks at the clock. 9:00. He listens to them leave. Sleep is pulling him back, but he resists it. The house is empty now. It's always best if he can do his waking up, his noisy lung clearing, when he is alone, nobody listening.

By the time they get back, he is washed, dressed, and sitting at the kitchen table sipping a can of Ensure. Rosy cooks breakfast. She brings over a plate of bacon, the grease saturating a paper towel on the plate, and sets it in the middle of the table. "How many eggs?" she says.

Maggie says she wants two, sunny side up. "Don't break the yolks."

"Yes, ma'am," Rosy says. She picks up a piece of bacon and puts it on Ryland's plate. "At least try one," she says.

Maggie tells them there are thirty-six padded folding chairs at the Knights of Columbus Hall, where the wedding reception will be. And sixty-five nonpadded chairs.

"That," Rosy says, "is a problem. Where are we going to get more chairs? The guest list," Rosy tells Ryland, "is completely out of control."

He thinks of Xanax. It's only ten o'clock. He promised himself not to have one today. Must ration. He's down to three, and they can't renew the prescription until next Wednesday. But it feels like it's going to be a long day. His back is out, and his throat feels like it's been lacerated. He told Rosy he slept wrong, and that's why he's walking crooked. She found him some Demerol. He took that the last time his back went out, something like four months ago, and apparently Rosy, thinking ahead, went ahead and got a refill even after the pain went away. For a rainy day, she said.

Raining in his throat today. He feels as if his body is sectioned out in acres. The acre on top is all right. No headache. There's a storm in the acre of his throat. Throat, lungs, lips, chin. They're all connected, and below that some sort of flood might be stirring the regurgitated bird food. His lower back is quicksand, the regular everyday pain of his kidneys jiggling back and forth sharpened by last night's calisthenics, and below the kidneys he's cotton. Cotton fields. A damned cotton-pecker is what he is. No trouble in the light-as-air acre below his kidneys and above his knees.

Ryland pushes his chair back, takes hold of the handle on his tank, and pushes himself up.

"Honey?" Rosy says.

"Just getting the newspaper," he says. He feels her eyes on his back as he wheels the cart toward the front door. Before he gets there, Rosy starts in about the senior citizens. How can they make sure the older people get the padded chairs?

"Children will scoot into those chairs," she says. A lot of her friends will be at the reception, and they need the padded chairs. She wonders if the padded ones could be designated "senior only," and how can she do that? Ribbons on the backs?

He opens the front door, then the screen. He stands on the porch, feeling the heat through his slippers. Heat shimmers above the pavement on the other side of the hedge, and his eyes are telescopes. No peripheral vision, doctor. It's a good thing he's not going to take his driver's test today. He can't see anything but what's in front of him.

He unhooks the tube from his nose, pulls the loop over his head, and leaves his cart on the porch. Dry grass crackles under his slippered feet. He stoops to pick up the paper in the middle of the lawn and stares at the headline. The Scorpions won, 48–10.

There's a picture of a big farm boy with charcoal smiles under his eyes. Big, thick-faced, bacon-fed farm boy with a winning smile, who smashed his way to victory in a preseason scrimmage on the local football field last night.

He walks back to the porch. Without his glasses, all he can see of the front page is the football player, the headline, and the score. He sits down on the porch swing anyway, hooks himself back up to his oxygen, begins flipping through the paper, reading the pictures, just like Teri.

He presses back into the swing, rocking himself a little. The plywood children stare solemnly at each other. They never smile, those two.

"Honey," Rosy says. She's standing at the door, looking through the screen. She tells him that she and Maggie have to run down to the reception hall real quick and will be back soon. He nods and looks down at the paper.

"Did you get enough to eat?"

"Yup."

"Just in case, I'm leaving the bacon. If you don't eat it today, you'll get it tonight in salad."

"Is that a threat?"

"Yes, it is." She stands staring at him through the screen so he'll know she means it, then she disappears. But in a few seconds she's back. "Lily might call. Please answer the phone if it rings. Will you?"

"Yup."

"Ask her where she'll be later this morning, and I'll call her. Or when I should call her, ask her that. I really need to talk with her." And then she's gone. He listens to the slamming of car doors.

Lily. Lily doesn't like to hear his voice on the phone any more than he likes to hear hers.

Heat from the sun seeps into his neck, an agreeable burn. He swings gently, letting his slipper soles scratch the porch. Down the block, the little cemetery dog is in a huff. Lady Finger's been barking all morning. Irritating.

If he took a Xanax, this day might be tolerable. He could, of course, take a half. Six halves, six days. But half doesn't do the trick. It was Rosy's idea that he take only a half—a child's dose. A whole will put him to sleep. He can still count on that.

Neck is turning to jelly in the sun. He is a useless fish. If he's going to die—well, it might not be so bad. If he were dead he wouldn't have to answer the phone, which is ringing. The ringing, and then Lily's voice on the answering machine sneaks past the open door and through the screen: Lily's sweeter-than-sugar, wouldn't-hurt-a-fly, do-I-have-the-right-number-sorry-for-the-bother voice wants to know if Rosy is screening her calls.

"She'll call you back," Ryland says. There. He did just as he was told.

Lily doesn't like him because she thinks Ryland could have saved her marriage. She had come to him in a rage the night she found out about Alice Atcitty, demanding to know when Ryland knew, accusing him of knowing for years and keeping it secret from her. Which is pretty much the case. With Sam there were always other women. Ryland figured they were Sam's business, not his, and anyway, he'd known Sam for years before Lily was in the picture. Why would he break Sam's confidence?

They were a bad match, Sam and Lily. She never got Sam. Once she came up to Ryland at one of the company potlucks. "Have you noticed I'm not speaking to you?" she said. He said, "You're not?" and she said, "I knew I'd have to tell you or you wouldn't notice," which made him laugh, but her lips were quivering, and he saw she was angry. They took their plates over to his truck, which he'd backed up to the basketball court.

They held the potlucks at the outdoor basketball court in Camp. Their first summer in Shiprock, Rosy had organized a "get-to-know-you." They set up card tables under one of the hoops and everybody brought food. It got to be regular, every third Sunday.

He asked Lily why she wasn't speaking to him, and she said it was because he was mean to Sam. She wanted him out of shift work. By then Sam had been with the company a good while. She wanted to know why he was still at the bottom of the ladder.

"He gets his raises, same as everybody else," Ryland told her, but she wasn't talking about raises, she was talking about a position with some kind of future and daytime hours.

Sam was playing basketball with some of the little kids at the hoop opposite the card tables. Ryland can remember him hotdogging, bouncing the ball behind and around himself. Ryland yelled, "Sam, you pick on somebody your own size," and Lily got up suddenly, spilling her plate on the sand.

"Where you going?" he said, and she turned to him. "You want to hold him down," she whispered. "You always have."

Right then and there he called Sam over, offered to promote him to day work in the office. He watched Sam size up the situation — Lily staring at the flies picking at her food on the ground, her face flushed. Ryland knew Sam wouldn't like Lily being in his business. Sam said just what Ryland knew he'd say, that he didn't mind shifts, that he liked mixing it up, changing the routine, versatile schedules, versatile jobs, and then he went back to the game.

"There isn't anybody holding Sam Behan back but Sam," Ryland told her.

She said, "I'm not afraid of you, Ryland Mahoney," her whole body trembling.

Lily. A little bit of high drama. He's such a scary guy.

The mail truck has just pulled up on the other side of the hedge, and the mailman's head disappears into the back of the truck. When he steps out, he's carrying three boxes. "Somebody getting married?" he calls as he walks up the path.

"Guess so," Ryland says.

"I can always tell. Because of the volume. Nine times out of ten, you get packages like this in the off-season, there's a wedding in the works." He plops the boxes down on the porch, then digs into his gray bag, pulls out the rest of the mail, and hands it to Ryland. "Have a good one."

Ryland stands, black dots swirling from his eyes. The phone is ringing again. He steps inside, carrying the envelopes to the kitchen table, letting the answering machine answer.

"Mr. Mahoney, this is Dr. Callahan. Listen, will you give me a call right away." He gives his number, and the machine beeps. Ryland stares at the blinking number 2 on the machine for a minute. He starts to press PLAY, then doesn't. Instead, he walks back to the door, unhooks himself from his oxygen, leaves the tank inside, and goes to collect the packages the mailman left. He carries them into the living room, where wedding presents have taken over an entire corner. He stoops, puts the presents on the floor, and stacks them neatly. He straightens up too quickly—the black dots rocket. He stands waiting for his vision to come back, breathing hard, thinks about Xanax, and decides.

On a day such as this when every breath he takes is a maggoty one, he needs a little help. Half a pill a day is better than nothing. He walks into the kitchen, takes the orange prescription bottle from the cupboard, and carries it into the bathroom. In the mirror he sees that his lips are not yet blue. Sometimes he unhooks himself from the oxygen, stands in front of the mirror, and sees how long it takes for his lips to turn from red to blue. Not long. Even now, as he watches, they begin to turn a little blue around the edges. Better hurry.

He thumbs open the childproof cap, shakes out a pill, puts it down, and takes a razor blade from the box in the medicine cabinet. He tries to rest the blade in the groove in the center of the pill. His hand shakes and the blade doesn't want to settle in, so he stabs, slicing it, and half of the pill goes skittering across the counter to the very edge, where it skids to a stop, a heartbeat away from a plunge into the toilet. He breathes deeply through his mouth.

He pops the half pill into his mouth, then picks up the other half and pops it in too. He tucks the bottle into his sweater pocket, walks into the living room, hooks himself back up to air, then pulls his cart to the answering machine in the kitchen and stares again at the blinking number 2. The doctor said he wouldn't call if it wasn't important. It's Saturday. Why is he calling on a Saturday?

There's a note pad and pen next to the phone. He picks up the pen. He puts the pen back down. His heart is thudding. He pushes DELETE.

He stares at the answering machine's red o. Rosy will know. All she has to do is check the caller ID box, which has its own memory. It makes him so tired, thinking about the boxes and their memories and the doctors, and how everybody has an opinion. He presses DELETE on the caller ID box, and just like that erases history.

15

D ELMAR DOESN'T show up Friday night. Becky calls her
aunt Alice again and again but gets no answer. Her aunt
keeps a trailer in Shiprock, but she's hardly ever home, and she
won't get an answering machine because she's superstitious.
Lightning once fried her answering machine, and instead of getting a new one, she found a new place to live. Alice won't live
where lightning has struck. Bad luck.

There's no answer all day Saturday, either. In the afternoon
Becky goes for a two-hour run through Fruitland to the bridge,
over the river, then up toward the lake, trying to exhaust herself.
She goes to bed early because she can't stand to be awake, she is so
mad at Delmar, but now she can't get to sleep. She ran too much,
has too much oxygen in her, and her father sounds horrible tonight, coughing and coughing, a dry, airless cough. It's after one
o'clock when she hears him get up. Her mother says something
to him, and he answers. The back door opens, and then Becky is
wide-awake. He has gone out to the hogan again. She and Delmar helped her father build the hogan years ago. He said it was
for them—their playhouse—but he has always used it. He prays
there.

It's cold out there at night. The silence he leaves is more disturbing than his coughing. She thinks her father believes he's
about to die. He believes that the living should not stay on in a
house where somebody dies, in case the spirit gets trapped in-

side. Most likely he sleeps in the cold so her mother won't have to tear the house down, even though Della has assured him that she won't do that. Becky thinks he worries anyway; he loves them and doesn't want to haunt them when he goes. And these days he seems resigned to going.

It's nearly two-thirty and she's still wide-awake when the phone rings. She rushes to answer, calling to her mother that she'll get it. She stands shivering, blinking, and trying to make sense of the voice, which is not Delmar's, on the other end. Finally her ears clear, and she hears somebody saying horses have gotten out. It's Vangie Biggs, who has the farm next to Becky's grandmother.

"On the side of the road," Vangie is saying. She's telling Becky that she almost hit one of the horses. They're grazing along the highway. "Somebody better come get them," Vangie says, "before they jump into somebody's car." Becky tells Vangie that she doesn't have any transportation. "Could you just get the horses in?" Vangie says. Becky is in the middle of saying she'll come out tomorrow and take care of them when the phone goes dead. She stands for a minute listening to the dial tone, staring at the empty phone cradle. Vangie Biggs doesn't care for her grandmother. Ariana doesn't believe in corralling or hobbling animals. For years the horses got into Vangie's corn and onto the highway and everywhere, and one day Delmar's horse, Luckyboy, went running down the highway and jumped on top of some white people's car. Amazingly, nobody was hurt. The horse landed dead center, found its ground, took a leap, and cleared the back end of the car, coming out without a scratch. None of the four people in the car were sitting in the center seats, where the roof caved in. Everybody was lucky except her grandmother, who had to pay. So Alice, Delmar, Becky, and her dad built a corral, and after that Ariana mostly kept the horses in it. Mostly.

She closes her eyes, trying to think of what to do. She decides to call Arnold.

"You want to go to my grandmother's farm and round up some horses?" she asks him. She can hear his TV in the background.

"Horses? Now? Sure. That's what I want to do. I was trying to think, what do I want to do tonight? Is Delmar going to be there?"

"If Delmar was there, we wouldn't be going."

"Well, I'll still come."

It's thirty-five miles from the house in Fruitland to the farm. They drive with the windows open, the cold night air rushing in, Marley on the stereo. Arnold likes opening the Saab up in the middle of the night on the mostly empty desert road, so they approach the turnoff within twenty minutes of starting out, but they slow to a crawl a mile or so before they reach her grandmother's land. The three-quarter moon tints the land bluish. They pass Vangie Biggs's house first, where a light is on, its yellow arc stretching from the window to the border of her cornfield. Becky can see the skeletons of stalks. She can't see any horses in the field. The crop should hold little appeal for the horses this time of year.

Becky switches the tape player off. She sticks her head out the window, listening to the Saab's tires crunch loose gravel near the shoulder, the chilly air making her eyes tear. Skunk is in the air. It's skunk season, but the scent is thin, the skunk probably far away by the river. She can smell manure, too, and the clean scent of cut hay. They're driving along the edge of her grandmother's farm now. She can see the ragged fencing, in most places just strands of barbed wire strung between wooden posts, but here and there the wires are missing and the posts bend down toward the ground. Crickets are singing to the wavering, high-pitched scream of the overhead telephone wires. There are so many wires now. When the whining started, five years ago or so, after the telephone company tripled the number of wires running along the road, her grandmother paid a medicine man to come and bless the farm to keep the ghostly voices from flying overhead. Now she believes the blessings have started to work, because she no longer hears the whine. Her family doesn't tell her that what's gone is the fine-tuning in her old ears. She no longer hears that high-pitched frequency.

"Looky," Arnold whispers.

Aunt Alice's two red roans are chewing weeds at the side of the pavement. The horses look up as the car approaches, then go back to grazing. A dog has begun to bark farther down the road, and behind them, at the Biggs' house, a chorus of dogs answers. The horses chew.

"How we going to do this?" Arnold says.

"I don't know," she says. "We should've brought rope."

"Don't worry. Horses like me."

She laughs. One of the roans lifts its head, looks back in the direction of the barking dogs. The barking comes closer. The horse takes a step onto the pavement.

"Don't do it," Arnold says. He flashes his lights, which the horse ignores, so he blasts his horn. Both horses jump and bolt to the other side of the highway, opposite the farm.

"Arnold!"

"Oops. Don't worry." He pulls to the side of the road, turns off the engine, opens his door, and steps out. "There's a flashlight in the glove compartment."

"Maybe we should go to the corral and get rope," she says, but he's already heading across the road. She hurries out of the car, turning the flashlight on, hoping that the dogs are not the Biggses' mean ones. Ariana keeps three dogs for herding the sheep and one farm dog that Becky herself named Denver — all mongrels. Right now the sheep dogs are with the sheep up in the hills. Her uncles and cousins will bring the herd down to the farm in a few weeks. Those dogs are smart and can hold their own with the Biggses' dogs, but Denver is old and useless now.

The horses are trotting in the ditch between the fence and the highway, and Arnold is trotting after them. From the barking, it sounds as if the dogs are even with her, moving across her grandmother's property, but she can't see them. The lone dog up ahead continues to call. She has a bad feeling about this.

A circle of yellow light from the flashlight bobs up and down as she runs after Arnold. They need rope. This is stupid. Up ahead, the white lights of an oncoming car bear down, lights so bright she has to look away, and she almost calls out to Arnold to keep the horses off the highway, but how in the hell is he going to do that? And anyway, horses running in a ditch will probably stay in a ditch; they're not likely to climb out of it unless pushed. Unless some stupid lays on the horn. She's laughing as she runs, nervous laughter. The car whizzes by. Down here in the ditch she is a floating head, at eye level with the pavement. "Hai!" Arnold is yelling just ahead of her. "Hey!" Now he's scrambling up the side of the ditch to the fence. She shines the flashlight on his back and beyond him, where she sees the silhouette of a horse turning sideways and then leaping over the fence. "Hey!" Arnold shouts again. She runs up to him. Arnold doubles over, holding his side, wheezing. The fence here sags. One wooden post angles forty-five degrees from the ground.

"Where's the other one?"

Arnold holds his knees. She sees his head nod toward the field. She shines her light on the horse that leapt and has now turned and is standing still, watching them. He puts his head down, as if taking a bow. Just beyond him, the other horse neighs. They both turn and trot away into the desert.

Arnold twists and sits. "I gotta get in shape," he says, still breathing hard. The dogs, yipping, seem to have reached whatever they were after. They're just a little way ahead on the other side of the highway. "Well, at least those horses aren't on the road anymore."

"Shh." There's something else out there. It might just be the humming of the telephone wires, which seems to ebb and wane, like human voices in conversation. Her skin is tingling, but she's not cold now, she's hot, her pulse noisy, adding to the dogs' loud barking, so she can't hear clearly, and in spite of herself, she's thinking of the stories her father has told her of skinwalkers, Navajo witches who don animal skins and take on their powers.

"What?" Arnold says. "Those dogs? They . . ." He looks up at her, then scrambles to his feet, grabs the flashlight, and turns it off. They stand listening to what sounds like a human voice — a high, nasal chant warbling in and out of the night noises.

Arnold slides down into the ditch, climbs up to the road, crosses, and walks along the fence in the direction of the barking. She follows. He doesn't turn the flashlight on. She can't see the ground she's walking on. She can feel weeds tugging at her jeans and knows her socks are already pincushions for the prickly goatheads. Moonlight shines on the pavement, making it glow like glittery coal. Not a stone's throw away, she can see a floating white cloud and now can hear, unmistakably, the sound of someone chanting in Navajo. Something leaden turns in her stomach. "Shit," she says. She runs ahead, grabs the flashlight from Arnold, turns the light on, and sees the floating cloud turn into the white swatch on 'Abíní''s back. 'Abíní' is her grandmother's palomino, and the voice, her grandmother's.

She calls, "*Shináli!*" and starts running toward the barking dogs, which explode with new vigor. "*Shináli!*" She waves the yellow light back and forth out beyond the pony. Only three dogs, that's all she can see. Making all that noise. They're in triangular formation, the Biggses' mean shepherd with one blue eye, the dog that always finds her if she tries to run around her grandmother's farm, stands point, and the flashlight catches his teeth, blue and bared.

"Hey!" Arnold shouts behind her, and suddenly the dogs scatter, one yelping. Arnold has picked up rocks and is throwing them at the dogs.

She shines the light toward 'Abíní' and sees Ariana's other palamino, Ak'ah. Both are nervous, rearing their heads, pulling against the ropes that her little grandmother grips, standing between them, chattering and squinting fiercely into the light. The old farm dog, Denver, stands next to her, barking at Becky as if she were a stranger.

"*Shináli*, what are you doing out here?" Becky says. Off in the darkness, the Biggses' dogs grumble. Her grandmother, just on the other side of the fence, doesn't answer or even acknowledge her. She's wearing the green bandanna that rarely leaves her head, a tiered skirt, and a sweatshirt that's at least three sizes too big — probably Delmar's. How did she manage to get ropes around the horses' necks? Becky pulls up the top strand of barbed wire, pushes the next down with her foot. "Go," she says, and Arnold steps carefully through.

"Ouch. Ow!"

She hears something rip, his shirt and probably the skin on his back, torn by a barb. She shines the light on her grandmother again. The horses pull against the old woman as she leans away from them, reaching for the ground with one hand. The horses keep yanking her back. She probably weighs ninety pounds. "Grandma, wait."

She once was tall, but she's no more than five-two now, shrinking every year. Her grandmother ignores her. But Denver now acts like he knows Becky. He walks over to her, tail wagging, licks her hand once.

Becky hands the light to Arnold and steps between the two horses, putting her hands on their quivering necks. They're both sweaty and hot, snorting. She pets them, saying, "Shh, shh." Her grandmother keeps reaching for something on the ground. When Arnold shines the light there, Becky sees her walking stick. Arnold picks it up and hands it to her. Becky tries to take the ropes, but her grandmother brusquely nudges her away, continuing her stream of talk. She jabs the ground with her stick, yanks the horses, and starts walking, the horses half following, half pulling away. "Speak English," Becky says softly, trying to take the ropes again, but her grandmother won't let her, so she falls in beside her. Arnold walks on the other side, shining the flashlight in front of them to show the sun-dried cracks in the land.

"What's she saying?" she asks Arnold.

"She's saying she doesn't need our help."

He looks over her grandmother's head at her. In the moonlight, she can see one eyebrow raised. Becky glares at him.

They trudge along, Becky and Arnold silent, her grandmother talking to the air. They're a good quarter-mile from the house, which is just a dark smudge against the navy sky. The sand is crusted and packed but softens a little as they get closer to the river. Here wild grass grows in patches. The sheep will crop it close when they come back, but now it reaches Becky's knees, and she keeps stumbling into it. It's stupid to walk through the desert at night in the summer, especially this close to the river, because on cool nights like this, when there's been no rain, rattlesnakes will make their way to the river. At the full moon she and her father used to go for a run but they always stuck to the road and never went near the river.

"Where's Luckyboy, Grandma?" Four of the horses are accounted for, Alice's two wayward roans and these two palominos, but where is Delmar's horse? Her grandmother stabs the ground.

The Biggses's dogs seem to have gone home to bed, and Denver has disappeared, too, having been relieved of guard duty. Behind them the horses crunch through the grass, breathing evenly again. They're crowding close, hurrying, as if going home were their idea. Ak'ah keeps sticking his head between her and her grandmother. She can feel his breath on her neck, a tickling warmth like the soft brush of horseflies. In summer the horseflies swarm the horses and their human riders, digging under hair and skin, stinging.

"*Deesk'aaz,*" Arnold says.

"What?" Becky says.

"Just talking about the weather," he says.

He looks amused, his eyes shining in the moonlight. Her grandmother continues preaching to the ground.

Arnold says, "*Dichin nishli.*"

"What'd you say?"

"That I'm hungry." She sees his purple teeth.

Her grandmother chants. Arnold continues to talk, sounding very agreeable, very conversational. Her grandmother stops speaking and begins to laugh, a high wheezy cackle. She stops walking, too, causing Ak'ah to try to shoulder ahead.

Arnold says something else, and her grandmother answers in Navajo. He says, "'*Aoo',*" and her grandmother hands Arnold 'Abíní''s rope.

They continue walking. And chatting. Becky stares into the leaves of the cottonwood next to the house. If she half closes her eyes, the leaves catching the moonlight look like a hundred little mirrors. They seem to flash but probably do not because there is no breeze. She is the one moving, not they. But she doesn't feel that she moves. These days, even when she runs she feels like she's standing still.

They stop in front of the house, a wood and adobe flat-roof that her grandfather built. Without a word to her but continuing her conversation with Arnold, her grandmother hands Becky Ak'ah's rope. Arnold, smiling, hands her 'Abíní''s. Arnold is having a real good time. Her grandmother picks up a lantern that she had left shuttered next to the door. She has no electricity on the farm. She wants it that way. The Biggses have electricity, but her grandmother likes old-style in everything.

"Where are you going?" Becky asks as Arnold starts to follow Ariana into the house.

"Coffee and breakfast," he says in his Eastwood voice.

Typical. Everybody likes Arnold. Everybody likes him but nobody knows him.

Becky leads the horses around the side of the house, past the adobe oven where her grandmother makes flatbread, past the wooden lean-to that smells of the plants — sage and aster — that her grandmother dries for medicinal teas, the sweet-smelling hut that always drew Becky and Delmar when they were children on this farm, because it's dark and cool and good for hiding. The corral is behind her grandmother's hogan.

'Abíní' neighs, and from the corral comes an answering neigh. The horses trot ahead toward the open gate, anxious to be caged again, and Becky lets go of the ropes. She can see the silhouette of a horse, small but broad-bellied, standing in the middle of the corral — Luckyboy.

The other two run toward the water trough. Becky follows, slipping the ropes from their necks while they're preoccupied. She lets the ropes fall to the ground beside the trough and turns to Luckyboy, who stands stone still. She walks closer to him, close enough to see his eye, open and staring at her. His tail swishes once.

She says, "Shoo."

Swishes again.

She raises her hand and slaps him on the rump as hard as she can, shouting, "Hai! Get out of here. Go find Delmar."

Luckyboy jumps and runs forward, stopping just short of the open gate. He looks back at her, turns, and trots to the corral railing, keeping his eye on her, giving her a wide berth, and veering toward the trough, where 'Abíní' raises his head and gives him a sniff.

16

DELMAR IS TO START his new job as the groundskeeper at Whitaker Estates on Monday, though they told him he could move up to his groundskeeper's cottage immediately. He doesn't need much. The cottage has furniture, linen, and dishes. The property manager told him that all he needs are some canvas gloves, a sturdy pair of work boots, and a good attitude.

He spends Friday afternoon after the interview taking care of business. At three he goes to see his parole officer, Mr. Xavier Happe. Officer Happy. Delmar has an appointment every Friday with Officer Happy. The man never looks up and never speaks when he comes in. There's always a plastic cup with a paper lid on the edge of the officer's desk, the name ATCITTY penned on the label. First thing, Delmar takes the cup down the hall to the bathroom and pisses in it.

Mr. Happe is a medium-built bald man with a high forehead, nicely spaced eyes, a bumpless nose, and thick, shapely lips. His chin is covered with peach fuzz. A handsome Christian, he says he prays for all of his clients because it doesn't hurt to enlist the Lord in a losing cause. Officer Happy knows the rate of recidivism for all kinds of criminals: city criminals versus rural criminals, blacks versus whites, girls versus boys, half-breeds versus full-bloods. "Do you know, Delmar," he frequently says, "that the recidivism rate for half-breeds" — when he asked once what Delmar preferred, half-breed or mixed-blood, Delmar told him he had no preference — "is higher than for full-blooded Indians?" It was news to him.

"What about your grandmother?" the man says when Delmar tells him about the job. "As per your conditions of parole . . ."

"My mom's helping with the farm."

Officer Happy opens a file on his desk and begins looking through the papers. He pulls out something Delmar recognizes, his mother's calendar. Alice signed off as his in-home supervisor at his parole hearing. When rodeo season started, she had to give Officer Happy a calendar showing the dates she'd be away. "It's good," Delmar says. "She's home."

He picks up the phone and starts dialing.

"I mean she's not home now. She took my grandma to Durango to the eye doctor. She'll call you when she gets back. She thinks I need my own money." Officer Happy stares at him. Delmar holds his gaze.

"Is she going to stay?" the man says. "Because you can't take a job one week and leave it the next."

"She's staying."

"Well. How are you going to get there? Pretty isolated up there on the mesa. You got your transportation figured out?"

"Going to get a bike."

"Bike's a good idea, though it won't work in rain or snow. What about in rain or snow?"

"I'll catch a ride. It'll be no problem."

"Because when do you turn into a pumpkin?"

"Three o'clock Friday afternoons." Officer Happy is a tough-love parole officer. He has told Delmar repeatedly that if he is even a minute late for his weekly appointment he'll have him arrested.

"All right," the officer says finally, tilting back in his chair and lacing his hands behind his head. He smiles. "I'm proud of you, kid. Step in the right direction."

Delmar drives out to his grandmother's farm. His grandma and his mom aren't back yet. He packs some clothes and a few other things, helps himself to some twenties from the stack in Ariana's cupboard — he needs some cash to see him through — and goes out to say hello to Luckyboy, who used to be skinny but now is very fat. The first time he ever saw Luckyboy, he thought he was a big dog covered in horseflies, with bulging eyes, visible ribs, and bowed legs, a walking skeleton of what turned out to be a little pony. The horse was a present from his father.

From the time Delmar was a baby until he was eight years old, he saw his father about once a week. Saturday mornings, after Sam worked the graveyard shift at the uranium mill, Delmar would wake to the sound of the dogs barking, a horn blaring, and Sam hollering, "Who wants breakfast?" They would drive the thirty miles into Farmington for pancakes at Pancake Alley. On Delmar's birthdays, Sam always gave him good presents: a ten-speed bike, a fishing pole, an underwater watch. Delmar doesn't have most of the presents anymore. He lost them along the way. Only Luckyboy.

"How come is it only the women in your family have horses?" his father wanted to know, and then, "I think we better get you one." It was his seventh birthday. They drove north toward the Colorado border, on dirt roads and wagon trails. For many years there had been herds of wild horses in the area; they caused trouble, eating crops, turning over garbage bins on the ranches below Mesa Verde. They didn't find the herds that day, but just as they were getting ready to head home Delmar saw Luckyboy. Sam said, "That is the worst-looking animal I've ever seen. You want him?"

The pony turned out to be a good runner. When they stopped the truck, Sam gave him a lariat, saying, "Go get him." The pony took off, tail straight up, and didn't look back, so they got back in the truck and followed him. When they caught up with him, Sam yelling, "Rope him, boy," Delmar rolled the window down and tried to rope him out the window. But the pony was a real good ducker, so Delmar climbed up to sit on the windowsill, while his father steered with one hand, the truck bucking all over the rough desert, and held onto his son's ankle with his other hand. Delmar tossed the lariat a couple of times, Sam laughing, yelling, "You'll never make a cowboy, kid," and driving so close to the doggy-horse that Delmar could see the pupils in his wild, frightened eyes. Finally, Delmar slipped the lariat over his neck like a noose. Later, during his bandit days, Delmar would remember that exhilarating moment when he saw the horse's wild eyes go blank with surrender and think that even though he'd probably make a lousy cowboy, he could make a very good hangman.

He puts out some hay and shovels some manure. Luckyboy is responsible for the ugliest manure. Alice's horses and his grandmother's produce nice, healthy clumps on a regular basis — what goes in comes out good — but Luckyboy has never been that healthy. What goes in sometimes takes a long time to come out, and sometimes it's a green stream.

Finished with his shoveling, Delmar says goodbye to the horses and starts back toward town, but then he remembers that this is the last weekend for the state fair in Albuquerque. It's been three years since he went; last year at this time he was in jail. He likes the fair.

He takes the western route, driving one hundred miles south to Gallup and then on to Grants, where he wants to stop at Stuckey's Pecan Shoppe and pick up Stuck. She's pretty much the only one from his bandit days he still likes to see. He met her at the halfway house in Farmington the first time he was busted for bootlegging car parts. He'd been trying to sell car radios at the Farmington flea market, but one of the original owners showed up and found his serial number on a radio. The man literally dragged Delmar by his ear to a security guard at the market, and the security guard made him sit on his hands and wait for the cops. It was a day Delmar doesn't like to think about. As for Stuck, she was at the halfway house for dropping yellow sunshine during gym at Farmington High. Delmar and Stuck spent a fun month in group therapy, then went their separate ways, she back to gym classes, he to skulking around the halls of Shiprock High, and for a while he tried really hard not to put himself in the position of getting dragged anywhere by his ear again. He hit the books and graduated six months early — he couldn't stand school. Stuck took two more vacations at the halfway house and didn't ever graduate.

She moved to Grants, following a speed freak named Jeremy, and got the job at Stuckey's Pecan Shoppe, where she's cashiered ever since.

It's just after six when he pulls into the nearly empty parking lot. Stuck's behind the cash register.

Inside and up close, he sees that she's looking not so good — like a zombie, with dark circles under her eyes and bluish lips and spider-web hair. She's wearing the tiniest of tank tops, and it looks baggy on her. Her jeans are belted around her hips, showing her stomach, which is concave. It is hard to believe that two babies have come out of that stomach, except for the scar that stretches from her blip of a navel on down. It looks like a bolt of lightning.

He tells her he's come to take her to the fair, and she tells him she's got to work.

"Get that other guy to work." He helps himself to a famous pecan log.

"He pisses me off so bad."

Two customers and their child are browsing among the hatpins, though they're not wearing hats. The hatpins are shaped like states. "You got Virginia?" the lady says.

"We got what's there," Delmar says, helping Stuck out.

"I was supposed to get last weekend off, but Stupid has to go to Phoenix to sell some of his stupid paintings, so I traded with him but nobody changed it on the schedule, and this morning —"

"How 'bout West Virginia?" the customer says. Stuck glares at her.

"Does that start with a W?" Delmar says. "I think it's with the Ws."

"I found Wyoming," the child says.

"— the phone rings and it's stupid Ginny saying why am I not at work and guess what? Stupid's nowhere and my name's on the schedule."

Delmar nods. He wants to go behind the counter and put his hands around Stuck's little waist. He wants it something fierce. He stares at the hatpin tree. It needs replenishing. There are a lot of blank spaces. Actually, the whole place is looking not so good.

The famous pecan logs need to be stocked, and the petrified wood does, too, and the fudge, and the life-sized porcelain cats. Maybe he should skip the fair, stay right here. Help Stuck do her job and have a sex spree, which is all he really wants, well not all. He'd like but isn't going to have some of the blow Stuck has clearly been dipping into. He wonders where she got it. She came to see him every few weeks this summer at his grandma's place, and every time she was clean. He can tell she's high now by the way her eyes keep drifting toward the top of their sockets.

"How far is the Petrified Forest from here?" Mr. Customer asks Delmar. The man lays a hatpin shaped like Texas on the counter, plus a miniature stone gargoyle from the gargoyle display. He picks out three famous pecan logs, seriously diminishing the stock, and lays them down, too. Stuck begins to punch keys in the cash register.

"Close. If you take the shortcut." He glances at Stuck, who smiles at the cash register. Making Stuck smile is something he likes. He's really good at giving tourists directions. He directs this guy to get off the freeway now and head through Zuni. He doesn't tell the guy that the Zunis will abduct his woman and enslave his child, which is something a Zuni guy he knows says about the Navajo. Instead he tells them that the Zuni are as playful as children and to be sure and take their pictures, they love that.

Stuck, happy now, tells the customer he owes her $24.95.

Stuck deserves help this weekend, Delmar decides, and she deserves a love spree. Everybody deserves a spree, especially him, since this is his last weekend of freedom before he starts his job. He plans to do good at his job and not leave the mesa until he's off probation, and then he plans to get out of Dodge, maybe go see his dad in Florida, he doesn't know.

After the customers leave, Delmar slips behind the counter and behind Stuck, puts his hands under her shirt and around her waist, touching the fingers of both hands in front and thumbs in back. He tells her that maybe he won't go to the fair, and he slips his hands down below the belt, under her panties, through the tangle of hair, to where she is already wet.

"Plus Jeremy's back," she says.

"Ah, dang," Delmar says.

She's leaning against him, bobbing up and down against his cock like a jumping jack—the coke gets her going. He wants some. He'd like to get going, too.

"Let Jeremy take care of the kids. Let's go to the fair." He pulls his hands out. "C'mon." He knows this is a reckless idea. He knows Stuck will pay if she takes off with him. But Jeremy, the kids' father, will hit her for nothing, so she might as well give him a reason. He goes around the counter, starting the getaway. She doesn't move. "Come on," he says.

She stands there, staring out at the highway. Behind her, a little round fan goes click, click, click. "Stuck, he is a fuck. You know he is." She just looks at the highway, her eyes roaming their orbits, hands squeezing the counter, and Delmar knows there will be no sex spree. She is a good person, his good buddy. He tells himself this as he moves quickly toward the door, because he sort of wants to hit her himself.

"Want to see what he gave me?" she says. Now she moves, all pep, around the counter, brushing by him to the door, locking it, taking his hand, and pulling him toward the stockroom, which is dim and cluttered with cardboard boxes, the cement floor sticky The place smells like sugar. Her purple sweater's on a hook. She takes the sweater everywhere because she's always freezing. From the sweater pocket she takes two small vials and hands them to him, and though it's too dark to see clearly, he knows he's holding some of Jeremy's famous coke.

"Gee," he says.

She's rubbing herself against him. "We've got half an hour. He's bringing the kids at seven. Come on." She takes his hand and pulls him through the room toward a desk in back, takes the vials from him, turns the desk light on, and shakes a little of the coke out onto a piece of paper, dividing it in four lines.

"I can't," Delmar says.

She doesn't stop what she's doing, which is bending over, holding one nostril, sniffing with the other. "Why not? Yes, you can."

She stands up, wipes her nose with the back of her hand, sniffing. He can almost feel the jolt as he watches her. "Why not?" she says again.

He tells her about the plastic cup, his Friday urine tests, and she says that's a bummer, drops to her knees, and unzips his jeans. He decides a little sex spree's better than nothing.

This one's on fast-forward, her lips and teeth scraping up and down his cock at lightning speed in a not unpleasant full-throttle kind of way. Energetic. Very like the first time when they were oh-so-young, seventeen. He lets his hands rest on her head like a pope blessing someone. He thinks he hears a knocking — his heart? Or maybe somebody at the door. He pulls her up by her armpits, pulls her tank top off, pinches her breasts, which are mostly nipple, and she steps out of jeans and panties. He likes this. Always he likes it when her clothes come off and she starts doing her goofy dance thing, stepping on his feet and climbing up. She is a little thing, Stuck, and he helps her, lifting her by her bottom so he can slide in — little gasp; he likes that. "Not on the desk," she whispers. The two lines are still there. He walks her around, hobbling because his jeans are around his thighs, back to the wall. He backs her up against it, which he knows she doesn't like — being trapped — but she deserves it for not going with him to the fair. Her little hands are tapping him on the back, reminding him she's claustrophobic, especially when high. He presses his chest into her face hard. She deserves this for being high when he can't be. After a while she stops tapping and starts clawing, trying to breathe. She is so weak, little Stuck, she has no muscles, and he is so hard. He pulls back a little, giving her air and also feeling for the back pocket of his jeans, where he has a bunch of Trojans, and he's glad he can't see her face too clearly, the roving eyes, because it's a little creepy, like diddling a jerking and very wet corpse.

He finds the packet. She says, "Just come in me."

"No."

She says, "I'm pregnant."

He says, "Jeez. Again?" And so he comes in her.

Afterward they don't talk. He zips up, she starts to dress. There is most certainly a knocking at the door. A pounding. He feels good, relieved, but also mad at her. She doesn't give a shit about herself. It's probably Jeremy at the door. It's probably another little Jeremy growing in her. He's glad it's dark and he doesn't have to look her in the face.

"He's moving us out to LA," she says. "He's getting a house on the beach that's big enough for us. I'm going to be a housewife."

Delmar wants to say, Again? but doesn't. With Jeremy it's always the same bullshit promises. "I'm going to go out the back way," he says.

Half dressed, she comes to him, hugging him, smelling like him and like acid blow sweat. She says, "When we move to LA, will you come see me?"

"Yeah." He kisses her on the top of the head and walks quickly toward the back door.

"Del?"

"Yeah?" He opens the door, sun and heat pouring in.

"How come they're testing you for drugs if you weren't busted for drugs?"

He looks back at her, a sad twig in the spear of sun, and he wants her again.

"I don't know." He shrugs, then grins. "It doesn't matter. I am an excellent pisser."

He hits the Albuquerque city limits just before sundown. Driving up Central, he sees a lot of tired drunks sitting on the low stone wall that edges the university and a lot of college girls in short shorts walking on the sidewalks. Hippies in long skirts and bra tops hug up against long-haired white boys and dreadlocked black guys, all drinking juice at the juice shop. Cowboys in hats and shades walk too carefully down the street, heel to toe, as if they have to concentrate — these are probably rodeo boys with sore bones, looking for bars.

At the fairground entrance, a cop directs traffic, waving cars in with his baton. The good smells of roasted corn and manure float out to the street. The Ferris wheel is turning, the roller coaster flying. He turns into the parking lot, staring straight ahead and not looking at the cop, who probably isn't even a real cop but a hand hired for the occasion. He tries to feel good about coming to the fair, but he still wants the blow—he's read that it stays in the blood system for only a couple of days. Why is he thinking of that now? He probably could've done a line, no consequence. It's Friday night, he's got a week before he has to piss in the cup again, he could've gotten high, but he hasn't in nearly two years. No blow, no GHB, no Smoke, no nothing. He started going to NA meetings when he was in jail. He liked listening to all those addicts congratulating themselves for cleaning up. It's good to accomplish things.

He parks the truck next to a Honda Accord. Out of habit, he looks in, sees at a glance that it's got a Bose stereo system. Why do people buy these cars? It's very easy to pop a Honda's window. He could strip this dash in two minutes if he were still in the business. But he's not. He's about to begin a new business, groundskeeper, and this is his last weekend of fun. He gets roasted corn and two chili dogs, heads over to see the animals, which are mostly snoozing now, the piglets zoned out, the lambs silent, the horses in their trailers.

He wanders through the Arts and Crafts building and the Ag building. Prizes have been awarded. Blue ribbons, Best in Shows, yellows, reds, and whites, ribbons on quilts and jam jars and cacti. Four-H Troop #238 got honorable mention for their interactive educational display. They have a board full of questions with multiple-choice answers. If you press the right button, a green light glows, the wrong, red. Delmar tries it. *What nutrients does a serving of beef provide?* He pushes the button next to Protein. The red light comes on. Hmm. He thought it was protein. He punches the other buttons: Vitamin B—red; Zinc & Iron—red; All of the Above—green. Of course. He should read all the choices before he pushes a button. He reads the other questions. Number six is an interesting one: *How many sheep are in New Mexico?* Wow. Did they count them? His grandmother has forty-five, but six of them are lambs. Did they count lambs? When did they take this count? If they counted before spring, they wouldn't have known about the six new lambs, which Delmar helped deliver, a bloody mess. He reads through the choices: a. 1,000. b. 10,000. c. 100,000. d. 1,000,000. He punches d. Green light. *Wow, that's a lot,* he thinks. He punches the others to see if the lights work, but they all glow green. Interesting. There are apparently no wrong answers here. He guesses this must be why Troop #238 only got honorable mention. All the answers can't be right.

He walks through the crowded, dusty grounds, past the merchandise booths, looking at the tiny tie-dyed baby shirts, the mirrored sunglasses, the canvas safari hats, past the amazing vacuum cleaner guy, and the pure mountain spring water guy, and the Sony guy. In the Sony booth, Garth Brooks blares from a new car stereo system, and the businessman behind the table looks well fed, little pot under his polo shirt, Dockers, five o'clock shadow, plenty of hair. Delmar stops to listen to him tell a wide-bottomed woman how CD players are selling faster than tape players now and she really ought to upgrade. "The compact disk is the fastest-growing consumer electronic product ever introduced in this country. The development of the CD player was a joint venture between two companies: Philips and Sony. Philips was the first to come up with the idea of optical-disk audio reproduction."

Making his sale. In the business. The guy nods at Delmar. Delmar folds his arms. He thinks Becky ought to get one of these CD players for her truck. She ought to upgrade. She's probably mad at him. He could get her one of these easy if he were still in the business, but he's not in the business, he doesn't get to be in the business anymore. How'd this guy get into the business, anyway? This guy looks younger than Delmar.

He moves on. The fact is, Delmar started out as a legitimate businessman salvaging car parts from the heap of junker cars at the base of Whitaker Mesa. There were a lot of good usable parts in the cars and trucks on the junk heap. Back in high school, during his warrior days, he and his buddies had races, and sometimes a car went over the edge of the bluff. You couldn't drive it anymore, but not every part got banged up. So he'd ditch school and return to the battlefield in the light of day, dismembering the wrecks, selling what was usable to salvage lots, keeping the electronics to sell at flea markets. He was pretty rich in high school. While everybody else was herding sheep and pumping gas, he was bankrolling parties. But then the city of Farmington started their own salvage business and put up a fence around the junk, put guard dogs inside. They also started patrolling the mesa at night, and the warrior days came to an end. The bandit days started. They'll force you into banditry. He'd been a legitimate businessman, and when they took his business away, he had to start thieving.

The fair isn't any fun. He wanders away from the exhibition areas and food booths, goes through a turnstile and into the carnival, where monkey music is playing. He sees a troop of little girls screaming in teacups while an old guy leans on the railing, watching them, his tongue between his teeth. Dirty old man. But Delmar likes it better in here. The Hammer is pumping, cages twirling. Woozy girls reel, draping themselves on each other, counting their tickets, wanting more — more tickets, more spinning rides. Girls in tight jeans and tight T-shirts, round breasts, eyes icky with mascara. They cut those eyes at him as they walk by, laughing behind their hands, glancing back after they pass, girls who smell like chocolate and strawberry and some like vomit. Boys follow them, teenagers, wannabe gangsters, suave, giving him the evil eye, like he already did it with those girls making eyes at him.

He goes up to a ticket booth and buys twenty tickets, a dollar each. Maybe some rides will cheer him up. He's been thinking about that question Stuck asked. Why does he have to piss in a cup if he wasn't busted for drugs? No reason. It's the system. The system will eat you alive. He's going to have to learn to be part of the system because it's better to be a cannibal than to be cannibalized.

His cousin's good at it. She has always been part of the system. She's got money and a truck. His friends used to call her Apple. Well, he still likes her. He should take her a present.

There's a hunting booth with BB guns chained to the counter. Two girls lean over the counter, aiming their rifles with the help of their boyfriends, who stand behind them, fixing the girls' hands on the triggers. They keep shooting and missing and laughing, shaking their butts in their boyfriends' groins.

"Five tickets, five shots," the barker tells Delmar. There are rows of moving chicks, ducks, rabbits, elephants, and bears. The girls shoot, the boys hoot. Delmar gives the man five tickets, picks up a rifle. He's a pretty good shot. His uncle Woody used to take him hunting, though with a bow and arrow, not a rifle. He aims, shoots, and a chick goes down. He can feel the girl next to him pause and watch. Her boyfriend, too. He shoots again, four shots in rapid succession, hitting two more. He puts the rifle down. The barker gives him a plastic whistle. Delmar holds it up for inspection, glances at the boyfriend next to him, who gives him a half smile, a shake of the head, as if to say "That's it?" But now they are comrades, just as long as Delmar keeps his eyes off the girl. Delmar knows the rules.

"Let me try," Boyfriend says, laying down five tickets, taking the rifle. When she moves, the girl cuts her eyes at Delmar, but the boyfriend doesn't see. He slays two chicks and a rabbit, and the barker gives him a little rubber duck. He grins at Delmar and hands it to the girl.

"What do you have to do to get one of those?" Delmar asks, nodding toward the stuffed animals arranged on a board at the side of the shooting booth.

"Hit all five in the same row."

"Oh, I want an elephant," the girl says.

"Everybody likes the elephants," the barker says. He's a wheezy, red-haired guy with shaking hands, a chain smoker.

They are cute Dumbos with long, floppy trunks and mild, dewy eyes. But the elephants are lined up on the second to the top row of the shooting range, and they duck randomly, whereas the chicks, rabbits and ducks don't duck. The elephants are a challenge.

The guys square off, all of them trying for the ducking elephants. These guys are pretty good shots. Whistles and rubber ducks begin to accumulate in three piles. Delmar quickly runs out of tickets and starts to go for more, but one of the shooters gives him five, very generous. When they all run out, they send the girls for more, Delmar digging in his pocket for a couple of twenties. They joke about how they could buy better elephants at Wal-Mart, but where's the challenge? And they discuss timing, which elephant disappears when, and at some point Delmar notices the girl at the end of the row do a little bob and dunk reaching over and down behind the counter while the barker is reloading, her hand coming back with a gray blur — she's quick. And so, without discussion, they go into business, he and these four strangers. The guys point, shoot without aiming in rapid-fire succession, and talk to the barker, keeping him busy, counting off intervals between disappearing elephants, hitting a surprising number, forking over tickets. Then the girls wander off, and shortly afterward, they all stop, gathering their ducks and whistles. They find the girls in line at the portable johns, laughing hard, legs crossed so they don't wet their pants, and the thief holds three handsome elephants.

"You're good," Delmar tells her.

"She's had practice," the boyfriend says proudly. They exchange names. Shannon, Noah, Roy, Ashley. The girls hit the johns; he and the other two guys go for candied apples, and the fair is fun again. They go on some rides together, the five of them. It's fun in the Hammer, where the cage is big enough for all of them. Delmar's thigh rides up against Ashley's, and he accidentally brushes her breast with his arm lots of times. It's a pretty big breast for a sixteen-year-old. Roy, Ashley's boyfriend, is a little dense, or maybe stoned, his eyes glazed. In the Tilt-A-Whirl, Ashley seems to be exaggerating each tilt and whirl, turning slightly toward Delmar, until he feels her erect nipple, and he starts thinking about and then can't stop thinking about what she'd look like without the T-shirt. But Noah is not so dense — or blind. When they get off the ride, Delmar sees Noah checking him out, and it's true: in the bright carnival lights the bulge in Delmar's jeans is fairly obvious. Noah says something to Roy, Roy's eyes narrow. They head to the Ferris wheel, where Delmar finds himself sitting alone and looking back at Roy and Ashley in the seat behind him. Roy has a pretty big hand. It completely covers Ashley's left breast. Ashley looks forlorn. She doesn't smile.

Well, he has a choice. Stay and rescue Ashley and get laid or go home. At first he thinks there really isn't a choice, but then he remembers Eduardo Martinez, a twenty-one-year-old he knew in prison, doing time for the statutory rape of his seventeen-year-old girlfriend.

Delmar decides to go home.

He stops for gas and a Coke at a Quik Stop before he gets on the freeway, and that's when he notices he has only three dollars left and less than half a tank of gas. He puts the three dollars' worth in the tank, but the needle still quivers below the half-full mark. This could be a problem. He decides to take the shorter eastern route home, up 550 through Cuba.

He drives with the elephant beside him, thinking about Ashley and what a bummer the straight and narrow is. He thinks of the people he knows who have followed the straight and narrow: Becky, who spends eight hours a day behind a desk and then runs her feet off instead of getting laid; Uncle Woody, who spent eight hours a day in a mill and now has cancer; Stuck, who doesn't really qualify because she isn't straight, but she's on the narrow path, was named employee of the month in July for perfect attendance, and now she manages to show up every day, take care of her two kids every night, and still stay high. He thinks he would have to blow his brains out if he ever qualified for employee of the month at Stuckey's. He's got six months on the straight and narrow to look forward to as groundskeeper and all-around handyman at Whitaker Estates.

According to the clock on the dash, it's just past midnight. It's an uphill drive, the truck climbing steadily through Zia and San Ysidro into the Jemez Mountains toward Cuba, where he slows down because the hills have eyes — always a state patrolman hidden in the shadows around the Apache rez; as he climbs, the needle on the gas gauge drops fast. He rolls his window all the way down, leaning half out, feeling the sting of cool mountain air. Stars paper the sky overhead in this glittering world. He comes up fast on a slow-moving car, its sleepy taillights weaving back and forth from the shoulder to the broken white line, and he lays on the horn as he passes, waking the driver up. "I'm already gone," he says to the answering horn.

He speeds up on the other side of Cuba, where the road flattens out and the mountains drop away, sailing around the cars he meets. Quite a few on the road for this time of night, fairgoers, he assumes, some going real slow, drunks trying to find their way home. Fewer cars are heading south. They turn down their high beams miles before they need to because distances always seem shorter in the flatlands. There's nothing but black space and headlights. He too turns his high beams down well before he needs to, then flashes them just before an oncoming car passes, helping the drivers stay awake with a flash of blindness. He pushes the truck up to eighty, eighty-five, as if by speeding he can outrace the empty tank. He's wishing he had money for gas; if he did, he could turn right and head on down to Florida, hide out on Sam's houseboat. He wonders how Sam would feel about that. He likes Sam and he thinks Sam likes him. If he had money, he might just do it.

The air smells like gasoline. Somewhere to the west, El Paso Natural Gas is pumping black gold, but the night's too dark to see the hammers. They're there, though, like giant cockroaches digging in the earth, right where the Anasazi used to plow and plant their fields. He can feel them, the cockroaches, busy feeding, not giving a damn about him heading toward the straight and narrow. He could use some of that gas. Why is it they get to just dig and dig and he doesn't have a dime?

Just at the top of Bloomfield Hill, the gas pump symbol on the dash flickers, a faint yellow, then black, yellow, black. He can see the tiny lights of Bloomfield and the glow of Farmington just to the west. Twenty miles to Farmington, thirty-five to Fruitland, where Becky is sleeping, and only fifteen or so miles to Whitaker Mesa, where he has his own cottage. How many miles does he get once the warning light comes on? Five? Fifty? He comes up fast on a slow-moving car, then downshifts, watching the speedometer drop to seventy, getting right up on the car, sixty-eight, shifting into neutral, coasting a bit to save gas. He's close enough to read the license plate. It's a nice car, a Mazda with a vanity plate. NM HUGH. Delmar turns his lights off. He's coasting. He's invisible. He glides behind NM Hugh in his cloaking device. Speedometer stays steady at sixty-eight. He turns his lights on, shifts back into gear. Turns his lights off. Presses the gas pedal and closes the gap between him and Baby Huey, leaving a three-car length. *Are you awake up there?* he wonders. Time to wake up. He watches the speedometer, which starts to climb. Seventy. He closes to a two-car length, the lights from the car ahead animal eyes, twenty-twenty, lighting his way. Oh, now he's awake. The Mazda pulls ahead. "Steady as she goes, sir." He wonders how fast a Mazda can go. Faster than this Nissan? Delmar watches his speedometer climb to seventy-five. Eighty. He closes in, breathing down the Mazda's neck, a one-car length. "Go, baby go." And the yellow gas light stops blinking, starts shining. Ninety. Fast little Mazda. Rocketing along the straight and narrow.

"Call you Zoom," he says, taking his foot off the pedal, shifting to neutral, and dropping back just before they enter Bloomfield's speed-trap zone, while the Mazda jets ahead, a decoy, should anybody be out there watching. Delmar knows this country. He's been busted here. This country he knows well.

17

THE SUNDAY AFTERNOON after her adventure with the horses, Becky is sitting with her mother on the front porch when Aunt Alice's white Chevy half-ton pulls into the yard. Her mother says, "It's the Pied Piper of Sin." Becky doesn't laugh.

Alice toots the horn, sticks her hand out the window, and waves. The truck, pulling a horse trailer, circles the willow tree where Arnold's old VW is parked, an orange boil on the dirt. Becky and Arnold went to his place just as the sun was coming up, and she drove the VW back. Two red horse rumps fill the trailer's rear window, two long tails hang out.

The wayward roans. Figures. Becky has had about three hours of very shallow sleep. She's been both dreading and anticipating a face-off with Alice about the lost roans, which, of course, are not lost. What a surprise. Things always seem to work out for Alice.

When Becky was younger, she secretly wanted to be Alice, who is everything a woman should not be. Her other aunts used to talk ceaselessly about a woman's place, which was in the home where she should rear children and abide by the righteous counsel of her husband. Or, if unmarried like them, she should serve the Lord.

As Becky grew up, people began to tell her that she looked like Alice, which delighted her, but when she examined herself in the mirror, she saw the resemblance but not Alice's beauty. Becky, her father, and Alice all have the same rectangular faces tapering just slightly into a squared chin, though Alice and her father have high, defined cheekbones and indented cheeks, which Becky, with her uninteresting slabs, has always envied. She thinks the hollows make her father and Alice look rugged and mysterious. Becky's nose is just a little wider than her aunt's, her lips a little thinner, and where Alice's hair is long, ropy, and very braidable — it's the color of sable but sun-threaded with copper — Becky's charcoal hair is coarse, electric, and copious, growing down her neck and in front of her ears like sideburns. Though her father and Alice both have thick brows, neither is nearly uni-browed, as she is. Arnold says he prefers Becky's Frieda Kahlo brow, her screwball face with its monstrous beauty. He thinks Alice's beauty is classic and forgettable, but he's the only one she knows who says that.

"*Yá'át'éhéii,* Della," her aunt calls, walking toward them. "*Yá'-át'éhéii,* Becky."

"Hello," her mother says.

Becky says nothing. A man gets out of the passenger's side of the truck. He wears a straw cowboy hat, plaid shirt, and tight jeans. Alice climbs the porch, smiling at Becky, stretching her hand out. Becky barely touches her fingers and can't bring herself to look in Alice's face.

She introduces the man, a wrangler from Sanostee who seems closer to Becky's age than her aunt's. Though it looks as if he's taken a few falls in the rodeo ring — his nose is flat, the bridge probably broken, and his left cheekbone is flatter than the right — he's good-looking in a scarred way. Her aunt's type. Becky has seen a dozen of his kind with Alice over the years.

Becky's mother moves over, making room for Alice next to her on the porch swing. "They were there this morning when I got to the farm," Alice says, nodding toward the trailer. "Sorry about the trouble. They know their way home." Her voice is jolly, as if last night was a fine joke. Her eyes are hidden behind dark glasses. She stretches her arms out on the back of the swing, crosses her ankles, spreading out. She's a little fleshier than usual, bulging around her blue-jeaned thighs, and she looks soft, sort of liquid. Becky gets the feeling she's watching the guy behind her glasses, though she keeps her face turned toward Becky. What it is? It's the languid softness of a good night's sex. Irritating. Next to Alice, Becky's mother seems shrunken and bland, her hair graying fast. Alice and Della are the same age, forty-four, but her mother is starting to look older. Her hair is badly curled, a dozen hoops all operating independently of each other, the hoops dull, the hair thinning. In spite of her effort to keep on top of her moods, depression has begun to ooze from her.

Becky looks at the horses' rumps. The tails don't swish. They're probably asleep. They had a hard night. Alice says she hasn't heard from Delmar, but it looked as if he'd been by the farm. Some of his stuff was gone. But he didn't leave a note. "Maybe he got the job."

"Where is it?" Becky says.

"I don't know. He just said it was a gardening job."

"So you want to lend me your truck?" Becky says. "Delmar took mine."

Her aunt presses her lips together, looking at the cowboy. Annoying. Becky gets the impression Alice is trying not to laugh. The cowboy smiles.

"Sorry, Becky. You know Delmar."

"I'm not kidding," Becky says. "We've got no transportation here." Alice looks at the VW. "That," Becky says, "is like a tricycle."

Alice puts her index finger over her mouth. Becky wishes she had the guts to slap her. Her aunt thinks Delmar is something. Clearly.

"Sure," Alice says. "Just as soon as we get back."

"Where are you going?" Becky's mother says.

"We have to go down to El Paso. *Yá'át'éhéii ánaaí,*" she says as she gets up. Becky's father is standing behind the screen door. Alice crosses the porch, opens the door, puts out her hand, which Woody takes and holds on to, leaning into her and coming out on the porch. She walks him to the swing. They speak to each other in Navajo. Becky glances at her mother and is glad to see a little fire in her eyes. Della does not appreciate conversations in Navajo, which exclude her, especially in her own home. Only Alice does this.

"What's in El Paso?" her father says after a while. He's wrapped in his orange Pendleton blanket, which he grips at the chest with fingers that are too bony. His concave cheeks no longer look mysterious and dangerous but simply skeletal.

Alice leans up against the porch railing next to the cowboy. "We're starting some training camps. We've got one in El Paso and one in San Antonio. Good money. We should be back in a couple of weeks. I was wondering, Becky, could you look in on *Shimá* until Delmar gets back?"

"And how am I going to get there!" Becky's mother's head rears back in surprise. Becky didn't intend to shout, but she can't stop. "Give me your truck and I'll look in on Grandma."

Alice stares at her feet. The cowboy looks at her feet. Becky's father smiles at his feet. Heat floods Becky. She bites her tongue.

The wrangler says something softly to Alice in Navajo.

"It's okay," she says. "He says his sister will look in on Grandma."

They sit in silence.

Becky watches cloud shadows drift across the dirt yard and thinks maybe it will finally rain. She decides she's not going to feel the shame she's feeling. How can Alice make her feel this way, as if she is a cute child having a tantrum?

"Don't worry," her aunt says softly. "He'll come back. You know Delmar." She takes her sunglasses off, cleaning them on her shirt. She has bags under her eyes, which make her look her age, but the expression in her eyes makes her look even older. Her teasing fit seems to have passed. She's looking at Becky with a heavy-lidded kindness, as if she understands exactly how Becky feels, as if she feels it, too, and Becky's temples begin to throb, the lack of sleep and the desire to cry swelling her sinuses.

"If he doesn't," she says quietly, "I'm calling the police."

Alice nods slowly. She puts her glasses back on. She links the index fingers of both hands into her jeans pockets and gazes at the section of porch floor between her and Becky.

Becky closes her eyes. She could be Alice's twin, and she wouldn't be as beautiful. Alice's beauty comes as much from her attitude and bearing as from her features. People don't mess with her aunt. Once when Alice was driving Becky and Delmar to their grandmother's farm, they had an accident. A gray blur, dog or coyote, slunk across the highway just as they were passing the Turquoise Bar at Hogback. Alice swerved, missed the blur, but nicked the back of some white guy's car, causing him to spin down the highway, while they plunged headlong into the ditch at the side of the road. The white guy's car nosed into the guardrail, collapsing the front and causing the airbag to inflate. Alice bumped her head on the steering wheel and cut her forehead, blood flowing into her eyes. Becky and Delmar were okay. The white guy was okay but angry, yelling at the people who came out of the bar that they better get a state trooper, he knew his rights. A Navajo cop showed up first, but the guy wouldn't let anybody move until a white state trooper came and tried to put Alice in the back of his car — the white guy screaming about the goddamned drunk Indians — but Alice did not get into the back of his car, and she did not scream at anybody, just said over and over again to the Navajo cop, as if the white one were invisible, "There was something in the road, I swerved to miss it," as the blood streamed down her face. Becky will never forget her voice and her poise, which seemed to cocoon and protect them.

"Well," Alice says, "he has to see his parole officer on Friday. Can you wait to call the police until then?"

Becky opens her eyes.

"If he doesn't show up for his appointment," Alice says, "his parole officer will contact the police. He knows."

"Is there a number where I can reach you if I need to?"

Alice looks at the wrangler. He stares at the ground. "I'll call you. Sorry for the trouble, Becky. We'll be on the road. I'll call next weekend."

After they've gone, Becky's mother goes in to start dinner. Her father pats the swing next to him, and she goes to sit with him.

"Are you going to No Fat?" He means the mesa where they run. Years ago she'd asked him why they call it No Fat. "Because everybody who runs there gets skinny. Look at you," he'd said.

"Too tired."

"You go yesterday?"

"Yeah."

"How far?"

"To the lake."

His eyes shine. "That's good."

"I'm thinking of registering for that fifty-mile race at Hopi."

He nods. She ran her first race with him when she was twelve, a 10K, and they've run two marathons together. He has only one rule: finish, even if it means walking, even crawling. But she holds her own. She came in twenty-sixth in her age group at the Green Valley marathon.

"Delmar should fix my car," her father says.

"Delmar doesn't know how to fix cars. All he knows how to do is steal them."

He laughs, wheezing, then coughing and sputtering. "That's true, that's true." He doubles over, gasping for breath. She holds his shoulders, gripping them hard, trying to help him hold himself together. When he can speak again, he says, "You tell him when he comes back he can have my car. You need your truck."

"You need your car," she says softly.

He smiles, closing his eyes, shaking his head, saying nothing.

18

O N MONDAY Dr. Callahan calls again. Rosy is outside watering the lawn. Ryland sees the doctor's name on the caller ID. He watches Rosy through the kitchen window while he lets the answering machine pick up and listens to the doctor say he left a message on Saturday and is calling again, that he really needs to talk to Ryland. He gives his number, gives it again, and Rosy is on her way into the house when Ryland deletes the call.

"A million things to do," she's saying. "Bone tired. Did it all last night in my sleep."

His heart is racing. The kitchen table is covered with chocolate truffles in red and blue wrappers, bags of cashews, rolls of breath mints. Maggie and George are coming over this afternoon to pack the stuff in colorful pouches that they'll leave for the out-of-town wedding guests in their hotel rooms. Rosy laid it all out last night and told him what it was about. He sits down at the table, taking the portable phone with him.

"Got to give this house a thorough cleaning before the hordes descend," she says. "I can't believe it's less than a month away. Edna, bless her heart, asked if she could send her maid down to help. That woman is an angel."

The phone rings. He jumps and answers. Rosy's eyes widen. He stares at her, watching her eyebrows knit, then hands the phone to her. He didn't recognize the voice. But after her first few words, he knows it's somebody from the uranium coalition. "Yes, I saw the announcement in the paper. You might be surprised. I think there's interest." They're having a meeting this Friday night at the Unitarian church. It's in today's paper. Rosy read the article to him and asked him to go. Nobody expects him, she said, but she wishes he would, because, she said, nobody knows as much about this stuff as he, and he said, "Good."

"Good what?" she said.

"Good that nobody expects me." Over his dead body would he help those people.

He runs his fingertip over the cellophane truffle wrapper. He pulls the candy toward him, then another piece, then another, arranging them in a line. He's on double doses of Demerol. His back's killing him.

When she hangs up, she puts the phone in its cradle on the desk. He waits until she leaves the room, then gets up and puts it on the table within his reach.

"Honey," Rosy says, coming back into the kitchen, "you're underfoot. Why don't you go to the living room and watch a movie or something. You look like hell," she says. "Didn't you sleep?"

"Slept good," he says.

"Well, you look like hell," she says.

"Thank you very much."

She puts her hand on his shoulder. He can feel her looking at him. He gets up and pulls his cart into the living room, where clothing has taken over. His good black suit is laid out on his chair, just a cloth socket waiting to be filled. And Rosy's new suit, which she has informed him is melon, not orange, lies on the sofa, with melon shoes on the floor. Billowy, lacy stuff, flower-girl headgear, covers the other furniture. More clothing and billowy stuff is scattered through the rest of the rooms. Rosy has been doing inventory, checking for rips or stains just in case something needs to be sent to the cleaners.

He walks over to his chair, picks up his suit pants, folds them, puts them on the footstool, sits down, picks up the remote, then puts it down again and stands back up.

He walks into the bathroom, stares at himself in the mirror, at the tiny blue veins under his chapped skin. He walks out of the bathroom, moves into the living room, and picks up the remote. He turns the TV on, watches it for a minute, puts the remote down, turns, and walks into his bedroom. She is running water in the kitchen. In less than a month the house will be full of family and strangers here for the wedding. He walks to the bed, sits, then stands again.

He looks at the dials and lights on his oxygen tank. He filled the tank this morning when he got up. The red light is dull, the green bright. He's used a quarter of a tank. He pivots, closes the bedroom door against the sound of the ringing telephone. Even when there isn't a wedding in the works, the phone rings several dozen times a day. She's popular, his wife. He walks to the window and stares at the cars moving up and down Cactus Drive. Across the street a young woman he doesn't know kneels in the grass digging tufted sprouts of dandelions. Digging in, pulling out, digging in.

In the afternoon, when Maggie and George come over to assemble party favors, Ryland sits with them at the table, his stomach numb from too much Demerol, the phone on the table next to him.

He is the main topic of discussion. Will he be able to walk Maggie down the aisle? "The question isn't," Maggie tells him, "whether or not you're giving me away." She pulls the two ends of a truffle wrapper, and the chocolate ball drops to the table. "He doesn't want to give me away," she says to George. She pops the ball in her mouth.

"That's not what he said," George says. "He said you have a choice."

"Eddy is not giving me away. Eddy is not my father." Chocolate squeezes around the corners of her mouth.

"Honey," Rosy says, "it's going to be a long Mass. Your father's going to be more comfortable if he can sit in the back by the door. He can't sit through the whole Mass anymore."

"Well, what about this," Maggie says. "What if he walks me down the aisle. Then he can go around to the side and go to the back of the church and sit there, and then when it comes time to stand up for me, he can come back up. What about that?"

"What does he do with his oxygen tank?" Rosy asks.

"What do you mean? He does what he always does. He pulls it in the cart."

"His oxygen tank embarrasses him," Rosy says. "He doesn't want everybody in the church looking at him pulling an oxygen tank."

"Daddy," she says, "will you dance with me at the reception? Daddy taught me how to waltz," she tells George.

"Honey, that was a long time ago," Rosy says.

"If I get the band to play 'Goodnight, Irene,' will you dance with me? That's his favorite," she tells George. She sings, "Sometimes I live in the country, sometimes I live in the town . . ."

The phone rings. Ryland picks it up. "Sometimes I take a great notion," Maggie sings. It's Lily on the phone. He breathes. "To jump in the river and drown . . ."

"That's a wedding song?" George says.

He hands the receiver to Rosy. Lily's voice squeaks through the receiver as it crosses the table.

He gets up, pulls his oxygen cart into the living room, stares at his footstool reflected in the TV screen.

He walks into the bedroom, closing the door behind him, and lies on the bed. He needs to calm down. He wonders if he's still efficient—if his mind is. *The man who considers himself unfit for combat flying or who is considered unfit by the flight surgeon or the unit commander is obviously inefficient.* He once had to make a tough decision concerning his copilot, Larry English. English had set up his pup tent, flap open, and was sitting half in and half out of the tent cleaning his rifle. It began to rain. Larry kept cleaning. The gun got wet. Larry got wet, his front half. His back stayed dry. For a long time, hours. It happened in a split second. Between unloading and opening the chamber, an efficient man lost his mind.

So. He needs to strategize. What does he know? He knows the test was positive. They don't call if it's negative. He doesn't mind knowing. He's glad to know. He just doesn't know why anybody else has to know. He doesn't want the family to have a conversation about it. What to do with Daddy.

His mother died in summer, and his father did, too. He always thought he would die in summer, but summer is coming to an end. His mother had been in the ground a year by the time he got back from the war.

His father died of lung cancer.

Today is Monday. Wednesday they'll refill his Xanax prescription. That was Rosy's idea. She went looking for the bottle, and Ryland told her he'd finished it. She's thinking about him. His nerves. He's grateful for this. He is. He listens to her muffled voice. Though he can't understand the words, he can tell from her voice that she's discussing all the ins and outs of the wedding. She loves planning and replanning, then doing and discussing it for days once something is over.

She is a good woman, Rosy. Sometimes it's hard to remember that. Hard to see the woman he married in the chatty old gal. No, that's not true. She's always been chatty. And tough. That's what he fell in love with. He remembers their first date. She called him, actually. He was just back from Guam. "Wouldn't you and a buddy of yours like to take the Walsh girls fishing?"

They took Sam's old Chevy, which handled the dirt road up to Electra Lake pretty good. They got a bag of worms at the tackle and bait, had it on the floor between the girls in the back, and Rosy said, he remembers this clearly: "The first time I ever saw a worm, I ate it."

"She lies," Lily had said.

"Just because you didn't see me doesn't mean I didn't."

"Nobody saw her," Lily told them.

"Just because nobody saw me doesn't mean I didn't."

Rosy kicked her shoes off. She had long, talented toes that she spread and wiggled for his benefit, he remembers that. She had personality. He knew prettier girls, but none who kept his eye like she did.

He said, "Let's see you eat one, then."

She just looked at the scenery and smiled.

So he said, "Who we going to believe? You or the fence post?"

"Believe the fence post, I don't care." She turned her nose up.

"You know, Sam," he said, "the lady in the back seat's got an upturned nose. Not like a pig, though. A little like a bulldog but not like a pig."

Rosy put her finger to the tip and pushed that nose between her eyes.

Later, in the boat, they broke open a watermelon the girls had brought and poured whiskey into it. They speared the melon with Ryland's army knife and fed some to the fish. He and Sam went swimming in their skivs, and the girls stripped down to their undies, which was a pretty sight, that pile of women's clothing there in the bottom of the boat.

He closes his eyes. He doesn't know how he's going to keep Rosy from finding out about the test. He really hopes he can. It would completely spoil her excitement about the wedding, and she's handling a lot already. He should show his gratitude. Something she'd never expect—his gratitude. He'll get Maggie in on the act. He'll give his wife a present or something. When everybody's giving presents, he should give one to Rosy. He doesn't know what. He'll let Maggie decide. He'll write the check.

19

ROSY IS IN HIS ROOM opening the curtains when he wakes up on Wednesday. It's eight o'clock and she's dressed to go out. She tells him that she needs to pick up Maggie's thank-you notes from the printer, and she needs to see about the nuts because nuts aren't covered in the caterer's arrangements and everybody agrees little dishes of nuts are just the thing for the tables at the reception. Maggie's afraid there won't be enough food.

"Honey, please answer the phone and take messages," she says. "I don't want to lose half the day returning calls." He says he will and promises to meet and greet the mailman and the UPS guy, too—especially the UPS guy, because he's new and won't leave packages on the porch like the mail guy will, and Rosy doesn't have time to go chasing after the UPS guy.

He gets up, bathes and shaves, and has Demerol for breakfast. He has the house to himself. Good. For a while, he's not going to worry about the doctor calling. Ryland stayed close to the phone all day Tuesday, but the doctor didn't call.

Sometime between nine and ten, the Demerol kicks in, and he falls asleep in his chair. He wakes to the sound of pounding on the door and gets up to greet the UPS man, who has five boxes. The mailman has been and gone, leaving three more boxes on the porch.

Ryland adds the eight to the mountain of presents in the corner of the living room. Some are wrapped in wedding paper; some are still packed in cardboard because Rosy hasn't gotten around to opening all of them.

The Demerol has left him tired. He far prefers Xanax because it puts him to sleep but he doesn't wake up in a fog. He stands staring at the blank TV. He decides that even though he's tired, he's going to surprise Rosy and open the mail for her.

He sits down on the floor, his back propped against the couch. The first package is from his sister Frieda. He cuts the packing tape with his pocketknife and lifts out a large square box, little pink Styrofoam peanuts clinging to it. The box, wrapped in nice silver paper with bells, is as light as air. He brushes the peanuts from the present, a dozen or so flying onto his lap and the floor, straightens the crushed silver bow, and digs through the peanuts for the card, which says MARGARET AND GEORGE in Frieda's block print. His sister's alphabet has always had corners, even on the round letters. He sees Frieda in her printing, a serious child. He always liked her. When she was a little girl, her face was constantly pinched in a worried frown. He remembers his dad teasing a smile out of her by pulling coins from her ears, doing fancy magic tricks. He remembers his dad teasing smiles from all of them at the dinner table when his mom's back was turned — a clown pulling his cheeks into hangdog jowls, rolling his eyes back, letting his tongue hang loose in an idiot drool; he'd have them in fits, while his mom, fussing at the stove, would say, "What? What?"

Ryland puts the present at the edge of the neatly aligned pile and puts the peanuts back in the packing box. He will do this job right. He will leave no messes.

He likes Frieda, but he's glad she and her family won't be coming to the wedding. One thing about his side of the family, he can count on them not to call, for the most part, and not to come, which is a relief. He likes looking at pictures of them. He likes hearing news of them through Rosy. He doesn't particularly want to see them — doesn't particularly want to see anybody, relative or not. Wouldn't mind seeing Sam.

One of the presents is from Lily. This surprises Ryland. He would have thought Lily would come to the wedding and bring her present along. Rosy's family generally shows up for things.

He slits through the packing tape, folds back the cardboard flaps on the box, and stares at something that has no wrapping. No silver paper, no crushed bows. Notebooks. Tied together with twine. He lifts the books out of the box, stares at them for a good minute before he recognizes them as his.

Five old green-backed logbooks from the mill and a manila envelope. He sees, in his own printed hand, his name on a white label glued to the middle of the book. Below his name, Uranium Corporation of America, and below that the year, 1964. He pulls the two ends of the twine, unleashing the bow, and opens one, thumbing quickly from the first yellowed page to the last.

The ink has faded to a fuzzy old blue. He lets the blue dots organize themselves into words and stares at his summary of that year:

> Processed 132,803.20 tons of ore.

He picks up a manual titled Operations:

> Milling process: a two-stage sulfuric acid leaching circuit, a countercurrent washing circuit, and a uranium and vanadium solvent-extraction circuit. Tailings from the washing circuit and yellowcake filtrates to be pumped to the tailings disposal areas and raffinate from the solvent-extraction circuit to evaporate in separate holding ponds.

He flips to the summary for 1965:

> In addition to the principal ore mineral, carnotite, the mill processed small quantities of the upgraded slimes.
>
> Tailings pile 400 feet from the edge of the terrace escarpment. Escarpment, 10 feet of silty to sandy gravel with cobbles overlying Mancos Shale.

He closes the book. Five of them. Up through 1969. But then, where are the others? If Lily has — had . . .

How did Lily get his logbooks?

He puts the logbooks aside, picks up the manila envelope, a heavy eleven-by-fourteen thing. He rips the top and pulls out a bound copy of reports. He'd found these reports himself when the

AEC and NRC started hounding him. Thought he needed to be prepared. Studies about toxicity levels at other processing plants around the country and in Europe, about levels of radiation poisoning, what was safe and what wasn't. The verdict was mixed, that's what he'd found out. One scientist would say no level was safe, the next would say the risk was minimal.

She'll use these for her meeting. That's what this is about. Rosy also has a couple of boxes of his medical records. She's going to read from those at this meeting on Friday, which is a fundraising event; bigwigs from the bank and the lawyer's office and God knows who else will be there — Rosy's counting on it. He's heard her say so on the phone a dozen times in the last three days.

He doesn't need to go to the meeting. He's already the starring attraction.

He reaches back to the couch and pushes himself up. Notebooks slip from his lap to the floor. He stands wobbling, feeling the pins and needles shoot from the soles of his feet into his calves, then pulls his cart into the kitchen.

He stares at the blinking answering machine. The number 2 lights up, disappears, lights up. Did the phone ring? He presses the ANSWER button. The first message is from Rosy, telling him he promised to answer the phone. She's checking in.

The second is from the doctor. "Ryland, I left a couple of messages. I hate to leave this kind of message on the answering machine, but I don't want you to worry." Something happened to the lung tissue samples. They got contaminated somewhere between the doctor's office and the laboratory, and Dr. Callahan regrets to say that Ryland will have to come in and get tested again. "Ryland, I'm sure sorry about this, and of course there'll be no charge. I wanted to get you in early this week because I'm going on vacation tomorrow, but we'll wait until I get back. No hurry."

And that's it. Ryland laughs.

He deletes the messages, turns, walks back into the living room, stares at the pile of presents, and remembers what he meant to do. He returns to the kitchen. There's a black address book on the table by the phone. He flips to the B's, runs his finger down a list of Behans, most of them crossed out — old numbers for Lily and a faded one in pencil for Sam. He picks up the phone and dials the number for the marina where Sam docks his boat. The man doesn't have a phone. The best Ryland can do is leave a message and hope Sam calls back.

When Rosy comes home, she is fit to be tied. He promised to answer the phone, and she called, and he didn't answer! She starts to lay into Ryland until she sees what a nice job he did of opening the mail, breaking down the cardboard boxes, and putting all the peanuts in a garbage bag, and then she is all smiles and compliments. Ryland doesn't look at her. He looks at the TV. In its reflection, he watches her walk to the stash. He left the logbooks neatly stacked on the top of the pile. He watches her back as she takes in Lily's presents. She turns and looks at him. He glances away.

She'll do whatever she damn well pleases. Always has. She pushes, and she pushes, and she pushes. He doesn't push. He doesn't care what she does.

He will not touch those logbooks again. Ever. They are not his. They are hers.

The TV. Hers. And the remote is hers. He's done with TV.

He struggles out of his chair, pulls his oxygen tank into the bedroom, closes the door behind him, stands looking at the bed, which he didn't make. It's been made, though. Sheets tucked in, bedspread wrinkle free.

There's a tap on the door, it opens, and she comes in. She sets an orange prescription bottle down on the dresser. "Here you go," she says. She smiles at him. Lips two-toned, just a pale nothing on the inside where the lipstick has worn away but lined red around the rims. He smiles back. She says, "Lunch?"

"Think I'll lie down a minute."

"Before lunch?" she says.

"Think so."

She leans toward him, her eyes narrow, peering at his chin and cheeks. She cannot, it seems, lift her eyes from the middle of his face to his eyes. Finally she says, "Just let me know when you get hungry."

"Okay," he says.

She leaves the door ajar, but as soon as he hears her in the kitchen again, he closes it, twisting the knob first so she won't hear the latch click.

He picks up the bottle of Xanax. He walks over to the bed, pushing his tank ahead of him, and sits on the edge of the bed. He puts the bottle of Xanax next to the bottle of Demerol on the nightstand. He sees that his hand is shaking, and he wants to cut it off. He twists, pulling his legs up on the bed, lying back against the pillows. The room is full of sunshine, hot yellow light.

He can sleep in hot yellow light, though he knows this is unnatural. He has no control over when and where he sleeps, not anymore. One ought to sleep in dark rooms. One ought to know when one is asleep and when one is awake. Sometimes she will tell him that he has been sleeping in his chair when he is certain he's been awake.

Once he slept for twenty-four hours straight and didn't know it. This was before he married her. Just after they'd taken Palau, or thought they had. Got a furlough to Guam. He and some of the other guys were going to get some chow, and he said he'd just take a short nap. Then he got up and told them he was ready to go, and they said, "That was yesterday." All the guys grinning, saying what a good sleeper he was.

He sits up, swings his legs off the bed, looks at the two bottles on the nightstand, one thin, the other a little fatter. He picks them up, pulls his oxygen tank to the door, opening it quietly, walks down the hall to the bathroom, closes the door, sits on the edge of the tub, twists the cap off the bottle of Demerol, and empties the bottle into the toilet. He tosses the empty into the trash can, presses down, and twists the cap on the Xanax bottle. He looks in. A full bottle, thirty pills. He can't see the bottom. He holds it over the toilet, tilts. Stops. Turns the bottle upright and listens to the pills inside shake.

He doesn't know why he shouldn't have a little relief. He shakes a couple out, pops them in his mouth, swallows.

20

T HE WEEK AT WORK is a disaster. In the VW, Becky's commute takes thirty-six minutes on a good day, twenty-six minutes longer than it should, and once there she starts making mistakes. She's more worried about Delmar now than mad at him. Her mother has been worrying about him, and Della's worry is contagious. Wednesday they call the state patrol to see if a gray Nissan pickup has been in any accidents. No. The police ask her if she wants to report the truck stolen or missing. No. She figures she'll know one way or another on Friday, because if Delmar doesn't show for his appointment, her father is on the list of people to be called.

Her sleep is ragged. She falls heavily into dreams that she has to claw out of, waking every hour on the hour with images of her truck on fire, in a ditch, going over a cliff . . . She feels constantly on the verge of tears, and on Thursday afternoon, when her manager jokingly tells her they'd be better off paying her not to come in, considering the time she's lost making mistakes and then fixing them, she does cry, to her horror, then makes a fast dash to the door. Arnold abandons his post and follows her to the parking lot.

"We're going out tonight," he says. "Dinner and a movie. No argument."

Arnold picks her up a little after six and takes her to Albondigas. He ends up eating her enchiladas along with his carnitas, and he doesn't even complain when she doesn't hold up her end of the conversation. He orders her a beer and makes her drink it, saying,

"Take your medicine," which is exactly how it tastes. It gives her a headache.

The movie is *Silence of the Lambs*. They're standing in line to buy tickets when somebody behind her says, "Shhht," and blows on her neck, and she thinks instantly, *Delmar*, because that's what he does, just like a backward reservation Indian; she whirls around, saying, "You jerk," and finds herself face to face with Harrison.

He smiles. "You didn't sign up for my class."

"No. Well, I thought about it, but . . ."

"You didn't either."

"I did." She laughs. "This is Arnold."

"Oh. The scary guy from the bank. *Yá'át'ééhii.*" They shake hands. "Do they let you keep bullets in your gun?"

"*'Aoo'.*"

"You know how to shoot?"

"Yeah. So don't try to rob us. Are you here alone?"

"Yeah. I just got through teaching." He frowns at her.

"Sit with us," Arnold says, stepping up to the window to buy their tickets.

Harrison watches her, and she thinks that her face must be the color of a pomegranate. "I don't want to interrupt your date," he says.

"It's not a date."

"Yeah, we're just friends. Really bad friends," Arnold says. "Popcorn?" Harrison says no, and Arnold says, "Thank God."

Later Arnold will say that she should always trust him in movies and men, because he could not have picked better: a gloriously gruesome film guaranteed to wrench her from her worries. And Harrison turns out to be a man who is serious about the theater, who will sit, uncomplaining, in the front row, who does not gross them out by eating, though Arnold could have forgiven this during the cannibal scenes, and who has the good sense not to say a word throughout the film.

When the lights come up, Arnold says, "Mmm, mmm. Hungry?"

"Actually, yeah," Harrison says. "I could go for a burger."

This, too, pleases Arnold, Becky knows. He hates opinionating right after a movie. He takes movies the way he takes meals. When they're over, it's time to move on, though he will expect Becky to get every little movie reference he makes for weeks afterward and will, in fact, remember every cutaway, every rocky or seamless transition.

"Take this one," Arnold says, nudging her. "She hardly ate any of her dinner. I ate hers and mine."

"How come?"

"A convicted felon stole her truck and she's depressed."

"Don't talk about me like I'm not here," she says.

"A convicted felon stole her truck that she gave him the keys to."

Harrison laughs. "Really?"

"It was my cousin."

"You have a convicted felon cousin?"

"Delmar Atcitty," Arnold says.

"No way. Delmar's your cousin?"

"You know him?"

"We used to party together. Back in my partying days. Before I became a teacher." He nudges her. Throughout the movie, his shoulder had been pressed against hers. "And I used to buy car parts from him. So he's out of jail?"

"He's out and on the lam," Arnold says in his Eastwood accent. "I'm out of here." Before Becky can stop him, Arnold gives a little wave and heads up the aisle.

"There goes my ride," she says.

"Hmm. We'll have to see about that." He jerks his head toward the exit.

They go to Chef Bernie's. She sits across from him in a lime green booth with ripped upholstery. She is no longer miserable; she's nervous. He makes her feel a little the way Delmar makes her feel, like her parts don't quite connect, like disaster could be around any corner. Like she is fully awake, the world tumbling toward her.

"So Delmar's your cousin," Harrison says. He leans forward, his laced fingers in the middle of the table. He wears the wedding ring. "You look like his mom."

"That's what people say."

"How come I never met you?"

"I grew up in Fruitland, not Shiprock."

"He speaks Diné. Delmar."

"I know. Weird, huh. He's mixed-blood and I'm full."

She leans forward, touching the wedding ring, his finger immediately hooking hers. "Why do you wear your wedding ring on this finger?" she says.

He laughs. "I told you I'm not married."

"Did you?"

He wraps his fingers through hers, their palms touching, but then the food comes and they unlace, burger and fries for him, just fries for her.

"It's my mom's. She pawned it, then I bought it." He doctors his hamburger—mustard, catsup, and onions—then seems to reconsider, scraping them off.

"She didn't want it?"

"Mom's MIA. Haven't seen her in years. Booze." He takes a bite.

"Oh. Sorry."

He shrugs.

"Your dad?"

"He's a weaver. Maybe you heard of him. Carl Zahnee?"

Carlee. The beneficiary. "No."

She squeezes catsup on her plate, dips a fry in, tries to eat. It goes down hard, sticking in her throat.

"What do you have against learning the language?"

"Nothing," she says. "I just wasn't raised that way. I've never even lived on the reservation. I mean I go there. My *nalí*'s there."

"I know her. Ariana, right?"

"'*Aoo'*."

He smiles, probably at her accent. He chews, hamburger pouching his cheek.

"I just feel self-conscious when I try to speak it. Anyway, I'm sure I'll never live there. There's no reason for me to learn it."

"Oh man, everybody's got to learn it. We all do. It's going away. We're going away. We're on our last days. If our generation doesn't do something about bringing the language back, and the ceremonies, who will?" He tells her he's building a house in a part of the reservation that has no water and no electricity. His grandmother's land. His father moved there after his mother left. Harrison's going to start spending his summers there. He'll have sheep, chickens, dogs, and horses. He's saving to move back permanently. He wants to start a school of his own, one that won't use public or tribal funds, cut through everybody's bureaucratic bullshit. He wishes the reservation would close its borders and become a sovereign nation, all bad news to her.

"I better not fall for you, Harrison Zahnee," she says. "We could never get along."

His eyes widen. "Are you falling for me?"

"I bet a lot of girls fall for you. All your students and the wife on the farm."

He smiles. Says nothing. She shakes her head and pushes the fries away. "You know why I really didn't sign up for your class? I don't want you grading me."

This makes him laugh and choke. He gulps water.

Later he gives her a B. They're sitting in his truck, C3PO barking on the porch, her mother peeking out the window, just like she used to when Becky was in high school, and Becky is reaching for the door when his hand grips her neck, pulls her over, and he kisses her, and he doesn't taste like onions. "You get a B," he says.

"Just a B?"

"I always give Bs to students with promise."

"Oh, give me a break."

"For incentive. Maybe you'll get an A tomorrow."

"Maybe I'll grade you."

"It's a date. I'll see you at the meeting. If I get back in time. I have to go to Albuquerque."

"Oh, God," she says. That meeting. She promised to speak.

"You'll do good," he says. "You got real good English." He laughs his funny airy laugh.

135

21

BECAUSE ROSY WON'T stop badgering her, Lily drives down to the meeting Friday night. Rosy told her she had rallied the forces, insisting that the whole family come and show their support. "If I cannot count on my own family to come to these things, who can I count on?" Rosy had said.

Lily hates to drive south of the Colorado border. Unlike most of the people in Durango, she never goes down to shop in Farmington, which is much cheaper. She's always afraid she's going to run into that woman or her son, Sam's boy.

She arrives a little after seven and stands in the doorway at the side entrance, scanning the room. She's surprised at the crowd. Though it's a large room — a slick hardwood floor and glossy white walls — the air inside is stuffy and smelly, acrid sweat mixed with the chemical sweetness of perfume and hairspray. On the other side of the room, a man is opening large windows near the ceiling, using a hook on a pole. Six ceiling fans rotate in lazy circles, stirring the hot air.

Lily scans the Indian people — about half of those in the room, clustered in the middle and back rows, with only a few Anglos sitting among them. There are a few old men, hair bundled and bound in string, turquoise bolos strung loosely over their shirts, and old women with scarves tied under their chins, wearing, despite the heat, long-sleeved velveteen blouses and ankle-length tiered skirts. Lily watches as they greet each other, touching but not really shaking hands. Rosy told her, "You don't shake a Navajo's hand. You hold it. If you haven't seen the person for a long time, you hold it for minutes, and if you saw the person yesterday, you hold it briefly." How did Rosy learn these things?

The younger people wear jeans and T-shirts. Lily looks for the boy's orange hair, a beacon, but she sees no orange-haired Indians, and she doesn't recognize his mother's face among the middle-aged women. She'll know the face when she sees it again, of that she's certain. Once Sam took Lily to the Shiprock rodeo. She sat on splintery old bleachers watching Indian cowboys rope calves, twisting the animals' necks so severely it looked like the necks would break. She didn't care for it, but she liked the barrel racing. She admired a woman who seemed to glide around the barrels, dipping in and out, her long braid perfectly stationary on her back while she moved with the horse so beautifully, nearly touching, nearly tipping the barrels, a woman whose strong legs seemed to melt into the obstacles without disturbing them. She was the woman Sam had been sleeping with for five years and whose three-year-old child was probably in the stands. Sam had put Lily in the stands to watch. Perverse.

Children are screaming, running up and down the aisles. "Aunt Lily," a shrill voice yells. She looks toward the very back of the room, where Maggie and Sue are organizing a refreshment table and waving to her. Eight-year-old Sandi, in shorts and a halter top, walks briskly toward her. "We're on KP. Grandma says so."

"Does she?"

Sandi pivots, walking back, a little soldier. Rosy is bustling around the front of the room, acting as if she's in charge, stopping to talk to this person and that, a pink-headed little man in khakis and cotton shirt, a round woman in a flowered summer dress fanning herself with a newspaper. Rosy wears a nice white pantsuit with a concha belt at the waist, turquoise nuggets around her neck. People used to say Lily and Rosy looked alike, but Rosy has gotten stocky over the years. She's always gone up and down in her weight. She put on pounds with the babies and had a hard time taking them off, but now her weight has crept up again, not just in her hips, where she has always gained first, but in her shoulders and face. She'd better take care. She's a short woman. If she keeps going that way, she'll be short and square. And she's let her hair go gray, wears it like a steel helmet. Fred told Lily she looks ten years younger than she is. She's been bleaching her hair for years, which Rosy thinks is deceptive. "We're not young, why pretend?" But why not?

"Everybody please find a seat," a man says through the microphone.

Lily goes to the refreshment table. "It's so hot," she says.

"The air conditioner's broken," Maggie says.

Maggie has pulled her black hair into a ponytail, the curls frizzy and wet with sweat. Maggie's got way more thick and curly hair than anybody deserves.

"How's the wedding coming?" Lily says.

Maggie rolls her eyes. "Why didn't we just elope?"

"I'm a flower girl," Pooh says.

"We all are," Sandi says. "Not just you."

"Well, that's a lot of flowers," Lily says.

"Good evening, ladies and gentlemen," the man at the microphone says, and he says his name, Bill Lowry. He begins laying out the plan for the evening. He motions to two microphones, one at the head of the room, one in the middle saying that anybody who wants to will have a chance to speak.

It's going to be a long night. Lily stands with her back to the wall, next to Maggie, who doesn't seem to notice that the meeting has started. She's whispering about the wedding. Lily tries to be polite and listen, though Maggie's chatter makes her nervous. It's rude talking while people are stepping up to the microphone, like talking in church or at the movies.

"Worried about Teri," Maggie whispers. "She's awful little."

Lily smiles and nods.

"Didn't have anything blue, so guess what Sue gave me." Maggie is wearing a sleeveless green shell that she now pulls away from her neck, showing Lily a star sapphire on a silver chain. "God, I love it so much I can't stop wearing it."

"Be careful you don't lose it," Lily says, then bites her tongue. Rosy calls Lily walking gloom. "Your first thought is always of disaster, Lily," she likes to say.

Fred doesn't say that, though. He calls her "pretty lady" and doesn't seem to get tired of hearing her stories. "Tell me something I don't know, Lil," he'll say, and she'll tell him whatever comes into her head, which always seems to entertain him. Suddenly she wants to scoot out of this meeting, get in her car, drive north to Fred's house on Rainbow Road, where she had spent the night last night. She wants to snuggle against the pillow of his flesh, which had felt momentarily suffocating when he fell asleep on top of her, but that moment passed, the moments pass, and in all, the moments with Fred have been good. They spent the weekend together in his lovely country home, which he designed himself. He had found an old barn south of Durango, just a stone's throw from the Animas, and converted it into a roomy, luxurious home. A talented man, and he can cook. He made her blintzes Sunday morning for breakfast. In the evening they sat on his deck and watched a pair of eagles hunting.

"I can't stop eating," Maggie's whispering. "I better stop. You don't want to know how much my dress cost. I've put on five pounds since then. Don't let me eat one of those," she says, nodding at a plate of Pecan Sandies on the refreshment table in front of them.

"Okay," Lily whispers.

An old woman has stepped up to the middle microphone. She is speaking in Navajo and not translating. This is one of the things that used to annoy Lily when she lived on the reservation. These people will talk behind your back. In the trading post, where she hardly ever shopped — she far preferred to drive into town if she needed groceries, but on those rare days and occasionally weeks when it snowed or rained, she had to shop at the trading post — it never failed, the cashiers would hold their conversations in Navajo. Lily knows one word, *bilagáana,* white, and that's how she always knew they were talking about her. She assumes every Indian in town knew about Sam and that woman.

"Wanted to get dresses the bridesmaids could wear after the wedding; can't please them," Maggie whispers.

They watch Rosy step up to the mike, and Lily finally holds up her hand. Maggie stops talking.

Rosy introduces herself. "My husband, Ryland Mahoney, first started in the uranium business in Durango shortly after the war." Her voice seems to boomerang around the room, quieting everybody. She is so confident. In any room it's always possible to find Rosy, for her voice carries a kind of jubilance into corners, and people always gravitate to her. It isn't fair. Lily has always felt like Rosy's sidekick. Yet she finds she can't go for many days without talking to her sister. She relies on Rosy's confidence.

"He worked his way up to foreman. Altogether Ryland was in the business for twenty-five years." She tells them that he's been sick for the last six, that she has stacks and stacks of medical records. "I want to tell you all right now, if you have a relative who's sick, start keeping a paper trail. I am sure that eventually we will win this fight, but we know that only the miners who had medical records got any compensation. We hope to change that. We know many of you have lost relatives who couldn't afford to go to doctors or who went to medicine men instead. We must find a way for everybody to be compensated. I just want you to know that a paper trail can make things a little easier.

"This is the kind of evidence a medical record can provide. I'm going to read just a few summaries. Here's one from three years ago: 'Mr. Mahoney is a debilitated gentleman with multiple medical problems including severe COPD and emphysema who is oxygen dependent due to past history of exposure to uranium and coal dust.' Here's another: 'The lungs remain very hyperinflated with chronic areas of linear scarring and emphysema.' Not only are his lungs damaged, but his esophagus has deteriorated, so he has difficulty swallowing solid food. We believe his kidneys have been damaged. His ankles sometimes swell so badly that the skin splits. I know many of you have relatives with multiple organ damage, too. If there is anybody in the audience who would like my help in contacting doctors, I would be more than happy. Hindsight is twenty-twenty."

She goes on, flipping through the years of Ryland's illness. Looking after him has made Rosy almost as housebound as he now. She used to be able to get out and exercise. That's the reason for the weight.

When she stops and steps away from the microphone, there is silence in the room. After a while, people begin to applaud, not by any means a wild clapping, but a metronomic slapping like marching feet.

Now a young woman steps up. She speaks loudly, the microphone shrieking. "My name is Susan Ray. I was born for the Tódích'íi'nii clan and from the Táchii'nii Clan. *Shinálí*, my grandmother, was born over there, on the mesa above the San Juan, just south of the old mill in Shiprock. She had two daughters and a son, but my auntie and my uncle have passed on. My auntie was forty-six years old when she passed. She had a little boy who was born with a tumor the size of a baseball at the base of his skull. They took the tumor out, but the tumors come back. He's six years old. He's had three operations. He can't move the fingers on his left hand, and he falls a lot. His balance is bad."

"My God," Lily says. She folds her arms over her stomach. Little children chase each other in the open space between the refreshment table and the chairs.

"I hope you can do something for the people who live around there. That land belongs to my family, but we can't live there anymore." The young woman sits down. The metronomic clapping goes on for a minute, the crowd warming to it, the noise gathering its own momentum.

Rosy begins making her way back toward Lily and Maggie. A tall, handsome young man at the front of the room stops her. He's wearing a cowboy hat, summer cotton shirt, and jeans. He leans down, listening. The emcee begins announcing the next speaker, and Rosy continues down the side aisle, pausing to talk — Lily stops breathing — to an orange-haired Indian standing in the doorway.

22

B ECKY IS THIRSTY. She forgot to bring water with her to this meeting. She had left work early and gone for a long run to calm her nerves, but she ran too long in the heat. She knows better. The line between relaxation and exhaustion is a fine one, and she didn't drink enough water. Her head is thick, throbbing, and her tongue seems bloated; it fills her mouth.

Harrison isn't here. It's after eight o'clock. She's almost relieved. It's bad enough having to get up and talk, but a thousand times worse is thinking of him in the audience. Grading her. She wishes she'd brought water.

She regrets not writing her talk. It would be a whole lot easier just to get up there and read something, like Rose Mahoney did.

Doo'ak''ahii. This morning she asked her father the Navajo word for No Fat Mesa. She wants to say something about running with him up there, and she wants to use the Navajo word. She wishes she could introduce herself with her clans. She wishes she knew her mother's clans. How many times in her life has she been in this position?

Her parents have been fighting. It's so odd. They never fight. Their nerves are frayed. Today when she got home, her mother was crying, and her father said, "Tell her Jesus Christ forgot to learn my name." He wants no more prayer circles in the house.

Terry Conrad is here. He came into the bank today and asked her to lunch, but she turned him down because she wanted to get her run in. He asked her to go out with him after this meeting, but she told him she had plans. He was pretty insistent, though. He has to go back to Dallas for a meeting tomorrow, and he wants to run an idea by her. She agreed to meet him for a quick cup of coffee after work. She drove to Denny's and, stopped at the light, she saw him sitting in the booth waiting for her. But she was wanting to run. When the light changed, she glided on by. She feels a little bad about that.

He has been talking to the people at the front of the room. He seems to be watching her. Now he heads her way. Tonight he's wearing a short-sleeved blue shirt that matches his blue eyes, seeming to magnify them, and a straw cowboy hat—he wears it well, like he's used to it.

"You stood me up," he says.

"Sorry," she says. "I couldn't get away."

"Anybody sitting there?"

She'd put her purse on the chair next to her, half thinking she was saving it for Harrison. She picks the purse up, and he steps over her legs.

"Good crowd," he says.

"Yeah."

He smells like cloves. A cologne-wearing businessman-cowboy. It's not unpleasant.

"How long you think they'll go?"

"It's supposed to be over at nine."

"I'd still like to get together with you. Can I buy you a beer?" He smiles, leaning toward her, his shoulder brushing her. "You owe me."

Overhead the ceiling fans turn, muted whirlybirds. She scans the back of the room. He is not here, and it's 8:20. It's a three-and-a-half or four-hour drive to Albuquerque. He'll be on the road eight hours. What's in Albuquerque? Who's in Albuquerque?

"Okay," she says.

"Great."

The microphone crackles. Bill Lowry has just said her father's name. He makes comments after each speaker. "People like Wood-

row Atcitty, who labored for years breathing radioactive dust ...."
It's her turn. She tries to focus. Will there be water up there for
her? She'll just say one or two things. That the new tumors are in-
operable.

People are clapping. She feels somebody's hand on her shoulder.

Harrison is looking down at her. "I made it," he says. She smells
coffee on his breath. He squeezes her shoulder, saying, "*Bee'-
ádíní.*"

And whatever it was she planned to say swallows her.

Standing at the podium, gripping it so her hands won't shake,
she is clear about only one thing: there is no water.

She says, "I am Becky Atcitty." She moistens her lips, swishes
her tongue to generate saliva. She can't look toward the east side
of the room where he stands, but she sees him on the edge of her
vision. He's wearing a black shirt.

She says, "This afternoon I went for a run."

She stares over the heads of all the people — so many!

"Up on the mesa near Fruitland, where I live." No Fat, no Fat.
What's the Navajo word?

She blinks and blinks again. "It was hot. No clouds." She licks
her lips. "I have been running since I was five years old. My father
used to take me up there with him. He taught me how to stretch
my hamstrings so I wouldn't get injured. Before we had good running shoes, he taught me to wear double socks so the bottoms of
my feet wouldn't get bruised by stones. He taught me how to run
slowly at first so as not to get winded. He taught me how to bend
and touch my toes if I got a side stitch and told me not to drink
soda before running because it's too acidic. 'Water,' he told me,
'is the best thing to drink.' He taught me to swish my tongue to
make saliva. 'Sometimes,' he said, 'saliva is all you have to drink if
you forget water.' I used to run close to the river, thinking I'd always have water, but it's not safe to drink the river water because
it could be contaminated." She swallows. Overhead the whirlybirds whirl. The only noise, children and the fans. The people are
listening, leaning toward her. Bill Lowry, sitting at the end of the

front row, is nodding and smiling. "It's better not to forget water. You've got to remember the important things, and I remember how he said if you go a little way one day, you can go a little more the next, and that's how you get places, but he will never run up there on the mesa with me again. He is too sick." She looks at the audience. They are very quiet. Bill Lowry smiles and nods. The black shirt near the wall is a speck in her eye. She says, "That's all."

They clap as she walks away from the podium. She walks down the side aisle, forcing herself to meet Harrison's eyes. He stands with his arms folded, leaning against the wall. He doesn't say anything when she stops next to him. "So?" she says.

"So?"

She takes a breath, turns, and lets the wall hold her up, leaving several inches between them. "How'd I do?"

"Good." She notices that he has a tiny bump on the bridge of his nose, and he doesn't look away and doesn't stop smiling. His sunglasses are in his shirt pocket. She takes them out, opens them, and puts them on his face. He laughs. Beautiful straight teeth.

"Look who's here." He motions toward the other side of the room, where her cousin stands below the clock watching them. Delmar puts his fingers together in a cross, as if warding off devils.

Outside, her truck gleams under the parking lot lights. He washed and waxed it. He's hoisting a bicycle out of the bed. Harrison stands next to her, his elbow touching her arm. "Nice bike," he says. In the weird light, she can't tell what color it is. It's got very skinny racing tires.

"He probably stole it," she says. Delmar straddles the bike and rides over to them.

"*Yá'át'éhéii*, Harrison."

"'*Aoo', yá'át'éhéii shiak'is.*"

"Yeah, I called Aunt Della. She told me you were here. I wanted to bring you back your truck. Good speech." He grins.

She says nothing.

"Yeah, I got the job up on Whitaker Mesa. Groundskeeper. You seen those houses up there?" he says to Harrison, who shakes his head. "I've been up there all week. Couldn't get back down until today, but I wanted to bring my cousin her truck."

He hands her the keys. He swings his knapsack around, pulling out a little stuffed elephant, which he tries to hand her. She doesn't move. He nuzzles the thing against her neck, and says, "This guy likes you." He leaves it in the crook of her neck, but it falls to the ground.

Harrison, laughing, scoops the elephant up. They watch Delmar zigzag through the parking lot. Harrison tucks the elephant under his arm, hiding its face and body, the trunk dangling over his forearm. He pinches the trunk with his other hand, wiggling it, nudging her, and says, "This guy's nasty."

"Don't get any ideas," she says.

"Like what?" The gray trunk flip-flops.

People have begun streaming out of the building. Between the two of them, they know a lot of people, who stop to say hello or comment on the meeting on their way to their cars, and then Terry Conrad is standing in front of her, bending down toward her. He says, "Ready?"

Harrison is talking to somebody from the college, but he stops midsentence, looking at her, his mouth half open.

"I didn't think you were coming," she says to him. He closes his mouth. The playfulness is suddenly gone from his eyes. "It's some sort of business thing. It'll only take half an hour. Come with us."

His jaw flexes as if he's grinding his teeth. His eyes look oily. Angry. Women probably don't tell this one no. It excites her a little, that he might see her as such a woman, but she definitely wants to see him tonight. Can she tell Terry to go away?

She doesn't get the chance. Harrison leans over whispering, "Three's a crowd," kisses her behind the ear, and walks away.

Terry Conrad sits across from her at a table in the Holiday Inn lounge. He orders a Budweiser, she water. The room is lit only by table candles and the lights behind the bar. A band is tuning up on the small platform on the other side of the room.

He wants to make small talk. He asks her what she thought of the meeting and where she thinks they should have the next one. She answers in single sentences. Her mind is racing. She wonders if Harrison's in the phone book. What is she doing here?

Terry doesn't have any sort of southern twang. He must be a transplanted Texan. His nails look manicured.

He begins after the waitress brings their drinks. He gives her a history of his company, a geological survey and resource development group. He tells her about research they've done on in situ leaching of uranium, saying again that most of the danger lies in ore extraction. He tells her that in situ leaching is especially effective in porous rock, through which chemicals like sulfuric acid can pass easily. "The trick is to use underground water sources for countercurrent rinsing, but then to restore the sources to their natural condition. That's been expensive in the past, but our engineers have developed cost-effective procedures to absolutely ensure a hazard-free environment both above and below ground." They've got the technology, he says, and now they're doing feasibility studies about how to cultivate resources on American soil that will ensure America's independence from foreign energy. "Other countries like Australia are rich in the ore, richer than we, and they want to get into the game, and they *are* getting into the game, and they'll be selling to unstable markets, to China for one. It's time to start thinking about safely resurrecting the industry here in order not just to be competitive but to continue to exert a governing influence on this volatile energy source. The fact is, the sandstone on the Colorado Plateau is porous. It would ensure maximum yield with an in situ leaching process."

He stops speaking, watching her in silence. He seems to be saying something more. There's something she's not getting.

"The Colorado Plateau? Monument Valley?"

"Well, for a start. And south. Southeast."

She begins to get it. He watches her gravely, his lips a straight line.

"You have got to be kidding me," she says quietly.

He takes a drink. The guitar plays a riff, the rest of the band comes in, and a man at the mike begins singing "Sweet Home Chicago."

"Were you ever going to tell us?" If she understands him right, he's talking about starting the mines up again.

"It's no secret. I've talked openly with Lowry about this. And I've signed up some members of the tribe as consultants. That's why I wanted to talk with you." He holds his hand up as she starts to speak. "Just hear me out. First of all, it's going to happen. If it doesn't happen on Indian land, it's going to happen on the border of Indian land. That's where the ore is. We want to do it right. I'm telling you, we've got a thirty-year record showing we know how to do it safely. But that's just in extraction. We need to make sure that we hear from people like you, people with a historical memory. Especially somebody like you, Becky. An educated woman. A businesswoman. A woman who knows, intimately, the risks. We don't want to deceive anybody. We want real, honest feedback. Come down to our facilities, let us show you what we're doing. Don't judge without having all the facts.

"If you like what we're doing and want to become a consultant, helping design educational strategies for your people, what we can do for you is something that the government cannot. I hope our efforts tonight are successful in prodding the legislature to take responsibility and to get some compensation for men like your father. But do you know how long it will take before you see any money? I wager ten years. And it will be pennies. That's a bad joke. An insult." He leans forward. "I don't mean to be cruel, but the dead are not going to wait for ten years — for pennies. We're in a position to put somebody like you on retainer as a consultant and to do it immediately. Anybody on permanent retainer, meaning more than a one-shot deal, will get a thousand dollars a month. The company's willing to engage in a long-term commitment. Somebody in your position — with your knowledge — would make twelve thousand dollars a year for, I'd say, at least five years, and all you'd have to do would be to come to a meeting now and again. Expenses paid, of course. And you'd be helping your tribe. Believe me, Becky, nuclear energy can be harvested safely. In the end, it will be safer and more reliable than fossil fuels. We will prove that to you. Your tribe stands to make a substantial profit. If the tribe doesn't come on board, McKinley County and the state of New Mexico will make that profit." He leans back. "It's going to happen."

He sips his beer. Her head throbs. She has drained her water but still feels dry. At the bar people shout over the noise of the band, the band amps up to compete. The singer sings, "Love me in the east, love me in the west, love me in the place that you know best."

Twelve thousand a year would go a long way toward paying off her parents' medical bills.

Terry is watching her. He wears that cowboy hat like he was born to it. She wonders where he's really from.

"Let me talk to my dad," she says finally.

"You bet. Take your time." He nods and sips his beer.

23

FRIDAY THE THIRTEENTH of September, 5:32 A.M.
Delmar steps out of his little adobe cottage into the smell
of sage, the mesa in front of him, shadowy in the blue predawn.
Stars are out but dimming. He carries a hot cup of Folgers instant
to the flatbed truck parked next to the electric cart. On Fridays he
drives the flatbed around the estates, collecting garbage. He prefers the electric cart, which is as silent as a sailboat on water.

Years ago, during his warrior days, Delmar used to spend weekend nights on Whitaker Mesa, which was just a mesa then, full of
tumbleweeds. Now it's a forest in the desert: piñon, sage, prickly
pear, yucca, all grown someplace else and brought in special. An
orange adobe wall encloses the estates, with a guard in a glass
booth at the gate. Little orange roads branch throughout the land.
The street signs are metal animals on poles: lizard, quail, snake.

In the warrior days, the only roads on the mesa were the ones
made by four-wheelers. Delmar knew several guys who died up
here, slain in battle. On party nights white guys from town would
come up here looking for rez rats, and the rez rats would come
looking for whites. They played tag in their trucks and cars, sitting in the dark, engines idling, headlights off. If you turned your
lights on and were spotted, or even if you lit a cigarette or a joint,
a horde of vehicles would zoom in like ants going for food, and
then you had to gun it, and if you got on the wrong road, too
close to the edge, the hordes could force you over it. You were a

goner if you didn't bail out in time. You were a goner, too, if you got trapped on the mesa outside your car. Then the ants swarmed and pulverized you with baseball bats.

The night was especially good if a town boy's tricked-out truck went over the edge and became booty during daylight hours. But the good days came to an end when the city started collecting the booty and forced him into banditry. The mesa changed, too. Everything changes, Delmar thinks. Except the ghosts. He sees them often when driving his little electric cart through the grounds, gray haze in the dawn and twilight, skulking along the quiet lanes, looking like coyotes. He wonders how the rich people up here would feel if they knew their houses were built on a graveyard.

Now, he gets into the truck, wedges the coffee cup between his legs, and turns the key. The flatbed is a noisy thing. Last week a guy complained to management about Delmar's early Friday morning drives, but he has to fill the dumpsters outside the estate gates by nine A.M., when the city collectors come to empty them. He figures the people up here can have either noise or garbage. Their choice.

He heads south down Quail Lane toward the complainer's house. On his rounds he wears headphones and listens to happy morning music, this morning Nirvana. He could've started in the north and finished in the south, which would've put him at the complainer's place later, around eight, but where would be the fun in that? He thinks of the complainer as Mr. VD, short for vodka drinker. Last week their trash was full of empty Skyy bottles and meat bones. They drive BMWs — she a silver, he a black — and never look at him when they drive past.

Last week he found cherry pie in the VD's trash. A smashed pie. Had just opened the lid and there it was, a dark goopy thing. A shame. He had had a piece of what was probably that same pie the day before. Elsie, the VDs' maid, gave it to him while he was trimming their hedge. The piece he'd had wasn't smashed. Who smashed the pie? he'd wondered. Why? These are the kinds of things he gets to think about these days. It's what makes him happy on the mesa. Such interesting things to think about and a lot of time to think, plus he gets to listen to Cobain: " I feel stupid and contagious, Here we are now, entertain us."

He likes to think about Elsie, too. He wonders if he has a chance with her. She is very cute, though she wears funny clothes — long skirts and peasant blouses with rickrack on the pouched sleeves. She's a mother of three, married to a tow-truck driver. The tow truck shows up at the front gate every evening at five sharp. Elsie walks out to meet it. Delmar once snuck up behind her in his silent electric cart, and she about jumped out of her skin when he asked if she wanted a ride. Now she's always looking over her shoulder when she walks.

On the day's agenda, after the garbage: Raid. It seems crickets have taken over Mr. Dildo's house. That's Delmar's nickname for the Delgados. Mr. Dildo has a young wife who goes jogging up and down Roadrunner Lane in nothing but a jogging bra and little shorts and always waves to Delmar, very friendly. He wonders how that old guy keeps her satisfied. Delmar plans to satisfy her later by getting rid of the wicked crickets, though it goes against his beliefs, wiping out a tribe of crickets just because they're noisy.

First garbage, then breakfast, and then the murder of crickets. He drives up and down the lanes, watching the land become visible, stopping at the inhabited houses to collect garbage, lingering at the Dildos' house because sometimes, early, he'll see that young wife standing in the open door wearing her workout clothes, eating something from a bowl.

Just a short jog past the Dildos' house he stops the flatbed at the center of the mesa, the old battleground, where something has just crept across the road. Blue lights are embedded in the ground along the road so the rich people can always find their way home. They can see the road, but do they see the dead guys looking for the party? He enjoys their company, especially the whites, ghosts of guys who never expected to die. White people don't expect to. Die surprised. Stupids. Now the Indians, the ones who die young, they always expect it, you can see it in their eyes. Fear. Maybe not of dying, but of lingering — of becoming ghosts. That bothers him a little, those guys he knew in the warrior days, who seemed to see their deaths before they happened. He is not like them. He tested death up here once. Got chased to the edge, floored it, and went over — kamikaze! But somehow death passed through him. He flew that night and came out of it without a scratch, he doesn't know how.

Cobain is singing about friends and old enemies. Farther down the lane, the something that slunk across is long gone.

Friday the thirteenth. Coyote on the path. Happy morning music. He takes a drink of coffee. The morning is good. The afternoon will be bad. He's got twenty-one Fridays left of pissing in Officer Happy's cup. Then he's a free man.

24

RYLAND FEELS LIKE an idiot, and what's worse, he looks like one. He stepped outside for the paper yesterday morning, and somehow his feet got tangled in his cart. The next thing he knew, he had blood running down his head and from both elbows. "Your dad took a little tumble," Rosy is saying to Eddy on the phone. Ryland has been sitting in the living room listening to her tell the story over and over to everybody who calls. "Got a pretty good conk on the head and skinned his arms. His poor battle-scarred arms. Fifteen stitches. They should be out by the wedding. I told Maggie not to worry. Scared us, though. Do you know what that pill did? No, not Maggie, your father."

She starts telling him about the contaminated lung tissue samples. When they went in to get him stitched up, Rae Freitag told her about the messages Dr. Callahan had left before he went on vacation. "Made me so mad," Rosy says. "We could've had this all over with before the wedding, but now we can't get another appointment until November. He fights me every step of the way."

He touches the gauze taped over his right temple, a thick bandage. He can feel the lump — can feel it from the inside because it throbs. He has a black eye, too.

"Oh, my Lord," Rosy says. "Oh, my Lord!" in a tone that chills him and makes him start from his chair — a tone that throws him back twenty-five years to when the kids were little and anything could go wrong. He stands, blinking out the front window at what looks like a truck parked just beyond the hedge. He grips the handle on his oxygen cart. Looks like Sam's old Chevy pickup.

Looks like Sam standing on the street looking in.

"You told me to come," Sam says, grinning. They sit at the kitchen table, cups of coffee in front of them. He looks exactly the same, a boy with blue-white irises, sheer white hair and eyebrows, but his skin is dry and papery, grayish, and the whites of his eyes are muddy.

"You drove all this way?" Rosy says. "Sam, why didn't you fly? You want sugar for your coffee?" She pushes her chair back.

"No thanks. Don't like planes." He cocks his head, gazing at Ryland.

"I'll be damned," Ryland keeps saying.

"You been brawling, Ry?"

Ryland just shakes his head and says, "Ssss."

"But Sam," Rosy says, her voice high and loud, the wedding's not for two weeks. You're early."

"Well, I needed a vacation."

"My goodness." She stands up. "We have cookies. Would you like a cookie?"

"Sit down, Rosy. I'm fine." She doesn't sit down. She crosses the kitchen, takes a plate from the cupboard, and starts piling on cookies from the cookie jar.

"Can't believe that old truck's still running," Ryland says. "How old is it? I remember when you bought it new."

"Thirty-one years old."

Ryland shakes his head.

"Paint's all rotten from salt in the air, and I had to convert it — you can't get leaded gas anymore."

"How's Florida? You ready to move back?"

"Crowded. It's full of jet setters. My old Kayot's the only tub in the marina. Raggediest rig in the water. Now the place is filling up with souped-up Leisurecrafts and Bayliners, and every year the rent goes up for my slip. Pretty soon I'm going to be priced out of the neighborhood."

Rosy brings the cookies over and the coffee pot, filling Ryland's cup, starting to fill Sam's, but stopping halfway when he signals. When her back is turned, Ryland watches Sam slip his old silver flask from his back pocket. He shows it to Ryland, offering. Ryland shakes his head, and Sam doctors his coffee, putting the flask away before Rosy returns to the table.

"How long is the drive?" Ryland says.

"Took me a week. I been taking my time, seeing the country. Down off I-10, near the Louisiana border? I got swarmed by palmetto bugs. Big as hummingbirds. The truck stops were thick with them. And people. There are so many people living along the freeway these days. Living in shacks like gypsies. You can see their campfires from the road. And the Rio Grande? In ten years it'll be a dry bed. Mark my word. I don't know. The country's changing fast."

"Changing here, too," Ryland says. "They're building gated communities outside of town."

"Sam, you wouldn't recognize Durango," Rosy says. "Lily bought the old Warnock house up on Crestview. You remember that place? It used to be the nicest in town."

"Big house," Sam says.

"They've got bigger ones now. They've got million-dollar homes by the river, right where Shantytown used to be."

"How's Lily doing?"

"Fine."

"Married?"

"No. She never remarried. She sees men. She dates."

"Well, I guess she probably doesn't want to see me."

"Probably not. She'll be at the wedding, you know." She grips the back of her chair and looks at Ryland.

"We're all adults," he says. "I think Lily and Sam will behave themselves."

Sam raises his eyebrows. "You think?"

"You better, Samuel Behan. I'll have no trouble from you at Maggie's wedding."

"Rosy, you're just the same," Sam says. "Isn't she?"

"She's a whole lot worse," Ryland says.

"And he's a mule," Rosy says. "I wish you'd talk to him, Sam. We've been organizing, trying to do something for the mill workers. Woody Atcitty. You remember him?"

"Yeah. Sure."

"He's sick. Lung cancer."

Sam glances at Ryland. "I'm sorry to hear that."

"And he's not the only one. That was dangerous business we were all in. It *was*, Ryland. Don't look at me like that. You would think this one . . ." — the back of Ryland's neck starts to burn — ". . . would want to do something for the old workers and their families, but," and now she looks at Sam, not him, her voice rising, "right now, we're just gathering material."

Sam meets his eyes and holds his gaze for a few seconds. He says, "I think I'll stay out of this one, Rosy."

"Oh, Samuel, they're just troubleshooting meetings to —"

"She makes trouble," Ryland says. "I try not to shoot her."

Sam grins. Rosy pivots, walking to the sink.

"You're staying with us, right, old man?" Ryland says.

Rosy's head jerks around, her eyes hard and bright. Ryland can see worry skitter through her. She doesn't know what to do with Sam. She doesn't know how to be with him since he broke Lily's heart. She thought Ryland should let the friendship go when the marriage busted up. She was mad at him when he wouldn't, but over the years, she's gotten used to their phone calls, used to Sam — as long as he stays three thousand miles away.

"If it's no trouble," Sam says.

Rosy smiles, but the worry line between her brows deepens. "No trouble at all," she says — with Rosy manners usually win — but then she says, "That dog!" venom in her voice.

"TGIF," Ryland says, winking at Sam, who is gazing at Rosy, his right eyebrow cocked in amused surprise. "We got us a little dog down by the cemetery who goes wild every Friday at this time."

"It's criminal the way those people let that dog go on and on," Rosy says.

"We suspect they're out getting drunk, celebrating the end of the week."

"Criminy," Sam says.

"Oh, you two," Rosy says, twisting her foot as if grinding out a cigarette.

In the evening, after supper, Sam pulls some of his hand-tied flies from a wrinkled grocery bag and dumps them on the kitchen table while Rosy noisily loads the dishwasher, clanging the dishes together. She's all worked up. Ryland knows she doesn't welcome a houseguest in the middle of the wedding preparations, especially not this one. He knows she's been turning it over and over in her head.

But after she finishes with the dishes, she goes into the sewing room, and Ryland can hear her fussing, pulling the sofa bed out, rummaging in the dresser drawers for clean sheets. Sam's flies are intricate, colorful bugs. Ryland plays with a pretty green item that looks like a dragonfly, flicking it back and forth on the table.

"The good thing about single-hook flies," Sam says, "is that I can find everything I need except the hooks right outside my door. I go scavenging along the beach and down at the nature preserve on the island."

"So you make a good living?"

"I do okay. Keep my overhead low. People are moving to artificial bait, especially for the big fish. These I call the Florida Ghost," he says. He pulls some white fluff from his bag. "Couple of months the mackerel will start running along the coast, and these'll bring them in. How're the trout this year?"

"Hell if I know. Lyle Terrano — you remember Lyle? In accounting?"

"Yeah."

"He brought us down some nice browns and a rainbow that he caught up near Creed this past spring, so I guess fishing's probably good in the headwaters, but the rivers have been low this summer."

"For trout flies, for the river trout, I like a blue-jay hackle and some gamecock. Gold pheasant for the tails. Actually, Ry, I thought I might tie a few flies special for the trout fishermen while I'm here, see if I can make a buck. Gas cost more than I expected coming up. You think Rosy'll mind if I set up here in the kitchen?"

"No problem," Ryland says. "You need money?"

"Nah." Sam pours from his flask into his coffee cup. They listen to Rosy moving furniture in the sewing room. "What's up with her?" Sam says. "What she was saying about Woody and all."

"Same old rigmarole. Trying to stir things up, like always. She isn't happy unless she's got some kind of a cause. Funny thing how this stuff never goes away. They want to rewrite history in regards to the uranium business. One minute they're telling you the stuff'll save the country, the next they're saying it'll kill us, and today's good news will be tomorrow's bad news, and then it'll all turn around again. What gets me are these people making a living off lawsuits." He tells Sam about the lawyer running the show. "Not that I'm saying we did everything right. I'm not even saying the business wasn't dangerous. It was. But look at you, buddy. You were up to your neck in the stuff, and you're doing fine, aren't you?"

"I guess."

"They, these lawyers, keep it stirred up. As far as I'm concerned, half the people creating a stir want compensation for getting old. We're not young. Things go wrong."

"Yeah, but Woody . . ."

"I know, I know. It isn't cut and dried."

"You seen Alice?"

Ryland pushes the plastic tube into his nose. "No. Why? She finally come to her senses and quit you?"

Rosy comes in with a folded towel and washcloth. "You're all set, Sam. I'll put these on your bed, and I cleared a towel rack for you." She picks up the portable phone and goes out to the porch swing, where she'll probably call Maggie to talk about Sam, the new kink in the wedding plans.

Sam flicks a Florida Ghost across to Ryland. "You know, why don't we go see Woody? Where is he? He was building a house in Fruitland when I left. Did he ever finish it?"

"So she finally quit you." Ryland grins. Sam shrugs. "Yeah. Let's go to Fruitland. See if we can find Woody." He shoots the fly back to Sam. "I know that's the Atcitty you'll be looking for."

It only happened once that Ryland rode shotgun while Sam chased a girl, and Alice Atcitty was that girl. They met her at the trading post the day after they drove down from Colorado. He got up to shave that morning and found Rosy hadn't remembered to pack razor blades. Sam's blades wouldn't fit his shaver, so they stopped at the trading post, and the girl at the cash register gave him little dainty blades for a Lady Schick.

"What am I supposed to do with these?" he asked her.

"That's all we've got." She wouldn't look at him. He thought she was lying. She'd dug the blades out from some box under the counter.

He stood there staring at her, and she stared at his chin. She was wearing a plaid cowboy shirt with pearl buttons, he remembers that, her hair one long tight braid. He remembers how her hair pulled her high forehead up into her scalp, the hair braided so tightly it looked like it hurt. He didn't know what to think. He wanted to go back behind the counter and look in the box. There was a line behind him at the counter, and Sam was at his elbow. He didn't want the blades, but he took out his wallet to pay and told her again what he wanted. She told him again that was all they had, but he could buy the shaver, too, if the blades didn't fit his, and she pulled up a dainty little Lady Schick shaver. The line behind him was three deep.

He almost walked out, but he had to shave. So he paid her, his ears and neck burning, seeing all at once that this was how it would be and regretting everything, the new mill that would bring revenue to the reservation and bringing his family here. Wanted to tell her he'd been all over the Pacific, met all kinds of people who were glad he was there and at least smiled when they cheated him. But he didn't say that. He said, "Thank you." She handed him the blades and shaver in a bag.

Sam, beside him, laughing.

They saw her again that weekend. They'd been listening to music wrangling down from the mesa just north of the housing compound, drums and a throbbing bass. They had a little to drink, whiskey before and after dinner, and Sam suggested they go find the music. It came from the Civic Center up on the mesa above Camp. They drove up there and threaded through a parking lot crowded with pickups, went into a dim square building that smelled like clay and sawdust and booze. All around him he heard the soft shushing of a language he didn't understand, and he felt like he was overseas and not in America at all. It was an agreeable feeling. A holiday, like they were on furlough. They stood on the edge of the dance floor, watching Indians dancing to country music, some fancy, fast dancing, different from the formal two-step he'd learned as a boy at Grange Hall dances, where stiff-legged couples would shuffle around the edges of the floor, each following the next like horses yoked to an invisible maypole. The center of the floor was always empty. But these people danced differently, kicking a leg out, dragging one behind, twirling into the center, then out.

She was there. She was not friendly. He saw her see them, and he noted her cool indifference. She was not a woman — a woman? She was a child. Sixteen, and Sam was thirty-eight, and so was he. She was not a girl to smile, not for men. She danced well, with lots of men, with girls and women. With the females she laughed, and they flung themselves wildly around. He couldn't stop watching her. She had that about her.

He remembers sitting in the truck after the dance. They'd been waiting to break into the stream of traffic when a young woman knocked on the truck window: "Hey, give us a ride." She was thin and small, hair tightly curled, her face a mask of makeup, eyes raccooned with smudged eye shadow. Behind her Alice. And leaning up against the bed of the truck, three other girls.

"Our car broke down," Raccoon said. The girls leaning against the truck were laughing.

They were flirting. All of them. He hadn't seen any harm. The wives would come soon enough.

"These girls need a ride," he told Sam.

"Tell 'em to hop in," Sam had said.

Three of them piled into the bed of the truck, and two sat up front, Raccoon and Alice. Alice next to him, the two girls nudging each other, laughing, talking in Navajo. He with his leg pressed tightly against hers, she staring straight ahead.

The next thing he knew, the sun was coming up and he and Sam were sitting dead center in the middle of nowhere, watching it rise. Later he wondered if the girls had had a strategy, if they'd huddled up and planned how they'd lure the white men into the desert and lose them.

"No, turn here. No, *here.* You missed it." The curly-headed one giving the directions, the ones in back hollering each time Sam hit a rut on one of those dirt roads.

Sam aimed for the ruts, and he met Sam's eyes over the girls' heads, grinning like a teenager. Both of them like teenagers.

She sat silent and prim, her leg in blue jeans solid against him. His hand on her knee. The urge to let it climb up her thigh.

Which he hadn't done. But Sam had, and not very long after that night. Ryland started seeing her in the parking lot at the mill, usually when Sam was coming off the graveyard shift and Ryland was just showing up for work. Ryland figured she spent more than a few of those shifts at the mill, against regulations. Those early mornings Sam would be slouched against the driver's door talking to her when Ryland drove up, and he'd nod to them, and she'd catch his eye, holding it for a few seconds, and he couldn't tell if it was mockery in her expression — it seemed a mixture of mockery and something else. Loneliness. He felt a little sorry for her — for any woman that would get hooked up with Sam. She stayed in the picture longer than any of the others. It surprised Ryland when Sam told him she wintered with him in Florida and had for all those years. Sam was usually a love-them-and-leave-them type — all but Lily, and he probably wouldn't have left her if she hadn't made so much noise when she found out about Alice. She'd gone door to door in Camp, demanding to know who knew what and when. Rosy went with her. Rosy had been so mad at him when it turned out she was the only wife in Camp who didn't know about Alice.

25

I N ROSY'S LITTLE sewing room that night, Sam feels brittle. He has felt odd since leaving the Gulf behind, a stone crab clawing his way inland against better instincts. He has lived so long by water it is strange not to hear the lick of it.

The room he's in is a small box. On the other side of the house, every so often, Ryland's wretched coughing rakes down the hall. The cough starts as a rattle and wheedles down to airlessness. It sets Sam's teeth on edge.

He sits on the sofa bed, legs stretched out, his bag of flies and tackle box next to him. He means to work tonight. Every day and every night since hitting the road, he has felt the pull of work, his hands itching for movement. He has been sleeping in truck stops, not sleeping much, a couple hours here and there, never stopping long. He has been looking forward to getting here so he can settle into it again.

The sheets Rosy put on the bed smell nauseatingly sweet — bottled scent. The curtains on the window are ruffled, tied in bows. The sewing machine table is a mess of wedding clothes.

There's a small TV perched on top of an old wooden dresser. He's been using the channel changer, flicking through the channels, lots and lots of channels. The only time Sam ever sees TV is when he's sitting in a bar.

He needs to work. He needs money. He had no idea how expensive it would be to drive that old gas-guzzler across the country. He has a hundred bucks left. He can't get back to Florida on that, plus he needs clothes. He hasn't bought new clothes in — he can't remember when. He'd been thinking about this on the road, about somehow getting new clothes before he sees Alice. On the boat it wasn't important. He likes his clothing worn and feeling like a second skin. But he's not on the boat now.

There's an old Stooges movie on TV. He watches Mo bonk Curly and Larry. He listens to Ryland cough. He puts the channel changer down and reaches for his flask on the floor beside him. The only light in the room is the blue light of the television, not bright enough to work by, but when he turns on the lamp beside him, the room seems to shrink, the pictures on the wall, collages of Ryland's children and grandchildren, leaning in toward him. He turns the lamp off.

He has always lived in small, boxlike rooms, but this one makes him antsy. It's probably because of Ryland's coughing, that and the cloying stench of fabric softener.

His old friend is bad off. When Ryland isn't coughing, Sam finds he's waiting for him to cough.

The boat is a box, the neighborhood noisy, but he doesn't know any of them, they leave him alone — and at his back is the ocean. It's different, not so closed in. As a boy, after his father died, he and his mother lived in a boxcar up on Red Mountain, the high Rockies. In winter the snowdrifts were taller than he, a world of white as far as Sam could see, not unlike the ocean except in color, smell, and temperature — a vast, formless world outside the door.

Once he and Alice were surprised by a snowstorm. They took off for a drive in the afternoon, and the storm swooped down from the La Platas, a blinding white sky that didn't clear. They lost the highway. Suddenly she said, "I think we're in a ditch." He kept a sleeping bag in back under his toolbox, and he kept a coffee can and candles, too, for a heater, a trick his mother had taught him. His mother had used candles in tins to heat the boxcar. He and Alice wrapped themselves in the sleeping bag, stretching the length of the seat, and made love by the light of the coffee-tinned candles, again and again and again.

Crawled into the sleeping bag together, and first they did it with clothes on, and then it got hot, and they took their clothes off, and the windows steamed up. The sleeping bag got too hot, and he held her ankles, put her feet to the ceiling, and fucked her again and again and again, and she came good, the only time he ever heard her scream during sex, and her nipples got so hard and swollen and every time he sucked them she got wet all over again.

From the other side of the house, the coughing begins. He sips from the flask. He watches Mo sneaking up a stairway, stopping. Curly and Larry plunge into him.

The last time Sam slept was at a truck stop outside Winnie, Texas, over a thousand miles from here. Slept locked in the cabin of his truck, the windows closed against palmetto bugs, bugs everywhere, under the windshield wipers and in his truck bed, bugs wiggling into the door cracks, and some dead, the ones he collided with on the road, smashed and baked into the grate.

His eyes ache. He sips, waits for the next cough.

He wakes to the soft click of the door opening. He half opens his eyes and watches Rosy tiptoe in. The room is bright with sunlight. She tiptoes to the sewing table and inches the drawer open, looking in his direction each time it makes a noise. She seems to find what she's looking for, but she doesn't leave the drawer open. Instead, she inches it closed again, freezing each time it squeaks. He had been dreaming of Stooges.

She tiptoes out, and he listens to the sounds on the other side of the door. There seem to be a lot of people in the kitchen. Rosy keeps shushing them. He can smell coffee and toast. It's ten A.M. He finally got to sleep at dawn.

Even though it's hot, he pulls a blanket over his head, trying to block the sunlight out. He wakes when the door opens again. He lies waiting but hears nothing. He looks out from under the blanket. A small child in a white veil stands near his face, her eyes a pretty cornflower blue.

"Are you an angel?" he says.

She squeezes her eyes shut, wrinkles her nose, throws her arms up, and runs out of the room.

"Teri!" Rosy says. And there she is in the doorway. "Sam, I'm sorry. Go back to sleep."

He says, "I'm up."

In the kitchen he finds Ryland, three children, Maggie, and a woman they introduce as Sue, Eddy's wife, a thin, hard-featured, stylish woman in a suit. The angel nestles against Ryland's leg.

"You didn't know you were sleeping in Grand Central Station, did you?" Ryland says.

"Uncle Sam, I can't believe you came for my wedding," Maggie says.

"Maggie, I can't believe how pretty you got to be. You used to be such a chipmunk." She laughs, her eyes sparkling. She's a mix of Rosy and Lily when they were young, the best of both of them —the dimpled Irish cheeks, the thick dark hair—but she's got Ryland's high color. She's fleshier than Rosy and Lily were at her age, and she wears it well. She is the picture of a happy bride.

Rosy wants to feed him. He tells her it's too early to eat, but she already has eggs frying. The smell turns his stomach.

"Rosy, I'm sorry to dump the kids on you like this," Sue says. "I completely forgot about this appointment today."

"It's fine," Rosy says. "We'll keep 'em busy."

"You girls be good," she says. She tells Sam it was nice to meet him and is off.

"I've got to go, too," Maggie says. She kisses him on the cheek, throwing her arms around his shoulders and hugging him tight. "I am so glad you came."

"Me too," Rosy says when Maggie leaves. "You know, Sam, it's really a blessing you came."

"Watch out," Ryland says.

"We could use your truck. Actually, we have a million errands that need a good hauling vehicle. Do you mind?"

"Say no now or forever regret," Ryland says.

Sam smiles. Rosy always was the General, everybody a member of her army. Through the kitchen window, he looks out over the town, across the river to the white bluffs and the reservation beyond. He will go there soon, no hurry. The prospect of finding Alice neither excites him nor raises any dread. Maybe this afternoon he'll drive to Shiprock and see what the situation is, and then he'll know what to do. Now he says, "Happy to help, Rosy."

She gives him a list of items she needs picked up and draws a map. The two older girls, Pooh and Sandi, want to ride in the truck with him — they're thrilled by the old truck, as if it's some sort of carnival ride — but Rosy says, "Absolutely not." He doesn't particularly want their company, but Rosy's "absolutely" surprises him.

"Let 'em come," he says.

She looks at Ryland, her brow furrowed. Alice never liked him to take Delmar alone in the truck either. The fact is, he's got a good driving record. Perfect. "They'll be fine," he says.

"I've got plans for them," she says.

"I imagine they'll be okay if Sam doesn't mind," Ryland says.

"Yay!" the girls screech.

Rosy shoots Ryland a murderous look, as if he's just invited them all to jump off a cliff. Sam smiles. Drinks his coffee.

They head out to the truck. Sam breathes in the smell of the crisp, dusty, thin air, the high desert, and experiences a dizzying sensation of stepping back in time. This air is as familiar as his own breath.

The girls dig out the seat belts from behind the seat, and he helps them strap in. "I'm the navigator," the older girl, Sandi, says. "Daddy always lets me."

"Okay then." He gives her Rosy's map. The girls' breath smells like strawberry.

This town that Sandi navigates for him, the hills full of neighborhoods and parks, the busy streets with carwashes and chain restaurants and Western clothing stores, this place he doesn't know — Farmington. He knows Main Street, which is also Highway 550 — an ugly stretch of roadside businesses, the main artery connecting two eras of his life: his childhood in Colorado and marriage to Lily, the mill and Alice in Shiprock. He used to come here with her for a night on the town occasionally, and he'd bring her and Delmar in for breakfast sometimes on Saturday mornings. He has only hazy memories of life with Lily in Shiprock, she always unhappy.

"Can we turn the radio on?" Sandi asks.

"Doesn't work."

"Ahh."

"What's wrong with it?" Pooh says, turning the dial. Static cackles through the speaker.

"It's old," he says, turning it off.

"What happens if I pull this?" Pooh says, putting her hand on the gearshift. "We don't have one of these in our car."

"You'll break the truck. Don't pull it. Here, I'll show you." He puts his hand over hers and shifts into third. She grins up at him, her gums and teeth red with the candy they've both been eating. The air in the cab has turned sugary.

"I like Madonna. I watch her on MTV. Like a vir-gin," Sandi sings, looking at him coyly over her sister's head. "Do you like Madonna?"

He and Pooh shift into fourth. "How old are you?" he asks Sandi.

"Eight."

"I'm six," Pooh says.

"Who do you like?" Sandi says.

"Captain Kangaroo."

"Who's that?"

"That's what kids like you used to watch before they started growing up too fast."

"Ahh."

"I know a kangaroo song," Pooh says. "Tie me wallaby bean, bean," she sings.

"That's not how it goes," Sandi says. "Our mom and dad taught us. 'Tie me kangaroo down, sport,'" she sings.

"You know that one?" Pooh says.

"I think I do."

"Tan me hide when I'm dead, Fred, tan me hide when I'm dead," Sandi sings.

"So they tanned his hide when he died, Clyde, and that's it a-hanging on the shed," they shout in unison, both of them tilting their chins up to him, as if expecting applause.

He says, "You're good."

The two chins, satisfied, turn simultaneously away, and Sam laughs.

"What else do you know?" Pooh says.

"I know that somebody made my gearshift sticky with her candy."

"Not candy. Gummy bears."

"We're addicted," Sandi says.

"Oh, that's bad," Sam says. "Addicts, huh. Can't quit?"

"I will never quit," Pooh says. "I have a whole pool full of them."

"In her head," Sandi says.

"Not just in my head," Pooh says solemnly. "In my dream room."

"That's in your head. She dreamed she was swimming in a pool of gummy bears."

Sam says, "I bet you were sticky."

Pooh's sandaled foot tick-tocks against his calf. "And that's it a-hanging on the shed," she sings softly. "I wish I could stand up. I can't see out the window. I can see out the window in my car."

"You can't stand up," Sandi says. "It's against the law."

Pooh looks at him, sticking her lower lip out.

He winks at her. "We got to obey the law. Where would we be without the law? I bet having a pool full of gummy bears is against the law."

"Not in your dream room," she says.

"Have you checked on that?"

"Sandi, it's not, is it?"

"He's pulling your leg," Sandi says.

"I'll pull yours," Pooh says.

"Try it," he says. "See where it gets you."

She slaps his thigh; he catches and grips her tick-tocking foot, and she shrieks.

"Don't get her started," Sandi says.

He smiles. She's such a little woman, that one. He squeezes Pooh's ankle. She shrieks again. Sandi shakes her head, her lips pursing in a smirk. "Your funeral," she says, and Sam laughs a full-throated laugh. The sound of it is odd in his ears.

They become a team. On the errands the girls are helpful. They know people at all of their stops, and Sandi steps up, his ambassador, introducing him as her "Great-Uncle Sam here all the way from Florida," which makes him feel both ancient and famous.

Now and again the girls put their heads together and whisper behind their hands. "What's the big secret?" he asks them. They don't tell. The little one hides her mouth with her hand, as if the secret might leak out, and the older gazes coolly out the window. He wonders when they get like this — gossipy and conspiratorial. He remembers the teenage Lily and Rosy when he was just back from the service. Lily was seventeen, Rosy a year older. They would cozy up, complicating everything, making a production of everything, and he dimly remembers enjoying that. He has begun enjoying it today. These little girls. His tour guides, planning in secret.

They drive to a Mrs. Gallagher's house to pick up centerpieces she's made for the tables at the wedding reception. Sandi warns him that Mrs. Gallagher is a chatterbox and not to encourage her, and Pooh warns him not to pet her Chihuahuas because they get excited and throw up, and Sandi tells him that the chatterbox really threw a wrench in the works, a phrase she must have gotten from Rosy, by insisting on moving the centerpieces out of her house two weeks before the wedding. "Where will we put them?" Sandi trills.

The woman's house is full of gilded autumn: pinecones, spray-painted leaves, and acorns, all glued to stands. They're big, delicate things that lose parts between the house and the truck, and the girls pick up the pieces for regluing. Mrs. Gallagher does keep up a steady stream of talk, while her three fat, pink-eyed Chihuahuas yap. She carries the smallest in her apron pocket, and because she trails after Sam on each trip to the truck, the yapping follows him. She tells him how to pack the items and how busy she is and what a bargain the centerpieces are, considering the time she put into them. Both girls keep their lips zipped, as does Sam, and they roll their eyes at each other when the woman's back is turned.

"Whew!" he says, when they're on the road again.

"Told you," Sandi says. "You need gas."

"Do I?"

She points to the gas gauge and tells him all about being on empty.

"It's broken," he says.

Her eyes widen. "How do you know when you need gas then?"

"Got a feel for it." But she's probably right. He shouldn't need gas yet, except these are town miles. The old guzzler drinks it up in town. He stops at a Circle K pump and goes inside to pay. He starts to give the clerk a ten, then decides on a twenty. He wants to drive to the reservation this afternoon. He'll need gas. He glimpses the stack of bills in the cash register. His goes on top of an inch-thick pile. In his wallet: three twenties, two tens. That's all he's got left. The clerk says, "You're good to go," and slams the cash drawer shut.

He needs to tie some flies, and then he needs to sell them. When he goes to Shiprock, he'll go to the river and look for material. Before or after he finds Alice? Maybe she'll go with him. The first time he ever got her out of her jeans was on the muddy banks of the San Juan.

Back in the truck, he drives to the reception hall, where they're going to store the centerpieces. A priest named Father Liam is supposed to let them into a storage room. On the drive the girls feed him tidbits about the priest. He learns that the man was once very fat but has been trimming down for his health and that once he fell asleep in the middle of a sermon but it turned out he wasn't asleep, he was having a stroke. Now he's fine, though. Sandi says she used to want to be a priest when she grew up but they won't let girls, so now she's decided to be a singer, and Pooh says she's going to be a dolphin, then tells him an elaborate dream about a dolphin who ate her, but it didn't hurt.

They stow the arrangements in the storage room, and while

they're walking to the truck, the girls huddle up. Back in, seat belts fastened, Sandi says, "Isn't it time for lunch?"

"Taco John, Taco John, Taco John," Pooh chants.

"You've been eating candy," Sam says. "You're not hungry."

"Candy makes you hungry."

"Taco John, Taco John," Pooh shouts.

"Shh," he says. "Where's the list?" Sandi hands him Rosy's crumpled list of chores. Last on the list, the word "lawnmower," and next to it the address of a repair shop. He wonders how they got the lawnmower to the repair shop before he showed up with his truck. He hands the list back to Sandi. She tells him that Taco John's is right on the way.

"We're not going to Taco John's," he says.

"Why not?" Pooh demands. "We're hungry."

"Shh," he says.

She crosses her arms. Kicks him. He starts the truck. She kicks him again — hard. He picks her leg up by the knee, and puts it on the other side of the gearshift. "Ow! Sandi! He hurt me."

"Shut up, Pooh," she says.

"Look!" There are two red spots on either side of Pooh's knee. The child begins to whimper. She leans away from him, huddling against her sister, and she rubs her knee. Sandi stares out the window.

"You're not hurt," he says.

"I am!" Her face has reddened. Her eyes are glassy with tears, which spill down her cheeks when he looks at her.

He takes his pack of cigarettes from his shirt pocket, taps one out, and puts it in his mouth. "No smoking!" the little one says. When he lights it, she starts coughing.

He pulls out of the parking lot and turns toward downtown. This is an older section. The houses all look frumpy, many in need of paint jobs, shotgun houses, long and narrow, probably built in the forties or fifties, most with square metal boxes on the roofs. Swamp coolers. A funny name for an item that wouldn't work in a swamp, where the air is damp, so much softer than the desert air.

"I can't see," Pooh whines.

She begins unbuckling her seat belt. "You've got to wear your seat belt. It's the law," her sister says, and he swerves over to the side of the road, stopping.

"Tell you what. How would you two like to ride in back?"

"Can we?" the little one shrieks.

"That's illegal," Sandi says.

"It is? Didn't used to be." He opens his door.

"I want to ride in back!" the little one shouts.

"Pooh! It's illegal." Sandi doesn't move.

He reaches over, helping Pooh out of her belt and pulling her across the seat toward him.

"Yay!" she yells. "Take us over bumps!"

Sandi stares at him, open-mouthed. She blinks rapidly, but when he hoists the little one into the truck bed, she scrambles out of the cab.

He goes around to help her in. She says, "I can do it," and puts her foot up on the tire. He scoops her up anyway, holding her under her armpits, swinging her up so her legs arc high, her feet landing with a thump. She scurries away from him. Her face is scarlet.

"Ouch. It's hot," Pooh says. She had just sat down but now lurches up, staring at the backs of her bare legs.

Hot. Yes. He pulls his sleeping bag out from under the toolbox, unties it, and scoots it toward the tailgate, telling them to sit on it. "If you see a cop," he says, "duck."

Back behind the wheel, he fishes his flask out and takes a swig, his first of the day. He turns onto Main.

Some places seem familiar: bridal shop, theater, courthouse. Many of the shops seem new. Novelty shops with straw dolls in the windows. Antique stores with polished rockers and carved headboards. New bank with a neon sign, blinking the time, 12:15, then the temperature, 96 degrees.

He glances at them in his rearview. They sit shoulder to shoulder, the little one chattering, the other staring straight ahead. When she sees his eyes in the rearview, she looks away. He smiles.

He thinks about the bait store where he and Ryland used to get worms when they went lake fishing in the Rockies. He wonders if it's still there. And will hand-tied flies move here like they do on the coast? There used to be a sporting goods store near the train station in Durango. Will it still be there? He's run into sonofaguns who will take merchandise only on consignment. He doesn't have time for that. He needs to find somebody who'll pay cash up front. Ryland will know somebody. The boss. He always knows.

He turns left off Main onto Schwartz, pulls up in front of the repair shop, takes a sip from his flask, recaps it, slips it into his back pocket, and goes in for the lawnmower, but it's not ready yet.

Back outside, the truck bed is empty. He looks quickly up and down the street. He sees no sign of the girls. "Goddamnit," he whispers. He turns around and looks back in the store. It's a small shop, just the counter and a few folding chairs. No customers.

He wasn't in the shop five minutes. Where could they have gone so fast? Sun glare on the windshield makes his eyes water. Down on Main Street, traffic is noisy, the air here putrid with car exhaust and garbage from a dumpster in the nearby alley.

He starts walking quickly toward the truck — where to begin to look? — then sees them on the sleeping bag, which they have opened fully and spread over the truck bed. They are lying flat on their backs, hands over their chests like little corpses.

"What are you doing?" he says.

"We saw a cop," the little one says.

"Oh."

"We didn't want you to get in trouble," Sandi says. "They could put you in jail, if you want to know."

He looks her in the eye. She glances away. "So you saved my hide."

"Yes, we did." She meets his eyes then, her lips pressed tightly in disapproval, a hard mistress, this one, except her eyes rebel, and she half lowers her lids coyly, blinking a couple of times, a flirty imitation of some doll somewhere, probably on the tube. He laughs. This one — watch out.

"Are you going to take us over bumps or what?" Pooh says.

"You bet I am."

He takes them to the river, where he finds a dirt road with plenty of potholes, and he guns it. They're sitting with their backs to the tailgate again. He watches them in the mirror. They hold onto each other, shrieking with each bump. Their heads and shoulders boing-boing above the tailgate. He zigzags, turning the wheel in abrupt jerks. They tumble left, then right, mouths open, eyes shut. This is a good ride he's giving them. They like it, he can see: little girls. His little tour guides.

Later, back on paved roads, the two of them straight-backed, glossy-eyed, and flushed, looking punch-drunk, he decides that there will be money. There has always been money. He's not going to worry about it. Instead of driving by Taco John, he turns in.

"Taco John!" they both holler. He tells them they can have whatever they want. But Sandi tells her sister not to order more than she can eat, that wasting food is a sin, and he smiles at what she already knows, the woman's talent for making and keeping rules.

They ride up front for the short trip back to the house, and he tells them that maybe they shouldn't tell Grandma Rosy about riding in the back of the truck.

Sandi rolls her eyes. "We know," she says, sassy and bored.

"We're good at keeping secrets," Pooh says.

"I know you are," he says.

26

I T'S GOING TO HAPPEN, Conrad had said. Becky cannot stop hearing him say it.

She is running along the edge of the mesa. She can no longer see the cracks in the ground where the dirt road has dried and separated. Evening is coming on. The sky in the east is the color of mercury, and she is far from her truck. It will be dark before she gets back to it.

Three's a crowd.

She squeezes her eyes shut for a few seconds. She will not think about Harrison. She is sick of thinking about him. Except he was so mean. Why'd he have to be so mean? *Three's a crowd.*

Her knees have turned watery. The big toe on her right foot hurts. There will be blood on her sock. When she runs this far—probably fifteen miles—the miles register in different ways. Fatigue at two, exhilaration at five, a pulse at seven, ankle and shin pain at eleven, watery knees at fifteen, and that's when she notices the pain in her toe, which means the nail has separated from the skin. The separation, she believes, occurs some time before she notices.

She feels as if she lives in disconnected moments, somewhere between what has already happened and its afterlife. A half-life. She has been reading about uranium's half-life, what they call the Radon Daughters, a term somebody, some man probably, gave to the radiated isotopes that lodge in the ground during mining. Invisible. Toxic.

In the valley below, a few lights have come on. The smoke from Four Corners Power Plant to her left is white against the graying sky, and the plant itself is lit up, yellow lights reflecting the stacks. The first stars have come out. Between this road she's on and the power plant, in that huge stretch of shadow, there are plants whose names she knows, healing plants. Gray grease, good for toothaches. Groundsel, good for rheumatism, arthritis, and boils. Navajo name, *azee'háátdzid*. Her grandmother taught her and Delmar years ago. Snake weed. *Ch'ildiilyé siitsoh*. For nervousness. For internal problems. Her grandmother had taught her many words that Becky has forgotten. Why do some words stick and others don't?

It's going to happen.

Her father won't tell her what to do. She told him about AGER's plans to reopen the mines. When he didn't answer, she tried to make a game of it, asking him four times, the way she did as a child. Her father used to say that if you ask a Navajo something four times, it means you really want an answer, and the person is obliged to give one. He has always given a direct answer if she asked four times. Not this time. In truth, she doesn't think he understood what she was telling him. He fades in and out.

She sees it in his eyes. He is preparing to die.

He did tell her, though, that he wants her to take care of her mother. He came to her room the night she tried to explain about the consulting and the money it would bring in. It was spooky. She woke in the middle of the night to him standing over her, and now she's not even sure if he was really there or if she dreamed it. He told her to take care of her mother.

What does that mean? Does he mean she should do this consulting and pay off the medical bills?

A siren, one of those that sound like Gestapo sirens in World War II movies, wah-wahs from the valley below, out near the new package liquor store on the highway. Red and blue lights reflect off the darkened mesa.

Sometimes she feels bitter toward her father, and she knows that isn't fair. He has never told her what to do. If she forces him, he'll give her an opinion, but it's always his opinion, never a clear direction for her. He has told her how to do things: *Go a little way one day so you can go a little farther the next; don't give up; finish the race.* But he won't tell her what to do. He has always left those sorts of lessons to her mother and her aunts.

She loves them, but she can't imagine how the house will be when it's just them. The prayer circles, the craft circles. Her aunts and mother, making crafts, selling them at bazaars. She driving her mother to church every Sunday. Driving her everywhere because her mother will never learn to drive and will never leave the house her father built, which is not in walking distance of any store.

God, she hates this place.

27

SUNDAY AFTERNOON. Sam and Ryland drive up through raw sandstone where the road has sliced into the bluff, Sam behind the wheel. On either side of the road the earth's innards flank them until they reach the bluff's crest, where the land levels out.

Yesterday afternoon Sam drove to Shiprock and found Alice's trailer. He recognized it because she had sent him pictures when she bought it and had told him where it was, up on the bluff behind the BIA school, which is not a BIA school anymore. Nothing is the same. But she wasn't home. The trailer was locked up tight. No cars, no animals. He had driven out there for nothing. Waste of gasoline.

Now he turns onto the Upper Fruitland Road. "Place has grown," he says.

They're passing a new ranch-style house with wood siding. Other houses are not so new: standard government issue, small, square, three- and four-room houses, some dingy yellow, others tarpapered, here a pink one with its door standing open, a goat chewing weeds in the yard. TV antennas sprout from some of the houses, and sunlight glints off satellite dishes in the dirt yards.

"Truck drives pretty good," Ryland says.

"Gas hound," Sam says. "You know what kind of mileage this old guzzler gets? Ten to the gallon. That's it. Probably could've bought two plane tickets for what it cost me to drive. It uses half a quart of oil every hundred miles. I went through a case just getting here." A steady shh, shh washes against the back of Sam's ears. Sand like glass spins up from the ground each time the truck veers from the paved road onto the dirt shoulder.

"Texas, that's what gets me," Sam says. "They make the goddamn gas in Texas, so you'd think there'd be a little price break, but it was higher around Houston than anywhere. Cost me . . ."

"You sure you don't need money, Sam? I can spell you."

"Nah. I'm going to get to work here pretty soon. Head up north, sell some merchandise."

"You know," Ryland says, "what Rosy was saying last night wasn't all wrong."

"What's that?"

"You paid in to Social Security for a good many years." Last night Sam sat at the kitchen table picking through supplies he'd scavenged on the banks of the San Juan. He'd found robin and duck feathers, rabbit fur. But he didn't make much progress tying. Rosy hovered, asking questions, wanting to know how many flies he made a month, how much they brought in, and also about his Social Security. He regrets telling her that he hasn't filed. She went on and on about how foolish that was, as if it was her business. After she and Ryland went to bed, he couldn't get the rhythm of work.

They sleep separately. He wonders whose idea that was. The only advantage to marriage: you don't have to sleep alone. Rosy seems more a nurse than a wife now. A fussy nurse. It took them an hour to get started today. She had to pack Ryland a kit with medicine, and she blew up a rubber pillow for his back, and there's an extra sweater, a blanket for his legs. And she had to call Woody's wife, Della, to make sure it was okay for them to go there. She wrote directions and the phone number, probably a good thing. Place has changed so much, he probably couldn't find the house. He's only been there once.

"It's not like the government's giving you anything," Ryland says.

"Don't worry about me."

"I'm just saying, you paid in."

"You saw to it."

"Yes, I did."

He turns right onto Power Plant Road, crossing the San Juan River into Fruitland, where he finds a property hedged by juniper. According to Rosy's directions, this is Woody's place. He slows and turns in at a gateless opening. They drive onto a large dirt lot with one shade tree, a tall willow. He and Alice drove over when Woody bought the place. It was an old rock hovel, a missionary's hut. Now the house is good-sized, half stone, half wood, a porch running its length. An old bluish dog stands on the porch barking. The young woman who comes out looks so much like Alice, Sam freezes. She puts her hand on the dog's head. But of course it's not Alice. Different hair. Too young.

Ryland opens his door and begins untangling himself from the seat. Sam takes a sip.

The girl, Woody's daughter, Becky, sits with her mother at the dining table on the other side of the room. Her mother is beading on a small loom. Sam and Ryland sit on chairs facing Woody on the couch. Woody is almost unrecognizable as the man Sam used to know. His arms and legs, once ropy with muscle, have shrunk down to the bone, and he looks like a white man—a gray man, his face the color of ash. His hair, which he has always worn short, is almost completely gray. It was black when Sam last saw him. Woody's on oxygen, too. He keeps opening his mouth to suck the air, making small, regular burping sounds.

"Can't believe what you've done to this place, Wood," Sam says. "How much this cost you?"

In a wobbly voice, Woody has been telling them how he has been building onto the house year by year. Now there are eight rooms and the two porches, front and back. He tells Sam it didn't cost much, just materials.

The girl walks over to sit next to her father on the couch. The dog follows, creeping to Sam, tail wagging lethargically, eyes rheumy; the dog licks his hand. It's a strong-smelling dog, a black patch over one eye, fur somewhere between Yankee blue and Confederate gray.

"That's Delmar's dog," the girl says.

"It is?" He barely remembers her, Woody's daughter. She would've been eight years old when he left. Same as his son.

"He's a good dog." Woody clicks his tongue and the dog crosses to him, lying down on his feet. He says, "What happened to you?" motioning to the bandage on Ryland's head.

"Cat got me," Ryland says. Woody smiles.

"Mr. Mahoney, what do they use vanadium for?" the girl says. She gazes directly at Ryland. In that way she's different from Alice. Alice wouldn't meet your eye unless you made her.

"Why?"

"Just curious. I've been reading about it — that you guys made uranium and vanadium at the mill."

"It's used to harden steel."

"Back during the war," Woody says, "they used it to harden weapons."

"That's right," Ryland says.

"So why did they continue to make it after the war?"

"We just processed the stuff. We didn't market it," Ryland says. Sam watches him push the tube into his nose again and again. Ry's nails are yellow and buckled. They look brittle, ragged. Woody's wheezing is getting louder.

"They used it for making cooking pots, anything that needed hard steel," Sam says.

"Yeah, but I read where the Atomic Energy Commission was your biggest customer. They weren't making pots."

"So, Woody," Ryland says, "where's your sister?"

Sam clicks his tongue, snapping his fingers, calling his son's dog over to him. The dog just looks at him. Sam watches Woody and the girl exchange glances. What does that mean? And what does Ryland think he's doing, jumping in?

"She's on the road. Running rodeo camps in Texas, I think," the girl says.

"When's she coming back?" Sam says.

"We don't know," the girl says. "Another thing I read?"

"Here we go," Ryland says quietly, looking at Sam.

". . . is that you don't have to breathe the dust in to be contaminated. It can be absorbed through the skin."

"Everybody had gloves," Ryland says.

Woody glances at his daughter, seeming to signal something with his eyes.

"That nobody wore," she says. "Right? But maybe somebody should've insisted they wear them."

Woody touches her on the shoulder and motions with his chin toward the door.

"That pillow?" Woody says, nodding at a large beaded pillow on the floor between Ryland's chair and Sam's. The pillow is checkered with little gray, black, and ivory boxes.

"Maybe somebody should at least say he's sorry," the girl says.

Woody says something sharply under his breath and slaps the back of his right hand against his left palm.

She looks at her father in surprise, her face coloring. She gets up and walks to the screen door, looking out.

"That pillow?" Woody says. "Do you know where Della got the pattern for that? From Taylor Newman. You remember how he used to organize the nuts and bolts in the warehouse?"

"Taylor?" Sam says. "Oh, yeah. The warehouseman. Right, Ry? He was a fanatic. He counted every damn nut."

Woody laughs, wheezing. "He used to . . ." He stops speaking, his lips sucking in air, fishlike.

"He used to arrange the nuts and bolts and nails according to color," Della calls. "Woody took a picture."

"What a weirdo," Sam says. "That's right. I remember. He didn't organize according to size or anything that made sense. He organized by different shades of gray. Remember, Ry? Old Taylor didn't want anybody messing with things out there. He took that job so damn seriously. If you wanted a bolt, you had to ask him and he'd get it for you. We didn't lose money on Taylor. I guess the mill may have had its problems, but thanks to crazy old Taylor, it was solvent."

"That's right," Woody says, laughing, wheezing.

Ryland says nothing. He holds the plastic tube against his nose.

Sam gets up and starts circling the room, looking at the beaded artwork on the walls. The room is full of beaded pillows and wall hangings. Some of the pictures are Bible quotes. The one over the sofa where Woody sits has a sky blue background with black lettering: AND THE GREATEST OF THESE IS LOVE. CORINTHIANS 13.

"Boy, these are pretty," Sam says. He stops in front of an intricate weaving of what looks like intertwined yellow stalks against a paler yellow background, orange streaks defining shadows, and again his hands itch to work. "Is this yucca? Looks like yucca. I didn't know Navajos did beadwork like this."

"We do. It's a Plains art, though," Della says. "You know, Delmar might know when Alice is coming back."

"Delmar? I thought he was in jail."

"He's out."

"He is? Where is he?"

"Working. Where's he working, Becky?"

"Up on Whitaker Mesa," the girl says quietly.

"You ready, Sam?" Ryland stands and walks over to Woody, stretching out his hand. "You take good care, Woodrow. We'll be seeing you, okay?"

"How long's he been out?" Sam says.

"Since February."

"Since February."

The wheels of Ryland's cart squeak as he pulls it over the wood floor.

"Nobody told me," Sam says.

The girl shrugs and seems almost to smile. He decides not to ask her how to get to Whitaker Mesa.

Driving home, Ryland slumps against the passenger's-side door, his face granite, hands shaking.

"You cold?" Sam says.

"Nope."

"I could turn the heater on. Except it doesn't work."

"No problem."

He decides to take the highway home, which is faster. Ryland's breath sounds sort of like a death rattle.

"How do you like that?" Sam says. "My son's been out of jail for six months and nobody told me."

Ryland says nothing. His eyes are half closed.

"I see what you mean, Ry."

"What?"

"The hostility back there."

"Damned if you do, damned if you don't."

"Eh, kids. Don't worry about it. Woody was a smoker, wasn't he?"

"Was he?"

"I think he was."

"I don't remember it."

"I'm pretty sure. Nights we'd go out, have a smoke. Yeah. Everybody makes their own choices, Ry. I don't see how people can blame you or the industry for the choices they made."

"That's what I'm saying." He pushes the tube into his nose, looks bleary-eyed at Sam.

"Don't worry about it."

Ryland leans his head back against the window and closes his eyes.

Alice could've at least written to say his son was out of jail.

"Where is Whitaker Mesa?"

Ryland says it's north of town

He hasn't seen his kid in seventeen years. He's seen pictures, that's all. Well, he'll go see him. They're in the same state now. Same town.

Sam smoothes his hand over his trousers, which are so threadbare he can see skin above the knee.

"You know, Ry," he says.

"Yeah?"

He wonders if she even gave the kid the money he sent. "Nothing. Just thinking." He sent regularly, every month, whatever he could. Hell, he sent more to the kid than he kept for himself. He just wonders if she gave it to him.

"Ry. How much you figure you have to make a year before you owe taxes?"

"No idea. Why?"

"Just wondering."

Highway 550 between Fruitland and Farmington is a solid string of businesses, convenience stores, gas stations, diners. They pass a cop, lights on his car pulsing, with two young Indian men, legs spread, hands behind their heads. The cop frisking one.

"Would be something, getting a Social Security check every month that you don't have to do anything for."

"Like Rosy says, you earned it."

"The thing is, I don't know if it's a good idea for the government to look too close at me."

Ryland frowns at him. "Why not?"

Sam doesn't answer.

"Sam? When's the last time you filed a tax return?"

Sam takes a sip from his flask, wipes his mouth with the back of his hand. "I guess that would be when Lily and I got divorced."

"Sam, Sam." Ryland shakes his head. "Same old same old, huh?"

"I guess."

"Remember how you tried to talk me into firing you, rigging a way to pay you under the table? You were always scheming how to stay under the table. Well, you probably don't owe much. You might have to pay a penalty for not filing, but I doubt you owe any taxes. What do you make? Ten grand a year?"

"Not even."

"I bet you're under the minimum. Like Rosy said, it's not the government's money. You paid in all those years at the mill."

"That I did. You saw to it."

"That I did."

"How do you suppose somebody goes about applying for Social Security?"

"It's simple. You just need your birth certificate or your army discharge papers. Something to show you're legit."

"Something to show I'm legit." Sam takes a sip from his flask. "I must have one of those somewhere, huh," he says. "A birth certificate. I wonder where."

Ryland smiles tiredly. "Sam, you're just the same."

28

ON MONDAY MORNING, twelve days before Maggie's wedding, Lily drives down to the Strater Hotel on Main in Durango to meet Fred for an early breakfast. They've been having a little disagreement about their vacation this November, not over where or when but specifically over how long they should go for and how much they should see. Fred has already begun to wrap up his business, and they've decided on a date. They'll have their first excursion outside the USA on November 15. Two weeks, no more. Touring can be taxing on a relationship, especially a new one — on this they both agree. So they want to go slow.

If Fred had his way, they'd be carted around on a dais, never touching ground, whisked in and out of Belize, Guatemala, Mexico, sampling but not, to Lily's mind, really experiencing these exotic places. Lily thinks they ought to choose a specific locale and really explore. Initially she thought she'd like a walking tour of some sort, but recently she has stumbled on kayaking tours, and they've captured her imagination. She wants to "paddle in hushed delight into one of the secret coves or spellbinding volcanic outcroppings of Baja's Sea of Cortez," just like the brochure says.

In truth, though, she has a secret agenda. If she can get Fred to agree to an active vacation, one that requires physical exertion, she plans to put them both on a fitness regime for the next two months to get in shape for the trip. She needs it, too. This is not just about Fred's weight. She has no upper body strength. Her arms are like noodles. She'd like to develop some muscle where she's never had any.

And so she goes to breakfast armed with brochures. From the sidewalk outside, she sees Fred in the window, reading a newspaper, and her heart skips ahead a little. Every time she sees him these days, she is surprised at how very glad she is to see him. Her gladness doesn't abate a bit when he tells her she's loony.

"Kayaking, Lily? What are you thinking?"

"I'm thinking, Fred," and she takes a breath, "that a hands-on vacation, one where we're forced to interact in all ways, physically, emotionally, all ways, would be so much more invigorating than one where we listen to a tour guide and ride around on a bus."

Fred, wide-eyed, stares at her, amazed but smiling. "Kayaking." He shakes his head. The waitress refills his coffee cup, pours some for Lily, and takes their orders. Lily is surprised that Fred doesn't order eggs Benedict as he usually does. Even though they've been going out for less than two months, she has begun to feel really comfortable with him. She feels as if they have "usuals." If they went on *The Dating Game* she would say with confidence "eggs Benedict" when asked what he likes best for breakfast, just as he could say, with confidence, "granola and low-fat yogurt" for her. But today he surprises her and orders granola himself. She wonders if he's dieting. He actually said something yesterday about wanting to drop a few pounds. She says nothing, though. She read somewhere that calling attention to a dieter's food choices can stymie the best intentions.

"Have you ever kayaked before?" he says.

"No. But that's the point. They say their trips are designed as perfect introductions to the sport. Plus, Fred, it's amazingly inexpensive. We could go for fifteen days, camping most nights, and they provide the food. Twelve hundred dollars each, and that includes airfare."

Fred shakes his head. "Nope. You might get me in a kayak, but you're not getting me to sleep on the ground. You and me, Lily, will be sleeping in beds. Big beds." He nods once. Lily puts her elbows on the table, props her chin on her fists, sticks out her lower lip, then laughs.

"Okay. No camping trips, but . . ."

"Yeah, yeah, we're going to do it your way, I've been thinking about it, it's a good idea, interacting, physical, emotional, whatever it was you said. You decide. I just insist that we eat in restaurants and sleep in beds, private beds with private baths." She smiles at him. He winks, stirs the yogurt and granola, spoons a mouthful, and chews.

Really, it amazes her how well they get along. As she drives home, she thinks about how much fun it is to disagree with Fred, because it's not like a disagreement at all, just a friendly spat, almost like he's only pretending to disagree. He is the only man she's ever met who seems completely comfortable with himself.

She has a lot to do. She's got to find the perfect tour, one that will combine day hikes, perhaps some boating, and dancing at night. He told her not to look at the cost — whatever it is, it'll be fine. He is so generous. She's buying the plane tickets, he's taking care of everything else.

As she turns onto Crestview Drive, she decides not to do this over the phone but to make an appointment with the travel agent. It's time to make some preliminary reservations, and she'd rather do that in person. She notices but doesn't really pay attention to the old truck parked in front of her house, a truck that on second glance seems familiar.

She pulls into her drive, hits the remote to open the garage door, and stops breathing. Sam is sitting on her porch.

"You look good, Lily," Sam says.

He sits across from her at the breakfast bar, turning his coffee cup around in its saucer. "So do you, Sam," she says. In fact, he looks precisely the same as he had the last time she saw him, and yet utterly different. His face is completely unlined, though his eyes seem more deeply set, eye sockets protruding, eyebrows thin and white, and his hair is snow white where it used to be white-blond. It's jagged, as if he cuts it himself. And he shakes occasionally. It's almost undetectable, like a very subtle tremor shuddering through his body.

"Nice place," Sam says. He looks around, taking in the sunny kitchen with its oak center island, the stainless steel grate hanging from the ceiling on which she has hung all of her copper pots and pans, the Spanish tiled floor, all of it.

"Thanks." Lily massages the warm coffee cup. Her fingers are freezing.

Sam shakes his head, his lips pulling into a thin smile. He says, "Good for you, Lily. You're doing good."

And his eyes are suddenly kind and warm, a look she used to wait for and hardly ever saw. He looks out the window into her backyard. She has a quarter acre of Kentucky blue grass backed by a thicket of ponderosa pine. "Nice yard."

"It's a jungle," she says. "We've been getting bears this summer, coming down from the mountains. A couple of weeks ago I saw the cutest little cub with its mom. They're getting used to people because people are invading the high country. But they're—"

"How'd you do this, Lily?"

"Do what?"

"This is a big house. You got a job? You didn't used to work."

"Oh." She shrugs. "Some lucky investments. That's all. My half of your pension got me started."

He gazes at her with an expression that almost looks like admiration. "Good—for—you." He nods after each word. "You know what, Lily, we were all wrong, weren't we? You're so much better without me."

She gets up and walks to the stove, where the coffee is on a warmer. "Well, we were young. You want something to eat, Sam?"

"Yes, we were. No thanks."

"Seems like a lifetime ago. How about you, Sam? Everything okay?" She takes the coffee to the table, pouring some into his cup, then hers. He's scratching his hand, up and down, up and down, like he used to when his eczema bloomed occasionally, a warning sign, always a warning sign that he was about to disappear, that she could expect to sleep alone for a while. Tics. She studies him. Every one of his little tics used to send her on an emotional journey that left her achy and weak. All the tics are still there. The scratching that would terrify her, the sudden kindness that would melt her, the shabbiness that would make her want to mother him. But she watches them from a distance. He seems like a dear toy that she has put away.

"Yeah, not bad. Everything seems so long ago. I was downtown this morning. Went over to the old neighborhood. You know where Little Santa Rita used to be? Now it's a park."

"Santa Rita Park."

"It's a different town," he says. "Where the mill was? They've put some kind of shopping center or something right where the tailings pile used to be. Remember that?" He laughs. "Remember me planting grass up there after we closed the mill?"

"And now Ryland's sick."

"Hell, we're all sick one way or another. Maybe not you, though, Lily. You've weathered well."

"So what are you doing in this part of the country, Sam?"

He tells her he came to watch Maggie get married. Which she didn't want to hear. *That* she didn't expect. Sam at the wedding. Meeting Fred. She has already played the wedding out in her head, introducing him to Rosy, to Ryland — but not to Sam.

Scratching. "Lily," he says, his voice hitching up a notch. "Lily, I was wondering, do you have any of my old records? Birth certificate? Army discharge papers? Things like that. Because I don't. I don't know where they are."

"I think so. I might. They might be in storage. I don't think I threw anything away."

He nods, his shoulders moving with his head. "I'd like to get them." He stands up.

"Okay. Well, I'll go out there and look. They're in a storage unit. I'm pretty busy today, but —" She starts to say she'll go tomorrow but thinks again. She doesn't want to see him tomorrow. It's very, very odd, because for years she imagined running into him, fantasized about him rounding a corner somewhere, rehearsed the encounter again and again. She'd gone into therapy. The therapist said that she and Sam never had closure, and that was a problem. It's time, she decides, for closure with Sam. "I'll go out today, Sam. I know right where to look. I can meet you this afternoon. At the park?"

"Okay. When?"

"Two o'clock. No, four." She has to call her lawyer. She hopes he's not on the golf course. "Sam? Well, this is a little awkward, but—" She doesn't know how to begin about the divorce papers, but now she's certain, absolutely, that it's time to get that business taken care of. Last week she ran her hypothetical situation by her lawyer, and he'd told her that a person would have to draw up new papers because the papers have to be filed within a certain period of time. She wonders how long it will take.

She begins haltingly to tell Sam about the little snafu with their divorce papers, and how she'll need his John Hancock again, and hopefully she can get everything together for him to sign by this afternoon. He listens, standing in the kitchen doorway, head down, staring at the floor. "So four o'clock?" she says.

He says nothing.

"Sam?"

"Lily?" His voice is a hoarse whisper. "What are you saying?" He looks at her now, eyes earnest and questioning.

"It's just a technicality, Sam."

He blinks several times, shaking his head, his mouth trembling, and suddenly he's laughing, holding himself, falling against the door frame, almost losing his balance, almost falling down, his eyes tearing. He sputters, "Lily, Lily, Lily," reeling around and staggering, knocking over a dining room chair in his rush to get out of the house and out the front door. Lily hurries after him. From the porch she calls, "Four o'clock, then." He waves his hand over his head, a two-fingered salute.

He's not there when she gets to the park a little before four. Nobody's in the park, which is not surprising, since it's the hottest part of the day. She sits in her car, the air conditioning running, watching the road for his truck. Her lawyer said he couldn't have the papers ready until early next week, a big disappointment. But at least Sam will be in the area for a while. She won't make him drive back up here. She'll make an appointment with him somewhere in Farmington and take the papers to him. She's got everything else he wanted, every scrap of paper she could find in storage that had anything to do with him. It's all sitting next to her in a box.

All day she's been rushing around, getting ready for this meeting, and now he's making her wait, just like old times. Was there ever a time when Sam waited for her? Never. She opens the car door, steps out onto the hot pavement, walks to the nearest picnic table. She's nervous, couldn't eat lunch. She's been on high energy all day, finds it hard to sit still. She leans against the picnic table, shading her eyes, watching the road, wishing she'd brought a hat. She looks at her watch every few minutes, wondering how long he'll make her wait and wondering just how angry he is, because certainly he is angry, which can't be helped. He's doing this deliberately, of that she's certain. Punishing her. She has waited days for him, lifetimes for him; this is just another one. She tries very hard not to cry, because she doesn't want her mascara to run, and she absolutely doesn't want him to know that he can get to her, that the old tricks still work. But she waits. And waits. And he doesn't come. When she hears the whistle from the narrow-gauge blowing into the downtown train station from Silverton, she knows she's waited long enough, that he won't come.

Driving back to the house, her throat constricting, she does not cry and not when she pulls into the driveway and waits for the garage door to open. But when it closes behind her, she sits there in her car, engine off, and cries until her stomach hurts.

At twilight she decides to go for a long walk, transferring keys from purse to fanny pack, grabbing a bottle of water, but she manages to go only half a block before she wants to flee, to be there in case he comes.

When Fred calls that evening, he tells her she sounds odd, far away, and she tells him she's just a little tired. It's a comfort to hear his voice, but she doesn't want to talk tonight, so she tells him she's not feeling well and she'll call him tomorrow.

Though she is exhausted and achy, it's a long time before she falls asleep. She sleeps fitfully. At one-thirty she wakes to something crashing, starts up from her bed, her heart thrumming, listening into the night. It's the bears. They've knocked over somebody's grill or trash again. She listens as the neighborhood dogs sound the alarm. They'll go on like that for an hour. She lies back down. Fred has helped her secure the house, she doesn't keep anything to attract them, but her neighbors insist on grilling on these hot nights. She falls asleep again to dogs barking.

She wakes late. Her head throbs. She feels waterlogged. She splashes cold water on her face, which is red, bloated, and creased with pillow lines. The lines are still there an hour after she gets up.

She has a huge list of things to do, but it's hard to muster the energy to leave the house. It's nearly eleven before she finally gets behind the wheel. Hitting the garage door opener, she starts to back up, but jams on the brake inches away from Sam's truck, which is parked in the driveway.

He is not in it. Her mouth is instantly dry and her heart quakes. She can't breathe. She feels as if she has rubber bands around her chest and forehead. She gets out of the car and creeps toward the garage door. She scans the yard, the street. Sam's windshield is badly pitted. The sun magnifies the pits, distorting the cab. He could be in there. She thinks she sees his head resting against the seat back. He could be sleeping. She creeps toward the driver's side.

"Lil?"

She whirls around. He's sitting on her porch.

"I think you left your keys in the car."

She notes, then, the ding, ding, ding coming from the garage. Yes. Her keys are in the ignition. The car door is open.

She retrieves the keys and takes several deep breaths before she goes to the porch, where he sits on the floor, his feet on the top step. He pats the space next to him, and because her legs are shaking, she sits down. "You scared me," she says.

"Did I? You scared me pretty good yesterday."

"I'm sorry." She clears her throat. "I'm an idiot. It's just a formality, Sam, filing the papers. No harm done."

"Well, I don't know. I've been thinking about it. It's not really just a formality, marriage. It's an institution. A sacred institution."

She laughs. "Never thought I'd hear you say that."

"Never knew how good I'd be at it."

"At what?"

"Staying married. Lil, this gives us thirty-seven years."

"What? Oh, Sam, we're not married."

"No, actually, we are."

She laughs again.

"We are."

She looks in his face. He's serious. "As if you'd want to be married to me," she says.

He leans over, bumping her gently. "I do."

She stands up, putting several feet between them. "We're not married, Sam."

He shrugs. "Pretty day. Yeah, I've been walking around the neighborhood. How long have you had this place, Lily?"

She doesn't answer.

"I'm glad you bought one of the old houses. I mean, the new ones are nice — big — but . . ."

"We — are — not — married."

"I think we are."

She crosses her arms, hugging herself tightly, and staring into his eyes, which are bloodshot and grave. He's trying to play her. "What do you want, Sam?"

"The fact is, Lily, it's been lonely on the boat. A few days ago I took a drive with Ryland's grandkids. Cute kids. Eddy's kids. I'm getting older. Wouldn't be bad to be around people more. Family, you know? Those girls? They reminded me of you and Rosy. I mean, I didn't know you when you were their ages, but I bet you were just like them. Spunky."

"Oh, Sam," she says. She goes back to sit beside him. He takes her hand, and she lets him. "We've moved on, you and me."

"So, are you saying you don't want to be married to me?" She smiles and shakes her head. "Because that's the only way I can put it together. Why would Lily not file the papers? Because she doesn't want to be divorced."

"Well, I can see how you'd think that, but you're wrong. We aren't married. You don't love me. I don't love you."

"I like you, though. That's pretty good after thirty-seven years. How many married couples can say that? How about it? Let's make a go of it."

"Oh, for Pete's sake. I saw your son a week or so ago. I heard you've been seeing his mother all these years. You think I'd ever put myself in that position again? No, if I ever marry again, it will be to somebody who's loyal."

"Mmm." He twists the ring on her right ring finger, a lapis set in silver that she wears for health and good luck. "Well, you've got a point. I guess we'll have to get divorced because I'm an old leopard and these spots probably won't change. So, what terms?"

"What do you mean?"

"Divorces always have terms. Like ours? I mean, the one we didn't have. The one that gave you seed money for this house. I gave you half of everything as settlement for a divorce."

She pulls her hand away. "Sam."

"Lily."

She stands again, stepping away from him. He's serious. She can see it in his face. "You've got to be kidding."

He doesn't speak.

"Oh, for Christ's sake."

"Don't worry. I don't want half. Just something for the insult. I mean, for seventeen years I thought I was an unmarried man. I could've married somebody else during that time, which would've made me a bigamist." He laughs. "Don't they put you in jail for that? Really, Lily, I'm very mad and very hurt that you deceived me. I deserve something for the insult."

A line of sugar ants marches across the sidewalk in front of her. She notices that her shirt and bra are wet, sweat seeping through, dripping over her ribs. "What do you want, Sam?" she says, her voice cracking, and when he doesn't answer, she says, "I keep some cash in the house. I'll give you some cash, okay? And then you sign the papers."

He doesn't answer.

She climbs the steps, not meeting his eyes but feeling them on her. She has a wall safe in the bedroom closet. She keeps jewelry there, some bonds, and about five thousand in cash, a precaution she learned from her father, who always warned her to take a lesson from the Depression and keep something aside for when the banks fail.

She fumbles at the combination, finally opens the safe, pulls out the stack of hundred-dollar bills. She's standing in the room, counting — she'll give him a thousand, she decides — when she sees him leaning against the doorway. Her heart hammers painfully again. She walks over, holding out the bills to him. He doesn't take them. He's looking at the larger stack in her other hand. "For the insult, Lil," he says quietly, and she feels as if the floor is sucking her in. Her whole body is shaking. She wants him out of her house. She holds both stacks out to him, her hands trembling violently. He takes them. "Thanks." He turns to leave.

"Sam! I want your signature on the papers."

He waves the money and is gone.

She doubles over, falling to her knees, dry-heaving.

Years ago a therapist told her that her body was smarter than she, that most animals understand this, even humans, but that abused women operate under a handicap, a disconnect between mind and body. Abused women, the therapist said, learn to short-circuit their instincts and so keep putting themselves in danger. Healthy people and animals tune in to even the subtlest warning signals: the barely noticeable pain at the pit of the stomach, the sudden tiredness or chill. Any of these could signal danger. But they come to the abused woman as delayed reaction, not the signal, the remembered signal.

She had thought she was past all of this, that over the years she had brought mind and body in sync, but now she remembers having stomach butterflies seconds before she told Sam — she should *not* have told him! About the divorce papers.

Twenty-four hours later, the warning sign registers.

It occurs to her that she probably doesn't need his signature. He has been missing for seventeen years. Divorce by default. She probably could have done this quietly, no fuss.

Well, she'll need the signature now. Now he knows. She told him.

Little humiliations. Little rapes. Self-rapes. The body knows what is intolerable and sends a thousand signals that the mind ignores. Years ago, did Sam put her in the rodeo stands to watch that woman, the mother of his child? Or did she put herself there? How many years did she live with this degradation when her body constantly screamed at her to leave him? Why didn't she file the papers?

She is wretched. She doesn't go out of the house that afternoon, and she doesn't answer the phone. She keeps repeating what the therapist, an abuse survivor herself, told her: "We live under a handicap. We pick ourselves up. We move on. We forgive ourselves."

This good advice will also register somewhere down the line. Now the words are empty. She can't stop thinking about how she's on Sam's schedule again. He'll sign the papers or he won't. Today. Next month. When he feels like it. And what if he comes back for more? Does he have a legal right? Colorado is a joint-property state. How can she keep Fred from finding out about this?

When the sun finally slips behind the mountain and the sky turns violet, she musters the energy to go out for a walk. She gets her fanny pack and water, and is just pulling the front door shut when she remembers that the keys are still in her purse.

Typical. Locked out. She reaches up above the door frame, where she always keeps a spare house key. It's not where it usually is. She runs her finger along the length of the frame. The key is not there.

She tries to think when she last used it—she's always locking herself out—but the sirens are going off now, every instinct screaming, reminding her that she and Sam always kept a spare key above the door when they lived together.

She rushes from the porch, adrenaline pulsing. The garage door is still open. Did she forget to close it this morning? She must have. She runs through the garage, into the house, to the telephone, and does what she should have done years ago. She calls Rosy.

29

DELMAR IS REPLACING burned-out bulbs in the ground lights on Jackrabbit Lane when his pager starts vibrating. It's the guard at the front gate. He heads over there and is surprised to find a truck he recognizes and, behind the wheel, somebody he knows.

"How you been?" Sam says. He sits at Delmar's kitchen table, a square wooden table painted orange. A flea-market special. The whole cottage, one room, is furnished with flea-market specials. The two kitchen chairs are old chrome items with plastic seats, thin and hard from years of use. There's a single bed against the wall opposite the kitchen nook, a rocking chair, a lamp, and a little shelf that Delmar has started filling with books. He's been riding his bike into town for supplies a couple of evenings a week. He tries to get there before the used bookstore closes. He has *The Man Who Melted* and *Planet of Whispers,* and he's been buying astronomy books. Each night he studies the sky, trying to learn heaven's map. He has started making charts and graphs, noting the stages of the moon, the sun's rising and setting. This is his favorite pastime on the lonely, quiet nights.

"Been good," Delmar says. "Excellent."

"It's good to see you."

"Good to be seen." From a distance Delmar thought Sam looked very fine, always his first impression when he sees his handsome father, but up close he sees that Sam's skin stretches tight over his cheekbones and is sort of see-through, the blue of his jawbone visible. His hair is cut very short; Delmar can see his skull under it. He's wearing brand-new stiff-legged jeans and new boots, fancy ones that look like snakeskin. His shirt looks new, too. It's a button-down, the color of old bone. He's wearing a sand-cast silver watch and a matching belt buckle.

"Thought you were in jail."

"They let me out. You want some food?"

Sam smiles. "What do you got?"

Delmar opens the cupboard. "Potatoes, onions, peanut butter, Hungry Man, vanilla wafers, apples, sardines."

"Okay," Sam says. "I'll have what you're having."

Delmar takes a yellow onion from his stash, peels and slices it.

"Cozy little place," Sam says. "This is just about the same size as my boat."

"Is that right?"

"You never been to the boat, have you."

"Nope." Delmar turns on the gas under a corroded cast-iron frying pan and pours some oil in it. He washes two russet potatoes and starts chopping them up.

"That wasn't my idea, you know. That was your mother's idea."

"I know," Delmar says. "She wanted me to do good in school." His mother always went to see Sam in November, when school was in session.

"Well, that's what she said anyway. You mind if I smoke?"

"Nope." When the oil smells hot, Delmar tosses the onion in, turning down the heat. He takes a hunk of cheddar cheese from the refrigerator and grates a pile of it.

"So, you got you a job," Sam says. "How is it?"

"It's good." Delmar tells him he's been working up here for three weeks, that he's a Landscaper I Specialist and got on-the-job training in prison. They let the minimum-security inmates go out and prune the highway median between Albuquerque and Santa Fe. He says he's thinking that when he has enough money saved, he might take some classes at the community college and try to get his forestry degree further down the line.

201

"Well, that's a fine plan," Sam says. "They pay well up here?"

"Minimum wage."

"Is that all?"

"Plus this house. I don't have to pay rent."

Sam says he ought to come to Florida, live with him, and tie flies. He could make twenty-five dollars an hour. No withholding. Cash on the line.

"Jeez," Delmar says. "That's about how much I get a day."

"I'm telling you," Sam says. He gets up and goes to look at Delmar's charts on the wall. Delmar dumps the potatoes in with the onions. Using a metal spatula, he turns everything, coating it all with the oil, turns the heat way down, and puts a lid on it. He goes to stand by Sam.

"See, the nights are getting longer," he says, showing Sam the sunrise/sunset chart. He also has a pinup of the seasonal skies, a black poster with star clusters. "If you come up here at night and look at the sky, you can still see the Archer. That's Sagittarius. But the Archer's enemy, the Scorpion, is beginning to straddle the horizon. That's me. I'm a Scorpion." From the smell, he can tell the onions are cooking good. Sam smells like wet aluminum, that bad drunkard smell. It makes Delmar a little sad. Sam's legs look skinny under the stiff jeans. His knuckles jut out, the skin thin, shiny, polished. He draws on his cigarette, holding it between thumb and forefinger like a joint. His fingers shake.

"What're you doing here, Sam?"

Sam looks at him, eyes half closed. "Can't I come see my kid?"

Delmar shrugs.

"You know," Sam says, his voice quiet, "it was never my idea for you not to come with your mom to Florida. She wanted you to herself. I told her you could go to school down there. She knew that. But you see it all the time with women, especially women with boys. They don't want the fathers to have a hand in the raising. I asked her to bring you to the boat."

Delmar used to wonder about that—about whether it was Sam's idea or his mother's idea to leave him behind. She always said the boat wasn't big enough and she wouldn't be there long enough for him to get used to the schools there. She never said Sam didn't want him, but he wondered.

He looks at the autumn constellations. There will be more night sky in the months to come. He's been doing some calculations. Over the next sixty days, the time that the sun spends below the horizon will increase by roughly one hundred and sixty minutes. "When's your birthday, Sam?" It's odd that he doesn't know.

"Third of January."

"Capricornus. The Goat." He points to it on the winter chart. "It's really the Sea Goat, because it's in the water part of the sky."

Sam drags on his cigarette, the ash tail growing. "She ever give you any of the money I sent?"

Delmar gets his tin ashtray from the kitchen counter and hands it to Sam, then returns to the potatoes, taking the lid off, scraping and flipping them. "I don't know," he says. They've got a nice brown crust and are pretty tender. He spreads the grated cheese over them, turns the burner off, and puts the lid back on. He takes two plastic plates from the cupboard and gets the little tub of diced green chili from the refrigerator, scoops the potatoes onto the plates, puts the chili and a spoon on the table.

"See, now that's what I mean. I sent money regularly. She probably never told you that, did she." His father's words are clipped, like punches, his voice high and tight, as if he's quarreling. Odd. Delmar has always thought of Sam as a cool cat. Once, when Delmar was pretty young, maybe six, Sam and his mom took him camping. He remembers finding a quart bottle of liquor in Sam's toolbox, carrying the bottle past Sam and Alice, who were sitting on logs by a smoky campfire, out in the open so they could see, and climbing up a large rock shaped like a ship, using both feet and one hand. When he got to the top, Sam said, "Don't you do it," but he did: dropped that bottle and listened to it shatter. Sam had said, "You little shit."

That was all. He didn't climb the rock to hit Delmar, which was what Delmar expected. But the next day Sam started shaking, and the truck stuttered out of the campground because Sam couldn't keep his foot steady on the gas pedal.

Delmar is not proud of the little shit he used to be. He can't remember now why he was so mad at his father and wanted to break the bottle. He used to get so mad he thought he would explode. His mother says he's like Sam, but he doesn't see it. He has never, in his whole life, seen his father angry.

"Wasn't very much, I'll give you that, but I sent money. Every couple of weeks."

"Time to eat," Delmar says. "You want a Coke?" He gets two from the refrigerator.

"As much as I could send." Sam stubs his cigarette out, leaving the ashtray on the counter, and sits down to the potatoes. "They look good. You know, I came into some money recently. You need some?" He digs in his pocket and pulls out a folded wad of hundred-dollar bills.

"Wow."

"How much you need? Couple hundred? How about five? We'll start you out with five. You need more, there's more where that came from." He peels off five crisp bills and hands them to Delmar.

"Thanks. Did you rob a bank?"

"Nope. I inherited it."

"Wow." Delmar puts the bills in his wallet.

"Maybe next year I could help you with college. You could quit this job, go to school full-time. Would you like that?"

"Sure." He piles chili on his potatoes and eats. They came out good. Sam eats his one chunk at a time, spearing, chewing, swallowing.

"Plus I'm going to start getting my Social Security. That might take a while, I don't know how long. The thing is, I paid in to Social Security for years. I tell you, Del, if you don't collect it's like bankrolling the government. They do take Social Security out of your checks?"

Delmar nods.

"Well, they shouldn't. It's a scam. But since they do, make sure you're in a position to collect when the time comes. Do you know where your birth certificate is? Because that's what you need—

proof that you were born in order to collect the money they take from your check, over which you've got no say—them taking the money." He spears, chews, swallows. "I'll tell you something I bet you don't know about your birth certificate. Where it says 'Father' on the form? You know what she wrote on yours? She wrote 'Unknown.' That's another thing I had no say over. I bet you didn't know that, did you?" Sam stares at him. His father's blue eyes are icy moons on red rims.

But Delmar did know that. His mother told him she did it because she wasn't eighteen when he was born and she didn't want his father to get in trouble. Delmar doesn't say that. They've had the conversation before. Sam used to bring this up to his mother in his presence. Delmar knows Sam knows the score. Unless he has forgotten. Heavy drinkers get forgetful. Sam seems a little uptight.

"I'll tell you something else I bet you didn't know," Sam says. "I offered to make you legitimate. Did you know that? That I asked her to marry me? Did she ever tell you that?"

"Yeah."

"She did?"

"Yeah."

Sam studies him. "Oh?" Delmar heaps on more green chili, scooping up the last of his potatoes. Sam laughs. He puts his fork down and looks out the window. "Guess she's got you trained to keep her secrets, huh?"

"She doesn't have me trained. She's not the marrying kind. Anyway, she said she wouldn't marry a drinker."

"Yeah, well," Sam says. He pushes his plate away, nodding. Sam's lips are scarlet but kind of rubbery, like a wino's. He fills his cheeks with air, blowing it out noisily, gazing at Delmar and shaking his head. He opens his mouth to say something, then closes it. He cranes his neck, staring out. "You got a little roadrunner out there."

"That's my pet." Delmar gets up and carries the plates to the sink. "He comes around every day. He likes apples. You want to feed him?"

"I got to get going," Sam says, standing up.

"Where you going?"

"I don't know. Colorado maybe. Go up, do some fishing."

Sam walks to the door and out onto the stoop. Delmar follows. The roadrunner has disappeared. He's hiding in the bushes, Delmar knows, waiting until he thinks he's alone.

Hands stuffed in his pockets, Sam stares off at nothing, looking sad. Delmar says, "You want to stay here? You can. I got a sleeping bag and a pad."

Sam smiles. "I'll be back this way. I've got a wedding to go to. Why don't you come fishing with me? The trout ought to be fat up there in the high lakes."

Delmar says he's got to work, plus he can't cross the state line and break parole.

Sam nods. "Del, you heard from your mom?"

"Nope."

"Where is she?"

"I heard she's down in Texas. She's teaching in these rodeo camps."

"When do you think she's coming back?"

"I don't know. Maybe a couple of weeks."

"She got a boyfriend?"

The roadrunner peeks out from under the scrub oak, where he thinks he's invisible. Delmar shrugs. "Grandma might know when she's coming back."

"Ariana? How is she?"

"Good."

"Maybe I'll go see her. I could take her some groceries or something. You think I'd be welcome?"

"Sure."

"She always liked me, your grandma. Maybe I won't go fishing yet. Maybe I'll go see Ariana first." He crosses to the electric cart. Delmar follows. They left his truck at the gate.

"I'm glad you came by, Sam. It was good to see you."

"Good to see you, too, kid. Del, I'm going to be a better dad. I'm going to find a way to help you through college." His voice rises a little. "If I can get my Social Security check, I'm going to have it sent directly to you. We're not going to have any go-be-tweens. When that happens, you think you can call me Dad?"

Delmar shrugs.

"You'll try?"

"Okay."

Sam sticks his hand out for Delmar to shake. He shakes it.

30

THE COFFEE TABLE is upended on the couch. Ryland's footstool and the piano bench have been moved to the kitchen. The carpet, which Rosy just finished vacuuming, bears the imprint of the vacuum wheels. Now the wheels begin colliding with the bedroom wall behind his head, an angry thump, thump, thump. She seems to be vacuuming the wall, not the floor.

In her efforts to "whip this house into shape," she has been moving him from room to room like a piece of furniture. He started out in the kitchen, but when the grandkids showed up and they all started cleaning the kitchen floor, she advised a retreat to the bedroom. Now he has been shooed out of the bedroom, and he cannot go into the bathroom, where he would like to take a bath, because Sandi is scouring it with a toothbrush.

The kids arrived just after eight and will be here all day. Sue and Maggie are down at the church. Or at the reception hall. Or up at Edna Friedan's, seeing about the rehearsal dinner. They keep dashing in and out, Sue and Maggie do.

Teri is sneezing. She sits in the middle of the living room floor, legs apart, red-faced, watery-eyed, sneezing at regular intervals — two, three, four, five, six sneezes.

"You better not be getting a cold," Rosy hollers, shutting the vacuum off and bustling into the room. "Are you getting a cold?" Teri sneezes.

Ryland doesn't think she's getting a cold. She's irritated by the dust Pooh is raising with the feather duster. He is irritated by it, too. Dust swirls in the sunlight in this room, gagging him.

"Want some juice?" Rosy says to Teri. "You're sure Sam didn't say when he's coming back?"

"He didn't say." Sam's been gone a week now, and each day he doesn't show up, Rosy gets madder.

She hustles toward the kitchen and comes back carrying a plastic cup with a duck-billed lid, which she hands to Teri.

"I think we ought to have him arrested," she says for the millionth time.

"We're not having him arrested."

"Ryland, it's extortion plain and simple."

"We ought to hear his side of the story before we go jumping to conclusions."

He opens Maggie's Bible. She has asked him to choose a Psalm for the ceremony. Rosy returns to the vacuum and begins attacking the wall. Each point of contact sounds like an explosion. He thumbs through the satiny pages.

She turns the machine off. "What side? He stole five thousand dollars."

"Who did?" Sandi calls from the bathroom.

"Never mind," Rosy calls. She comes back into the living room, stands by Ryland's chair, and says quietly, "I don't want him at the wedding."

"Rose, wait until we hear from him before you start getting on your high horse."

"If he's at the wedding, I won't be."

"Don't give me ultimatums."

"Ryland, this is our only daughter's wedding. He's already spoiled it. He's got me so mad I can't think straight. I don't need this right now. And Lily. My God. Lily does not need this."

Sandi comes in, her face screwed in a horrible grimace, as if she has been eating soap. "Are you through in there?" Rosy says.

"The floor is wet. Ugh. I hate cleaning bathrooms."

"How long's it going to be wet?" Ryland says.

"I don't know," she wails, as if his question makes everything worse.

"Don't talk to your grandfather in that tone, Sandra," Rosy says icily.

"I — don't — know," the child says in a sugary voice that makes him want to smack her.

"Well, let's inspect." She glares at Ryland as she and Sandi go off. "Oh, honey. You did such a good job."

"Don't walk on it," Sandi shrieks.

"It certainly is wet. Honey, get some paper towels and dry it. Your grandpa wants to take a bath."

Today is Tuesday. Thursday begins it, people arriving from out of town. Eddy will make airport runs, chauffeuring guests to the Holiday Inn. The rehearsal. The rehearsal dinner. Saturday the wedding. Sunday it's over. Sunday is the day Ryland wants.

Where is Sam? And what in the world is he up to? If he needed money, why didn't he take it when Ryland offered?

Rosy pulls the vacuum back into the living room, dragging the cord behind. "Bathroom's yours," she says. Ryland stands up and pulls his oxygen cart into the hall. As he passes her, she whispers, "I still think we ought to call the police."

"We're not calling the police."

"Somebody ought to do something about getting my sister's money back."

"I'll get it."

"If he shows up here."

"He'll show."

He stands in the bathroom doorway, looking at Sandi on her hands and knees, a wad of paper towels in both hands. She swashes the floor in wide, exuberant strokes.

"I think that's good enough," he says. She looks over her shoulder at him, squinting and scowling, then pushes herself up, brushing past him and yelling to Rosy that Grandpa says it's good enough.

He walks in, closes the door, and locks it. The room smells like a mixture of ammonia and rotten flowers. On the back of the toilet is a new dish of dried flower petals. He turns the hot water on in the tub full blast until it drowns out all of the sounds on the other side of the door.

Perhaps he slept. The open Bible balances face-down on the edge of the tub, where he laid it when he closed his eyes. The water was steaming then. Now, just tepid, it is the temperature, perhaps, of saliva, which he was reading about in the Bible — the inconsequential spit of a lackadaisical believer. Lukewarm. He toes the hot-water knob, but the water that gushes out is cold. He must have run the hot-water tank dry. He toes the knob back off. His feet have wrinkled, his fingers too. He should get out, but that seems like such an effort, and the voices on the other side of the door have multiplied. Maggie and Sue are back. He hears Maggie say they might as well open the presents. Rosy tells Maggie they really should wait for George. He can hear exaggerated gaiety, a tone that tells him that behind it all, she is seething. Maggie says George doesn't care.

He picks up the Bible. His glasses are speckled with water drops.

"Let me open one," a voice squeals.

"Everybody gets to open one," Maggie says.

"It's like Christmas, isn't it, Ter," Sue says.

"Ooh, look at this. Ooh la la."

"Don't get it dirty. Pooh, look at your hands. Go wash them."

"Grandpa's in the bathroom."

"Still? Ryland? You okay?"

"Okay," he says.

"Ryland?"

"Okay," he shouts.

"Just checking, just checking."

He closes the Bible and puts it on the side of the tub, pushes his glasses up on top of his head, and closes his eyes.

He wakes to a pounding. "If you don't answer, we're taking the knob off," Rosy yells.

"Dad!" Eddy.

He tries to answer, but his teeth are chattering. He can't stop them. His hips have locked up or something. He can't move.

"Get a screwdriver."

"Dad!"

He tries to speak, and he tries to push himself up. The Bible is in the water. His arms have turned to fins. He watches the doorknob shiver. He listens to the grinding of screws. They are taking the doorknob off.

"My God, my God." Now Rosy is on her knees beside him, plunging her hands in the tub. "Call an ambulance."

No, he tries to say, but his teeth are chattering, and he can't speak.

She releases the plug, and the water begins to drain. She rubs his upper arms vigorously.

"Eddy, we've got to get him out of here."

"I don't think we should move him, Mom."

"My God, he's blue," Maggie says, and he feels such shame at his daughter seeing him naked.

He stares into Rosy's eyes. She seems to understand, because she says, "Maggie, keep everybody out of here. Eddy and I can handle this. But get a blanket."

She pushes his oxygen tube up against his nose. "We've got to get you out of there," she whispers. She slips her hands under his armpits and tries to lift him. He can hear her breath in his ear. He knows her cheek is against his, but he can't feel it.

"Mom, I really don't think we should move him. He may have fallen. Injured his spine or something."

"Ryland, wiggle your toes." She stares at his feet, bending down closer to them. He thinks he's wiggling them. Can't tell.

Now she grips him by the shoulders, bringing her face inches from his, her pupils pinpoints. "Did—you—fall?" She shakes him.

It seems ridiculous. He fell asleep, he got cold.

She puts her hand over her mouth, her eyes suddenly watery. She blinks rapidly. Her nostrils flare.

The water has drained out. Rosy is tucking the down comforter from his bed around him in the tub. She begins rubbing him through the comforter, his arms, his torso, his legs. "Got to get you warm," she says. Her tongue's sticking out between her lips, a habit of hers. When Rosy works, the tongue comes out. This makes him want to laugh, and he does, his teeth knocking together.

She sits back on her heels. The tongue goes in. Her chin is trembling, her lips, too, and it looks like she's going to cry. He tries to remember the last time he saw her cry—not since the kids were little, not since then. "Look at you, you're all pruned up." She takes his hand, rubbing his fingers. Their eyes lock, her eyes filmy, blinking, blinking, and her lips tremble.

She puts his hand back under the comforter and goes to rubbing his ankles and calves. "Here," she says. "We can do this. You getting warmer? I don't think you injured your spine."

"Nope," he manages to say. A thousand pins have started pricking his feet.

Eddy peers over her shoulder. "You okay, Pop?"

"Tell them . . ."

"Tell who what?" Rosy says.

"No ambulance." But already he hears the siren. Shame washes over him again.

A doctor he doesn't know is talking to Rosy and Eddy and someone else outside the blue curtain. He's lying on a gurney. The blue curtain separates him from a couple of other gurneys in the crowded emergency room. The doctor is telling them that the EKG showed no sign of heart attack, and the MRI no sign of stroke. He thinks Ryland got a touch of hypothermia.

They have been waiting for Dr. Callahan. The doctor on duty had told them that Dr. Callahan wouldn't officially be back from vacation until tomorrow, but Rosy has his home number, and she insisted on calling, and now Ryland recognizes the doctor's voice. The emergency room doctor tells Callahan that he sees no sign of stroke, and Rosy says, "Don't you want to monitor him overnight?"

The curtain parts and Dr. Callahan comes in. He's wearing a white polo shirt and khaki pants. He has a good tan.

"How you doing, Ryland?"

"I'm fine."

"Gave everybody a scare, my man." The doctor leans over Ryland, pulling his eyelid up, his lower lid down, and shining a penlight in his eye. Ryland can smell garlic on his breath.

"Guess I interrupted your dinner?"

"That's okay."

He uses a stethoscope to listen to Ryland's heart.

"Got a headache, Ry?"

"No."

"Noticed any pain in your arms?"

"No."

"Neck?"

"No."

"Is this wedding a pain in the neck?"

Ryland smiles; the doctor smiles.

"Did you take pills, Ryland?" He stares him in the eye. Ryland stares back. Says nothing. "I know this is a stressful time, but you don't want to overdo the sedatives." Ryland holds his gaze.

"Well. I think you're fine. I think you just got cold."

"Man freezes to death in his own bathtub. Pathetic," Ryland says.

"In ninety-degree weather." The doctor smiles and slips outside the curtain. Ryland listens to him tell Rosy to take Ryland home but to remember that he's not at the top of his game, and anything she can do to reduce stress she ought to do. He says that if Ryland seems confused or if at any time he has trouble speaking or understanding speech, or if he loses his balance, to call immediately.

"And Rose, keep an eye on his medications." He says that Ryland must have been sleeping heavily for the water to have gotten so cold.

Like a kid fibbing to his mother, Ryland tells Rosy he doesn't know where the bottle of Xanax is and then feels so ridiculous he immediately fishes it out from under his shirts in the dresser drawer and gives it to her, which makes him feel like a kid owning up. She watches him ceaselessly. Eyes dim with fatigue — it's a fear-tinged fatigue, like he used to see in the eyes of sleepless soldiers — she examines him, looking for evidence of what, stroke? Has he had a stroke? Will he? It is odd to think that if he does, she'll know before he does. That's the nature of strokes. The body and the mind separate; an open-eyed witness gives evidence. What is his wife if not open-eyed?

Suddenly the house is empty. Tuesday evening he listens to her hushed conversations on the telephone as she relocates Wedding Headquarters Central to Eddy and Sue's house. He's just getting into bed when she comes in and sits on the mattress next to him, searching his face. He wants to tell her to stop looking at him like the grand inquisitor, but he knows that'll just make her self-conscious — or mad. He is so tired. Is tiredness evidence of stroke?

"I think maybe we ought to have Eddy walk Maggie down the aisle," she says. "It's enough that you're at the wedding."

"I'm walking Maggie down the aisle," he says.

She blinks, swallows; eyes unfocused, she stares at the oxygen tank in the corner.

"You scared me, Ryland."

"I know. I'm sorry."

"I don't know what I'd do if . . ."

He takes her hand, squeezing it. "I'm okay, Rosy."

She stands up, threads of pink bleeding into her wan cheeks. "Thursday will be such a long day, Ryland. You could skip it. Skip the rehearsal. The rehearsal dinner. Just rest up for Saturday."

"I'll be fine."

And yet when has he been so tired? He doesn't remember sleeping, but it's almost noon when he wakes on Wednesday to Rosy's fretful face inches from his, telling him he's been asleep for over fifteen hours and asking him if his shoulders ache or if he has a headache.

Everything does ache, though no more, he thinks, than yesterday, or any other day of his life, for that matter.

He had been dreaming about the mill. Woody was in the dream, his leg splashed with sulfuric acid. But that never happened. It happened to Ryland once in Durango. Ryland has a brown burn patch on his right calf and has had it for thirty years now.

Eddy is at the table having lunch when Ryland goes into the kitchen. "You off today?"

"Until Sunday. I'm taking a few vacation days."

"Where's your mom?"

"She had some errands."

By midafternoon, when Eddy, who has stationed himself in front of the television to watch soap operas, shows no sign of leaving, Ryland realizes that his son is on duty. Eddy must have a million things he should be doing. He most certainly should not be spending his vacation days before the wedding watching soap operas. Except he's not really watching them, not closely, because every time a car passes he looks out the window. When Rosy comes back, Eddy goes into the kitchen and Ryland strains to hear their conversation. It becomes clear that Eddy has been watching for Sam. If he can, Eddy will intercept Sam without Ryland knowing. In that way they will save Ryland whatever stress Sam might cause. And probably have Sam arrested.

Ryland sets up a vigil of his own, though he is so tired — when has he been so tired? Every time he feels himself drifting, he struggles out of it, keeping his eyes on the front window, his ears tuned to the traffic on the street. He sleeps badly Wednesday night, waking every half hour. At breakfast Thursday morning, Rosy tells him he looks like death warmed over. She invites him again to skip the rehearsal, and he considers that, because then he could be alone, and maybe Sam would come. But when she says that if he skips, she'll skip, too, he rallies. He may never be alone again.

The rehearsal is chaotic. No one told the church cleaners about it, and four Mexican women are scouring the altar area when they arrive, one pushing an industrial vacuum with an engine that sounds like a B-52. Father Liam and Rosy both holler directions over the clatter, and Mrs. Gruber, the organist, plays the Wedding March over the noise of the vacuum.

All of the young people — George and Maggie, Sue and Eddy,

the best man, who is George's brother — wear jeans and T-shirts. This bothers Ryland. Why it should bother him, he doesn't know, except it's a church. Their costumes seem a study in disrespect. The little girls are wearing summer shorts, halter tops, and thongs, and they're chewing gum. Which bothers him.

His job isn't hard. The hard part is waiting in the noise while Sue and Rosy argue about letting Teri walk alone down the aisle. Sue thinks she ought to walk with Teri and help her keep pace, but Rosy says Sue's place is in the procession ahead of Ryland and Maggie, that it has to be that way, that's where the matron of honor always is, and it doesn't matter if Teri runs down the aisle because she's so cute and little. They argue about this for fifteen minutes, Rosy finally winning.

It has been decided that Ryland will leave his oxygen cart at the back of the church. Unencumbered by the tank, he'll walk Maggie up the aisle, and his other, smaller tank will be with Rosy in the head pew, where he'll hook himself back up.

Finally they start. He doesn't remember the aisle in the church being so long. He leaves Maggie at the altar, handing her to George, steps into the pew next to his frowning inspector-general wife.

Then they have to rehearse it again. Why again? Nobody else seems to wonder.

It's on the third long walk that his knees buckle. It's the noise, he thinks, that caused it. He was leaning toward Maggie, trying to hear what she is saying about her petticoats, which will make her twice as wide on Saturday, but the organ music was so loud he couldn't quite hear her. Everybody was chattering. His knees buckled, and he fell into Maggie, who fell into a pew.

They all swarmed, Rosy grabbing his wrist, checking for a pulse, and wanting to look in his eyes. "Enough," he yelled.

Now he sits in the pew, the church utterly silent, everybody watching him. Maggie squats next to him. "Daddy," she says, "maybe Eddy should walk me down the aisle. You could just wait in the pew with Mom and give me away when the time comes. Or Eddy could do that. Really, all that matters is that you're there. If you want, you can sit in the back of the church. Quick escape, you know. If you want to."

He looks at his daughter and thinks about explaining that he's really okay, it was just the noise that got to him. But why did it get to him? Why did it seem so loud?

He simply says, "I'll be fine."

It's late by the time they get out of the church and head up to Whitaker Mesa for the rehearsal dinner at Edna Friedan's house. Edna, an old friend from Durango, was a mill wife who came with them to Shiprock with her first husband. She has been married four times since, widowed each time. The last one, Friedan, a real estate mogul from Los Angeles, left Edna very well off.

The sun is just slipping behind the horizon when the wedding party tops the mesa. It's 7:45. They're driving in a caravan, Eddy and Sue in the lead, Ryland and Rosy behind them. Approaching the security gate, squinting against the setting sun, Ryland sees something that makes no sense: Sam's truck, with Sam and somebody else — Alice? — inside.

He and Eddy are out of their cars simultaneously. "Ed!" Ryland calls. "I'll handle this." Eddy looks back at Rosy. Ryland unhooks himself from his oxygen and covers ground.

Not Alice but an old Navajo woman sits on the passenger's side of the truck.

"Ry. You know Ariana Atcitty? This is Alice's mother." The strong smell of liquor-soaked sweat wafts through Sam's open window. Sam is badly sunburned, his nose peeling. Red dirt cakes his neck and throat above his T-shirt.

"Can I talk to you?" Ryland says, motioning for Sam to step out of the truck. "Where the hell you been?" he says as soon as they're out of earshot, though where Sam has been is clear. He's found Alice.

"Been camping out at Ariana's place, helping her rig an irrigation system."

Sam looks at the line of cars idling at the gate. "What's with the parade?"

"So I guess you found Alice."

"Sort of. She's due back—"

"What, are you just sitting out there roosting?"

Chin raised, eyes half closed, Sam looks at him and doesn't answer.

"Lily called."

"Oh?"

"What do you think you're doing, buddy?"

Sam purses his lips, nodding, taking his time to answer, finally saying, "What does she think she's doing? Did she tell you the story?"

"Yeah, we heard the story. Sam, if you needed money, I told you . . ."

"It's not about that."

"What's it about?"

"For the insult, Ry. I mean, what the fuck. Seventeen years I think I'm divorced and then find out I'm not. Anyway, she can afford it. You've seen how she lives? Christ, she's got more than you and me put together."

"It's not your money, Sam. You're not entitled."

"What do you care?" Sam says. "Why are you so pissed?"

Ryland swallows. A young man whom he recognizes as Sam's son—he's run into the kid now and again over the years—has just driven out of the gate in a little white go-cart. He parks near the adobe wall that encircles the estates, starts toward Sam's truck, but detours when Rosy gets out and calls him over to her.

Something that feels like a vise steadily tightens around Ryland's chest.

"Wouldn't think you'd give a damn," Sam is saying.

"I don't. Rosy does."

"Ah." Sam smiles. He takes his flask from his back pocket and sips. "Rosy." He recaps the flask. "So you're her messenger?"

"What do you mean by that?"

Sam shakes his head, smiling. The boy walks over to the pickup and gets in on the passenger's side, as Alice's mother moves over.

"I want Lily's money."

"Or?"

"Or I'll have you arrested."

Sam laughs. He starts walking toward the truck.

"Sam. I mean it."

"Have me arrested."

"Don't think I won't," Ryland says through clenched teeth.

Sam stops, turns, and they look at each other. "You do what you've got to do, Ryland."

His head aches. It's the lack of oxygen. He needs to get to it. Sam turns back toward the truck.

"Sam."

"What."

"We don't want you at the wedding."

Sam stops again but doesn't turn around. His head bows toward the ground. "You know why I'm up here, Ry? Woody died. I came to get my boy. I don't think I'd be making the wedding anyway. I figure we'll be burying Woody that day."

Edna's large living room seems to undulate. Furniture blooms from its center — bold, thin-skinned chairs and chaises without arms or edges but with rolling lips top and bottom. The couches and chairs are organized around a low black table that seems to Ryland to be miles from the walls, which are decorated with metal wall hangings. Everywhere, pillows seem to crawl with color, bright tropical flowers, tropical birds. The floor is red clay.

"Mister, you look good," Edna says.

"No I don't," he says.

"You look good to me," she says, leading him to a chair, handing him champagne. She looks pieced together, hair a patchy metallic red, little mangled coils with bits of bald shining through, two rouge dots on cheeks that have lost their roundness, streaking into creased folds of skin. "I have always told your wife she married a good-looking man."

The vise squeezing his chest hasn't loosened. It's distracting. He finds he has to concentrate to understand what people are saying.

Rosy sits in the middle of a purple chaise opposite him. Her clothes seem to have shrunk. The fabric of her green pantsuit stretches over her middle, and the shoulders pull up toward her chin.

A young Mexican woman wearing a black and white server's outfit comes through a door that must lead to the kitchen. She begins to tour the room with cocktail napkins and a platter full of little pigs in blankets and tiny pies with what looks like spinach in them. When Ryland gets a whiff, his stomach turns.

Father Liam's voice booms, telling everybody how happy he is to be here. "Doesn't Maggie look good? Here's to the bride."

The grandkids scream, running up and down the halls. Five halls branch off the main room, three to the west side of the house, two to the east. In some other room — the kitchen? — somebody is saying Sam's name. Ryland leans back in his chair, looking at a thin metal structure mounted on the western wall. Something that looks like a boxy man faces a smaller version of himself; the miniature doesn't have the edges of a face or body, just the hint of them.

"So you sold Edna this house," Father Liam is saying to Sue.

"Got two more pending," she says.

"Sue, your daughters are taking over Mrs. Friedan's house," Eddy says.

"They're your daughters tonight, Ed."

People — first the Mexican girl, then Maggie — keep sticking the pigs in blankets in front of Ryland. Rosy's face looks like it's made of ice and if she stops smiling her lips will melt.

"I miss having children around," Edna is saying. "Now I remember, was it Maggie? Twirling the baton. Do you remember, Rosy, the little girls and their batons in Camp, running from house to house, putting on shows for us? We had a nice life, didn't we? A nice little neighborhood."

"You ought to see it now, Edna. The houses are falling down. We've got pictures."

"Don't show me any pictures. I don't want to see any pictures of falling-down houses. It was a lucky life for me. Me, I was lucky in bingo and lucky in love."

"Edna, how can you say that? How many husbands have you buried?"

"Five. Each one the love of my life. Here's to you, Miss Maggie and Mr. George. May you find your luck."

"And long life."

Ryland holds the handle of his oxygen tank to push himself up, watches the black dots shoot from the center of his eyes out into the room, where they dive into color that is blurry now. He steers around the furniture. George's mother's voice floats up to him, "And I fell right through the ice," the priest booming, "A miracle." "We have lots of baby pictures," Eddy is saying, "Mags crying in every one." From the back of the house, a child's piercing laughing scream — "You kids! Stop it." Ryland winds around people he doesn't know, George's people, and he nods at their chins when they try to speak to him.

The room has no corners, Ryland notices. All of the corners are rounded, and the walls have many alcoves. He puts one foot in front of the other, moving to an alcove with a display of knives, where he stands swaying, touching the alcove's edge, the adobe cool and soothing. Old relics. Knives and swords. Fancy knives, some with jeweled handles. They put him in mind of another time, another world. He saw a man knifed in the throat when he was in the military. Early on in their campaign against the Japanese. He was one foxhole over, and in the dead of night, somebody crawled through the dark and slipped a knife from point to hilt through a man's throat. Left the thing there. It was Ryland who pulled the knife out. He can remember the feel of the handle, solid and smooth like a good kitchen knife.

Behind him, he hears the whispered names: Woody, Sam. They think he can't hear. They're exchanging news.

Edna is next to him now, saying, "Ryland, would you like to wash up? Let me show you." She takes his arm and leads him away. He can hear the scraping of his shoes as he walks. Pick your feet up, soldier. In a barely audible voice, Rosy is telling George's people who Woody was.

They go down a narrow hall. To their right is a wall, to their left glass, and on the other side of the glass a tiled patio opens to the sky. Holes have been cut into the tile, where various types of cactus have been planted. In the center a huge prickly pear has dropped its fruit, and the fruit, he sees, has pruned up and rotted. The plant shouldn't grow at this altitude. Should it? The patio must have a humidifier and temperature control.

"Too bad about Woody," Edna says.

"One of the best men I know. Knew."

She opens a door, and he goes into a bathroom.

The back side of the door is mirror. The skin under his eyes is thick and puffy, the whites pinkish, his cheeks blue.

He reaches into his shirt pocket for the pill he put there.

But there is no pill. He wanted to put one there, but he couldn't because he doesn't know where they are.

He steps away from the mirror, turning his back on it.

This room is full of reflections. The entire wall above and below the counter with two sinks is mirror. The floor is the same red clay as the rest of the house. There are levels to this room, three steps leading up to a tiled platform and a tub as big as a small wading pool. The wall behind the tub: mirror.

The commode is tucked into a little nook, away from the rest of the room and surrounded by thick, sweet-smelling green plants.

The nook walls are sea green, no mirrors. The tucked-in place looks out onto an enclosed cactus garden, a miniature of the larger, more public one.

A pleasant and private place for a commode, pretty view.

Ryland crosses to it and sits on the closed lid, looking into the garden, where a gray lizard is quickly disappearing as darkness deepens. Do lizards see color? Is he himself disappearing here in the middle of the sweet-smelling plants?

"Grandpa," one of the kids yells. "Time to eat. Grandpa, Grandpa, Grandpa."

He doesn't want to eat. But he has to eat. But he doesn't want to get up. But he has to. His kidneys have been tugging for half an hour. The lizard has slunk away, gone off to look for a warm place to spend the night.

He stands, lifting the toilet lid and seat, unzipping, propping himself up by anchoring one hand against the wall, listening to the pitiful sound of his water kerplunking, and without warning, he is coughing, convulsing with it, dropping his cock, which continues to fire wild and spray the sea green wall with piss. He spews spit all around, covers his mouth with the back of his arm. "Grandpa!" one of the kids yells, and knocks on the door. He stands gasping, trying to blink the haze out of his eyes.

He sits in a straight-backed chair against a wall in a room tight with people. A long table nearly fills the room, his family and George's crowding around it — the table a shiny Christmas red. A thick-lipped, eyeless salmon has been laid out on a bed of greens. Goopy swarms of red and black fish eggs nestle in the greens. Edna, loading her plate, says, "You sure you want to go through with this?" and George says, "Kill us now." Rosy says, "There'll be no killing on my watch."

There are cheeses on the table, and fruit, and some potato-looking thing, and a turkey, its inside stuffed with something orange.

Maggie stands in front of him. She's saying something he can't quite understand and handing him a box wrapped in silver. "Hey, everybody," she says. She picks up her champagne glass and clinks it with a fork. "Daddy has something he wants to say." They all wait. He looks at the box, then at Maggie, her eyes bright and eager. She says, "Mom, Daddy got you a wedding present."

"Isn't that nice," the priest says.

Ryland stares at the silver box. He hands it back to Maggie, who hands it to Rosy, who at first doesn't look like she wants to take it. "Honey," she says. "How nice. Whatever it is, you spent too much."

They all watch her open it, and they ooh and pass it around. Maggie holds it under Ryland's nose. She's joking about how it's a surprise to him, too, but his checkbook has a bigger surprise in store. He stares at a clear blue stone in a silver setting on a silver chain, a tiny four-point star shining like the star of Bethlehem in the middle of the stone. Rosy comes over and kisses him on the cheek.

"It's a smaller version of the one Sue gave me, Mom."

A child stands next to him, her hand on his knee, looking into the box. For the life of him, he can't remember her name. He knows he loves this child, but just now her name has flown from his head.

31

I T WAS STILL LIGHT Thursday evening when Becky came in from her run, and her mother asked her to go check on her father, who was in the hogan. She stopped to change out of her running shoes. She believes that was the minute he died, because he was still quite warm.

She found him lying next to the wood stove in the middle of the round room, stretched out on his back, eyes closed, hands fisted at his sides, feet pointing west. She was not afraid to touch him. She had been anticipating this moment for so long. Among the mix of emotions that swept through her, she felt relief that the struggle was over. She knelt next to him, uncurling his still warm fingers one by one, the only part of his body that betrayed any struggle at the end. She was not sorry that he had faced death alone because she knew that was what he had wanted, but she was sorry for herself and, oddly, mad at him, not at *him* but at the clenched hands, a gesture that left her out so completely. For a while she held his hand, just as he had held hers when she was a little girl. She tried to pray but had no words, only relief and, behind it, the urge to blow something up. She felt the heat of him leaving. Before he was completely cold, she straightened his arms by his sides and covered him head to ankles with his Pendleton blanket, which was not long enough to cover all of him. Then she went into the house and told her mother.

The struggle, though, is not over. Becky's mother began making calls right away, first to the undertaker and doctor, then to Aunt Pip and Katie, and then she handed the phone wordlessly to Becky, who called her father's relatives. But it was her grandmother who arrived first. It was odd. Ariana had the farthest to come, and she has no phone. It was as if she'd been hovering just around the corner. Delmar's father brought her and Delmar, too.

They wouldn't come inside, so Becky went out to them, and that's when she saw the casket in the back of the truck. A simple pine box.

"Mom has a coffin," she told them.

Ariana didn't speak. Delmar did the talking. He said that their grandmother wanted her father buried at their sheep camp on the hidden mesa, where his ancestors were. Becky told them her mother had a plot at Desert View Cemetery in town. Her grandmother wanted him laid to rest in the Navajo Way, lodged in a shallow grave, from which the spirit can easily get out and find its way west. Her grandmother believes that's what her father wanted.

Becky went back in and told her mother. When Aunt Pip and Katie arrived, they decided to call the undertaker back and tell him to wait until morning while they resolved the problem. Nobody wants a fight.

But the problem has not been resolved. Instead, they've settled into stalemate. Becky's mother tried to explain to Ariana that she wants her husband close, in the cemetery, where she can visit him. The hidden mesa is fifty miles from here, twenty of them a steep, rutted wagon trail. And if they take him there, the men will cart the body off and not tell anybody where it is. But Becky's grandmother sat stonily through the explanation, acting as if she didn't understand English.

All night her father's relatives drove in. This morning they sit parked in the yard, waiting in their cars; some of her clan cousins lounge around the stone fireplace at the edge of the yard. Her grandmother and Delmar moved to the porch, and Delmar's father stayed in his truck.

All night her grandmother talked to herself in Navajo, telling and retelling the story about their ancestors, and Becky sat on the swing listening. Delmar translated. Becky has heard the story her whole life, of the lucky band of boys who became known as the lost boys, except they weren't lost, they were hiding in the hills when Kit Carson enslaved the Navajo and forced them to walk to Fort Sumner. The band, her great-grandfather and great-uncles, lived quietly, hunting in the hills around Mesa Verde while so many of her people starved or froze to death on the Long Walk. Her grandmother says that the Diné spirit runs strong in their family; when relatives pass, their spirits can best find their way west from the hidden camp.

Now Delmar sits under the willow playing with C3PO. The minister from the Baptist church and his wife are in the house. Occasionally Becky can hear them praying with her mom and the others inside. They have called her in a few times, but she doesn't want to join the circle. She feels leaden, rooted to the swing.

She has been reading and rereading the bumper stickers on Aunt Pip's car. The new one seems especially appropriate: AS SURE AS GOD PUTS HIS CHILDREN IN THE FURNACE, HE WILL BE IN THE FURNACE WITH THEM. Becky hopes this is true, because the day is going to be hot as hell, and though the hogan stays cooler than the house, it gets stuffy, too, by the middle of the afternoon.

The sweet smell of baking pastries comes from the house — the aunts are baking again. It's just after ten. She's thinking of changing into her running clothes, going for a quick run while it's still cool and before anything happens. She watches Delmar's father get out of his truck and let down the tailgate. He says, "Del, help me," and begins to pull out the pine box. Almost simultaneously, the screen door bangs open, startling Becky. Her mother yells, "We have a casket at the mortuary!" She has probably been waiting for this.

Sam stops what he's doing.

"We don't need that!" Della screams. She holds her stomach. Her body is shuddering, almost convulsing. Becky lurches from the swing, puts her arms around her mother. Tear streaks have dried on her face, looking a bit like war paint. Della says, "I'm through with this." The door slams behind her. A minute later, Becky hears her mother on the telephone with the mortuary.

She feels as if she's been filled with sand, dry and heavy. Becky gazes at her grandmother's feet, stretched out in front of her in the dirt, looking like a child's in holey tennis shoes. Her grandmother would not want the heavy cherry wood box they bought, which could trap the spirit inside.

C3PO walks slowly out into the sun to get the stick Delmar has just thrown. The dog looks sad. And hot. He knows about death, animals know.

Delmar's father leans against his truck, smoking. His hair looks like it's been recently cut. Short, even fringe lies flat on the top of his head and high over his ears, like a boy-god, a Greek statue. The cut emphasizes his long forehead, making it seem bulbous. He tosses his cigarette and walks heel to toe across the yard, as if he has to think about it. He leans up against the porch railing. "Just tell me what you want me to do and I'll do it, Ariana," he says. He seems very chummy with her. When she was little, Becky remembers seeing him a couple of times at barbecues on her grandmother's farm. She didn't understand how he could be Delmar's father, since her grandmother didn't treat him like a son-in-law. Becky knew it was considered taboo for a man to look his mother-in-law in the eye, but with Sam the taboos didn't apply. Her father said it was because he never married Alice, that Sam was, in fact, married to somebody else. On the farm nobody acknowledged him as a relative. He was Delmar's father, that's all.

Now another vehicle is pulling in at the gate. Becky's fingers hurt. She's been clenching her hands as if fighting the battle before it happens. She thinks of her father's body, of his fists, and feels suddenly dizzy, her knees turning watery.

The new truck is blue. A Ford.

Harrison.

He's wearing a green shirt, hair loose. He parks near the opening in the hedge, gets out, and stands, hands in his pockets. There's a dog on the passenger's side. A brown lab.

She crosses the porch and the yard. "What are you doing here?"

"I went by the bank. Arnold told me about your dad. I'm real sorry, Becky." He touches her arm.

She swallows, looking quickly at the ground, because if she looks in his face she'll cry.

"What's going on?" he says quietly.

The dog crosses to the driver's side, sticks his head out the window, and sniffs her shoulder. She runs her hand down his head, massaging under the collar, and the dog reciprocates, nuzzling her.

"Looks like a powwow," Harrison says.

She tells him the problem.

"Old Indian standoff, huh?"

"It's about to bust open." She tells him about her mother's fury and the phone call to the undertaker.

"Want to get out of here for a little while? This is the boss, my dog, Naat'áanii. We could take you for a ride. You look like you could use a break."

She laughs hoarsely. "I would," she says, "but three's a crowd."

He bows his head, shaking it a little. She watches a smile flit across his lips. Suddenly he grabs her wrist, saying, "*Hágo!*" and pulls her toward the road, out beyond the juniper hedge. When they're out of sight of the house, he puts his arms around her, pulling her close, and the move starts her crying. He tightens his grip, and she cries harder. He smells like wood smoke.

He kisses her. Cars whiz by. She feels very visible. The ground has turned soft, like quicksand. She feels her father's eyes on her, but she kisses him back. She wants to pour herself into him, to obliterate herself.

He licks the edge of her mouth, smiling at her, his eyes full of light. "Mmm." He licks a tear track. "Salt." She laughs, wrenching away. He links his arm through hers and they walk along the hedge. She feels drunk.

Harrison drapes his arm over her shoulder, and she lets hers creep around his waist. He's got a little roll. He doesn't work out. Take him to No Fat Mesa, her father seems to whisper. *Why is it called No Fat? Because everybody who goes there gets skinny. Look at you.*

At the edge of the property is an open field. He steers her into it, following the hedge away from the road, trailing his hand down her back and into her jeans pocket. They have set the field's cicadas off. Well away from the road, they stop again, shouldering into the bushes out of sight of the road, he kissing her, his tongue swishing around hers. He tastes like maple; the cicadas clickety-clack.

She turns her head so he's kissing her cheek. She says, "What would your wife say about this?"

He bites her ear.

"Ow."

"You," he says, "are the most suspicious woman I've ever met." He runs his tongue over the top of her ear and says, "I am not now, nor have I ever been, married."

C3PO starts barking, Naat'áanii answers, and she can hear Delmar's father talking.

They lean against the bristly pine needles that snap like live electric wires and feel like tiny knife pricks against her arm, cheek, hand — which ages ago unfurled her father's cooling fingers. He enfolds her in a bear hug, and she is crying again, burying her face against his chest. She can smell the long night's watch in her salty breath and sweat. His sweat is sharp and dark, musky. The world is made of juniper. He is in it, her father, who planted these bushes. She has smelled the tang of pine most of her life. She's grateful it hasn't died, that at least she has the sting and smell of it, and for now she has this groping, hot-blooded man.

A horn beeps on the other side of the hedge. She gasps. He pulls back, his dark eyes glossy, forehead glistening with sweat. The horn beeps again. He smiles, putting his forehead to hers. "Gotta face the undertaker," he says. He begins pulling pine needles from her hair, and she from his.

They walk slowly. Her legs and feet feel liquid. Grasshoppers, full-grown browns and yellows plus new little greens, scoot out from under their feet. She can hear crows calling from the river, where they always go to complain as the day heats up.

"Your dad never told you what he wanted?" Harrison says.

Tell her Jesus Christ forgot to learn my name. She watches the ground.

"What do you think he'd want?" Harrison asks.

It makes more sense to hide his body away in some shallow place. If the spirit lingers or returns, as she thinks he believed, she supposes it would want to be running and not trapped underground.

"Why is everything a struggle?" she asks him.

"Not everything's a struggle." He pinches her side and bumps her hip, smiling at her. "I heard about the renegade Indians. I thought they were a myth. The band that evaded Kit Carson."

"My grandma's been telling the story forever."

"So you're related to the renegades. Cool."

"There are pictographs on the canyon walls up there. You can see where they made camp."

"Very cool. Can we go up there sometime?"

She thinks about that. Probably not after today. It's her grandmother's land.

"It's complicated," she says. She explains how her grandmother holds grudges and she may not be welcome on her grandmother's land if her mother gets her way.

"Don't let it happen."

"My mother's got her rights."

They're nearly to the road. She can feel the burn of the sun on the back of her neck and in her scalp. It will be over soon, she thinks. She doesn't want to think beyond today, what this walk and this man mean.

"You side with your mom? You believe what she believes?"

"No. I don't know. I think a wife has a right to tend her husband's grave."

He nods, then says quietly, "Christians have been exploiting our people for years."

"You don't understand," she says, her voice low, shaky. She is furious all of a sudden that he thinks he gets an opinion. Mr. Sovereign Nation. "It's complicated."

He stops, takes her face, and kisses her lightly. He says, "*Bik'i'diishtiih.*"

The sound of the language grates. "What?" She stares at his throat. The word came out harsher than she meant it.

"It means I'm trying to understand," he says softly. He takes her hand. She holds his loosely. They start walking toward the driveway, where a hearse is parked half in and half out of the yard.

She can hear chanting coming from the other side of the hedge, Navajo voices. Her legs ache terribly.

At the entrance they see the hearse driver and his helper walking across the yard toward them. "Listen," the driver says, "I can drive back and forth all day. But does your mother understand that it's an expensive ride? And there's no refund on the casket. And you've got the viewing room whether there's a body to be viewed or not. I don't mean to be disrespectful, but somebody ought to make a decision here."

She glances at Harrison. He watches her. There's warmth in his eyes but also something else. Some distance.

"Don't leave," she tells the driver and lets go of Harrison's hand.

32

B ITS OF SUNNY SAND and dust swirl in the yard, drifting up, floating down. C3PO has brought Delmar the wet
stick. He says "Shht" to the dog, making as if to throw the stick
but then not throwing it. C3PO walks out after the invisible stick,
stopping in the sun, looking back, and giving Delmar a mean
look, then continues walking toward the porch.

Delmar has been thinking about the times he's partied with his
cousins. He wonders if he will party with them today. He doesn't
want to, but he might want to later, after Officer Happy. He hopes
he doesn't want to, but just thinking about it makes him want to.
All night his clan cousins stood around the stone fireplace near
the edge of the lot and fed cedar to the fire. Delmar stayed away
from the fireplace. They're younger than he. He had taught them
the trick of disguising the smell of marijuana with cedar smoke.

A little while ago, one of them dropped a joint, as fat as a
Tootsie Roll, in Delmar's hand. "Mexican stuff. Mostly pesti-
cide," he said. "Works, though." Delmar put the joint in his T-shirt
pocket.

Delmar remembers a funny story he heard about draft dodgers
during the Vietnam War. They had to take urine tests to make sure
they didn't have hepatitis or something, and one guy told how he
snuck in vanilla cream soda and poured it in the pee cup. When
the army physician saw it, he said, "That doesn't look right," and
the guy said, "No, it doesn't. Better run that through again." And

drank it. The guy didn't get drafted because they thought he was crazy. Delmar wonders what Officer Happy would do if he peed cream soda this afternoon, and he wonders, too, how he's going to make his three o'clock appointment if they have to take his uncle's body to the sheep camp.

Becky has just gone out of the yard with Harrison. Harrison's a good guy. Harrison and Becky. That's a combo Delmar never would have predicted. Good. But surprising.

His father is leaning over, listening to his grandmother. Now Sam straightens and walks over to him. "C'mon, Del. Let's do this."

"Now? We should talk to Becky."

"Your grandmother wants us to do it quickly because if we don't it'll be too late."

The people in the house have huddled up again. Through the front window, he can see their backs as they stand together in a circle, heads bowed. "*Má sání,*" he calls to his grandmother. He motions with his head toward the back of the house. His grandmother nods at him, then begins struggling to her feet.

Under the porch he can see a pair of sleepy eyes. That dog. That robot. That spy.

For his grandmother, Delmar knows, Sam has his uses, and so does he. At times like this Delmar is white. None of his relatives in the yard would want to deal with the body, though they would have to if his father and he weren't here, and afterward they would have ceremonies to purify themselves. He doesn't mind dealing with his uncle, though. He'd rather be doing something than just waiting.

At the pickup Delmar takes the foot of the pine casket, balancing the other end on the truck bed while Sam throws in the stuff they brought, sheepskin, a shovel, and a pick. Sam balances the lid on top. Delmar feels a pinching at his elbow and turns. His grandmother squints up at him, holding out a small leather pouch, which Delmar takes. There is corn pollen blessed by a medicine man in the pouch. He starts to put it in his T-shirt pocket, but then remembers about the joint, and instead ties the pouch cords around his wrist. His grandmother turns and, using her stick to keep her up, walks toward the backyard, her skirt swishing around her ankles.

They carry the casket around the east corner of the house, past a row of saluting sunflowers, to the backyard, which is quiet and empty. A rug nailed at the top covers the hogan doorway. Delmar props his end of the casket on his knee, flips the rug up, and enters backward, looking over his shoulder, watching where he steps. It's pretty dark inside. The only light comes from the door and a small opening in the middle of the rounded roof that the stovepipe doesn't completely fill. He sees a blanket next to the stove in the center of the room, and underneath the blanket the shape of a body. Delmar steers to the other side of it, and they put the casket down. Feet and ankles stick out from under the blanket.

The stove is cold. There's a lantern by the door, which Sam opens and lights. Then he lets the rug drop back into place, closing off the east entrance. Some flies have gotten in. Delmar hears them before he sees them, then sees three of them zigzagging above the blanket. The room smells like Vicks VapoRub. There's an open jar of it balanced on the shelf of the cast-iron stove. The place smells a little like the beginning of death, that stale perfume, sweetish in the early stages, a smell he knows from a funeral parlor. He has been to one parlor for the funeral of a fallen warrior from back in the warrior days — an old friend named Harry. He has been to two other funerals, though, Navajo ceremonies, and at one, his grandfather's, he and his father did this same service. His mother had gone to the mill and gotten his father especially for the job. Delmar thought that was weird. His father barely knew his *cheíí*. His mother explained that if the spirit lingered, it would not harm his father since Sam is not Diné, and though Delmar is Diné, his white side would protect him. As a child, Delmar didn't really believe her. He thought she was making that up. But he has tested this theory since then, and death does pass through him. There must be something to it.

His grandmother had instructed him, telling him his *cheíí* must not leave the hogan through the east, where the living enter, so they made an opening in the north wall and took his grandfather to a remote spot a few miles south of the sheep camp. That was a long time ago, and he was just a boy, barely strong enough to help. He supposes they'll take his uncle to the same place. They'll have to hurry.

The time doesn't add up. Two hours to the sheep camp, two hours back, at least two hours to find a place for his uncle. By then he will have turned into a pumpkin. He's going to have to figure this out.

Delmar unties the pouch from his wrist and sets it next to the Vicks jar, then takes the pick and shovel out of the casket. Sam kneels down next to the casket, removes the sheepskins, begins lining the box with them. Delmar moves toward the north side of the hogan. His uncle's feet point outward, forming a V. Sam makes a funny sound while he fixes the sheepskin, humming and breathing through his nose. He hums only when he breathes out, one note. Delmar looks over his shoulder. Sam is rocking, just a little, back and forth on his knees.

Delmar swings the pick up to his shoulder. His shadow, long and thin, stretches up the sloping wall, the shadow of his head stopping near the hogan's apex, and when he swings the pick into the adobe wall, cracking it, he swings directly into his shadow's center. He pulls the pick back, adobe crumbling at his feet.

"Couldn't have been forty-five," Sam says. "Let's see, your mom was sixteen when I met her, and she's — how old is she now? Forty-three? Guess he could've been near forty-five. Forty-six."

Delmar swings again, piercing the wall, sunshine pouring through the gap.

"He was, what, three years older than she is? Poor old Woody. Hmm. Hmm."

Delmar swings again, cracking and crumbling a section of wall from top to bottom, sand and dried mud falling on his head and shoulders.

"Here," Sam says. "Let's put him in."

Delmar puts the pick down. Sam is squatting at the head. Delmar squats at the feet. The bottoms of the feet are gray. The toe-nails look like shells curving around toes that are long and flat. Delmar grasps the ankles, which are as hard and cold as ant-lers. A fly lights on his hand. He tries to jiggle it off but it sticks to him.

"One, two," Sam says, and they lift. The blanket slips because Sam is stepping on it, exposing the face. Delmar drops one ankle, the heel thudding down to the earth floor, and the flies rocket up-ward. He picks up the blanket and throws it over the face, which, he sees in a quick glance, looks nothing like his uncle, whose face had broken into a mess of worry lines over the last year. This face is smooth, calm, and blue. Eyes closed.

Sam gazes at him. "Hey, kid. You're not nervous, are you?"

"No." A fly lights on his uncle's ankle. He waves it off. He picks the ankle back up, lifts and lowers the body onto the bed of sheep-skin in the casket.

Sam is gazing at him. "Maybe we should get him something better to wear."

Pajamas, the color of the cloudless sky at noon. "It's okay."

"Because we could dress him in his Sunday clothes," Sam says, smiling weirdly. Delmar says nothing, and Sam laughs. "I think you're nervous, kid."

He holds his father's eyes for a few seconds, then turns away, wiping his hands on the front of his jeans, taking up the pick again.

"I guess that'd be too much work," Sam says. "Getting him un-dressed and dressed. We should've thought of that earlier before he started stiffening up."

"Whatever you say," Delmar says and swings the pick forcefully into the wall. He has torn away enough adobe to make a small doorway, about five feet high, two feet wide. Loose sand sifts down steadily. Outside, people have begun arguing, and he can hear singing, *Nizhónigo naniná.*

Delmar puts the pick down and takes up the shovel, scraping the pile of debris at his feet off to the side, out of the way. He glances behind him. Sam is doing nothing, just sitting on his heels rocking and watching him, holding his flask. In the ragged sun shaft, Sam's sunburned face looks raw.

The dirt floor before the opening is now clear. Delmar puts the shovel aside and wipes his hands on his jeans. The feel of antlers in his palms, the desire to squeeze something, to strangle something. The singing has stopped. He can hear his grandmother's voice and Becky's, but he can't hear what they're saying.

"Del?" Sam says.

"Yeah?"

"Your mom got a boyfriend?"

Delmar stares at him. "You already asked me that."

"What'd you say?"

"I don't know."

Sam nods and doesn't stop, as if his head's on a spring. "That's not what your grandma said."

Delmar sees a flash of silver—a quick flick of the wrist as Sam sips from his flask. His father is drinking that stuff in here. That is not right. Again, the urge to strangle something, but then he remembers the joint in his pocket, and the memory makes his arms go weak.

"You didn't think you could tell me?"

The buzzing flies are invisible but noisy, arguing in the dim room, and outside several people are arguing in the yard. One voice Delmar doesn't recognize, but he believes it must be the preacher, a baritone with a southern accent, and Becky, his grandmother, her voice high, like a scream.

"Tell you what?"

"Christ," Sam says. "How long has she had this boyfriend?" He drinks again.

"I don't know."

"Well, is it serious?"

"We should just do this now. Okay?" Delmar picks up the corn pollen pouch and lifts the blanket enough to place it on his uncle's chest. He tucks the sheepskins around and over the body. Then he lowers the lid onto the box. There are no nails or hammer. They'll have to nail it later.

Sam has just been kneeling there watching him, rocking; now he jumps to his feet in one movement, putting the flask away, stooping to grip the box.

There is only the noise of the buzzing flies inside. The yard outside is quiet. Delmar squats, picking up the foot of the casket, and Sam picks up the head. They start out, Sam moving fast, almost pushing Delmar over, forcing him to sort of trot backward out the opening he's made.

33

Becky walks through the opening in the hedge. Aunt Pip, standing on the porch, seems to have been waiting for her. She runs down the steps. Delmar is no longer under the tree.

"Honey," Aunt Pip says, "your grandma . . ."

"Where is she?"

"In the backyard. They all are."

Becky jogs toward the backyard, noting Sam's empty truck bed. She finds her grandmother standing between the house and the hogan, chanting, turning slowly in a circle, and sprinkling pollen in the four directions. Her father's relatives form a semicircle around her, all of them with heads bowed. She sees a flash of steel above the hogan, and now she knows where Delmar is. She can't see the part of the hogan where he's making the northern door.

She looks at her mother, who stands with Aunt Kate, the preacher, and his wife on the back stoop. Her mother's face has collapsed into an expression Becky has never seen. She looks hopeless. She has lost. He is dying again for her.

"*Shinálí*," Becky yells. She walks quickly to the center of the yard. "*Shinálí, Shipá* told me he wanted to be buried in the cemetery." She looks quickly at the side of the house. Harrison has followed her. She sees his eyebrows rise.

Her grandmother stops turning. She says something in Navajo to the relatives, her voice eerily high, and the relatives nod, saying *'Aoo'*, and Becky shouts, sputtering, "You guys, you can't come on my mother's property and disregard her wishes. He was her husband!"

Her grandmother looks at her, the expression in her bluing irises befuddled, as if wondering who Becky is. "*Shináli*," Becky says, trying to soften her voice, "he told me he'll get too lonely without Shimá." She glances at Harrison. His face is solemn, unreadable. "He wanted her to be able to visit him in the cemetery," she says.

They stand in silence. Her grandmother's eyes drift toward the ground. She bows her head. Delmar's father is talking in the hogan, and she can hear cars passing on the road in front of the house.

After a bit her grandmother draws the string on her pollen pouch and tucks it in her sleeve.

34

WHEN DELMAR EMERGES from the hogan, he is surprised to see Becky standing close by. She's very pale, lips dry and gray, hair a mess, strands floating skyward in the charged air. The white people from inside and Becky's mom all stand watching from the back stoop. Two strange white men, one in a suit, the other in work clothes, are there, too.

Delmar's grandmother is walking toward Harrison, who stands at the corner of the house.

"What's up?" he asks his cousin.

"Dad told me he wanted to be in the cemetery." She licks her lips and doesn't look at him. She's lying, he can see that.

"What do you want, Ariana?" Sam yells. But his grandmother has disappeared around the corner with Harrison.

Delmar watches his cousin. Something about the way her shoulders bow makes him see her when she was a scared little girl following him around. He could make her flinch just by looking at her. He's not proud of that.

He puts his end of the casket down. He reaches out to touch Becky's arm, but she pulls it out of reach, stepping back, glaring at him. "You can take Dad now," she yells. The two men start across the yard.

Delmar sits next to the open window of the truck, his grandmother between him and his father. He's glad for the hot wind brushing the side of his face. Poor *má sání*. His grandmother looks all caved in, her face shriveled but very beautiful to him. She smells like the plants she dries in her herb shed, the way she always smells; when he feels crazy, as he does now a little, her smell helps remind him that he walks on the earth. The flies followed them out. As they turned onto the road, he saw one rubbing its legs on his hand. He stuck his hand out and let the wind carry the fly away.

He feels *má sání*'s sadness. She had two children, and now she has only one. This is outside the order of things. Your children and your grandchildren aren't supposed to die first. She told him often when he was younger and stupider that he better be careful and stop getting into trouble because he had to be around to say goodbye when she was ready to go, that it was his job as her *tsói*. His uncle went before her and now will be put deep into the ground, which is okay, because his spirit will not be there. It is in the wind. Go home, Uncle, he prays. He rubs his hand where the fly's legs had played.

They drive through Fruitland and past the turnoff to Navajo Mines, past the butcher shop, MUTTON painted in red on the dirty white sandwich board outside. Two pickups are parked in the lot near the road, tailgates down, watermelon in the beds. On up through grassy land and cornfields, corn stalks yellow and brown and tall, past four-cornered Mormon hay bales stacked in neat squares and rectangles, past nicely curried horses and mud-spattered pickups, on toward Hogback. Just this side of the mountain is the new package liquor store across the road from the old Turquoise Bar, which is not turquoise anymore. Somebody painted it white and hung a sign on the door — NO TRESPASSING. Rolls of barbed wire circle the bar, which is not a bar anymore, it's a prison. They have locked up the wraiths there. When Delmar was little, his mother pointed out the wraiths drinking rotgut in the ditch on the side of the road and warned him never to go there, which he never did, because he is not a fool. Cops watched that place like hawks.

Sam hums just under his breath, saying, "Poor old Woody,"

every so often. He's smoking. Occasionally Ariana waves the smoke out of her face. When he was little, his mother was constantly waving Sam's smoke out of her face, and if he was in a good mood, he'd blow it at her, and if he was in a silent mood, he'd pitch the cigarette out the window. The silent moods always made his mother mad.

"Do you know that song?" his father says.

"What song?"

"Hank Williams. I can't remember how it starts."

He hums. Delmar doesn't know it.

"The chorus goes, 'She sent his saddle home.' Your mom knows it." Sam, red-eyed, looks at him over his grandmother's head, and he can see that it's neither a good nor a silent mood he's in. Though he has never seen Sam lose his temper, he has seen temper run across his face a thousand times. It runs, a fast shadow, there one instant, gone the next, and it always used to make Delmar feel his littleness. He's got five inches on his father now. But still.

"Your mom used to say I look like Hank Williams. You think I do?" Sam tilts his chin.

Delmar shrugs. "No."

"Well, I was younger then."

He drags on the cigarette. "Sent his saddle home," he sings, smoke leaking out the sides of his mouth. "You're thinking of the younger Hank. Wrote 'A Family Tradition'?"

"'*Aoo*'."

"Just a shadow of his old man. Believe me. No, that's not the one your mom meant. The senior is who she meant."

On the Indian side of Hogback, the land is beige and bristly with tumbleweeds and sage. They drive into Shiprock, past the ugly government houses, people's laundry hanging on lines, skinny red dog running in the ditch, slouching basketball hoop on a pole in cement, no net. Past Harry's house on the hill, Harry, Delmar's old cruising buddy, but Harry doesn't cruise anymore because he died on Whitaker Mesa when he was fifteen — ten years ago. Just ten years ago he and Harry were fifteen, and he didn't know Officer Happy then, and he didn't have a job. And Harry didn't know he wouldn't make sixteen.

"You know why Hank Williams was so good? The best."

Past the boarded-up elementary school, where Delmar went and got spanked for stringing wire across his desk, playing the strung wire like a guitar. That wasn't right — spanking a little kid for making music.

"I said, you know why Hank Williams was so good?"

"Why?" His grandmother whispers to him. "She doesn't want you smoking, Sam."

"This bother you, Ariana? I'm sorry." He tosses the cigarette out the window.

Past the Uranium Corporation of America, those houses behind the cattle guard, the letters UCA in twisted wire on the cattle guard gate. Sam used to live in one of those boarded-up houses, Delmar doesn't know which one because he never went there, not once, and doesn't remember if he ever even knew where his father lived until he didn't live there anymore. The roofs have caved in on the houses facing the highway and look like nests for large birds. When he was little, Delmar thought Sam lived at the mill. He and his mom sometimes went up that way to the Dairy Queen and got Dilly Bars, then went to the mill parking lot. Sam would come out and talk to them. And would never let him go into the mill to see the machines, though he wanted to.

"Because he ate the world. Not many have that courage. His kid? Money ruined him. He didn't have a chance from the beginning. Money'll ruin you. People with too much money ought to be relieved of it."

Sam drinks from his flask, steering with his wrists so he can screw the cap back on.

"*Háni' yigaat. Adláanii.*"

"*'Aoo'.*"

"What, Ariana?" She doesn't answer. "What'd she say?" Sam says.

His grandmother wants Sam to go, to leave the farm. Delmar doesn't want to tell him in the truck. Not while he's driving.

"*Shik'is,*" his grandmother says.

"She says you've been a good friend."

"That's right. We've gotten along just fine, haven't we, Ariana. We've been improving the irrigation system to the garden."

His grandmother closes her eyes, her lips moving again. Where is his mother? His father has been out there alone on the farm with *má saní'.* Delmar didn't know that until yesterday. His father has never been on the farm without his mother. He hadn't meant for his father to stay there. He thought Sam was just going to visit.

They drive up the mesa, cross the bridge, turn onto the Teec Nos Pos highway, and drive slowly past the new high school.

"He ate the world," his father says. "Old Hank." He holds the flask, saluting. "It all came out in his songs."

His grandmother's eyes are closed, and her lips are moving. She prays, "*Nizhónigo naniná.*"

It's 1:40 when they pass the Biggs place and turn onto the dirt road leading to the farm. The truck jitters across the rain welts, which sound like machine-gun fire because Sam's going a little too fast. Delmar puts his arm across his grandmother to keep her from pitching forward when Sam brakes hard, the truck fishtailing. Denver comes out from the shaded herb shed to bark at them.

"Come on, I'll show you the irrigation system," Sam says.

"Okay, but I need to get back. I have an appointment in town at three." His father has slammed his door and is walking quickly across the yard toward the river. It'll take forty minutes to get to town. They should leave no later than two to be on the safe side.

He follows Sam past the corral and through the weeds by the dry irrigation ditch, toward the garden by the river. "I guess this is your work, huh?" Sam says.

Delmar and Alice had dug the irrigating canals from the river. His father seems to have deepened a couple of them. Trickles of water run through the deeper ones and into the garden. The melons and pumpkins look fat and healthy. The deeper trenches have little wooden traps. "See," Sam says, squatting and pulling a knotted rope to lower the door on one and cut off the water supply. "During the spring, all she has to do is close these gates and she won't flood the garden. But for the dry season, like now, you need the deeper canals."

"Good," Delmar says. He looks at his watch. It's two o'clock.

Sam picks up a discarded shovel, wedges it into a ragged edge on one of his canals, and shaves off some dirt. Delmar squats. He looks back toward the house, where he can't see any sign of life. The horses are hidden in the shady part of the corral, and his grandmother has gone in. Denver is probably asleep in the shed again. The second hand on Delmar's watch sweeps past the 12 once, again, again. He licks his lips. The muscles in Sam's back strain against his T-shirt. Delmar thinks of the time Sam wanted to teach him how to pitch. He came by with new gloves and a ball, but Delmar couldn't get it right; Sam could pitch line drives, but Delmar's balls kept curving, and Sam kept saying, Just hit me, just aim at my chest. For a long time he said that, hours, it seemed, and Delmar's arm got tired, and finally Sam walked up to him, handed him the ball, and in a weary, frustrated voice said, "Just hit me, kid," and when Sam turned around, Delmar threw the ball as hard as he could, hitting him in the back, knocking his wind out, causing him to double over and gasp for a long time. But then Delmar couldn't tell if he was gasping or laughing, because when he stood up, Sam was laughing like crazy, saying, "I guess you hit me."

Delmar stands up. "This appointment. I can't be late."

"Plenty of time," Sam says. "I'm almost through here."

The air is full of cotton picked by the wind from the cottonwood trees. The shallow canals are threaded with white puffy veins. Delmar says, "The thing is, Dad, the appointment's with my parole officer, and if I'm even a minute late . . ."

"Oh, now it's Dad," Sam says. "When you want something." He tosses the shovel aside, turning to face Delmar. "Your mother used to do that, too. When she wanted something, she always knew the right words. Didn't mean anything. Just words." He starts back toward the truck, pulling his flask out of his pocket. "Savages," Delmar thinks he hears him say.

Several feet away, Sam looks over his shoulder. "Are you coming?"

"That's all right. I'll find another ride."

"Oh, come on."

"*Má sání* doesn't want you here anymore."

"Ariana? Nah, we're good. She likes me."

Sam turns and starts walking at a clip toward the house. Delmar's grandmother has come out and is standing by the back door. "We're good, aren't we, Ariana?" Sam calls. His father beelines for her, and Delmar runs, positioning himself between them, steeling for a collision, but Sam veers off, saying, "Tell you what, you find another goddamn ride." He goes into the hogan, and a minute later comes out, tackle box and duffle in one hand, a sleeping bag in the other.

"You think you're the only man?" Delmar says as quietly as he can. He wants to yell it. "There've always been other guys. She's always had men. Boyfriends. You're just a boyfriend."

Sam stops a few feet away from him. He laughs. "Well, I guess I was the only fucking sperm donor."

"Donated to a sixteen-year-old." He can't help it. He yells, "You know what they call that in prison?"

Sam opens his mouth. White spittle in the corners. He closes it.

He hurls himself past Delmar so close Delmar can feel his heat. Seconds later, dust roils up behind the truck as it speeds toward the road.

Delmar is running across the field toward the Biggs's house. The dogs leap around him, nipping at his heels, the shepherd with the blue eye gurgling, gleefully enraged. He kicks at its teeth. He yells as he runs, "*Yá'át'éhéii!*" Vangie Biggs stands in the yard watching him. "Can I borrow your truck?" he says, but even as he says it, he sees engine parts all over the ground around the truck. All of the other vehicles are gone. "Can I borrow your phone?" he says. She doesn't like him, Vangie Biggs, and he doesn't like her, so he just pushes past her, opens the door, runs into the house to the phone in the kitchen. She follows him, standing in the kitchen doorway, a stick in her hand, which makes him want to laugh — what does she think she's going to do with that stick? He dials the number, staring at his neighbor's face, her lips slightly parted, eyes focused on his chin, her chin quivering, and the phone is ringing. He counts the rings, saying *pick up pick it up pick it up* to himself, four, five, six, and then she does, she picks it up.

"Beck?" he says. "I really, really, really need a ride."

Now and then a car or truck whooshes by. Delmar stands on the side of the road, still in view of his grandmother's farm. He puts his thumb out. Nobody stops.

He has passed the safety zone. He doesn't know what time it is anymore, though his watch says it's 2:25. He doesn't really know what that means, except that he's late, which is funny, because his whole life he's felt like he's been early, as if he lives in a flood and is trying to catch hold of something and always having it slip by. He knows she won't come — why should she? Anyway, he's late. Even if she comes it will do no good.

He squats. The sun is now directly overhead. He has slipped into his shadow. The pavement, practically at eye level, has rivers of hot tar melting between tiny asphalt rocks. Looks hot. Is hot. He takes the joint out of his pocket. If he had a match, he'd smoke it. He twists it between his fingers. He watches the second hand make its rounds.

It's 2:45 when he sees something that looks like his cousin's truck come over the hill, rolling toward him soundlessly, a mirage, and then a sound, rubber on pavement, the smooth, even hum of an engine, and he stands just before she passes, she looking surprised out the window, as if he had snuck up on her. He watches her brake, sees the cloud of sand rise as she pulls off the road several yards beyond him, turns the truck around, heads back. Just before she reaches him, he rips open the paper on the joint and lets the weed fall out.

When he gets in, he says, "*'Ahéhee'*." She gives a little nod. Her face is bloated and dirty, streaked from tears. He says, "Beck?" Her eyes are full of sadness, and he thinks she is the only person in the world he really loves. He says, "Could you hurry?"

35

THEY TELL RYLAND he looks dashing in his wedding suit and boutonniere. They don't tell him that his suit is two sizes too big and his shoes a size too small. The boutonniere is a yellow rosebud. Rosy is dashing, too, in her melon dress and melon shoes. The skin of her feet fits nicely into her shoes, doesn't ooze over the tops like his skin does. But her face looks starched today. She has painted her eyebrows so they'll stay up. She said she didn't sleep a wink, worrying about all the ins and outs of this day.

He is one of her worries, he fears, the major one. Rosy now sits alone in the head pew, marked by a huge satin bow, and he sits in the back in an unmarked pew. The rest of the wedding party is waiting for the bride out on the church steps.

Everything is wrapped in cellophane. The people entering, the statues in their alcoves, the Eucharist in its chalice. His feelings.

He watches the altar boys light the candles. He has ample oxygen — they filled the tank at his feet and the one in the front pew with Rosy before he came. He has two clean handkerchiefs, one in his breast pocket and one in his back with his wallet. He'll do his best not to fill the handkerchiefs with the hardened ball of spit in his throat, and if he must cough, he will try to do it under the muffle of organ music. He will try not to think about coughing because it's the thinking that always brings it on. He will try not to think.

Father Liam, dressed in white and gold vestments, comes bounding out of the vestibule and down the aisle, bowing and waving to people. He stops beside Ryland, saying, "What a blessed day this is," and sticks his hand out. "A blessed, blessed day."

The cellophane rips, the ball in his throat quakes, and Ryland's hand closes. The priest shakes his fist. Ryland can smell his holy aftershave, a fruity stench. He swallows and listens to the priest explain that he doesn't need to come to the altar for Communion, that they'll bring Communion to him and Rosy, which makes Ryland's head spin. He begins sputtering. He can't take Communion. He manages a "No thanks." In a puny voice, Ryland says he hasn't been to confession, is the reason he can't take Communion. The priest's mouth purses in a little o.

Father Liam walks on, out to where the wedding party is organizing. Rosy keeps turning around and looking back. Now she stands and hurries down the aisle, just as one of the ushers escorts Edna Friedan in. They meet halfway, and Rosy says something to Edna. The usher turns her around, and they walk back down the aisle, Rosy returning to her pew. "Is that seat taken?" Edna says, stepping over Ryland's feet to sit beside him.

"Are you my babysitter?" he says.

"Absolutely not," she says, patting his knee. "I'm your date."

"I guess Rosy thinks I need looking after." He smiles tiredly at her.

"She did tell me to tell you it's not too late to back out of this."

"She did, did she?"

"Don't tell her I said so. It's supposed to be my idea. I'm supposed to say, 'Sit here with me and rest. Let Eddy step in.' Don't tell Rosy."

"Mum's the word."

Edna is dressed in clothes from another time, a navy blue suit that Ingrid Bergman might have worn for a date with Bogart and a wide-brimmed straw hat that nearly engulfs her little face.

Ireland is all around them. In the choir loft the Austrian lady, Mrs. Gruber, plays "Danny Boy" at Maggie's request. Over and over again.

"Does Maggie know this is a funeral song?"

"She knows. She doesn't care. She wanted it. Irritating song."

"Not as irritating as 'Amazing Grace,' do you think?"

Ryland tries to smile. That's Mrs. Gruber's standard Sunday opener.

"I think she's an impostor," Edna says. Edna's perfume reminds him of Christmas, why, he can't say. He tries to place the scent. "That's a Protestant song if I ever heard one. I think the only reason she's here is because she gets to play a nice organ."

Now Ryland does smile. He's glad for Edna's company. She's a good friend. Has always been a good friend to his family. Unlike some he could name.

They're probably burying Woody today. Sam will be there.

Father Liam goes bounding back to the altar, stands at its center flanked by altar boys. Mrs. Gruber stops playing "Danny Boy" and sounds the first chord of the Wedding March. They all stand. Ryland places the perfume scent. Plastic, like a child's new toy.

Here comes little Teri, throwing her sunflowers, her face solemn, legs stiff.

The church is packed. He loosens his tie.

Here comes Sue, who looks quite pretty except for the severely made-up face. Here's Sandi with the Offertory gifts, the wine and water, and Pooh with a satin pillow and the rings. Here's Eddy with Maggie. Ryland pulls the oxygen tube over his head, steps out into the aisle, and relieves his son from duty. Maggie's eyes brim with tears when she looks at him. He smiles at her. "Pick up your feet, soldier," he says. And he walks her down the aisle, stepping as lively as he dares, turning her over to George and stepping into the pew beside Rosy, where he hooks himself back up to air.

Half sleeping, he listens to the priest charm them all in a language they understand, and he regrets the Latin they've lost. Once he could recite the whole Mass in Latin, both the priest's parts and the congregation's. Though he didn't understand the language he felt its meaning, and faith was easier.

At the Offertory, before the Consecration, somebody in the choir loft sings "Ave Maria." Maggie takes a single yellow rose, places it at the feet of Our Lady of Guadalupe, and kneels until the song is over. Ryland thinks of his mother, who never knew his children, but he had felt her presence at their baptisms, their confirmations. He doesn't feel her presence today. He doesn't feel anything much, just the rock in his throat.

He should go to confession. It's been so long. If he confessed and took the sacrament, maybe he would feel something again. But what should he confess? Where to start? Should he start with Woody? Woody's family? Make a list of the people he has let down? Might as well atone for his whole damn life.

He knows what his mother would say to this line of thinking. She'd say, "Self-pity is a sin, Ryland. Go to your room and get rid of it."

After Mass, after Maggie and George and all of them run back down the aisle, after pictures at the altar and on the church steps, Rosy says, "Ry, you don't need to go to the reception. I'll drive you home." But Edna, standing by, says, "Run along, Rosy. He's my date," and he lets Edna take his arm. They walk to the reception hall, leaving Rosy to herd the wedding party.

"Let's sign in," Edna says. They stop at the guest book and sign under a supervising photo of Maggie and George, the date printed on the bottom of the picture: Saturday, September 28, 1991.

They sit at a round table covered with a white cloth and a small, ornate centerpiece: a little horn of plenty, gilded flowers, and, in a vase at the center, live mums and sunflowers. Next to the vase is a placard that says NO SMOKING PLEASE.

People stop by, telling him it's good to see him, people he hasn't seen for years, mill people who seem to have crawled out of the woodwork — Howie Beeker, a welder, and Chris King, a mechanic, and the wives, more wives than men — they all stop by and say hello.

"Rosy's the same old gal, isn't she. She has so much energy," Edna says. Rosy bustles around the room, moving from the guest book to the present table to the band on a platform. The band members are dressed in what look like matador costumes.

"She's energetic."

"I wish I had half her gumption," Edna says.

"She has more than her share."

"How about some whiskey, mister?" Edna says. At a bar in the corner, Pretty Boy from across the street swirls liquid in a glass and talks to the bartender.

George, passing by their table, says, "I'll get it."

"Whiskey and water," Edna says.

"Neat," Ryland says.

Lily and her new boyfriend stand in the doorway. Lily clutches her handbag in front of her stomach, looking in their direction. Edna waves her over. Lily takes the boyfriend's arm, steering him toward a little table on the opposite side of the room from them.

"She didn't see me," Edna says.

"She saw you."

Edna looks at him curiously. "Here comes the bride," he says. The bride makes her way toward their table, carrying her train over one arm, her cheeks flushed, eyes glittery.

"What'd you think? Was it a great ceremony or was it a great ceremony?"

"Everybody was great," Edna says.

George brings the whiskey. "They're waiting for the trumpet player," he tells Maggie.

"I don't care. He can be late. Guess what? We're going to Ireland for our honeymoon. This lug has been keeping it a surprise. We're going to stay in a castle!"

"Ireland. Well, take a little boat ride to Scotland, then," Edna says. "I honeymooned in Edinburgh with Tommy, my third husband. What a lovely city."

The band tunes up, the drummer brushing the cymbals. The trumpet player comes rushing in looking crumpled, hair tousled, costume wrinkled as if he's been sleeping in it. He looks pleased with himself. He has accomplished something. He has arrived. "Time to dance," Maggie says. "Get ready, Dad."

"I think I'll sit this one out."

"Oh, a father's got an obligation to dance with the bride," Edna says.

"Get Eddy," Ryland tells Maggie.

"Coward," Edna says.

"Yup," Ryland says.

The trumpet player jumps onto the platform, spits a few notes, gives the band a wave. George and Maggie swirl away into the middle of the floor, and the rhythm in the room takes on a spiky Latin beat. People group around the dance floor to watch the leading couple. Heads move to the beat.

Now Eddy cuts in. Playing the part of the father. George starts dancing with Rosy. "George looks like he's stamping out a fire," Edna says. Rosy takes three steps to every one of his. "Look at our girl. She'll never let that boy know he can't dance." It's true, Rosy is chatting and smiling just as if she's not aware of the two hundred pounds behind George's feet, which could crush the bones in hers with one misstep.

"I hope she holds up. No use having two cripples."

"I bet you've still got a few moves, mister. I used to enjoy watching the two of you dance. Remember when we had dances in Camp out on the basketball court? Those were good times, weren't they?"

"Were they? Nobody seems to think so."

"Who? Who doesn't think so? You're talking to the wrong people, buddy." She squeezes his arm. He pats her hand and smiles tiredly at her.

But the whiskey has kicked in. He's beginning to feel a little buzz. "Let's have a couple more," he says. When Eddy comes over after the dance, they send him to the bar.

The room is a stew of wedding clothes and made-up faces. All the faces strain toward one another, laughing and talking, sipping champagne. The servers Maggie hired wander around with platters of tiny sandwiches and champagne in plastic champagne glasses. Kids dash in and out of the crowd, but so far only one platter of drinks has gone down.

The second whiskey turns out to be a good idea. He should drink more, Ryland thinks. It could take the place of Xanax. It's good sipping whiskey, so he takes this second one slow.

Midway through the reception, Maggie and George smear wedding cake on each other's faces, and then the servers start passing out cake. Maggie and George bring them theirs.

"Oh, yum," Edna says. "A yellow cake."

"With butter frosting."

"I love butter."

"Mom thinks it's scandalous."

"At our age? Who's counting the calories anymore?"

"No, she thinks a yellow cake is scandalous. She says traditional white indicates purity, but white cake — yuk. I wanted chocolate. We compromised with yellow, even though Mom says it means I'm not a virgin."

"That's just like Rosy. Of course you're a virgin," Edna says, laughing. Maggie rolls her eyes; George blushes. "My, look at Lily. They're tangoing."

"That guy can dance."

They do dance well, Lily and the new boyfriend. Long Lily. Rubber Lily. The guy dips her and spins her and her limbs lope along gracefully. Her face is the color of cantaloupe. "Looks like somebody's had a little champagne," Ryland says.

"If she's drunk, then he's talented," Edna says. "He sure makes her look good."

"Can Uncle Sam dance?" Maggie says.

"Nah."

"Oh, no," Edna says. "You couldn't get Sam on the dance floor. Lily traded up in that respect."

They watch the dancers silently. Though she hasn't said it, he thinks Maggie is disappointed that Sam's not here. She was so thrilled that he made the trip.

The music stops. Rosy's at the bandstand beckoning toward their table.

"We're wanted," George says, and the trumpeter says, "Let the toasts begin." Maggie and George go toward the platform, where a gaggle of well-wishers are lined up at the mike to make drunken toasts.

"I am mad at Sam," Edna says. "I would've liked to see him."

"Maybe you can visit him in jail."

"Ryland. You didn't have Sam arrested."

"I'm thinking about it."

He glances at her. She swishes the liquor around in her glass, lips pursed. "I think, Ryland Mahoney, that you could no more have Sam arrested than one of your kids."

"You think?"

"Yes. I do. Anyway, what he did wasn't so bad. No worse than what Lily did."

"No? What Lily did was stupid. Not illegal."

"Oh, who makes these laws? I think they were just flirting with each other."

He looks at her, incredulous.

"I bet it happens more than you'd think. People can't bring themselves to take the final step. I mean divorce. Especially when the marriage was a long one like Lily and Sam's. I should think it would be like cutting off a limb. We're lucky we've never had to do that, you, me, Rosy. Take it from me, death is cleaner. I miss my men, my husbands. But grief is somehow pure. Divorce. A dirty little business."

"I don't think Sam sees it that way."

"You think not? If Sam cared about the divorce, he would have just signed the papers. He did something certain to get Lily's attention. No, I think Lily's been carrying a little torch for Sam all these years. She was so gone on him. And maybe she didn't plan it this way, but she certainly kept a road open, and Sam, well, what he did guarantees he's on her mind. They're flirting."

"Whoo. Now that is a creative way of looking at it. Edna, you're kooky."

She smiles. "That's what all of my husbands said."

"I'll bet they did. Yes indeed, Miz Friedan, there's nobody like you. I can see why so many men wanted to marry you."

She leans over, putting her hand on his arm, and he gets that whiff of Christmas. "No, you can't," she says. "But if you ever find yourself alone, come on up and I'll show you."

Ryland laughs, throwing his head back, coughing and sputtering at the ceiling.

Edna beams at him. "You know, mister, that's the first time I've heard you laugh all week."

The crowd is thinning. Mill people start coming up to say goodbye and to congratulate him on getting Maggie married. The trumpeter says they have a couple more songs in them, and this one's by request. They start a waltz. It's a song Ryland knows, not Latin music, and here's Maggie in front of him, holding her hands out, saying, "Daddy taught me how to waltz to this," and Edna says, "Give it a go, Ry. Don't turn a girl down twice." He doesn't see how he can say no.

He unhooks himself from oxygen and follows Maggie to the floor. They do a three-step. Maggie sings in his ear: "Last Saturday night I got married, me and my wife settled down, now me and my wife are parted, I'm gonna take another stroll downtown." And maybe it's the whiskey, but he seems to be leading.

Then he is dancing with Rosy. He feels the doughy roll of flesh at his wife's waist that didn't used to be there. It embarrasses her, he knows, so he barely touches her at the waist. Anyway, they know how to dance together — they've done this a time or two in their lives. Rosy looks over his shoulder as she always used to when they danced, and she doesn't smile, because waltzing is serious business.

People in the room are singing: "Stop rambling, stop your gambling, stop staying out late at night. Go home to your wife and family, and stay by the fireside bright." It is a sad song. He doesn't know why it makes him happy. But it does.

36

IN THE DAYS following her father's funeral, Becky and her mother are rarely alone. Becky comes home from the bank each afternoon to find one of her aunts there. They seem to be on shift, a different one supervising the afternoon and evening hours each day. It's canning season, and the kitchen windows are always murky with steam from pots of boiling water, the table full of cucumbers and beets to be pickled, the first of the pie pumpkins to be cooked and frozen, the new crop of gourds to be hollowed. Last year's gourds, which for months hung drying on the back porch, have been taken down. Her mother has begun decorating them with woven beadwork, and they'll be featured in the Christmas bazaar.

Becky spends her free time training for the upcoming race at Hopi. Each evening she comes in ravenous from her run to find dinner on the table, her mother and an aunt sitting down to piñon-studded meatloaf, roasted yams, homemade bread. Her aunts tease her about her appetite, and hold her as an example for her mother, who has none. They tell Della she has an obligation to eat, even if she isn't hungry, because her body is not her own, it is borrowed for only a little while to do the Lord's work, and eventually he will discard it and call her spirit home.

Becky feels as if she can't eat enough. She's always hungry, even after eating. It's comforting to come home to the smells of food, to chatter, to the mess of beading all over the dining table. Three nights a week several church women come for craft nights, the living room filling with women who knit and crochet. They always invite Becky to join them. "It's so therapeutic," they'll say, "the making of things," and she does join them many nights, preparing the gourds for her mother, organizing the beads, but mostly eating the delicious desserts, oatmeal cookies, apple pie, almond tarts.

When the women leave in the evening, the smell of sugar lingers. Becky and her mother clean up the dessert things, and it's only when the house is tidy, both of them ready for bed, that they face each other's naked panic. Becky recognizes the wild fear in her mother's eyes, which she suspects reflects her own, a fear of the quiet dark, the absence of his coughing, the tricks on their ears: a middle-of-the night imagined opening of the back screen door; the music of his chanting in the broken hogan. And the horror of severed ties: her grandmother's averted face, the shame of their lies. Becky doesn't see how either of them could have done otherwise, how she could not have stood up for her mother, how her mother could not have stood up for herself.

She runs a minimum of an hour a day, sometimes three hours. It's the only time she can stand to be alone. If she runs to exhaustion, she can almost forget her grandmother walking out of the backyard, Harrison by her side. The memory replays itself all day, every day. Hoping for reconciliation, she and Arnold drive to her grandmother's farm one day. She wants Arnold with her as a buffer. "Use me," he'd said. "That's what I'm for." They bring groceries, enough canned goods, flour, grains, and coffee so that her grandmother won't have to worry for a month. But when they get there, they find a crowd of people and a tepee in the yard. Her grandmother is having a ceremony. For what? Becky doesn't know. "Let's go see," Arnold says, but she wants to hide. She has not been invited, hasn't even been notified. Why are they having a ceremony? For her father? They do not have ceremonies for the dead. Do they? They? Her people? She feels entirely foreign, out of place. "Let's go," she orders Arnold. They turn back and do not deliver the groceries.

She frequently finds herself in a rage that leaves her breathless.

The Sunday after the funeral, the newspaper had a full-page account of the plans to renew "uranium cultivation" in the southern part of the reservation, and her name was listed along with a dozen others as a consultant for the tribe. She couldn't believe it. She tracked down Terry Conrad, who was back in town, and ranted at him: "Since when did 'I'll think about it' become yes!" He assured her it was a mistake, that he didn't even know how the paper got the list, which was tentative, only tentative.

She hasn't seen him since. He's probably taken her off his list, which, she tells herself, is good, though it's not going to help her mom pay off her loan.

Harrison doesn't come to the bank anymore. She didn't know how he was depositing his checks until Arnold goaded her into looking at his account, and she saw a deposit at another branch, which made her feel awful, and she snapped at Arnold, as if it were his fault.

She cannot stand herself.

One day she goes home to find the minister and his son at the house. Aunt Pip and Katie are there, too. They are leveling the broken hogan, raking chunks of adobe into a pile. Her mother sits on the stoop, watching, and Becky screams at them all: "What do you think you're doing?"

Her mother buries her face in her hands, and Aunt Katie rushes to Becky, trying to embrace her, but Becky pushes her away. "It was too hard on Della to have to look at it every day, Becky. It reminds her of him too much." Becky bolts. She gets back into her truck and drives for hours.

When she gets home, her aunts want to talk to her. "This is no life for you," Aunt Pip says. "You need to get back to your own life. Don't worry about your mom. She's in good hands."

She knows they mean well, but she feels as if she's being discarded, as if they are punishing her for losing her temper.

She moves back to town, into a furnished one-bedroom apartment in the new complex near Farmington High School. The apartment has popcorn ceilings and plaster walls painted Navajo white, walls that disintegrate if punctured with nails for pictures.

It has a dishwasher, a garbage disposal, a stacked washer and dryer, wall-to-wall carpet, beige, and the front door opens out onto a large communal patio with a gas barbecue and picnic furniture bolted into cement.

Alone in this place, she can't sleep. It's her torment. The only time she can stand being in her body is when she's asleep. She falls asleep easily enough, but wakes moments afterward, heart pounding, mouth dry, in such a rage she feels she will explode. She is furious at Harrison. She keeps thinking about how he just walked away that day. Who does he think he is, judging her? She begins to fantasize about tracking him down at the college. She tells herself she doesn't care if he loathes her, but his avoidance angers her so much. As if she were diseased. She wants to have it out with him. One night, at two A.M., she gets out the phone book to see if he's listed.

Of course he is not. There are five Zahnees, no Harrisons, no initial H. She's tempted to call them all. She can't sleep. Why should they? She looks up San Juan College, but only administrative numbers are listed.

She thumbs through the book, stopping in the Ms, scanning for the name Mahoney, which is listed, right there, number and address: Ryland and Rosy Mahoney.

She stares at the number until her eyes go blurry. She picks up the receiver. She's suddenly shivering. She presses the numbers: 3-2-5-4-2-1-3, listening to the music of the mechanical tones. It begins to ring. She pictures them in their house. Where is their phone? Do they have a phone in their bedroom? She can see the house, the living room, where she sat on a soft sofa, the kitchen, where she sat on a hard chair. Soft, hard. That's all she remembers. She closes her eyes, trying to visualize the phone, which rings and rings and rings until it becomes not a sound but a pulse.

But then he picks up. "Hello?"

She clutches the receiver so hard her fingers throb.

"Hello?" His voice is raspy, weak. Like her father's had been, a voice that slides back into itself. That can't seem to climb out of itself.

"Sam? You there?"

She puts the receiver down on the counter. His words leak up to her. "Buddy? Sam?" She crosses the room to the front door, which is opposite the phone. She stands with her back against the door, then slides to the floor. She can still hear the man's ghostly voice.

She balls her hands and presses her knuckles into her eye sockets. She wonders what the Navajo word for murderer is.

On the last Friday of October, Harrison comes to the bank. She sees him immediately, even though the bank is crowded. He doesn't appear to see her. Actually, he seems to make a point of not looking in her direction. He stands in the line for the tellers.

Arnold, at the door, gives her his high sign. He motions toward the tellers' line, his head jerking like a bobble on a spring.

Harrison is wearing a brown corduroy coat and faded jeans, his hair messily braided. He finishes his business with the teller. Halfway to the door, he glances her way, hesitates. Turns and walks in her direction.

"What's up?" he says, sliding into the customer chair.

"Not much. You?"

"Same."

"Haven't seen you in here much," she says.

"No."

An onyx stud in his left lobe gleams like a tiny animal's eye in the artificial light.

"How's your mom?"

"Fine. I guess. I moved out."

"Oh?" Then, "I read about you in the paper. Your consulting job." The edges of his lips are white, and his eyes are nearly black, cold. Hostile.

She opens her mouth to explain, then closes it.

Two customers are sitting on leather couches around a low glass table in her waiting area. Harrison cut in front of them, a young white couple. The guy stares sullenly at Becky; the girl flips through loan brochures.

"What *is* that noise?" Harrison says, clipping his words.

"What noise?"

"Like grinding gears."

"Change counter." She looks at the tellers' line, which has grown way beyond its rope boundaries. "See that little man in the green stocking cap? He came in fifteen minutes ago with one of those roller carts. He was pulling four gallon jars of coins. Stupid. Friday is the busiest day. Everybody needs to deposit their checks. It never fails. Some jerk-wad comes in with some ridiculous business that could be handled any other day of the week and jams up the line, and then the customers lose it with the tellers, but it's not their fault, and it never fails!" She is suddenly furious at the man in the green stocking cap.

Harrison turns, taking in the crowded bank, the tellers' line, the waiting area behind them, the sullen guy, his girl, and now a third sits down.

"I should go," he says quietly. "I'm making your busiest day busier."

"Don't go." She's surprised to hear herself say this. He looks a little surprised, too. He leans back, folding his arms.

"I'm not consulting."

"The paper said—"

"I know what it said. It was a mistake. I'm not saying I wouldn't or I won't, but I'm not. Not yet, not now, maybe not never."

He smiles, his eyes do. He says, "You got real good English."

She tries to smile. Her face feels like it's made of glass. "I thought you were avoiding me."

"'Aoo'. I couldn't believe you were working for him."

"I'm not."

"Good."

"I thought it was because of that day. What I did."

"What? At the house?"

She nods.

He shakes his head. "No. That day was tough. I felt sorry for you. I should have called you. But—I detest that guy, and when I read you were working for him . . ." He shrugs. "You know, don't take this wrong, but you look rough."

She bites the inside of her lip. She's afraid she might cry. She hasn't cried since she saw him last. She looks at Arnold, who is staring at the monitor on his security desk. "Wave to Arnold. He's looking at us."

"He's not."

"He is. See that monitor? He can flip through channels and see every corner of the bank. Right now I bet he's looking at us."

Harrison waves. Arnold smiles. Nods to the monitor.

"See?"

The sullen guy in the waiting area stands up, banging his knee against the coffee table. He says, "Damn it!"

"You still going to Lowry's meetings?" Becky says.

"'*Aoo*'. Last week he went over the budget. We raised five grand at the meeting."

"Not bad."

"Yeah. Then next week we're having a meeting at Naschitti. I figure we'll raise maybe three hundred out there in the boondocks. At this rate, you and I will be elders before there's enough money to get anybody's attention."

"You sound like Terry Conrad. Wait—don't look at me like that. He says it'll be ten years before anybody sees any compensation from the government and that it will just be pennies."

"Oh, is that what he says."

"I didn't say it."

"Yes, you did. Just now." He frowns. She frowns back, and he laughs.

"You know, we should do something some time," he says.

"Like what?"

"I don't know. Movie?"

She smiles. "That's three."

"Three what?"

"Three times you asked me to do something. Maybe four, depending on if you count the time you wanted me to take your class. There was the time you wanted to grade me, but that may not count either, since you were mean that time."

"Who was mean?"

"You were."

"*You* were."

She clears her throat. Looks at the ceiling. He laughs. "Anyway, we can definitely count the time you and your dog were going to take me for a ride. One more and I'll know you mean it."

He raises his eyebrows.

"You never heard of the four-times rule?"

"What's that?"

"It's something my dad told me. He said if a Navajo asks you something or tells you something four times, you know he means it. You never heard of that?"

He shakes his head.

"What kind of Indian are you?"

He squints at her, smiling a lopsided smile, holds his chin with one hand, puts his index finger over his mouth, and studies her. He shakes his head slowly, smiling behind the finger. After a bit, he reaches into his back pocket and pulls out his wallet. He removes what looks like a business card, stands up, picks up a pen from her desk, and writes something on the card. He slides it, face down, across the desk to her, pinning it with his finger. He smells like autumn. He says, "*Hágoónee'*, Becky Atcitty," and turns, walking toward the door.

It is his business card with the college address and his contact information, a little mug shot of him in the corner. At the bottom of the card he has written Home: 327-0693.

"Hey!" she calls.

Halfway to the door, he turns around.

"Is this three or four?"

He laughs, shaking his head. "You tell me."

37

L ILY," FRED HAD SAID when she told him about Sam. "Aren't you a mystery. How many other husbands you got hiding in the woodwork?"

"I could kick myself for not telling you from the very beginning," she said. "It's such a load off my mind. No more secrets."

Given the circumstances, her lawyer thinks they'll have no trouble finalizing the new divorce papers — the circumstances being extortion. Lily doesn't want to put Sam in jail, but now that the secret is out in the open, she can certainly play that card if she likes. She has put it all in writing for her lawyer; should Sam attempt anything like it again, they'll take whatever steps are necessary. For now, he'll draw up papers that don't need Sam's signature, listing abandonment as the grounds for divorce. If Sam doesn't show up again, the divorce will be finalized without him. If he does, the lawyer will have a little talk with him, explaining why it's in his best interest to let things be. He can keep Lily's money. She told the lawyer she doesn't care about the money.

So all Lily has to do is bide her time and see Chichén Itzá with Fred as they had planned. They'll fly out mid-November. The week following the wedding, Lily finds herself sailing through the days, shopping for breathable lightweight hiking clothes and sun-filtering hats. She falls in love with gadgets like the all-in-one hiker's pocketknife with bottle opener, nail clipper, and corkscrew.

On Saturday she nabs Fred for a shopping excursion. They drive to the mall in Farmington, browsing through sportswear at Dillard's.

"You think we ought to get his-and-hers matching outfits?" Fred says, holding up two handsome maroon rain jackets, a small and an extra large.

"You're kidding, right?"

"How else are they going to know we're American?"

"I don't think his-and-hers outfits are particularly American. Not that I want them."

"I think you should think about it. If you get lost I could say, 'Look for my twin,' and show them the jacket.'"

"I'm sticking with you. I'm not planning on getting lost."

"One never plans to get lost, honey. That's what it means to be lost."

"Well, I'm not getting lost."

They move on to the shoe department. Fred says, "How about matching hiking boots?"

"No, no. I have researched hiking boots." She tells the salesclerk that Fred will want a wide toe box because his feet are shaped like a duck's, whereas she has long, bony toes and weak ankles. "Our feet might as well be from different countries."

Once she gets them shod, the clerk tells them to wear the boots for a little while each day. "You don't want to break them in on the trail. And stock up on moleskin."

It's a heavy traffic day on 550. Driving home, Fred decides not to fight it and pulls back behind the slow drivers on the two-lane sections, waiting for the passing lanes rather than getting adventurous. At the state line he says, "You know, back-seat drivers make me nervous."

"Me? I'm not a back-seat driver. Am I?"

"You're a side-mirror driver."

"I am?"

A few minutes later he asks her if she's worried he's going to sideswipe somebody, because she's still doing it.

"Am I?" She settles back, closes her eyes, and doesn't open them again until she feels the car speed up. They're in the passing lane on Bondad Hill, passing a string of cars. Still several cars behind the first one, they pass the sign that says their lane is ending. She holds her breath. They cap the mesa, veering back into their lane, and a clear highway in front of them.

It's four o'clock. They've got tri-tip marinating at Fred's house. She's thinking about garlic-roasted mashed potatoes. Fred loves them. She loves them. Fred has dropped about five pounds. He seems comfortable talking with her about diet. They've decided portion control is for them. They will not eliminate any of the foods they love but will make friends with moderation.

They're almost to the fish hatchery turnoff when Fred says, "I'm a good driver, Lil. You can stop helping."

She catches herself. "My. It's like instinct. I don't even know I'm doing that."

"Well, you didn't used to."

"I didn't?"

"No."

He signals, turns left, and drives down the steep gravel road that leads toward the Animas and his house at the end of Rainbow Road.

In the kitchen, she puts garlic in a clay dish to roast and starts the potatoes boiling. It's still warm enough to sit out on the deck. Fred mixes martinis and puts out pretzels. She's just sitting down when it dawns on her that the side-mirror driving meant something. Her body is telling her something her mind needs to acknowledge.

"He's here," she tells Fred quietly. "Sam. That's who I was looking for in the mirror. In case he was following." She explains what her therapist said about the fracture between instincts and consciousness in survivors of abuse. "Even though our instincts try to warn us when we're in danger, it takes our minds a long time to get the signal. He's in the area."

"You're sure of it?"

"Absolutely."

"You think you're in danger? I mean, he wasn't violent with you, was he?"

"He never was, but . . . I don't know. He also never stole money from me."

Fred sips his drink, shaking his head, staring out toward the river. Gunshots resound down the river valley this time of day. Hunters. It's elk season. Fred thinks they're inside the county line, which is off-limits to hunters.

"Tell you what, Lil. Helping people figure out what they need to feel safe is my specialty. That's what life insurance is all about. Of course, to a certain extent it's a matter of hedging your bets, but a good deal of circumstance and outcome is in your control. I ask my clients how much they want to invest in protecting their assets. If they can sustain a loss, a minimal investment's okay, but if they really care about what they have, they ought to carry a policy with clout. The same thing applies here. You've already lost more than is acceptable. We ought to do what we can to insure you. You have a right to feel safe. What I suggest? I suggest we make a list of everything we can think to do that will make you feel protected. And the first thing on your list? We're packing you up and moving you in here. It'll be good practice for traveling together anyway. We ought to get used to each other on a daily basis. Don't you think?"

She smiles. "Whatever did I do to deserve you?"

So Fred gets paper and a pen. She has already had the locks changed at her house. "As if a little lock would stop Sam. When he's determined, nothing stops him. I should get all the valuables out of my house safe and put them in a safety deposit."

Fred writes it on the list.

"You know what I've never done, Fred? I've never made a will."

"Lily. That's extreme. Nobody's going to die. But yes, you should have a will." He puts it on the list. "It's good to think prevention. What can you do that might prevent an encounter? What about installing an alarm system at your house, one that's connected to the police? Let's put a policeman between you and the burglar."

It's costly, but she decides it's worth it. They add it to the list.

He looks at her steadily. "And what about filing charges, getting the law involved."

"I don't know. No. I don't think I want to do that."

"Why not, Lily? Be proactive. If they can find him before he finds you, well, there'll be no unpleasant surprises."

She looks out over the pines, all brown at the tips. Somewhere nearby a woodpecker is tapping an agitated drum roll behind the rifle shots. The hunters seem to be on the other side of the river. "It was just not like Sam to do something so, well, outlandish. He was always an oddball, swimming against the tide, but not like this. He's not himself, Fred. I think he's in a bad way."

"My point exactly. People in bad ways do extreme things. I really think you ought to get the law involved."

"Well, let me think about it."

"At least get a restraining order. You know, we can post a copy on your front door. That way he'll know a third party has been contacted, which can be a deterrent."

"I guess we could do that."

She spends the next few days checking items off the list. Fred insists that whenever she has to go to her house to get something or meet the alarm company, he'll go with her. "You have a right to feel safe, Lil. I'm part of the package." Even in the middle of the day, if she has to go to the house for some reason, he takes off from work and accompanies her.

She's very sorry that Sam knows the car she drives. It makes driving into town difficult. She tells Fred she's an accident waiting to happen because she finds herself constantly checking the rearview for Sam's truck. She begins to remember things she hasn't thought of in years. He could be very, very quiet. She remembers falling asleep nights without knowing where he was, then waking up to him sleeping beside her. She would see signs in the morning that he'd been in the house for hours while she slept: cigarette butts in an ashtray, a glass in the sink, a dogeared book on the coffee table. His shoes under the table. His socks, always filthy with yellow dust, stuffed into his shoes. "He could walk as quietly as a cat. Actually, he liked to sneak up on me in the early years. I think he found it arousing to make me jump," she tells Fred. And she did, too, which she doesn't tell Fred. That bite of fear seconds before she knew the hand on her breast was his, her nipple erect before the hand found it.

"Well he doesn't know my car," Fred told her. They decide that when she has to go to town, he'll drive her. That means she has to plan ahead. She doesn't want to take advantage of Fred's good nature; she doesn't want to make him miss work because of her bad planning.

She decides Monday will be her town day because she has a weekly appointment with her stylist that day. The second Monday in October, Fred drops her downtown at the stylist's on his way to work; after her appointment, she does her downtown errands, and Fred meets her for lunch. The plan is for her to drive his car in the afternoon to the grocery, the dry cleaner's — but the plan backfires because a worry worm niggles the minute she gets behind the wheel. Within a block of the insurance company, she has to pull over, shaking so badly she's afraid she'll crash. She returns to Fred, who takes her into a back room and holds her until she stops shaking. "What if he sees me driving your car?" she says. "He could follow us. He could follow you."

"What, he's going to extort from me?"

"I don't know," she says. "I just have this feeling."

So they change the plan. She'll stay home, do her own hair for a week or two. Fred will do the week's shopping. And they return to the checklist. She racks her brain trying to think of anything else that will short-circuit these panic attacks, and it occurs to her to get in touch with the marina in Florida. If he's back in Florida, well, then her instincts are all off.

She makes contact with a receptionist at the marina named Candy, who tracks down a dock worker named Raul, who tells her Sam's boat is moderately secure, the moving parts tied down or stored inside, more or less ready for hurricane season, but Sam hasn't put it in storage. Then again, he never puts it in storage. Raul hasn't seen him in a month.

Which means her instincts are correct. Which is a relief of sorts, except that more than ever she feels that Sam is nearby.

Fred teases her about being his kept woman, his captive, and he warns her not to leave the house while he's away, which isn't all that funny because she has to force herself to leave. The minute he drives off in the morning, her temperature drops. Trembling, she'll return to bed and try to warm up, wondering whether the chills are natural in the big drafty house, just an indication that winter is on the way, or whether her instincts are rattling, telling her to pay attention.

In the afternoons she makes herself get out of the house and walk the half-mile down the dirt road to Fred's mailbox. On the way back one day, she glimpses a streak of white out in the trees on the hill to her right. She drops the mail and bolts toward the rain gutter, her stomach churning. She scans the hill, the thickets of ponderosa, but her mind's eye sees Sam, she feels him there in the trees, watching her. The streak of white triggers a memory of the young Sam, hair bleached white from the sun, a white fish slipping headfirst through the white waters of the Animas, dodging rocks, and mixed with the fear she feels a longing for that young boy. She remembers him pulling himself out of the water, triumphant, running back upstream to dive in again. It surprises her how vivid the image is, how intense the memory, because for a second she is in the memory, worrying that he'll crack his head.

That evening Fred tells her that what she saw was probably a husky in the dog run. His neighbors train sled dogs for the winter races up north. The runs are mostly hidden by the trees. He asks her if she heard barking. She remembers no barking. She tells Fred about the memory it triggered of Sam slithering, eel-like, head first among the river rocks. "I guess I'll always worry about that little boy. Our connection was really more mother and son than—"

Fred interrupts, telling her it's getting a little tiresome, her needless worrying. "I really think you ought to file charges, Lily. Let's get this guy caught and stop worrying."

This peeves her a little. She's on the verge of snapping at Fred, telling him she's very sorry if her fears are inconvenient for him. But she says nothing. She does not explain again about the psychic schisms in an abuse survivor, the suppressed instincts that erupt in their own time and trigger memories that might not be pleasant but that nonetheless need to surface. Instead she snips, "Okay. I'll file charges," and then is more peeved when he simply says, "Good."

She files charges, a warrant is issued. They alert authorities in New Mexico, Colorado, Texas, and Oklahoma. She waits by the phone. A week goes by. No word. No sighting. She and Fred don't talk about it. He doesn't ask when he comes home in the evening, and she doesn't bring it up. But she's distracted, and when Fred tries to draw her back into planning their trip, she mostly agrees with whatever he wants, and he tells her she's no fun.

One night she wakes from a dead sleep with the memory of Fred's business card under a magnet on her refrigerator. She had scrawled his home address and phone number on the card when they first started seeing each other. Suddenly, as if from photographic memory, she sees the refrigerator but not the card, and is utterly certain the card wasn't there when they installed the alarm. That Sam has the card, along with her spare key. She's out of bed and half dressed when Fred turns the light on, sleepily asking her where she's going, and she explains why she's certain that Sam is in the area and knows where she is, that he's just biding his time, waiting to take her by surprise.

"You're crazy," Fred says. "If you've got to go to the house, tomorrow's soon enough." But she cannot sleep, and he, groaning, says he won't let her go alone.

They drive in silence. The night is cold, a chilly wind blowing down from the north. Fred is upset, she can tell by the way he leans away from her and into the door. He thinks she's silly. She is not silly. She won't be a sitting duck.

When they turn onto her block, she sees that the house is dark. She always leaves the porch light on. "Drive past," she says. They scan the block, looking for Sam's truck, which is not parked in front.

"If he's in there he would've triggered the alarm," Fred says.

"I didn't turn the light off. Did you?"

"Maybe the alarm company did."

"Maybe. Let's see what we can see."

They park a few houses away and walk down the dark sidewalk, waking the neighborhood dogs, who send out an alarm. On the front porch, they stand listening, looking at the restraining order taped to the front door.

"Let's go around to the side," she whispers. "Shh!"

"You shh. This is ridiculous," he says.

She says nothing. They creep around the house, opening the side gate, unlock the glass patio door, which slides noiselessly open. Once inside, they have a minute to disarm the alarm. She can't see its blinking red light from here. Fred says he'll turn it off, and she says, "Shhh."

The patio leads into an open dining area and the kitchen. Immediately, she notices an odor. A fetid odor, a rank odor, an odor she does not associate with her house. *He is dead,* she thinks. She switches on the wall light.

From here she can see the refrigerator and can just make out Fred's business card, exactly where she left it.

"What's that smell?" she whispers to Fred, now standing in the doorway.

"Garbage?"

She crosses the room, turning on lights as she goes, down the hall to the master bedroom, where the bed is made and the adjoining bathroom clean. In the laundry room, she opens the door into the garage, which is empty.

"I found what's rotten," Fred calls, his loud voice sending a jolt through her. She hurries into the kitchen. He hands her a paper bag of oranges, a half-inch of fuzzy green mold covering them. "He's not here, Lily. It doesn't look like he's been here."

"What about the porch light?" They go into the front hall and find the switch in the on position. The light has burned out.

She holds her stomach. It aches.

"You're all nerves, Lil." He slips his arm around her. "What do you have to drink? Or when he broke in and forgot to take my card, did he drink all the liquor?"

She tries to laugh. "Let's see." The bar is fully stocked. She pours some Scotch.

They sit at the kitchen breakfast bar, she with her feet in Fred's lap. "You know what I just did, Fred? I did what I always used to do. I didn't think I was, but now ... I thought I was staying ahead of the game. You know. Being proactive rather than reactive. Thinking about it though—proactive, reactive. I could never anticipate him while we were together. What makes me think I can now? Once ..." She swirls her Scotch, the ice clinking. "I've never told anybody this. I knew there was something wrong with the marriage. I thought I could fix it. I decided to surprise him. You know. So one evening I take my clothes off ..."

"All?"

"All."

"All right, then."

She laughs. She closes her eyes. "God, that house. Those houses down there in the desert, they were always full of sand, so grimy." She opens her eyes. "So I'm standing in this godawful filthy house, not a stitch on. It was in the summer, the house still full of daylight, even though it was dinner time. He was late. I stood just waiting. Seemed like forever. Finally, I hear his truck pull into the drive, and every instinct in me is telling me to cover up, but I don't, and then he's on the porch, opening the screen, stepping in. And then he's gone.

"I don't even know if he completely saw me, because he turned around so quickly it was almost as if he wasn't there at all. He got back in his truck and went away."

"He was an asshole."

"Yes, he was, but I left myself wide open again and again, and tonight he's not even here, and I let myself get worked up. My God, I got you out of bed—"

"Oh, stop it, Lily." He stands, slipping out from under her feet. He takes his glass to the sink and rinses it. For a long time.

Finally he turns the water off, walks into the living room, turns the light off in there, then goes back into the kitchen. "Let's go to bed," he says.

"Here?"

"Yes. Here."

"Not here, Fred."

"Lily. I'm tired."

He turns off the kitchen light, the laundry room light, and the dining room light, leaving her in the dark. He goes into the master bedroom. She listens to water in the master bathroom. When she hears the toilet flush, she gets up quickly and follows him.

In bed, the light out, he lies on his side, turned away from her.

She lies very still, flat on her back. Blinds scissor the moonlight, drawing blue bars on the ceiling. "Fred?"

He doesn't answer. He's not asleep. She knows the difference between his sleeping and his waking breath. Hot air hisses through the furnace grate in the wall above her head. Her house is so much less homey than his, with its wood-burning stoves — the house he designed himself. She is going to lose that, she is suddenly certain, a house she has grown fond of ... "Freddy," she says, "tell me something I don't know."

He doesn't answer. She can't hear his breath at all.

Outside the dogs have set up another alarm; there's the crashing of metal cans. The bears are uprooting the garbage again.

38

Sam walks along the banks of the Animas carrying a crumpled paper bag. In the bag are bits of fur from mule deer and raccoon, from rabbit and fox. Blue jay feathers, crow feathers, wild rooster hackle. Coyote hair. He has been scavenging for hours. Soon he'll lose daylight, so he heads back toward the truck, picking his way around thickets of tamarisk, which Alice is allergic to. She told him about the tamarisk. "Everywhere you go, all along the San Juan, the Rio Grande, the Animas, tamarisk has taken over. It's choking everything else out." It makes her sneeze.

Selectively, he can believe what she says, what she said, used to say.

He hears voices up around a bend in the river. He heard them, saw them yesterday at this time, too. Yesterday and every day. This time of day along the Animas people begin moving in, hobos setting up camp under cover of the overgrown bushes, hiding from park rangers or cops or whoever they are, the green-uniformed patrollers he occasionally sees. In the air marijuana smoke mixes with sweet sedge.

Tamarisk. It's not a bush he's seen where he scavenges in Florida. There, along the water's edge, guava trees grow wild, dwarfish and gnarled nearer the sea, trees that will seem to sleep through the hot months, but when it cools, the fruit matures and drops, rotting on the ground, and then the whiteflies come, and the thicket by the marina will buzz. The flies are there now, Sam knows, their larvae mulching on the leaves' moist underparts, but the little flies will hatch and rise. Come winter the thicket will be full of them humming around his ears. He's never seen anything like the hordes of whiteflies in Florida, they're nothing like the pygmy blue flies here in the high country or the tough old horse-flies that swarmed the horses on Ariana's farm.

He should not have pushed Delmar. Delmar is not to blame for that bad moment. But Sam wonders if what the boy said was true. Did Ariana really want him to leave, or was the boy speaking from anger? Certainly, what he said about Alice is true. Of course there have been men. Why shouldn't there be, beautiful woman like that.

Maybe she taught the boy her bad habits, what a liar she is, but . . . He has a system now. For Alice. He needs to remember to reverse whatever she says, that whatever she says, the opposite is true. Selectively speaking. Not about the tamarisk, but about him and her. She liked to say they were kindred spirits. Was what she liked to say.

Two scantily clad teenagers sit on boulders jutting out of the river. They wave sleepily at him. Olive-skinned, a boy and a girl with sandy dreadlocks.

"Blessed be," the girl says.

"What?"

"Blessed be," she says.

"Blessed be what?"

"You, man," the boy says.

"Whatever," the girl says.

After he passes them, he calls back, "What's the date?"

They wave.

The days and nights have begun to blend together again, like they do on the boat when it's just him, him and the flies. He thinks it's Tuesday. Might be Wednesday. Maggie was married last Saturday. Might have been a week ago Saturday. He's waiting for the right time to pass before he goes back through and tells Ryland goodbye and then heads east. His poor old friend is bad off and will surely only get worse.

As he approaches his truck, he remembers the bugs on the

headlights and mucking up his windshield. He needs to wash the truck. He tosses the bag of supplies onto the seat. The floor is littered with packaging from his new clothes and with money.

He heads up Main looking for a car wash. He hears the Silverton train. Must be around five. Over the bridge, past the old Malte Shoppe, the old bowling alley, he sees a car wash near where Lucky's Drive-In used to be, where he'd take Alice for milkshakes.

Not Alice. Lily.

A million years ago. He passes the car wash and goes on, heading north on the Million Dollar Highway. To keep himself awake while he drives, he keeps his hand in the bag of supplies, pressing his thumb against hook points. The old flies he brought from Florida mix with the new stuff. The new ones feel gritty, the old oily and scummy; the feathers have lost their buoyancy.

Throw them out, Alice would say. They won't float. The fish will know they're fake.

A wasteful woman. He can take them apart, reuse the hooks.

Through Trimble, Hermosa, along Goulding Creek. Into the high country. He could drive this route in his sleep. He was on this road when it was new and he just a tot, with his father and mother in an old Model T, which they had for about a year until his father traded it for land, Ute land the government opened up for homesteading. His father tried farming when Sam was very young, until the '29 crash, when he lost the farm, and they all hit the road, his father looking for whatever work he could find, mostly in the mines but the mines were used up. Only the Idarado at Red Mountain limped along, opening and closing, then opening again. They'd been at Red Mountain just two weeks when his father fell through the floor of that old shaft.

They stayed on, he and his mother, living in the boxcar, and he fished the Uncompahgre with Ryland that summer, where browns and rainbows should be fat right now. He wonders if that old boxcar is still there.

He moves into the switchbacks, turning the wheel left and right and left and right, the truck weaving in toward the mountain, out toward the gorge.

He lets the road do the work. Has a good driving record. The best. No reason to worry when the kids are in the truck. Gin softens the road.

It's a long haul back to Florida. November's coming up. He wants to get back no later than mid-November, when the mackerel will be running south, and will she come to meet them? He better hold on to these old flies. His Florida Ghosts. Mackerel don't discriminate when they run, they'll bite at anything.

This road's better than it used to be. More passing lanes. But the mountain is just as sheer, little waterfalls slicking up the rock face, rivulets watering the road, and the gorge is just as deep. He slides over into the southbound lane, looking down to glimpse white water, sliding back to the blare of a horn.

Lily always thought he drove too fast. "Don't drive fast," she would say. "It may be your last."

Why did he get tired of Lily? Did he get tired of her? He should go back to Lily. With Alice, it's only going to get worse. He'll keep getting older. She'll keep not coming. Why should she come? What's in it for her, young woman like that.

The aspens have already turned. He missed it. He and Lily used to come up to watch the season change. You get a week, sometimes less. In the gully at the base of the cliffs, the fallen leaves look like gold coins.

She never cared when he talked about Lily. Why didn't she care? That's unnatural.

She used to say they were just alike, he and she.

Was what she used to say. What she said — he should've told Del — was that she didn't want other kids because she only wanted one: he the wanted, Delmar.

She may have been young, but she was always old.

Was? Is?

Only going to get worse.

He pokes his thumb into the hook he's holding.

Might as well just head east. Hasn't been much of a hurricane season from what he's heard. Go back. See how his old tub has weathered. Some things he should do before he goes, though.

Should apply for Social Security. Should have it sent to the kid. They'll make it up, he and the kid. The kid's young. Should go back to Lily's place and get his birth certificate.

Go check out the Uncompahgre before everything freezes, then head south, then east.

The long mountain twilight is almost gone, stars coming out. It'll be dark by the time he hits Red Mountain — there is no moon. He thinks of his mother, the time they spent, just the two of them after his father died, in the boxcar down below the Idarado mine. They heated it with coffee-can candles, seemed like hundreds of them, glowing like votive candles, and his mother would get up in the middle of the night to relight them so they wouldn't freeze to death.

He could sleep there tonight if the boxcar's still there. Will probably have to kick the rats out. Field mice. Used to find their way into the supplies. Always had to watch out for that, come winter when rodents foraged. Little tracks everywhere on the snow.

He's weaving in and out of the hairpin turns. Comes up on a sheer wall of rock that falls away like magic into the road.

And there were other tracks, too, men's track. In the summers he listened to them on the other side of the curtain that separated her space from his. He never saw them enter, never saw them leave. Three or four a night. In winter their footprints muddied the snow, three or four a night, then three or four the next night, the snow melting midday, forming ice by night, freezing, thawing, and refreezing. The footprints of a herd. There was only one winter, though. Mining was finicky then, like everything. You couldn't count on it, and they moved to Montrose, where she worked in a diner. Still, the men came.

He doesn't blame her. Single woman. Raising a kid. His mother did what she had to do. Just like Alice. She didn't want him around the kid. She had her reasons. She did what she had to do, and he does what he has to do, and what he's got to do now? He pinches the hook. Got to get to work.

Got to get a permit. Ryland told him to be sure and get a permit if he's going to fish, because fines are sky high for what used to be free and was their goddamned legacy, fishing the Uncompahgre, the Animas, the Dolores . . . Fished pretty near every damn river in Colorado before they were eighteen. This is the land of plenty. Used to be, they'd just put a string in the water and the fish would bite. Now you got to bait them, tailor-made bait for fish full of mercury or lead or what have you.

He needs to work. There will be elk hair. Crow feathers. Marmot. Screaming marmot. A lonely, eerie sound. Winter nights at Red Mountain he'd hear the marmot scream. Worst sound he ever heard. He pinches a hook. It pierces his thumb.

At Bear Creek Falls, above Ouray, he pulls over and gets out. He walks to the bridge overlooking the falls. Far below, white water froths, the racket of it as noisy as the mill when it got cooking. A frigid mist rises and feels good on his skin. He reads a sign that says it's a 250-foot drop. Not so far. For a fish. A long haul upstream, but what a ride down.

Due west, a shimmering halo, the sun's afterthought, caps the mountain. Nice. If she were here, she'd think so, too. But she's not. The problem with that woman — he sees this now — is that she spoiled solitude for him. Should've stayed with Lily. Being with Lily was like being alone, which was good. But then Alice came along. Made him feel human for a couple of months out of the year at least.

Never asked anything of her. Not really. Which now, it turns out, was too much, and that's a paradox, how too little can be too much. Just over the mountain due west there's a town called Paradox, right in the heart of uranium country. Ry and he used to poke around there.

Poor old Ry. "It's only going to get worse, pal."

"Pardon me?" A young man is standing nearby. Sam didn't notice him in the dark, but now he sees there are lots of people clustered around the overlook.

"Nothing," Sam says.

"Have a good night, then."

The road is crowded. A pickup pulls off behind his truck, the cab light coming on. Two men look at a map. A rifle hangs from a rack on the back window. It's October, elk season. Laughter wafts from the bushes below. It sets his teeth on edge. Tourists in this wild place.

He gets back in his truck and continues north, but now that he has felt the spray of water, he yearns for it. He starts looking for a place to pull off and camp. He passes the organized campgrounds, looking for someplace away from people. He finds a dirt road that threads through dense pine toward the river, then disintegrates. His headlights shine on a circle of stone, an abandoned campsite. He drives beyond it, into and over bushes — raspberry? huckleberry? A fruity smell. The bushes screech against his truck, clawing the underbelly. The truck finally refuses to go any farther.

He gets out on the passenger's side, which opens to a little clearing. He can hear cars passing on the road behind him, but he can't see headlights, so they can't see him, and this is good. The louder noise is in front of him, the clamoring river. He's been thinking of going for a swim. Used to be, when he was a younger man, he never passed a river without going in. At home he swims around the island, but ocean water is different, warm, the tidal pull both deeper and gentler.

He follows an animal trail down to the water's edge. Even in the dark, he can see rocks puncturing the foamy pools, dozens of rough hatchets in the water — a dry year, a very dry year, yes, he's surely seen this river higher. But the gorge is narrow, the water deep enough.

He begins to take his clothes off, the expensive boots, the stiff jeans, the dirty t-shirt, all of it stinking of days on the road. He balls the clothes up, tucking them under a bush and, naked, takes a step into water that burns, it is that cold. Jolts through him, sending electric shocks into his skull. But he numbs quickly and ignores the jagged stones piercing his feet. He wades toward the river's center. Water doesn't feel wet when it's this cold. It feels solid, painful, brutal, and it wakes him up, it creaturizes him.

If he were a younger man and had the energy he used to have, he'd swim upstream and let the current bring him back. He doesn't have that kind of energy anymore.

Anyway it's time to head south. Where he has friends. And a wife. Ha!

He stands in the middle of the river. It's no little effort staying upright here. The water spars with the middle of his back. For balance, he stretches his arms out to the sides, letting them float.

What amazing little creatures they are, the river fish that battle this strong current, tough little buggers, rainbows, browns.

He brings his hands down to his sides and, as he's done a million times before, he lets the river take him, torpedoing head-first into white water, sluicing in and out of rock-lined channels, tucking himself in, hands gripping his thighs, legs straight, toes pointed, the back end of him a streamlined tail staying the course, following the current. Eyes open in the watery dark, mouth closed. It could never get any better than this.

Heading south. Through the Uncompahgre Gorge toward Bear Falls. In the middle of the San Juan Mountains, which long ago took his father and now are all mined out.

39

NOVEMBER 1. This is the month of Fridays. Usually there are only four, but this month has five. It seems to Delmar that he should get one off, since there's an extra one, but no. There are no free Fridays until February.

The morning was good. He spent the early hours collecting the garbage. Mr. and Mrs. VD either got up very early, which is not like them at all, or they were up all night, because all the lights in the house were on, and Mr. VD came to the door, opened it, and shouted something at him when he backed the flatbed up to their cans. Delmar doesn't know what he shouted, though, because he was listening to his morning music, oldies today, the Stones.

He thought it was going to be a hungry day because he's completely out of supplies, but just as he was driving his load of garbage out to the dumpsters, he saw Angie walking in, her husband driving away. Angie brought her lunch today, green chili that she made herself, and when Delmar stopped to say hello, she pulled a little Tupperware dish out of the paper bag and gave it to him, saying she brought extra — for him.

He thinks he might have a chance with Angie. She's starting to get that look in her eye.

So he had the chili for lunch, the best he ever ate. At one-thirty he starts getting ready for his trip down to the flatlands. He's got to do his shopping before meeting with Officer Happy because the days are short, and he doesn't like riding his bike home in the dark. He's just putting on his empty backpack when his mom drives through the clearing.

"Hey," he says, walking over to her. She rolls the truck window down. "You back?"

"I'm back." He hugs her through the open window.

"How long you been back?"

"A few days. So this is where you work. Fancy."

"Yeah."

"Well, I guess it keeps you out of trouble."

He grins. There's a big paper bag on the seat next to her. "Did you bring me something?"

She smiles and hands him the bag through the window. In the bag: a boom box.

"Cool."

"I didn't know what you were listening to these days, but I thought we might go down to Hastings and get you some CDs."

"Great. But I've got my appointment today."

"I know. I thought I'd give you a ride. We can go shopping afterward, and then maybe a movie?"

"Cool. What's playing?"

"*Silence of the Lambs.*"

"That's been there a while."

"I guess it's popular."

"Seen it."

"Oh."

"It's good. I'll see it again."

"No, we can see something else." She hands him a newspaper section with movie listings. He scans it.

"How about *Beauty and the Beast*?"

"Isn't that a kids' movie?"

"I hear it's good."

"Let's go to the cheap one, then shopping, then Mexican food." She smiles at him. "We'll make a night of it."

"Well, we can't go to the cheap one because I won't be done until five."

"Oh? Did they change your appointment time?"

"No. I have to be there at three."

"Two hours at the parole office?" She pushes her sunglasses down on her nose, looking over the rims at him. "Why?"

"Because I turned into a pumpkin."

On the way down the mesa, he tells her about showing up almost an hour late for his appointment the day Uncle Woody died, and the only reason he's not in jail is that Becky went in with him and told Officer Happy what had happened. But as punishment, Officer Happy keeps him waiting for two hours now. He doesn't tell his mom everything, though, because she seems sad.

"I shouldn't have gone away. I didn't know Woody was that bad off. I thought he'd still be around when I came back. Grandma tells me he's at Desert View Cemetery. That's not what he wanted."

"'*Aoo'*. It's not a bad place, though."

"How do you know? Have you been there?"

"Sure." During his warrior days. It got to be a test of courage for Indians to go into the white cemetery, especially after they noticed a pattern; things started happening to the brothers who went there. Like Harry died right after he visited the cemetery. Delmar went to test his courage, and it was spooky. He could feel the dead crowding in. But he just talked to them, the way he talks to the ones on the mesa, and so far they've let him be. Maybe it's because he's a half-breed, he doesn't know. The dead pass through him.

"I heard your dad's in the area."

"He was. I don't know if he still is."

"Boy, I leave town and everything happens." She downshifts, slowing for the stop sign on Thirtieth Street. "How'd he seem?"

"I don't know. Not too good."

"That's what *Shimá* said." She turns right onto Thirtieth. She smiles, shaking her head. "Sam. I should've gone there this year. To Florida. But you were in jail, and *Shimá* needed help, and . . ."

"How come you stayed with him so long, Mom?"

She shrugs. "We have fun. He was always fun. Mostly. He's a free spirit. I always felt like we were kindred spirits. And he's your dad."

They pass the college, gleaming white buildings in the desert, and she turns onto Butler. Delmar has begun looking into night classes for the spring. It will be hard, though, riding his bike, especially if it snows. By February he should have his uncle's car running. Becky told him Uncle Woody wanted him to have the car. He's been hitching to his aunt's house on weekends and working on it.

"You're a little like him, Del. Your dad."

"I know. You told me."

"The best of him. There's a lot of good in him." Delmar shrugs. "Maybe we should go see him when your parole's up. You'd like his boat. You want to?"

"No."

She pulls to a stop at Twentieth and looks at him across the seat, and he looks at her. She nods and says she understands.

She drops him off at 2:55, saying she'll be back at 5:00. At exactly 3:00, he walks into Officer Happy's office and picks up the plastic cup on the edge of his desk. It has occurred to him that he could wait until, say, 4:30 to do his business, and then he wouldn't have to sit in the hall holding his piss for two hours, but he's pretty sure that would backfire. There's a small round mirror in the corner of the hall. Officer Happy's office window looks out onto the hall, and Delmar can see a miniature Xavier Happe in the mirror, and he knows Mr. Happy can see him. He's pretty sure the public display of his piss is part of his punishment.

It was embarrassing at first. It started the week after he turned into a pumpkin. He got the cup and pissed in it, but when he went back for his appointment, somebody else was in there, so he sat down to wait. But then the 3:30 appointment showed up, then the 4:00, and he finally figured out that he now has two appointments, the one at 3:00 when he picks up the cup and the one at 4:45 when he delivers it.

He doesn't mind so much now. It's amazing the things you can get used to.

There's a chunky secretary, Yolanda, who goes out for a smoke about every half hour. She says things to him coming and going, like how they'll probably fire her but she's got to have her smokes, and she's tried nicotine gum, nasty stuff. She has never said one word about the cup, which he appreciates. He likes politeness in people.

At exactly 4:45 Officer Happy calls his name. He puts the cup on the edge of the man's desk and wipes his fingers on his jeans. The cup is wet on the outside because it's filled to the brim and the paper lid doesn't fit so good. Some has leaked over the side.

"Just three months to go," Officer Happy says.

"Thirteen Fridays," Delmar says. "Twelve after today."

"Think you'll make it?"

"Hope so."

The officer nods at him. He's looking at the cup, which has made a little wet spot on his wooden desk.

"So what'd you do this week?"

"I got my application from the college. I've got to take an entrance exam. I'll ace it. I'm good at tests. They've got lots of forms. It'll probably take a month just to fill those out." He started on them last night, just answering the easy questions, like name, sex, age, ethnicity — they never have a category for his ethnicity so he always marks Other, which makes him feel like an alien from *Planet of Whispers,* which makes him feel good.

"If you need any help with them, Delmar, bring them in."

"Okay."

"Anything else?"

"Nope."

"All right, then. This time next week." Delmar gets up to go. "And Delmar?" the man says. "You don't have to fill that cup so full. A little sample will do."

"Oh, that's okay," Delmar says. He grins. "I am an excellent pisser."

40

R YLAND, WAKE UP," Rosy is saying.
He opens his eyes. "I wasn't asleep."

"Yes, you were."

"I was resting my eyes."

"Oh. The girls and I are going to church."

"Today?"

"It's All Souls Day. Did you forget?"

"We're going to get some lucky stiffs out of purgatory," Sandi says. He and Rosy have been watching the girls this afternoon while Eddy helps Sue with an open house.

"You want to come?" Rosy says.

"No." He has a two-ton weight on his chest today.

"What are these?" Pooh calls from the kitchen, a note of hysteria in her voice.

"Get your coats," Rosy says. "It's chilly. Fish sticks. They're defrosting."

"Fish sticks! Do we have to have fish sticks? I'm not eating them," Pooh whines.

"You better change your attitude," Sandi says, her voice trailing off. The back door slams.

The kids had been watching the cartoon channel. Ryland hits the OFF button on the remote. Down the street Lady Finger barks angrily. Been barking. All afternoon. The dog is lonely. Used to be she could count on him every day to come down and say hello on his way to visit his pals at the cemetery.

He stares at the plywood children in the ash tree and runs his finger over a mole on his arm that has started to go funny. He's been sleeping here in the living room for the last several nights. For a while after Sam called — that strange, silent phone call — Ryland kept dreaming that he called again. At least that's what Rosy says. That it was a dream. But he's not sure she's right. Rosy has been taking sleeping pills. Neither of them has been sleeping well. It's very possible she sleeps too heavily to know. Several times he struggled out of a dream to what he's certain was the last ring of the phone.

So he's camping out in the living room, closer to the phone, hoping Sam will call again. He's left a few messages at the marina in Florida, but if Sam has gotten them, he's not returning the calls. He wishes the man would check in. He doesn't like the way they parted, especially after that strange phone call.

Ryland figured Sam was on the reservation or wherever Alice is. But then Rosy tried to find out, mostly because Ryland's new bedroom drives her crazy. She wants to get back to normal. It upsets her notions of order, him sleeping in the living room. She says it upsets his sleep cycles. Probably true. Nights on the sofa he mostly just dozes, days in his chair he dozes some more. Just after the phone call she asked around and found out that Sam had left the reservation.

The ocean in his throat heaves. He swallows, and his eyes tear.

He should have gone to church with them, done his part to pray the dead free. He just doesn't want to miss Sam if he calls.

Where is he? It has been almost two weeks since that night. The call left Ryland feeling turned inside out. Not at all like Sam to do a thing like that. They listened to each other's silence for half an hour before the battery on his portable went dead.

The ash leaves have turned. Skinny spears shroud the plywood children, like a yellow feather coat. Soon the leaves will drop, and Rosy will take the wooden children down so they don't dry and crack in the winter air.

He closes his eyes. The pooch barks furiously. One block beyond her, the skeleton crew is waiting. Woody has joined their ranks. He and Rosy sent a check to Woody's wife a month ago.

Wanted to help with the funeral expenses. The check came back within a week. Rosy doesn't know this. Ryland got the mail that day. Woody's wife probably doesn't know it either. He doubts she would have returned it. Ryland is pretty sure the girl sent it back. Becky Atcitty, whose birth they toasted twenty-five years ago. Funny how things turn out. She has no use for him, that girl. That's okay. He doesn't have much use for himself.

Ryland tore the check up and put cash in an envelope, addressed it to Woody, and sent it without a return address. The cash didn't come back.

Ryland would like to see that man. Woodrow. He would like to ask if Woody holds him responsible. Didn't seem to that day when Ryland and Sam visited. But maybe he was just being polite. Navajos. Never could read them. If Woody holds him responsible for — everything. For all the mistakes they made every minute of the day on the reservation . . . *Self-pity, Ryland, is a sin. Go to your room and get rid of it.*

Down the block the pooch rat-a-tat-tats.

If Woody holds — held — him responsible, then probably he is. Woody was a pretty straight shooter. Seemed to be, anyway. Except Ryland doesn't really trust "seemed to be." He tries to think of the times in his life when what seemed to be actually was. Never. There are always surprises in the shadows. He plays with the funny mole on his arm.

He just wishes somebody would tell him if he is or if he isn't. Responsible. He can't seem to figure it out on his own. On this, the day of atonement, it would be a good thing to know.

He closes his eyes, sleepiness tugging. Little flea-head. Little barker. In his mind's eye he can see his driver's license on her side of the fence.

Poor little thing can't help but bark. She has no brain.

He should go see his pals.

He begins to drift into that half-dream state he knows too well, thinking it would be nice to get up and take a walk, then doing it in his mind, pulling his cart behind him, thinking as he does that if it were true sleep, he could leave the cart behind, as he sometimes does in those rare liberating but disorienting dreams when he steps back in time and has self-sufficient lungs. But in the half-dream the cart goes with him everywhere. It's autumn, the tail end. The sidewalk will be messy with drying apples. The cart will catch in goo. Almost, he can smell it. Almost, it smells like apple-sauce. Crabapples rotting under foot.

Bury me in applesauce. Bury me in butter.

They buried you in Grace Cemetery, Mama. I couldn't go.

He jerks, waking, tears stinging his eyes.

He wipes them away.

He takes a drink of water from the glass on the TV tray next to him, then switches on the tube, tuning it to the black-and-white channel, muting the sound. It's almost five o'clock. He can tell by the noise of traffic on Cactus. Every day the traffic revs up at this time, and every year the revving gets louder — louder cars and more, so many more. The house fills with the smell of exhaust this time of day, and in the living room, which is closest to the street, it never goes away completely.

The mole. Rosy wants him to have it burned off, but he's decided to keep it. See what happens. He's had moles go funny for years. He's betting nothing will happen. He seems to live in a strange vacuum where things go wrong but never wrong enough.

Sam has the skin of a Norseman, thin and white, but he never had trouble with moles, though he was in the sun just as much as Ryland. There, too, Sam beat the odds.

Rosy'll give him trouble about this mole. *I warned you, Ryland. How many times did I warn you not to take your shirt off and get burned to a crisp?*

Guilty. Guilty as charged.

The cemetery dog is singing. Exhaust coats his tongue.

Apple guts squish under his shoes. He doesn't have the energy to change direction. Pick up your feet, soldier.

The back door slams. He hears one of the kids say, "He's asleep." He opens his eyes.

"He's not asleep," Rosy calls from the kitchen. "He's just resting his eyes."

He closes his mouth, licks his dry lips, pushing the oxygen tube against his nose. Pooh perches on the couch opposite him.

"Guess what, Grandpa." He straightens up. A lace beanie is bobby-pinned to the top of her hair. "I got two out."

He clears his throat. "Two what?"

"Two souls. Out of purgatory."

"Two. That's good."

"What you have to do is go in and out of church six times and say six Our Fathers, six Hail Marys, and six Glory Bes each time."

"Well, that sounds easy," he says.

"It's not so easy. It takes a long time. You have to do that for each soul. Next year I'm getting three out. Guess what else?"

"What?"

"We get pizza for dinner because we were good at church."

"Oh, happy day."

"That dog," Rosy says, coming into the room, still in her car coat and holding Teri. "You'd think it was Friday."

"TGIF," Ryland says.

"What does that mean?" Sandi says from the doorway.

"That means," Rosy says, "that every Friday the dog's owners celebrate the end of the week and don't do what they should do, which is take care of their dog. I wonder if something's wrong over there."

"Eh, the dog barks at the wind," Ryland says.

"The wind is picking up. I think it might storm," Rosy says. "Ry, I don't have enough hands, so I'm going to take the girls with me to pick up pizza. Can you watch Teri for half an hour?" She puts the child down. "Come on, honey, let's take your coat and hat off." But Teri runs to him laughing, out of Rosy's reach. "Ry, take her coat and hat off," she says, heading for the back door. "Let's go, you two."

Teri slouches against Ryland's leg, watching the silent TV. He unfastens the strap under her chin—her cap, a woolly blue helmet. He unbuttons her coat. "Want some juice? Let's get you some juice."

They go for juice and look for one of her books, then settle in, he in his chair, she on her footstool reading to him. The dog's yapping syncopates the rattle of Teri's nonsense. Yes, it's irritating, the yapping. On the TV Claude Rains, all bandaged up, is terrorizing his partner. Ryland turns the mute off and the sound up, trying to drown out Lady Finger. Rains says, "If you try and escape by the window, I shall follow you, and no one in the world can save you."

Teri frowns while she reads, her voice quarrelsome, high-pitched, a little screechy, the way she gets when she's tired. She didn't have a nap. He puts his hand on her head. She looks mournfully at him, letting the book sag, scooting and leaning against his calf, her head against his knee.

Has always been an irritation, that dog's barking.

Outside the front window, the wind is undressing the ash tree. Ryland closes his eyes, resting his head on the wing of his chair. Rains says, "Would you mind getting the car? It's a bit cold outside when you have to go about naked."

He can make the barking stop. Lady Finger and he have an understanding. When she sees him, she shuts up. Over that dog, he has some sway.

He begins to drift, walking in his mind, pulling the cart. His nose itches. The wind will be blowing smoke in from the Four Corners Power Plant. His nose would like to register a complaint. Why not?

In the south, smoke always fills the sky. Smoke from Four Corners, from Navajo Mines, and, an eon ago, from his own place, the mill on the reservation, where he used to walk along the garden path between the acid leach and the clear, cool water. It makes him dizzy even to think about trying to stay balanced on the narrow strip of land.

In dream he turns north, away from the smoke and toward an irritation.

He can't see her yet. Can't see the gleam in her eye, but he knows it very well. From the dog's point of view, anything can happen. Possibility abounds. This is what he does for the little Lady Finger. Big dog on path opens up a world of possibility for the cemetery dog. His cart wheels keep a rhythm: pow pow pow. Slo-mo machine gun, rat-a-tat. There's a throbbing at the back of his ears and in his neck. He looks straight ahead toward the things he can't see.

The barking stops. Has she seen him? She must have. He can't see her. He savors the sudden quiet. Does she fly in a tizzy up and down behind her fence? Is she furious? He pulls air as hard as he can.

Behind him a car is slowly approaching. He can hear the hush of tires sneaking down the hot pavement, and he can hear the engine. In his throat a tickle. He swallows, licks his lips, lips cracked and swollen because he breathes through his mouth. He swallows again, but the tickle bucks in his throat. Don't cough.

The cemetery dog has backed away. Big dog coming, big dog coming. The car flanks him. He burns with the effort not to cough. "Ryland," somebody whispers, and the ocean heaves, the cart skitters away, and he is falling, a torrent of hard nothing rising in him, behind it the thing that never comes, and just before he wakes up, he catches a glimpse of his own face on a rectangular card staring up at him from the grass, his ten-years-younger face without the bruised skin and blue lips, the man with a license to drive.

"Ryland!" Rosy is saying. "You missed it!"

"Missed what?" He opens his eyes.

"Say it again, honey."

Teri leans against his leg looking at him, eyes milky, cheeks flushed, as if she's about to cry. "What are you watching?" Rosy says.

Just now a pair of pants without a body is spooking the village people.

"Ah, honey," Rosy says, picking up the remote and flipping to the cartoon channel. "Is that a scary movie? Ryland, I'm not leaving you to babysit anymore if you're going to fall asleep."

"Teri talked!" Pooh yells.

"I wasn't asleep."

"Then what'd she say?"

"She said . . ."

"Shh." Rosy says to Pooh. "Don't tell him. He doesn't deserve to know if he's going to sleep through it."

Teri leans against him, both arms pressing into his thigh, the tears retreating, that cunning spark he loves moving in. "What'd you say? What'd she say?"

"I'm not gone thirty minutes, and you fall asleep."

"I wasn't asleep."

Rosy tosses her head, turns, and walks into the kitchen, the older girls following.

"What'd you say?" he whispers.

Teri laughs, rocking back and forth, his chair swaying with her. The back door slams. "Guess what, Daddy," Sandi says.

"What?" Eddy says.

"Your daughter just said her first words, but your dad missed it," Rosy says. "She was trying to have a conversation and he was asleep in his chair."

"She said —" Pooh says.

"Shh," Rosy says.

Then, after a beat, Eddy says, "She did? Hey Ter, come here."

"If I hadn't come back, we would've all missed it," Rosy says.

"Say it again," Ryland whispers.

But she's absorbed in the cartoon now. They watch a big grinning cat pussyfoot toward a yellow bird. Teri grips his trousers.

In the middle of the night, he wakes thinking he is sleeping next to water. The wind has picked up. Eyes closed, he listens to dried leaves scoot along the pavement, sounding like a babbling brook. There's another sound, closer. He tries to place it. He opens his eyes, staring through the murk of sleep. Somebody is in the room. He can barely make out the shape of a figure sitting in his chair. "Sam?" he whispers hoarsely. The figure sobs. "Rosy?"

He swings his legs to the floor, blinking, heart thudding. "Rose, what's the matter?"

She's crying. Is she crying? He can just see her in a shaft of light, the streetlight shining through a narrow strip where the curtain isn't quite closed. She brushes both hands under her eyes. "What's the matter, Rosy?"

"Nothing," she says. "Just blue." She blows her nose. "I'm sorry I woke you."

"Couldn't sleep?"

He thinks he sees her face spasm, teeth bared in a crying jag, her upper body jerking with it. Did he see that? Rosy? He waits, and he listens to her strange shuddering moan, which gradually dies away. They sit in silence. She sniffles occasionally, and he hears her tugging Kleenex tissues from the box.

"You know what I was thinking of?" she says after a while.

"What's that?"

"Horses." She clears her throat, garbled with phlegm. "Those old hobbled horses that used to come into Camp. Remember them?"

"Yeah. Sure. You cold? It's cold in here."

She gets up and walks to the curtain. He sees her fumbling for the cord, and then the curtains open. "What a wind. Maybe we'll get rain."

"Come sit under the blanket."

She crosses to the couch, sits down next to him, and he pulls the blanket over her legs. He reaches for her hand, which is freezing. He holds it in both of his. They sit listening to the leaves in the street. "You always get blue in the fall," he says.

"That's true. It takes me by surprise every time."

Cloud shadows race across the wall. There won't be rain, and there won't be snow. The clouds are empty. The autumn air carries no moisture, just friction, electricity.

"They scared me to death, those old hobbled horses. In the mornings, when it was still dark, I'd be packing your lunch, and I'd look out the window for the dawn and there would be one of those horses looking in."

"It was the grass. That's what lured them."

"Except they always came in fall. You remember? I got to where I'd listen for the crunching of dead grass so they wouldn't surprise me. And then in winter. I remember once, it was the first winter we were there. The kids were both sick. You'd been called in to work. One of the ore roasters had blown. I had this bad feeling, like something was going to happen that night to the kids or you, and I was standing in front of a window, it was all frosted up. On the other side it seemed so bright, like day in the middle of the night. And while I watched, these two little black holes appeared on the window. And they grew, and they grew. I didn't know what to think. And then I saw I was standing nose to nose with a horse. Scared me so much, because I hadn't heard a sound, and then I realized it was snowing, that was the reason for the quiet.

"Nothing did happen that night. Nothing happened the whole time we were on the reservation, nothing that bad anyway, not until the end, when Sam and Lily broke up. But it seems like it's been happening ever since, doesn't it? Little pockets of trouble. Do you know what I mean, Ryland?"

He doesn't answer.

"I mean Woody . . ."

"I know." He squeezes her hand.

"You think Sam's okay? I mean, not that I care."

He laughs a little. "Yeah, I know you don't care."

"You think he's in trouble?"

"I don't know."

"What does your gut tell you?"

"My gut?" He thinks about that day on the mesa, Sam turning his back to him, something he hadn't done since he was a boy. "Yes."

She takes a ragged breath.

"But when has my gut ever been right."

"Well," she says, "I guess he's a big boy. He can take care of himself."

"Been doing it for a lot of years."

"I just hate not knowing."

"I know it."

Except for the wind, it's a quiet night. Not much traffic on Cactus. He can hear the clock on the wall ticking, the oxygen tank in the bedroom gurgling. An efficient metal animal, his roommate, more reliable than he. It will go on to be somebody else's room-mate when he's gone. And yet he could live another thirty years. He's not that old. Sixty-five. Rosy read him an article yesterday about some oxygen-dependent sonofagun who outlived his machine, God forbid.

Could be worse. What if she went first?

"Ouch. Loosen up. You're hurting my hand."

He loosens his grip.

"Well, we should try to sleep. It's a big day tomorrow."

"Oh?"

"Don't you remember? You've got a doctor's appointment first thing."

"I do?"

"Ryland. I told you a week ago. I swear I think your memory's going."

"You're my memory."

"Hmph. We're going to get your blood work done. And the bronchoscopy."

Ryland laughs.

"I told you. Don't pretend I didn't."

"No," he says.

She looks at him. "What no?"

"Just no. No more doctors." She tries to pull her hand away. He holds it firmly.

In the dim light he sees her lips part. The canyon between her eyes deepens. She wrenches her hand away. "What do you mean?"

"I mean I'm done with doctors."

"Oh, that's ridiculous." She leans toward him, closing her mouth. Her chin begins to quiver. She starts to get up. He grabs her wrist, pulling her back, hooking her arm, clamping it against his ribs.

"I mean it, Rosy."

Voice shaky, barely audible, she says, "As far as I'm concerned, buddy, you don't have a vote. You might not care what happens to you, but I do."

"Mine is the only vote. It's my body. And Rosy? If I'm not able to speak for myself, I rely on you. Do you understand me?"

302

"No, I don't understand you."

"I mean it."

She takes a deep breath, starting to argue, but he cuts her off.

"Do you understand me?" he says.

She inhales, holding it. For a long time. Finally exploding, "Yes! But . . ."

"No buts."

"Let go."

"No."

She pulls. He holds her hand firmly. She pulls hard. He tightens, and she suddenly goes limp, hissing, "I don't care."

He laughs softly. "Of course you don't."

They sit there linked together, she fuming, he wheezing, listening to the wind and to the oxygen tank percolating in the bedroom. After a while she leans her head back on the sofa and closes her eyes. He squeezes her hand. "What did Teri say?"

"I'm not going to tell you."

"Come on. Tell me."

"No."

"Come on," he says.

He thinks he sees a nerve twitch at the edge of her lip.

"You don't deserve to know."

"What'd she say? It was something about the movie, wasn't it." He nudges her. Flicker of a smile at the corner of her mouth. "She didn't like the movie. That's what she said, isn't it?"

Her chin puckers. She's trying not to smile.

"Am I close?"

"You're so far off the mark."

He leans into her. "I'm close, aren't I." She smiles. He says, "There's my pretty girl."